The Retribution Conspiracy

The Rise of the Confederate Secret Service

A Novel Alternative History of the Lincoln Assassination Plot

Samuel W. Mitcham, Jr.

The Scuppernong Press

Wake Forest, NC

The past is a foreign country ...
They do things differently there.
— L. P. Hartley

The Retribution Conspiracy
The Rise of the Confederate Secret Service
A Novel Alternative History of the Lincoln Assassination Plot

©2021 Samuel W. Mitcham, Jr.

First Printing

The Scuppernong Press
PO Box 1724
Wake Forest, NC 27588
www.scuppernongpress.com

Cover and book design by Frank B. Powell, III

International Standard Book Number ISBN 978-1-942806-32-5

Library of Congress Control Number: 2021907166

‚Ö CONTENTS ‚Ö

—᠔ INTRODUCTION ᠔—

Did the Confederate Secret Service murder Abraham Lincoln? A few years ago, I wrote a book about the Red River campaign of 1864. In the process, I uncovered some striking information which eventually led me to conclude the Confederate Secret Service had more than a hand in the assassination of the U.S. president.

My investigations led me to John A. Stevenson, director of the Louisiana State Bank, which was located behind Federal lines and continued to operate with Union Army permission. Stevenson bought 19,000 bales of cotton from the Confederate Trans-Mississippi Department's Cotton Bureau and somehow secured a permit, signed by Abraham Lincoln himself, to ship his cotton from New Orleans to Europe. Unknown to the Yankees, Stevenson was a captain in the Confederate Secret Service. The cotton was sold, the funds were transferred into a Confederate treasury account, and the money was used to buy war supplies for the South. Captain Stevenson apparently did not personally profit one dime from the transaction.

How did Stevenson manage this deception? Unfortunately, important details of this shady transaction have vanished into the mists of history, just as with many other Rebel undercover operations. General Nathan Bedford Forrest, for example, usually knew exactly what the Yankees were going to do before they did it. "We never know where Forrest is or what he intends to do, but he always knows where we are and what we propose to do," whined one Union general. Forrest had access to a very efficient spy network, keeping him apprised of his adversary's every significant decision. In December 1862, he crossed the Tennessee River, beginning one of the most successful raids of the war. He did not have enough supplies and was especially short on percussion caps. As soon as he crossed the river, however, he was met by one of his operatives, who delivered to him thousands of percussion caps. The contact then promptly disappeared. We don't know who he was, where he came from, where he went, or anything else about him. My attempts to recover the details of this operation yielded absolutely nothing.

All of this was very annoying to me as a historian until I thought about it for a while. Then it occurred to me that, if a historian can trace the activities of a secret service 150 years after it ceased to exist, you don't have to ask if that organization was any good; you know it wasn't worth a hoot. The Confederate Secret Service was phenomenal. One source estimated it had nearly 1,200 agents, most of whom were sophisticated, had money, and knew more than one language. Even today, historians are not entirely sure who was in charge, although it is certain that some of their top agents met with John Wilkes Booth at least once in 1864.

This fact naturally led to other questions. How deeply was the Confederate Secret Service involved in the plot to assassinate Abraham Lincoln? We know it transferred $1,500 ($40,000 in today's money) to Booth. John H. Surratt, Jr., was a courier and a spy for the Secret Service and a close associate of Booth, with whom he planned to ambush Lincoln's carriage. Just before the Lincoln assassination, Surratt escaped to Canada. Then, with the assistance of the Secret Service, he went to Europe under an assumed name and joined the army of the Papal States.

Lewis Powell, a former Confederate soldier who was wounded and captured at Gettysburg, was definitely associated with the Secret Service. On the night Lincoln was shot, Powell's mission was to assassinate Secretary of State William H. Seward. He stabbed the Republican politician several times and left him for dead. Miraculously Seward survived, if only barely.

So, we continue to rightfully ask, how deeply was the Confederate Secret Service involved in the plot to kill Abraham Lincoln? The facts uncovered in researching this question raise more questions than they answer. The conspirators planned to kill Lincoln, Vice President Andrew Johnson, and Seward. Why these three? Why was the cruel and Machiavellian secretary of war, Edwin Stanton, absent from their list?

An incident which occurred in 1923 provides us with a clue. Two old friends — golfing buddy Horace G. Young and Nichols Murray Butler, the president of Columbia University, called upon Robert Todd Lincoln, Abraham's oldest son, in his Vermont summer estate. They found Robert at the fireplace, burning some of his father's papers. He had discovered confirmation of treason in his father's cabinet and was committed to destroying the evidence. His friends implored him to stop burning the documents.

Why shouldn't he burn them, Robert asked.

"For the sake of history," one of them replied.

"Yes. For the sake of history," Lincoln responded and consigned another sheet of paper to the flames.

The Retribution Conspiracy

To whom was Robert Todd Lincoln referring when he spoke of treason in his father's cabinet? Stanton is the most logical candidate. He was undoubtedly ruthless, ambitious, and undeniably dabbled in the obscure world of espionage.

Only during the last week of his life did the president show any interest in his personal security due to a premonition of his own death. On April 14, 1865 — the last day of his life — a worried Abraham Lincoln visited the War Department. He told Secretary Stanton he was going to Ford's Theater that night and requested that Major Thomas T. Eckert, the chief of the War Department's Telegraph Office, act as his bodyguard. Eckert was a perfect choice. He was wholly devoted to Lincoln and was a large and powerful man. Had he been on duty, it is unlikely that John Wilkes Booth — armed only with a knife and a single shot Derringer — would have gotten to Lincoln that fateful night. But Stanton declined Lincoln's request, claiming Eckert had too much work to do that evening.

Shortly after Lincoln left the War Department, Stanton told Eckert that he had no pressing work and released him for the day. The secretary later told reporters and a congressional investigating committee that the last time Lincoln visited the department was April 12th.

Why did Stanton lie to Lincoln and later lie to Congress? These are just two of the questions that never were satisfactorily answered.

Until after Lincoln was assassinated, Stanton rarely had anything good to say about the president. After Abraham's death, Stanton's behavior toward the conspirators was peculiar, to say the least, and as secretary of war, he certainly did nothing to protect Lincoln on the night of his death. Why was Stanton not on the conspirators' list for assassination? It is clear Stanton would benefit most if Lincoln, Johnson, and Seward all died on April 14, 1865. Widespread murder was his best chance to become *de facto* ruler of the United States, if not the president himself; in fact, it was his only chance.

There is a lot we don't know about the years 1861-1865 and the shadowy events of the spring of 1865 in particular. What we do know is the Confederate Secret Service was lurking around the edges of Lincoln's assassination. How deeply it was involved, we don't know. But novels are governed by their own rules and, in this book, the Rebel Secret Service is in it up to its neck.

The majority of this book is true. As with most historical novels, some of the characters actually existed; others did not. Most of those who live in this book were real people, and I have tried to portray their characters as accurately as possible. Our protagonist, Rance Liebert did not exist but, in a sense, he is the composite of several people who did. Sally Mae/Guinevere never lived — but it is not hard to imagine that she did. The role of women in the Confederate war effort has long been overlooked; however, it was she, the "Ole Miss," who kept the Southern armies in the field for four long years. She ran the plantations and farms while the men were off fighting the Yankees. She was a lot tougher and more powerful than most people today imagine. Without her, the entire Southern war economy would have collapsed, long before the Union Army arrived. Although it is a matter of dispute, there are those who believe Ole Miss (i.e., the University of Mississippi) was named after this determined, indefatigable and incredibly capable woman. So it would not be so far-fetched to imagine a Southern woman playing a vital role in the anti-Lincoln conspiracy. Certainly the Lincolnites thought one did; otherwise, they would not have hanged Mary Surratt.[1] Guinevere is, I think, one of the more interesting characters who emerges in this novel.

I should note that this novel is not just about the Confederate Secret Service and its operations, which culminate in the Lincoln assassination. Parts deal with the Old South and its culture, as reflected by some of the fictional personalities in the book — especially Grover Liebert and his grandson, Rance. Both Lieberts led interesting lives, which were not atypical of the Old South planters, and I felt that a fictitious biography of Rance would make an excellent vehicle for conveying their mindsets to the reader. (Grover was perhaps less typical than Rance and more the frontiersman than his grandson, who became something of an old-school aristocrat, but even in his case the violence of the frontier did not lurk too far beneath the surface.) The Old South culture was certainly not all magnolias and rose bushes.

It should be understood the "Gone With the Wind" version of the Old South is accurate — but it sprang from a frontier culture. The southwest[2] was only one generation removed from the frontier. Frontier ideas and attitudes still prevailed in many cases and had not yet been replaced by more civilized cultural mores. The Wild West culture

---

1 Although Mrs. Surratt was not involved in the death of Abraham Lincoln, she did run a safe house for the Confederate Secret Service.
2 The "Southwest" in the Civil War era included western Tennessee, Alabama, Mississippi, Arkansas, and Louisiana.

The Retribution Conspiracy

did not, in fact, originate in the West — but instead moved west. The colonial records of South Carolina, for example, speak of brandings and cattle drives, roundups and cow pens, gunfights, rustling and vigilantes, and hangings. The South of the 1850s and the South that went to war in 1861 were grounded in the Old South culture, but the frontier culture formed a major part of its subconsciousness. The astute reader will perceive this from time to time as the novel progresses.

I have discovered — somewhat to my surprise — that another fact needs to be pointed out. *Retribution* is a historical conspiracy and romance novel. The first word here is "historical," which stems from the root word "history." The reader who wants a formula romance ("Okay, we're in Chapter Seven, time for the two lovers to have a fight") is likely to be disappointed. A great many people don't like history; they were last exposed to it in high school, and it was taught by boring ol' Mr. or Ms. So-and-So, who was dry, dull, and terminally unexciting. The history they taught mainly consisted of memorizing dates and was therefore dry, dull, and B-O-R-I-N-G. It was doubly bad if it was the last class of the day. I happen to love history. I fear for the soul of someone who could make Pickett's Charge, for example, dull. Nobody who was in it, faced it, or was anywhere close to it found it at all boring, I can assure you. Real history loves and sweats and bleeds.

Did I just mention history and love in the same sentence? You bet I did. Everybody involved in Pickett's Charge, for example, loved somebody. If they didn't love, they wouldn't have been there. I hope the Pennsylvania soil rests lightly upon them. The person who reads this novel must expect to pick up a little history along the way. We'll take it on faith that it won't cause anyone's head to explode.

I should also mention that I do not believe that the story of a love affair, historical facts, and the evolution of an assassination conspiracy are mutually exclusive proveniences. I spent most of my career trying to educate people historically, so I do not mind people learning a little history, or about past cultures, even if it is in the context of a novel.

I do not intend this book to be a one-dimensional love story or formula romance, where boy gets girl, boy loses girl, boy gets girl back. I believe the conspiracy gives it another dimension, and the so-called historical facts give it yet another.

But are they historical facts?

At the time they occurred, the historical facts presented here were not historical facts at all. To Abe Lincoln, Robert E. Lee, President Davis, *et al.*, they were current events. They were affected by them, and they had to deal with them.

Many people look at history from the present to the past. Their view of history is therefore corrupted because they are allowing present-day social and cultural mores to influence their view of the past. But you do not live that way. None of us do, e.g., we do not live from the present to the past. We all live from the present to the future. History should be viewed from the past, looking toward the future, because that is how the people of the past lived. And that is what I have tried to do.

This book is also, to some extent, a war story. Rance Liebert (and Jefferson Davis, for that matter) is a Christian and an educated, well-traveled, sophisticated Southern gentleman and bourbon aristocrat, but he could transform himself into a killer at the drop of a hat, when necessary. A warrior lurks below the surface and sometimes not far below the surface at all. This applies to a great many of the boys who wore the gray.

In 1861, a frustrated Abraham Lincoln turned to his general-in-chief, Winfield Scott, and asked: "Why is it that you were once able to take the City of Mexico with 5,000 men, and we have been unable to take Richmond with 100,000 men?"

"You want to know? I will tell you," Scott replied. "The men who took us into the City of Mexico are the same men who are keeping us out of Richmond."

Although Lincoln fired him shortly after that, General Scott was telling him nothing but the truth. Robert E. Lee and Stonewall Jackson (both of whom battered their way into Mexico City and stood defiantly in front of Richmond) are the personifications of those men. Also, I hope, in the fictional sense, is Rance Liebert.

I would like to thank everyone who helped in the production of this book, especially Frank Powell, Benton Arnovitz, Natalie Guerrero, and my long-suffering wife, Donna Mitcham, who took time away from her edited, proofreading, and ghostwriting business to help edit and proofread this book.

—◌ CHAPTER I ◌—
THE GLASS BALL

Second Lieutenant Rance Liebert stared at his reflection in the mirror and grinned. This was the best he had ever looked. True, he was never a remarkable physical specimen. He was of average height, brown hair, brown eyes, and very much suntanned, which was not considered a positive feature in 1847. On the other hand, the Mexican War had burned off the moderate amount of excess weight he had bragged he never had, and he looked resplendent in his brand new uniform. He grinned again. It was definitely not designed with camouflage in mind: black slouch hat, white dusk pants, and a bright red shirt, with the epaulets of a brevet first lieutenant of infantry.

Rance felt a little embarrassed, as if he were a boy pretending to be a soldier, and he had felt that way since he returned home. True, he had fought in the American victories at de La Teneria, Monterrey, and Buena Vista, and he had exchanged fire with the enemy, but they had not hit him, and he had not hit any of them, either. Liebert, in fact, had fired only one shot in anger and he had no idea where it went. He doubted if his wild pistol ball even came close to one of Santa Anna's men, and he rather hoped it didn't. He looked down and shook his head. Despite his self-proclaimed rather dismal performance, however, people now looked upon him as a war hero. This was because he had served as adjutant to Colonel Jefferson Davis, the daring commander of the elite 1st Mississippi Rifle Regiment. Adjutant! He smiled ruefully. That meant he was mostly a paper pusher and spent the majority of his time sitting behind a desk. He wondered how people would treat him if they realized that. He smiled again. Well, he thought, I may not have seen a lot of action, but I was a pretty good adjutant, and I never got myself shot, although I did get a somewhat nasty paper cut once.

Liebert's face turned a little pale and deadly serious as he thought about his evening. He felt more fear now than he had at Buena Vista. Tonight was the big night. As soon as the regiment returned, the local officers of the Mississippi Rifles and other military and militia units were invited to a ball at Windrow, the plantation of Richard Glass, a very wealthy planter. Other distinguished locals were also invited. For the first time in his adult life, Rance Liebert would be forced to face head-on his biggest fear: women. He had already discovered that, when confronted with a member of the opposite sex at or near his own age, he tended to freeze. He had also noticed young women preferred men who could talk charmingly, or in a witty manner, or at all. But this he could not do. He would usually make a few vowel sounds, and then the girl would go away. Even so, he was attracted to Marguerite Glass, the oldest daughter of the host. She was a beauty: hour-glass figure, long, black hair, beautiful, clear complexion, sparkling personality, perfect teeth, and truly impressive cleavage. Unfortunately, dozens of other young men felt the same way. Rance nevertheless decided to sweep her off her feet the night of the ball. Lamentably, two dozen or so rivals made precisely the same decision. The butler did not say: "All young men who intend to try to sweep Miss Marguerite off her feet should get into the line on the right," but he could have.

The ball was something out of a fairy tale. Despite the fact it was only a short distance to the Glass mansion, the entire Liebert family piled into two carriages and rode to the dance. Other carriages were already lined up out front, where footmen helped the distinguished guests dismount. A majordomo announced the arrival of each person. Rance immediately noted there were flowers everywhere, on every mantel and bracket, in ubiquitous silver vases. The staircase was garlanded with roses. The lighting was provided by waxed candles in crystal chandeliers and in silver candelabra. The civilian men wore frock-coats or dark tail coats with white linen or cotton shirts, highlighted by light-colored vests and low standing collars. Their ties were knotted in a wide pointy bow or in the Osbaldiston fashion, featuring a barrel shaped knot under the chin. The officers naturally wore their dress uniforms, with or without swords. (Rance had his uniform specially made; this was the first time he wore it. He didn't wear his sword. He considered himself a little clumsy and shuttered to think of the carnage he could accidentally cause with a sword on a dance floor. He did, however, wear his Bowie knife. That was safe enough.)

The men were a handsome lot but paled in comparison to the women, who sported gorgeous costumes of silk, lace, jewels, and plumes. Their hair was parted in the center and beautifully arrayed in long, "sausage curls," which often extended to their shoulders. They wore magnificent gowns, featuring plunging necklines and hooped skirts that dropped to the floor. They swirled around the dance floor with their lucky partners while white-gloved musicians played the Quadrille, the Scotch Reel, the Schottische, the Valse a Deux Temps, the Redowa, and the Varsouvienne. All these dances were characterized by ease of movement and naturalness except the Quadrille, whose steps were too intricate for Rance. He did not know any dances when he returned from Mexico; fortunately for him, his sister Penny knew them all and was delighted to help Big Brother. To his surprise, Rance Liebert enjoyed dancing, but he was afraid to try the Quadrille.

The Waltz was also a popular dance among the younger people there. Some of the older women, such as Rance's grandmother Elizabeth, disapproved of it, because they felt it was too intimate. Fortunately for others, Mr. Glass's musicians did not consult the Baptist Ladies' Auxiliary before choosing what to play; otherwise, the entire evening would have been spent dancing the Polka or listening to gospel hymns, and singing *Blue Tail Fly* or the *Star Spangled Banner*.

Rance dutifully joined the line on the right and watched the couples glide across the floor. Finally his opportunity came to speak to the Goddess Marguerite. The conversation was remarkable only in its brevity. She declined his request to dance, saying her card for the evening was full, and perhaps he should ask a girl who was less popular than she. She then walked off with one of the other young men. At least she spoke quietly, so Rance was not completely humiliated — but it was close enough.

The deflated lieutenant walked to the punch bowl in a daze. All of his carefully laid plans had gone right into the cesspool. The reddish drink tasted like sugar water. Well, this evening certainly was massively disappointing, he thought, kinda like when you bite into an apple and find half a worm. He decided to go home early. He sought out the host, Mr. Glass, to tell him good evening but found him arguing with his six-year-old daughter, Sally Mae.

"Oh, please, Daddy, let me stay up a little longer!"

"No, Sally, it's your bedtime!"

"Please, Daddy! Ppppllllleeeeeaaaasssssseeeeeeee!"

What the devil, Rance thought, and heard himself say: "She can't go to bed now, sir. I believe she has promised the next dance to me."

Mr. Glass did a double take.

"If you don't mind, sir?" he grinned and bowed slightly.

Glass quickly recovered from his surprise, smiled widely, and tried not to laugh. "No, of course not, lieutenant."

Liebert looked down at Sally. "Would you grace me with a dance, young lady?"

"Oh, yes! Yes, Mr. Rance!" She bubbled. She had hopes of watching the ball, but it never occurred to her she might be allowed to partici-

pate in the dancing, especially with a young war hero like Rance Liebert.

Without further ado, Rance literary swept her off her feet. He lifted
her up, held her in the crook of his right arm, with her right hand in his
left, and grandly swept across the floor, much to Sally's delight and that
of the other dancers. After the dance was over, he kept her on the dance
floor, and they had a second dance. She laughed much of the time and
couldn't stop grinning.

After the second dance, Rance lowered her to the floor, took her by
the hand, and walked her back to her father. At that moment a butler
announced: "Dinner is available."

"Can I eat, Daddy? Can I?"

"You've already eaten, Sally ..."

"I would love some dessert! Would you escort me, Mr. Rance?"

"He hasn't asked you, Sally," Richard Glass said disapprovingly as
he gave his youngest daughter a stern glance.

"But I was just about to," Liebert declared. He liked the little girl
and, for the first time in the evening, he was actually having fun.
"Would you do me the honor of joining me for dinner, Miss Sally?"

"I would love to, Mr. Rance!" She exclaimed before her father could
answer. She curtsied and quickly grabbed his hand and began pulling
him toward the table before her father could react.

"Well ... I guess it's okay," Glass muttered, somewhat reluctantly. His comment was superfluous. The matter was already out of his
hands.

Served from early evening until the wee hours of the morning,
"midnight supper" was a buffet of enormous size. It included a central table with cold meats, whole hams, salads, and galantines, a Polish
dish of deboned meat (fish or poultry), poached and served cold, and
coated with gelatin. A multitude of specialty dishes covered the side
tables. Fruits and several cakes stood in layers, and there were numer-
ous pies, custards, jellies, and creams. One of the several homemade
sponge cakes topped with raspberry jam and a mountain of whipped
cream dotted with red cherries was Sally's first choice. Other options
included towers of caramel or nougat, along with various ice creams
and sorbets, some of which featured candied orange peel topped with
sugared rose petals or violets. Also available were many wines in cut
glass decanters and iced champagne served in gold-traced or Bohemi-
an glasses, and served by skilled waiters in tail coats. When they finished here, the older gentlemen retired to the sitting rooms to smoke

The Retribution Conspiracy

cigars and sip brandy, Scotch, bourbon or Irish whiskey.

Rance pulled out a chair for his "lady" and pushed it up to the table after she sat. He then sat by Sally and listened to her talk as if she were an adult. Marguerite noticed this and decided to divert his attention to her favorite subject — herself. But Liebert would have none of it. He let her ramble on, but he only paid attention to Sally, whose topic of conservation was dolls. Rance pretended he was fascinated.

"I have an opening in my dance card now, Rance," Marguerite purred suggestively. The thought of ruining her half-sister's evening by stealing her only "beau" appealed to Marguerite. She could always dump young Liebert later.

Although what Rance Liebert didn't know about women could have filled volumes, he saw through this particular maneuver immediately and would have none of it. "I'd like to, but I'm occupied at the moment," he allowed, without even looking at her. Take that, Miz Narcissist, he thought. Rejected for a six-year-old, Marguerite left in a bit of a huff.

For the first time in her life, Sally Mae Glass felt like a grownup. She was flattered by the attention given to her by a dashing warrior. All too soon — for her — the dessert was finished (even though she ate it as slowly as possible) and it was time for Rance to return her to her father. Mr. Glass shook his hand and thanked him for making Sally's night.

"The pleasure was all mine!" The young adjutant declared with a slight bow. Since she couldn't reach his neck, Sally hugged his leg, while the adults laughed.

None of the amused guests or the jovial host had any idea they were witnessing a pregnant moment in the history of the Southern Confederacy. In eighteen years, the United States secretary of war would call these two the most dangerous couple in the history of the western hemisphere. Sally Mae, alias Guinevere Spring, would be a beautiful woman, a much sought-after actress, and an highly successful secret agent. Tonight's escort would eventually be her boyfriend — and her superior officer. As head of the Confederate Secret Service, Colonel Rance Liebert and his girlfriend would be a major asset to the Southern war machine, would plow a row of carnage across the North, and would plot the successful murder of Abraham Lincoln. But that was all in the future.

———

For a few days after the ball, Liebert was the target of some good-natured ribbing from his peers for "robbing the cradle." He turned the tables on them by remarking he paid special attention to Sally "because I wanted to have some intelligent adult conservation for a change," and this they, unfortunately, were unable to provide. Within a week or so, Rance had all but forgotten the whole incident.

But not Sally. She went to bed and was tucked in by her nanny, but it took her a long time to go to sleep. In her mind's eye, she danced and danced and danced. And for the rest of her life, she would have a soft spot in her heart for Rance Liebert. Only many years later would he reflect on this night and conclude that little girls grow up someday, and some of them became beautiful women ... One should always be nice to them.

Like many Belle's Balls in the antebellum South, the Glass Ball lasted until morning. Some of the partners danced until dawn. The hostess then served strong black coffee, and the guests took the long carriage ride home. Many of them fell asleep on the way. The Lieberts had already been back for hours.

∽ CHAPTER II ∽
GROWING UP SOUTHERN

The seeds of what became the Confederate Secret Service were planted many years before. Rance Liebert, its director throughout its existence, had a grandfather, Grover Liebert, who was a bedrock of his life. Grover was the toughest man most people who met him ever knew. In an era in which the average man stood just over 5' 7", he was more than six feet tall and was broadly built. He had a fierce temper and was not afraid of a fight or a duel. Few people called him Grover. It was usually Mr. Grover, Mr. Liebert, Boss, or Master. His close personal friends called him Sir, or at least they would have if he had any close, personal friends. He was almost always ornery, sometimes mean, and occasionally violent, not to mention that he threw pennies around as if they were anvils.

Grover's main passion in life was the pursuit of money. He was good at it and had a talent for seizing an opportunity. As a teenager, he saw the potent combination of cotton and slavery could make a man rich and he took full advantage of it. By the late 1830s, he was wealthy and was the squire of Fusilier, the most extensive plantation in Rainbow County, Mississippi.

As a young man, he proposed to Elizabeth. She was much smaller than he and — in her youth — was petite and presentable, if not exactly pretty. What attracted him to her is not clear, because there certainly was no profit in it. What attracted her to him is even less clear, although he was a fine figure of a man and did genuinely care for her.

Elizabeth was the opposite of Grover. She was a Christian, which he definitely was not. Their courtship was brief. He proposed on their fourth meeting, and she accepted on their fifth.[3] She was soon the administrative head of the plantation and handled all of the farm's bills and paperwork. The children came early and often, starting with Ambrose, who would one day be Rance's father.

After only a few years, Grover owned more than 5,000 acres. At Elizabeth's insistence, he built a magnificent mansion in the Greek Revival style, featuring six Doric columns. The plantation was run by the patriarch, Grover Liebert. It was based on the model of the English

---

3 Proposing on the fourth meeting was not uncommon on the 19th Century American frontier.

Cavaliers, who were descended from the knights and lords of the Middle Ages. They brought with them their ideas of economics and privilege, as well as the medieval codes of gentility, chivalry, and honor. Liebert's ancestors were not among the original Cavaliers; they came later. But when they did come, they adopted the Cavaliers' codes, hook, line, and sinker — especially Grover, the patriarch. His word was law on the plantation, and no one defied it, except Elizabeth, who ignored it from time to time and usually got away with it.

Every Sunday morning, Elizabeth had one of the male slaves hitch up the horse to the buggy and drive her to Rainbow, where she attended a home church. As the community's prosperity increased, she and the other ladies hired a part-time preacher.

"Why?" Grover wanted to know. "Dang near anybody can read a Bible," he snapped at Elizabeth.

"Because I don't want our babies to grow up in no heathen town," Elizabeth snapped back. She was already angry because her efforts to shut down the local saloon had failed.

Grover muttered something indiscernible and ambled off. He grumbled at her overly lavish contributions (or at least he thought they were), but he never actually tried to stop her from giving generously. As a result, her generosity only increased. He said no only when she wanted to build a church, using materials from the Liebert Lumber Company and slaves from his plantation as the carpenters and construction workers. It took her two weeks to wear him down. She did this by inviting the home church to their house for Sunday services — morning and evening. To Grover's chagrin, Wednesday night prayer meetings were held there as well. They quickly broke his resistance. Two dozen Baptist women screeching loudly and off-key would wear down anybody. He agreed to fund the construction of the church if the home church group was forever banned from their home, a permanent ban which actually lasted almost two years. Next came the parsonage. Elizabeth wanted a full-time preacher for her church.

"I ain't payin' for that!" Grover snapped.

"You ain't got to!" Elizabeth declared. "I am!"

Grover's mouth fell open, but this time he held his ground. It took her three weeks to get the bricks and lumber for the house next to the church and a full two months to obtain funding for the minister, with Grover footing about half the bill — although he was convinced he was funding 140 percent of everything, including the Vatican, the Baptist

The Retribution Conspiracy

Missionary Society, the Lutheran Synod, and the Papal States of Italy.

In the evenings, Elizabeth would sit and read the Bible or a story-book to her children and later to her grandchildren. Sometimes they would just sing hymns or songs, while Elizabeth (and later Penny, Ambrose's third child) played the piano. Although Grover never said much, he was deeply touched by these evenings. They produced wonderful memories which lasted a lifetime for all concerned.

This was the family that sired Rance Liebert, and he saw nothing wrong with it. As the oldest grandson, he received particular attention from his grandfather, who was the man he admired more than any other.

"Rance, it's time you learned somethin," Grover said.

"Yes, Granddaddy," the five-year-old boy replied. He was eager to please and always felt a sense of awe when his grandfather was present. He wanted people to respect him that way someday.

"Follow me," he said. Then he turned to one of the maids and said: "Go to the kitchen, git me a large butcher knife, and meet us in the chicken yard."

Like the chicken coup, the kitchen was in a building separate from the Big House, to minimize the danger of fires. When they got to the chicken yard, Grover handed Rance a piece of stiff wire, about three feet long. The end had been bent back to form a hook. "See that fat chicken with the black feathers?"

"Yes, sir."

"Catch 'im for me! Hook 'im by the foot, just above the claw."

Rance grinned and immediately set off after the chicken, as fast as his legs could go. He was proud that he hooked it on the first attempt, even though he realized it was blind luck.

The maid arrived with the butcher knife about the time Rance handed the chicken — still on the hook — to his grandfather. Grover walked over to a wooden block, wrung the chicken's neck, and stretched the bird out on the block. The head was held in place by a bent nail. He handed the knife to Rance.

"Cut its head off," he ordered.

Rance didn't even hesitate. He took the knife and decapitated the fowl without further ado. He watched with fascination as the headless chicken ran several feet before it keeled over. "Ain't that somethin," he exclaimed with amazement. He never saw a headless chicken run before.

Grover smiled widely. He was pleased that did his chore without having to be coaxed. He didn't want to raise any squeamish grandsons who were afraid to shed blood. Grover then ordered one of the slaves to pluck the feathers off the bird. In his opinion, it was fine for white boys to kill; but they did not pluck. That was beneath them. Slaves or women did that.

From then on, beheading chickens was one of Rance's duties. He knew Elizabeth or most of the slaves could swing a chicken over their heads a few times and pop their wrists, instantly snapping the head off. But he loudly proclaimed that was his job. He enjoyed watching the chickens run without their heads. Besides ham, blackeyed peas, and cornbread, fried chicken became his favorite food. And when the boy became a man, he was not squeamish about shedding blood — just as Grover planned.

"I want a Bowie knife," Rance announced to his grandfather a few weeks later.

"What for?"

"Kill chickens."

"Waste of money," Grover declared. "We got plenty of butcher knives."

"Don't want them. I want a Bowie knife."

"You willin' to work for it?"

"You bet! I mean, yes, sir!"

Grover grinned. Rance was his favorite grandchild, although he tried not to show it. "Are you willin' to milk cows for it?"

"Yes, sir!" He declared, after a moment's hesitation. Rance was crossing a social line here, and he knew it. In the Old South, men did not milk cows if there was a woman around to do it. This applied to slaves as well. If a male slave and a white female were the only people available to milk a cow, the white woman pulled up a stool. This was the only duty on the plantation about which that could be said.

After several weeks of milking, Grandfather Liebert and Rance rode into Rainbow, and Rance proudly purchased his Bowie knife. He couldn't stop grinning. Grover and Ambrose showed him how to sharpen it, and his father showed him how to throw it. For the rest of his life, it was his favorite toy.

With the land filling up, bricks were in high demand, so Grover took what, for him, was a logical step: he established a brick manufacturing plant and a brickyard. It was located in the small town of Rainbow, Mississippi, and was run by William, whose father Jonathan was the plantation overseer. (Jonathan and his family were Grover's first slaves. Initially, he treated them as property. By now, however, Jonathan was looked upon as a member of the family and ranked higher with Grover than most of the cousins.) Both Jonathan and William turned out to be pretty good managers, and Grover quickly took advantage of that fact. Because William was black, some of the redneck white farmers occasionally tried to treat him with disrespect or bully him in some business matter, usually in an attempt to get bricks more cheaply. William would simply say: "We's gonna have to take dis matter up mit Mister Grover." The redneck would immediately become more reasonable. One, a coward named Bishop, did not. He demanded credit but, because of his poor reputation, William knew that Bishop would never pay it back. When he was denied his bricks, Bishop slapped the Negro, who immediately reported the incident to his owner.

Grover instantly flew into a rage. "Nobody hits my darkies but me! At least not without my permission!" He roared. It flew all over him when people tried to bully someone who was powerless — a responsive trait he passed on to his children and grandchildren.

"Saddle you and me a horse, Rance, and another one for yo' daddy!" Grover commanded. "You're goin' into town with me!"

Rance, who was now eleven, was excited. He loved the infrequent trips to town, especially with his hero, Grover. He liked the change of scenery and getting some maple or hard rock candy, and maybe even some gumdrops. He ran to the stables, his knife banging against his hip, and didn't ask any questions. But Elizabeth did.

"Whatcha gonna do, Grover?"

"Beat the fire out of some white trash."

Elizabeth didn't see anything wrong with that, so she let the matter drop. But Grover wasn't entirely forthcoming with her. He intended to go much further than that.

Grover didn't have to tell Ambrose what to do. He knew his job was to cover his father's back, so he showed up with a brace of single-shot pistols. Grover carried three. He gave one to Rance. "Now, you don't even draw that thang 'less I tells you to!" He commanded.

For just about the first time in his life Rance Liebert felt like a man. He was riding into town with two other armed men on dangerous business. He swelled with pride. In his young mind he was sure he looked like a real desperado.

On the road to Rainbow, he asked: "What are we gonna do, Grandpa?"

"You ain't gonna do nuthin' but learn. I'm fixin' to show you how to deal with cowardly white trash."

Bishop was in the tavern when the Liebert trio entered. He scowled as Grover strode up to his table.

"You like slappin' people, manure brains?" Grover roared, and then slapped him halfway across the room.

Before Bishop could get up, Grover roared: "Pistols! Dawn! In the graveyard, so we won't have to carry your dead carcass very far. And don't make me come and get you!" He turned on his heel and stalked out the swinging doors, covered by Ambrose. Rance — who was so excited he almost wet himself — fought back the urge to draw his pistol. But there was no need. None of the other men in the tavern showed any inclination to take up for Bishop or tangle with Grover Liebert.

Ambrose and Rance served as Grover's seconds, much to the displeasure of Elizabeth. But on this rare occasion, she lost the argument. "He's too young to witness a duel, much less be a second!" She cried.

"He's a Liebert!" Grover retorted. "And he urinates standing up! Time for him to grow up!" He didn't say it, but the elder Liebert was afraid Rance was growing up too soft and sensitive, and that later, as an adult, he might not act with an appropriate level of violence when the situation demanded it. It's time to get that out of his system right now, Grover thought.

"I'm old enough, Grandma," Rance assured her. With tears pouring down her cheeks, Elizabeth bent over and hugged her grandson. She was more concerned about him than about her husband. She knew Grover would be the victor and considered Bishop's death a foregone conclusion.

"You might say a prayer that I kill the blackguard on the first shot," Grover suggested as the dueling party left.

"I most certainly will not!" Elizabeth retorted. "I will be on my knees until you come back, with my Bible in my hands, praying for your eternal salvation!"

Grover grunted. Although it was only a short distance to the traditional Rainbow dueling ground, they rode in the back of the carriage. A duel, after all, was a formal affair, which is why all three men wore their Sunday "go to meetin'" black suits.

Remarkably enough, Bishop actually showed up, although he was pale with fear. Ambrose expected him to flee the county during the

The Retribution Conspiracy

night, but he did not. He had convinced himself he could talk his way out of this mess, but that got him nowhere.

"You want free bricks? I'll have them put on your grave, moron!" Grover shouted. "Start the duel!" He yelled at Ross Yeldell, the newspaper editor who was also the umpire.

Yeldell, who like most people despised Bishop for his arrogance and selfishness, nevertheless made a half-hearted attempt at getting the two parties to reconcile, but it was plain to Ambrose he did so only because, as umpire, that was what he was expected to do.

Ambrose interrupted Yeldell's exhortation. "A resolution is not possible," he declared. "A Liebert Negro has been struck without justification or provocation, and we demand satisfaction. Proceed with the duel!" He demanded.

"But he's only one of those Africans!" Bishop cried in astonishment.

Ambrose sneered at the cowardly Bishop. He could have explained that William was one of the Liebert Negroes, and people laid their hands on them only at their peril but, since he considered Bishop beneath contempt, he did not waste his breath. Besides, why bother explaining anything to Bishop? He was going to be dead in five minutes anyway. "Start the duel!" He snapped at Yeldell.

Rance watched all of this from four feet away. For once, he felt immensely proud of his father. He hoped he could give orders with that kind of authority someday.

The editor did as he was told. He even smiled a little.

Bishop was pale and trembling. His legs shook as he walked off the traditional ten paces. Then he turned and fired first, but his hand was trembling so badly that he didn't even come close to hitting the much bigger target. The witnesses to the duel were in more danger than Grover Liebert. With tears pouring down his cheeks, Bishop fell to his knees. "Please, Mr. Grover …"

"Oh, go to the devil, you stupid peckerwood!" Grover Liebert was not a merciful, turn-the-other-cheek sort of man, but he was a fine shot. Bishop's head exploded like a ripe watermelon. One second later, Merv Bishop was dead.

"Did you see that, Rance?" Grover asked, with the smoking gun still in his hand. "That's how we handle white trash who try to abuse our people, especially our women and our darkies. We put 'em in the ground and relieve ourselves on their graves! Always remember that!"

"Yes, sir, Granddaddy!"

"We also defend helpless whites, especially poor whites, if we think they're bein' bullied and they're worthy of our protection," he added.

"Yes, sir, Granddaddy," Rance said, and he took the lesson to heart. It began to dawn on him that the duty protecting the weak and helpless was a responsibility which came with his station in life.

"And you ain't always got to fight fair, like I done today!" Grover added, smiling at the boy.

"Yes, sir."

Meanwhile, a crowd of adults gathered around the body. Rance moved hesitantly in that direction.

Mr. Yeldell put his hand on the boy's shoulder. "You don't have to observe the body, son," he stated.

"No, sir. That's okay. I want to," Rance declared. He didn't really want to but, as a second, he felt it was his duty to do so, so he did. A good part of Bishop's head was blown off, and his eyes were staring into space, but seeing nothing. The sight gave Rance a couple of nightmares over the next year, although he never told anybody. He was afraid the older Lieberts would think less of him if he did.

The sheriff didn't want to pay for the funeral with the limited county tax funds, so he approached Grover and asked him to bear the expense.

"I ain't gonna pay for it!" Grover snapped. "You should pay me for performing a public service. Why should I pay?"

"You killed him!" The sheriff declared, using typical frontier logic. Grover paused to consider this. He tried to think of a counterargument but could not.

"His wife and kids left him years ago, so there's no family to pay for it," the sheriff said.

"Well, I can't blame her for that …"

"And he dang sure didn't have a dime."

"He wasn't worth a dime!"

"I know," the sheriff replied. "But if you don't pay for it, the county will have to. You don't want everybody else to have to pay for something you done, do you?"

Grover thought for a moment. "Why bury him at all?" He asked. "Buzzards got to eat, same as worms!"

"Nope," the lawman replied. "That won't work. The Baptist Ladies Association would never stand for it."

"My foot!" Grover snapped. He wasn't about to mess with that bunch if he didn't have to. Defeated at every turn, he agreed to pay for the funeral. He had his slaves construct a coffin out of rejected boards and dig the grave. Coffins were normally lowered into the grave by ropes, which were then tossed into the grave and covered with dirt. To avoid the expense involved in losing two perfectly good ropes, Liebert ordered his slaves to simply nail the coffin shut and flip it into the grave upside down. They then covered it with dirt, and Grover ordered them to place a boundary of bricks around the fresh grave. "He wanted bricks!" Grover snapped, "but make sure to use only broken bricks," he told William. "Don't use nuthin' we might be able to sell."

"Yes sir," William replied, smiling broadly.

Before very many days, there was a faint smell of urine about Bishop's grave, suggesting Grover had paid it a nocturnal visit or two.

Everyone expected the grave to remain unmarked. Grover surprised them all. He ordered Bishop a tombstone, made from the cheapest stone, of course. It read: "Here Lies A Stupid Fool Who Crossed a Liebert." Grover was not an easy forgiver. He intended to have Bishop's name carved on it but decided to forgo the extra expense.

As on most plantations, the white children and the black children assigned to them at Fusilier grew up as virtual equals. They fished and gigged frogs together, played marbles and make-believe, fought each other with sticks that served as sabers, built forts out of mud or cotton lint, climbed trees, made sling shots and popped cows, dogs, and chickens, and occasionally a sibling. They also went skinny dipping together in a nearby pond or bayou, played hide and seek, and generally had a wonderful childhood. "Soldiers" and "Cowboys and Indians" were also popular games. The girls played dolls, house, and held tea parties, where they took turns serving each other. The "tea" very much resembled water.

Gradually all of this changed. Father and grandfather taught Rance and his younger brother Billy how to shoot, ride, and hunt. Their black companions knew they would suffer the severest punishments if they even touched a firearm; they were not even allowed to watch. In the 1790s the blacks in Haiti revolted and killed most of their white masters. The few who survived ran for their lives and, in most cases, escaped with only the clothes on their backs. Tales of horror, rape, and murder spread throughout the United States and shook the Deep South to its core. There was nothing a white Southerner feared more than servile insurrection. It was later a major factor contributing to the Southern secession movement because it was feared (and rightly so, in some cases) that Abolitionists and Republican Party leaders were encouraging slave revolts. Any slave caught conspiring to revolt was immediately hanged from the nearest tree. "Better to hang one too many than one too few!" was the governing principle. Any white child who allowed a black to hold a firearm could count upon a severe beating — and that was one beating neither Rance nor his younger brother Billy ever deserved or got. As for teaching a black how to load a gun — well, that was simply unthinkable.

By the time the Lieberts reached mid-childhood, the blacks walked slightly behind the whites. At the "tea" parties, the blacks now served their white friends but were served by them no longer. The close friendships which existed in childhood gradually deteriorated into more acceptable master-servant relationships. Then the white boys went to boarding schools and the white girls went to charm or finishing school. The blacks went to work. Every time the white boy returned from school the gap between him and his black childhood companion grew just a little bit wider, until there wasn't much left of the old relationship — just an occasional smile the white and Negro shared, as they remembered the golden days of their happy youth.

Only much later did it occur to Rance that he grew up advantaged, but his parents and grandparents never let him know it. They instilled in him the principles that privilege implies responsibility, difficult decisions naturally came with his station in life, and that character — the willingness to keep every commitment and to accept responsibility for one's actions — was the ground from which self-respect grew.

This is the world in which Rance and his brother Billy grew up. They never questioned a minute of it. The slaves felt much differently, of course, but to Rance and Billy, defending it was a cause worth fighting for. Worth dying for, if need be.

─◌ CHAPTER III ◌─
JEFFERSON F. DAVIS

Αt about age 12 or before, most plantation owner's sons went to boarding school. For many, this meant a school in the North. For Rance Liebert, it meant Jefferson College in Washington, Mississippi, because Grover wasn't about to spend the sort of money required for a New York or Pennsylvania institution. Tuition at Jefferson was $60 a year. Corporal punishment was administered at no additional charge.

Jefferson consisted of three large, ugly, multi-story brick buildings. These housed residential and classroom areas and a refectory (mess hall). It was a strict school, academically and in other respects. Classes began at 6 a.m. and continued until late afternoon, Monday through Friday. Saturday was a study day — all day. Failure to learn a lesson quickly enough usually earned the dullard a beating with a hickory switch.

Like Jefferson F. Davis — an earlier student — Rance hated Jefferson College. He hated the lack of freedom, the harsh rules, the terrible food, the uninterrupted work, and especially the frequent whippings. He could return to Fusilier only twice a year: Christmas break (two weeks) and August (summer vacation). At age 17, he looked upon his graduation day as one of the happiest days of his life — an opinion he never altered. In 1863, when the Yankees swept through the area, Colonel Rance Liebert openly hoped they would burn the place; after all, they were burning almost everything else. But in this hope Rance would be disappointed.

Meanwhile, Rance Liebert had made the transition from child to young man. He was very different from his father and grandfather in several ways. Though unquestionably a member of the Southern bourbon aristocrat class, he was not typical of it. He tried to like hunting, for example, and even though he was a reasonably good shot, he simply had no interest in sitting still for hours in order to kill an animal that had given him no cause for anger — especially when the mosquitoes were out, or the weather was cold. He liked to ride but was an indifferent horseman. He loved to fish but, to his chagrin, was never very good at it. He practiced throwing his Bowie knife and was very good at that, but it was more a result of repetition than of any natural ability. He rarely drank more than a single beer, didn't smoke, chew, or dip snuff. He enjoyed chess at Jefferson, but found few opponents in Rainbow, and thought checkers was too simple. He liked low-stakes poker, although he rarely was a big winner and more often than not was a modest loser. He never told anyone, but if his opponent were a poor Cracker, he occasionally would lose on purpose. They, after all, needed the money more than he. Although certainly not as charitable as Elizabeth, he did not mind helping out an impoverished family or down-and-out man or widow if he liked the person. Often the recipient would declare "I'm gonna pay you back," to which he would answer: "Naw, don't worry 'bout it," because he knew it never would happen, and he didn't want the party to feel guilty or obligated, or to avoid him because money was owed. He would usually end the conversation with the words: "This subject is closed. We will never discuss it again." Rance Liebert was, in short, generally kind to everyone when not aroused, whether a slave or a governor, and he definitely did not have his grandfather's temper — much to the relief of both the slave and the governor.

For a while, Elizabeth hoped, and Grover feared, that he would go into the ministry, but that didn't happen. He was, however, a bookworm. He loved to go to Natchez, Vicksburg, or Jackson for supplies and come back with a wagonload of books — or at least so it seemed to Ambrose and Grover. Actually he usually bought five or six volumes. They criticized him and occasionally berated him but to no avail. At one point, Grover and Ambrose refused to give him money to pay for his books. Elizabeth came to the rescue immediately. She loved having a man in the house with whom she could discuss the Bible and the finer points of scripture, and Rance purchased a Bible compendium, which gave her hours of pleasure. He also bought a religious dictionary, several books on church history, and biographies of Martin Luther, St. Thomas Aquinas, and other religious leaders and philosophers. The two of them enjoyed hours of theological discussion — and often alone. Grover, Ambrose, and Billy immediately found other things to do. Sometimes Jonathan and Rance's younger sister Penny would join them and, although they rarely spoke, they seemed to enjoy listening. In any case, as far as Elizabeth was concerned, not buying books was just unacceptable.

The next time Rance and one of the slaves prepared to drive a wagon to Natchez, she rushed out and handed Rance $40 in gold pieces — a huge sum. "Here's some money fur yo' books!" she declared loudly, right in front of Grover and Ambrose. "And don't bring none of it back!" This was a direct challenge. The two astonished Liebert males just stood there with their mouths open, but they didn't dare say anything. That ended the financial prohibition, but not the beratings. "You gonna fill up the stinkin' library with books!" Ambrose snapped.

Rance soon developed a tactic to deal with his father and grandfather. When they criticized him for being too much of a reader, he would just look up from his book and stare at them. He had read somewhere that silence was the most effective form of scorn, and he discovered that was sometimes right. He would let them exhaust themselves; then he would quietly return to his reading. After he got back from Jefferson, he spent the entire summer immersed in books. He especially enjoyed military history.

Grover Liebert sat in the rocking chair on the huge front porch of Fusilier, holding a mint julep and staring at his oldest grandson with his mouth wide open. He was utterly astonished by what the young man had just announced. He wanted to say, "What do you mean you don't want to be a planter?" But the words just would not come. All he could manage was "Huh?"

"I said 'I don't want to be a planter,' Granddaddy."

Ambrose Liebert frowned at his boy and waited for the explosion. Grover Liebert finished his drink in one gulp, but he said nothing. He just glared at young Rance.

"Want me to git you another, Mr. Grover?" The butler asked.

"No! Bring me a bottle of bourbon and a pitcher of water."

Rance smiled. He knew the bottle would empty faster than the pitcher.

Grover rapped his fingers on the arm of the rocking chair. He had intended to give Rance a section of land in Rainbow County and lease him some slaves to get him started. Then he could build a house, procure a wife, and begin producing great-grandchildren, preferably at a rapid pace. Shucks, that boy could do anything. And now this.

"What do you want to do?" He asked the recent Jefferson College graduate. "Become a lawyer?"

"Good heavens, no! I mean no, sir."

Grover smiled slightly. He didn't like lawyers — or carpenters, tailors, railroad conductors, dress makers, bookkeepers, stagecoach drivers, or much of anybody else. Especially the Irish. And Catholics. And

Jews. And the Chinese — even though he had never met one. And Protestants of all denominations. And … He focused on the issue at hand. "What then?" he asked Rance.

"I don't really know …"

Then Rance threw his grandfather what later generations would call a curveball. "I think I'd like to try my hand at soldiering."

A frown extended across Grover's face but he didn't say anything. He was thinking hard. The boy wants an adventure.

"The Mexicans crossed into Texas last week and killed some of our boys. They need their rumps kicked. I'd like to help."

That could work the other way 'round, Grover thought. He had heard that Santa Anna had a hech[4] of a big army, and although everyone glorified the Alamo, Grover remembered that every American there (except for the women, children and some of the slaves) ended up dead.

"I don't know …" Ambrose responded.

"Oh, hush!" Grover snapped at his son, who went silent immediately. After a pause, he turned to Rance and said, "Yeah, but you don't want to enlist as a private. Once you do that, you can't get out." Grover would never know what a curveball was, but he knew how to handle one.

Rance hesitated. He was obviously unsure how to proceed. Grover, as usual, had an idea. His brain worked rapidly, but not usually in the most pleasant manner, and what he thought and what he said weren't always the same thing.

"I'll write to my friend Jeff Davis at Brierfield. He's forming a regiment. He owes me more than one favor. He'll get you a commission if I ask him to."

"Okay," Rance responded uncertainly.

"He gave a speech at Natchez Thursday. He'll be at Brierfield now. You can meet with him there tomorrow."

"Excellent," Rance declared, although he was a little overwhelmed at how rapidly things were moving.

"You go get packed for three days," he ordered. "I'll have the letter writ before you're finished."

"Yes, Granddaddy," Rance said, and headed upstairs. He was a bit stunned at the speed of events. He would be on the road within 10

---

4 Originally a Scottish word for annoyance or surprise, it was the forerunner of the word "heck," which was first used about 1887.

hours of the decision being made. Grover Liebert was an "action this day" sort of person.

After Rance went upstairs, Ambrose dared to speak again. "What are you thinkin', Daddy?"

"The boy wants adventure," Grover allowed. "There ain't nothin' we can do about that. So let's let him git it out of his system. Colonel Davis will take care of him as much as he can 'cause he owes me. And, as an officer, Rance can get mad and quit. As a private soldier, all he can do is git mad."

"So you think he'll quit?"

"Sure. Probably won't take long, if I know the army. Most likely long before he gits to Mexico."

"But what if he doesn't?"

"Then I reckon he'll have to take his chances like everybody else," Grover reflected.

"What if he gits kilt?"

"Then he gits killed. Would you rather he run off and fight Indians?"

"No."

"Maybe sign up on some ship and hunt whales or something stupid like that?"

"No," Ambrose said. "I'd rather he stayed here and planted cotton."

"Ain't gonna happen," Grover declared. "At least not yet. Let's let him go. We're goin' to have to do that anyway. The army and the Mexicans will knock this nonsense out of his system. Then he'll be ready to come home and plant cotton." Grover revised his own plans. *I'll just give him half a section. When he gets back from Texas, he'll be happy with that.*

Rance and Chuckatuck, Jonathan's youngest son, were up and on the road well before dawn the next day. By early afternoon, they were near Davis Bend on the Mississippi River and went to the Big House, to see Colonel Jefferson F. Davis.

They went to the wrong house. The Big House was Hurricane, which was owned by Joseph Davis, Jefferson's older brother by 23 years. It was a massive, two-story structure with twin wings. It was ornate and awe-inspiring, so Rance and Chuckatuck naturally assumed it must belong to the congressman. They were set straight by Joseph's butler. Brierfield was nearby and was much more modest. But the colonel wasn't there either. He was in Joseph's library, which was located between Hurricane and Brierfield. So Rance made his third stop in an hour.

Joseph Davis' library was off the main road by several hundred feet. Joseph had built it for his wife, but both he and Jefferson used it extensively. It was constructed with huge glass windows (to facilitate reading during daylight hours) and easily could have accommodated a family of four in luxury. A black servant opened the door, received Rance's card and Grover's letter, and asked him to wait. A few minutes later, Rance was escorted into the presence of Jefferson F. Davis.

Davis frowned when he read Grover's request. The last thing he wanted right now was to do another favor for a constituent. He had to organize and equip his new command and prepare for embarkation to Texas. Still, a request from Grover Liebert could not be ignored, and the young man waiting outside was a Liebert. He, therefore, could naturally be expected to relish a good fight. It was even possible he had the senior Liebert's talents for organization and seizing an opportunity, in which case he might be a tremendous asset, despite his youth and inexperience. He hoped he didn't have Grover's temper.

Jeff Davis was a tall, slender man who was cleanly shaven except for a short beard extending from his chin. Although it was not apparent to the casual observer, he was not in good health. Davis suffered from malaria and a chronic eye infection which made bright light very painful for him. He also had trigeminal neuralgia, a nerve disorder that caused severe facial pain and is considered one of the most painful of diseases. He had the reputation of being an unemotional, cold fish. In fact, Jefferson Davis had a very complicated personality. He was warm, aloof, thin-skinned, affectionate, obstinate, petty, witty (when he wanted to be), vindictive, fearless, bitter, and loyal to a fault. Unfortunately, he was a very private public man who kept his better side hidden from all except his family and closest friends. He did not open up to strangers, but he could be quite warm and even friendly to people he liked. He just didn't like many people. Similar to his father, he felt affection but repressed the expression of it.

Born in Kentucky, his family moved to "Rosemond," their plantation near Woodville, Mississippi Territory, when he was very young. He was sent to boarding school in Kentucky at age nine. He returned home when he was 11, but only for a few weeks. Then he attended Jefferson College, where he soon received an assignment he could not complete. After the instructor beat him severely, he left the school and returned home. His father, Samuel Davis, said that was fine — he could go to work instead. He picked cotton for two days, from daylight to dark ("Can see 'til can't see" as the slaves said.) He then eagerly returned to Jefferson.

Jeff Davis was good in Latin and Greek and at least adequate in everything else. He wanted to follow in the footsteps of his brother Joseph, who was a father figure to him and his beau ideal in all respects, and he already wanted to be a lawyer, like his brother. So Jeff attended law school at Transylvania College in Kentucky. After he graduated, Joseph had a surprise for him: he proudly announced that he had secured Jefferson an appointment to the United States Military Academy!

Jeff Davis bowed to his brother's wish without the slightest objection, even though he really did not want to go to West Point. There he was a mediocre cadet and a wild one. He received one court-martial conviction, almost got a second, was found guilty of repeated infractions, had a below average academic career, and almost got himself killed. He was visiting Benny Havens Tavern, which was strictly off-limits to all cadets, when word arrived that the duty officer was on his way. Davis tried to evade the captain by making his way through the woods but, due to a combination of alcohol and darkness, fell 60 feet off a cliff and spent the next four months in the hospital. He also spent six weeks in the guardhouse for his part in the Egg Nog Riot, for which 19 cadets were expelled. He ended up ranking 23rd in a graduation class of 33. In conduct, he finished 163rd out of a cadet corps of 208. He was commissioned in the infantry — the least desirable of all branches.

Second Lieutenant Davis distinguished himself almost at once. He went directly into action in the Black Hawk War against the Sauk Indians, a conflict he considered unfair, unjust, and one-sided. On his first mission, he personally captured Chief Black Hawk and ended the war without firing a shot.[5]

Lieutenant Davis was a favorite of his regimental commander, Zachary Taylor — until he fell in love with Sarah Knox "Knoxie" Taylor, the colonel's daughter. Then their relationship rapidly fell apart, and the Taylors denied Davis permission to marry their daughter, or even to enter their home again. Jefferson resigned from the Army and

---

5 Abraham Lincoln also volunteered for the Black Hawk War, was given command of a company and was promoted to captain. He was such a hopeless soldier, however, that he was soon demoted to private. It was his only military service, and he served only three months. Like Davis, he did not hear a shot fired in anger.

married her anyway. This elopement led to the turning point in Davis' life. In a hurry to wed the 21-year-old beauty, Jefferson persuaded her to move the wedding up three months — which meant they were in the Mississippi Delta in the middle of the malaria season. While on a honeymoon visit to his sister's plantation in St. Francisville, Louisiana, both of them contracted the disease. He nearly died from it, and she did die. They were married for three months.

Her death broke Davis' heart. It took him a long time to forgive himself for Knoxie's death — if he ever did. He became a recluse for several years and never was the same fun-loving, carefree young man after that. When he finally emerged from his self-imposed exile, he was cold, distant, and formal to almost everyone.

Knoxie undoubtedly was the one true love of Jefferson Davis' life. His second marriage, to Varina Banks Howell, was much more tumultuous. They separated twice and, despite six children, had more than their share of tragedy and strife. They were going through one of their periodic fights when Rance Liebert arrived at Brierfield. Davis responded as he always did — he threw himself into his work. Now, this included interviewing young Liebert.

"How old are you, Mr. Liebert?"

"I am 18 years old, sir. And you can call me Rance."

Davis ignored this attempt at informality. He asked the standard interview questions, which haven't changed since Caesar's time. He inquired about Liebert's military experience (none), his motivations (patriotism), and what made him think he'd be a good officer (plantation management experience and attention to detail). Finally, he asked: "How did you like Jefferson College?"

This was the moment Rance Liebert had been dreading, and he faced the age-old dilemma: tell the truth or tell the interviewer what he thought he wanted to hear. The devil with it, Liebert thought. Since the interview wasn't going particularly well anyway, he decided he might as well tell the truth.

"I hated it."

Jefferson Davis sat up, startled.

"What?"

"I said I hated it. I hated every minute of it."

There! He said it. The cat was out of the bag.

To Liebert's amazement, a huge grin broke out all across Congressman Davis' face. "I hated it also!"

As if by magic, the ice broke. Suddenly, the older man and the young aspirant had something in common. They began talking to each other like old friends. Davis lamented about the beatings he received and commented that any owner who beat his slaves as often as the instructors beat their students at Jefferson would be a sorry master indeed. He went on to compare Jefferson unfavorably with Transylvania and West Point. Jefferson Davis could be quite charming when he chose to be, and Rance Liebert thoroughly enjoyed listening to him. The interview ended with Davis inviting Rance to dinner. He also wrote out a pass for Chuckatuck, instructing Joseph's butler to feed him and put him up in the guest slave quarters for the night.

After dinner, Davis and Liebert talked well into the night. (Rance did not realize why, but Davis preferred talking to the younger man instead of arguing with his wife.) However, it was more than that. In each other the two found something for which each of them was looking. Rance found a leader he could follow. Grover was and would remain something of a role model, but the senior Liebert wanted to spend his life on his own little empire (Fusilier and the town of Rainbow, of which he owned about half). This Rance did not want to do. He wanted to see the wide, wide world, and visit some of the places about which he had been reading. Colonel Davis would be a willing guide and something of a second father.

In young Liebert, Jefferson Davis saw a more youthful, if somewhat tamer, version of himself, as he was before Knoxie's death. He also saw a valuable subordinate and collaborator. He saw someone in whom he could confide, as well as a man who would not be afraid to take drastic action should the time come. He instinctively understood Rance would be a loyal if inexperienced friend and colleague. Experience could be gained; loyalty, efficiency, and intelligence were innate. And Jeff Davis needed all the friends he could get, because he didn't have very many.

To Liebert's astonishment and delight, over breakfast the next morning, Davis named him regimental adjutant. His rank would be second lieutenant of Mississippi State Troops (i.e., of volunteers) as soon as Governor Quitman signed the commission. He told Liebert to go home, have uniforms made, and then head for the regiment's encampment at Camp Independence near Vicksburg. Davis was precise about how the uniforms should look. The colonel himself would join them in about a month.

"You won't be joining us immediately, sir?"

"No. I have to make a quick trip to Washington. I leave by steamboat this afternoon."

Liebert looked up from his coffee. "Congressional business?" he asked.

"Yes and no," Davis responded. He thought a moment and decided to tell the young man the whole story. After all, if he were going to be his adjutant, he might need to know it. "I've made a political deal. I want to equip the regiment with M1841 rifled muskets, which are superior in all respects to the old smoothbore muskets the other regiments will have — especially regarding range. General Scott, our army commander, tried to block me on this, because the M1841 has not been sufficiently tested. But President Polk needs my vote on the Walker Tariff. If I delay my resignation from Congress until after the tariff passes, he has agreed to equip us with the rifled muskets."

Liebert smiled. He saw Jeff Davis wasn't above doing a little political horse trading and would take care of his men, even if it meant earning the lifelong enmity of a powerful man like Scott. He also got a preview of Davis' future military success in Mexico. In the open field, his men would shoot the enemy to pieces before they could get close enough to do any damage at all to his regiment. This, in turn, would give them a confidence and a swagger the other volunteer regiments would never have. It would also make Jeff Davis look very, very good. Soon the governor renamed the regiment "the 1st Mississippi Rifles" or just the "Mississippi Rifles." Although it was manufactured in Connecticut, the M1841 became known as "the Mississippi Rifle," and the 1st Mississippi became the best volunteer regiment to fight in the Mexican War. It later occurred to Rance Liebert that, at the beginning of his military career, he had been fortunate indeed. Davis even gave him three books to read on military tactics, drills, and formations.

Finally, it was time for future Second Lieutenant Liebert to return home. Davis walked him to his horse and Rance mounted. To Jefferson Davis' surprise, he hated to see him go. The two men were already developing a father-son relationship. But instead of riding away, Rance asked a question.

"What does the F stand for?"

"Sir?" Asked a puzzled Davis.

"You are Jefferson F. Davis. What does the F stand for?"

Davis smiled. "Finis. I was my father's tenth child, and he didn't want any more. He gave me the Latin name for 'finished' to underline that fact."

The Retribution Conspiracy

Liebert grinned. "Did he have any more?"

"No!"

Both men laughed as Liebert nudged his horse with the toe of his boot and began the long ride back to Fusilier.

—✌ CHAPTER IV ✌—
MEXICO

Second Lieutenant of Volunteers Rance Liebert joined his regiment at Camp Independence and, after a stop in New Orleans, was on a boat headed for Mexico. Veterans considered the trip down the Mississippi and across the Gulf of Mexico to be uneventful, but 18-year-old Rance Liebert loved every minute of it. Before now, he never saw anything like the Gulf or ventured very far from home. Now he discovered he liked traveling, and he relished new experiences and seeing new places. When not engaged in his duties (and there was little to do on a sea voyage) or in studying military manuals, he was constantly on the deck, day and night, watching the waves and the sky and the sea. Grover Liebert would have been irked: his plan was miscarrying.

They ended up at Port Isabel on the Rio Grande, where they pitched camp and remained for several weeks, along with 5,000 other soldiers. Jeff Davis drilled his men in formation fighting every day, morning and evening. The hot sun and white sand made life miserable for the troops, as did the flies, sand fleas, and the constant drill, musket and manual-of-arms practice, but Davis was going to be sure his men were ready when the time came. Meanwhile, Rance Liebert learned his new profession rapidly. Colonel Davis was pleased the young lieutenant was a quick study and exhibited none of the infamous Grover Liebert temper. He devoured the three books the colonel had loaned him, asked for more, read every regulation and training manual he could get his hands on, and was rapidly becoming the master of his job. Although generally humorless, Davis showed occasional flashes of charm and wit and even took to calling him "Rance" when they were alone. On the other hand, Rance discovered Davis was what in another century would be called a micro-manager. He supervised everyone very closely, and no detail was too small to attract his attention. Although this occasionally annoyed Rance, he was too inexperienced to realize this was a fault. He assumed that, because Davis acted this way, perhaps that was the way adults were supposed to act. Only later, as he learned more about the world, would this trouble him.

While they were in the Texas desert, the rifles arrived. As Davis had said, they fired a five-ounce, .54 caliber conical bullet, which was considered huge in 1846. The rifle's maximum range was 1,100 yards. The best muskets of the day had a maximum effective range of 75 to 100 yards. It had no slot to mount a bayonet. The designers calculated that, if they were facing a regiment armed with M1841, the enemy would never get close enough for the Americans to need cold steel.[6]

They were right.

—⁂—

Rance Liebert's first battle took place at de La Teneria, a fort on the outer edge of the fortified city of Monterrey. It was a former tannery constructed out of stone and improved by Mexican army engineers. Rance fought on foot, armed with only a pistol, a saber, and his ever-present Bowie knife; he did more cheering than actual fighting. The Mississippians with their superior rifles cut down dozens of Mexicans long before Rance got within range with his puny little single-shot pistol, and his saber was even more useless. Once the enemy saw how effective the M1841s were, they kept their heads down, and the onrushing Southerners just ran right over them. Liebert leaped over a low spot on the wall with the first wave, only to find himself face to face with two dirty, unshaven, Mexican privates, armed with ancient muskets. They were holding them at port arms, not in firing position. The first man was older, so Rance instantly decided he must be the leader. He thrust his pistol into the old man's face, cocked it, and yelled, "Hands up!" It is almost certain the adversary did not know a word of English, but he dropped his musket and threw up both hands, his eyes wide with terror. The younger man immediately followed suit. *Hech, they're probably just a couple of Santa Anna's recent draftees, Liebert thought, possibly a grandfather and his grandson. They'd rather be home, planting corn, than here. In fact, I'll bet they'd rather be just about anywhere than here.* It occurred to him later they probably had never fired a shot in anger before — but then neither had he. He took them prisoner and sent them to the rear. He then examined their muskets. They were old, heavy, and so cumbersome they could not be lifted to the shoulder and properly aimed. They would have to fire them from the hip! The weaponry with which Santa Anna sent his men into battle was appalling. By the time Liebert finished his brief inspection, the entire garrison had surrendered, and Jeff Davis was accepting the Mexican colonel's sword. *Not much to brag about in my first battle,* Rance thought. Still, he had "seen the elephant," as the Civil War generation would call it, and he

---

6 Later models would have a bayonet slot.

The Retribution Conspiracy

had risked his life; he was proud that he felt more excitement than fear.

Two days later, Taylor's army was fighting house-to-house in Monterrey. It was the American army's first experience in urban warfare, and it did not go well. The U.S. 5th Infantry, a regular army regiment, charged down the narrow streets toward the plaza. Its men were slaughtered by the Mexicans, who were firing from rooftops with their muskets and cannons. The seriously depleted Regulars retreated in disorder and the Texans and Mississippians replaced them.

The Texans actually knew what they were doing when it came to street combat. Many of them fought at San Antonio in 1835, where they destroyed an entire Mexican army in house-to-house fighting. Unlike the Regulars, they disdained the streets; instead, they knocked "mouse holes" in the adobe walls and moved slowly but steadily from house to house, clearing one building after another. Watching the Texans, the less experienced Mississippians also figured it out quickly. Using their superior weapons, they waited until a Mexican sniper or artillery spotter raised his head; then they shot him. This the Regulars, armed with their antiquated muskets, could not do. The fact such wounds were almost invariably fatal demoralized the Mexicans, who now kept their heads down — in most cases until the bottom floors of their buildings were overrun. Before very long, isolated and pinned down on the roof, baking in the hot sun with no hope of escaping, they chose to wave the white flag. One building after another fell to the Southerners.

At one point, a sergeant named Leonard was running from one edifice to another when a Mexican on the roof shot him through the shoulder. He lay bleeding and helpless in the street. Lieutenant Liebert, who saw the whole thing from a mouse hole, realized Santa Anna's soldier was almost certainly reloading his musket for another shot. "Quick!" He yelled to four of the Mississippi Rifles. "Into the street! Keep that tortilla eater's head down while I carry the sergeant inside!"

Although not under his direct command, the Rifles obeyed immediately. As Rance lifted the wounded man, he heard two shots. Looking up, he saw the Mexican's musket falling to the pavement and a red haze floating in the gentle breeze. He knew what happened: the enemy soldier had raised up to finish off Leonard and was shot in the head by the Mississippians. They quickly reloaded while the other two riflemen covered them and Liebert carried the sergeant to the nearest mouse hole. Once they were inside, Leonard's comrades ripped off his shirt and tried to stop the bleeding.

"Good work, lieutenant!" Colonel Davis exclaimed. Rance beamed with pride. He always welcomed praise, especially from Jefferson Davis or Grover Liebert.

The house-to-house fighting continued all day, with the Texans and Mississippians slowly clearing block after block. At one point, Jeff Davis and Rance Liebert watched as a soldier kicked in a door, broke into the house, and immediately turned around and ran away. Davis yelled at the boy, who shouted back something indistinguishable and kept running. The colonel and Liebert drew their pistols, ran inside, and then also turned and ran away.

They had entered a house of ill repute. A fat and obviously drunk Mexican was trying to pull up his trousers when they broke in. Seeing the two Americans pointing their pistols at him, he raised his hands to surrender — dropping his pants and exposing himself in the process. Two singularly unattractive naked women in the bed laughed uproariously as the future president of the Confederate States of America and the future head of its Secret Service ingloriously fled as rapidly as they could, with Liebert moving faster than the older man. He later told a group of officers that it was the most horrifying sight he saw during the whole war, and the only time he ever saw Colonel Davis run away. Jefferson Davis just smiled, blushed a little, and shook his head. He never said a word.

Meanwhile, the Mexican garrison surrendered on September 24.

In 1846, the United States Army did not pass out medals; instead, they rewarded courage in one of two ways. The first was to issue "brevet" (honorary) promotions. (Captain Robert E. Lee would earn three during this war.) The other was to mention a particular soldier in dispatches. "Mentioned in dispatches" was a conspicuous honor, but not as high as a brevet. To his delight, Rance Liebert was "mentioned in dispatches" for his "conspicuous gallantry" during the Battle of Monterrey.

Other than that, the winter of 1846/47 was an unhappy one for Second Lieutenant Liebert. It was a very rainy winter, and two-thirds of the tents furnished by the army were rotten and offered little protection. The cold rain poured through and made everybody miserable. The food was also horrible — usually just a slab of beef or pork and a piece of hard bread. Before long, diseases, including yellow fever, malaria, dysentery, measles, and smallpox swept through the camp. Nearly 87 percent of the American army deaths in Mexico were from disease — seven men for every one killed by a Mexican bullet, shell or sword.

The Retribution Conspiracy

The Americans had already achieved their objectives and were ready for peace, and assumed the Mexicans would be also. Santa Anna, however, refused to accommodate them. He intended to retake northern Mexico, including Texas, New Mexico, Arizona, and California. So the war went on.

President Polk decided Mexico City would have to be captured before the war could end. To accomplish this, he established a second American army under General Winfield Scott. It was to assemble at New Orleans and launch a seaborne invasion of southern Mexico, an operation which would end in the capture of the Mexican capital. To man this army, he took nearly all of the regulars and some of the volunteer regiments from Zach Taylor's force, reducing its strength to 4,700 men. None of the remaining regiments had seen combat except the Mississippi Rifles. Santa Anna read all about it in American newspapers. He decided to recapture northern Mexico and assembled an army of 20,000 men for that purpose. He intended to strike Taylor before Scott could launch his invasion — and he did.

In February 1847, Taylor took Saltillo (50 miles west of Monterrey) without a fight and pushed out 30 miles to the south. Then scouts from the Texas Rangers warned General Taylor the Mexicans were coming. He fell back to Buena Vista, the name of both a mountain pass and a hacienda, seven miles south of Saltillo, where he made his stand. It was an excellent defensive position.

On February 22, the Mexican generalissimo launched a massive frontal assault. After three hours of heavy fighting, the 2nd Indiana Volunteers broke and ran, and Santa Anna pushed through Taylor's front, while the rest of the army streamed to the rear. All that stood between it and total destruction were the reserves: the 1st Mississippi Rifles and Captain Braxton Bragg's artillery battery. But Colonel Davis had also selected his position exceptionally well. The Mexican cavalry set out in pursuit, only to run into an ambush and a crossfire. It was a slaughter; horses and men went down by the dozens. Then came the infantry. But Davis rested both his flanks on ravines in a "V" formation. As the Mexicans advanced, they met a devastating converging fire from the Mississippi Rifles. Meanwhile, Taylor rallied the rest of his army, regrouped, and counterattacked. By the end of the day, the Americans possessed the field.

Rance Liebert spent the entire battle on horseback at Jefferson Davis' elbow. As adjutant, that was what he was supposed to do, so he did it. Although he hoped to be given command of a company — and on rare occasions, second lieutenants did receive such a command — it did not happen for him. Once a musket ball flew between him and Davis, and Liebert's only thought was that it made an odd sound. Only later did it occur to him he might have been killed. He fired his pistol only once during the entire battle, toward an oncoming phalanx of Mexican infantry. He couldn't tell if he hit anything, and at that range, it was extremely unlikely he did, but it made him feel better.

Jeff Davis spent the whole battle riding a horse. He had to ride because he couldn't walk. Early in the day, a musket ball slammed through his foot near the ankle joint. He flinched but never said a word about it. As the enemy began their retreat, Rance Liebert noticed the colonel was pale from loss of blood. He and another officer lowered him from his horse (despite Davis' weak objections) and, using a door as a litter, carried him to the rear. They were briefly stopped by General Taylor, who uttered some of the most gratifying words Jefferson Davis ever heard. "My daughter was a better judge of men than I was," he said, referring to Knoxie. A tear rolled down the colonel's cheek as Liebert and his colleague carried him off the field.

In terms of killed and wounded, Buena Vista was the costliest battle of the Mexican War. It also left the United States in undisputed control of northern Mexico, including what became the American southwest. The war in northern Mexico was over. After a few more miserable weeks in the Mexican desert, the enlistments ran out. The Mississippi Rifles had no interest in signing up for the duration. They marched north, toward the boats which would take them home, where they were discharged.

It took Colonel Davis five years to fully recover from his wound. It would be two years before he could walk again without crutches. He wrote his final report from his hospital bed. In it, he recommended Rance Liebert be given a brevet promotion to first lieutenant for gallantry at Monterrey and Buena Vista. General Taylor concurred, and the brevet was granted. So when Rance Liebert returned home, people looked upon him as something of a war hero, even though he had never held a command, never killed anybody, fired only one shot in anger, hit nothing, and had been routed by a pair of ugly prostitutes and a drunk, overweight, overage Mexican.

The Retribution Conspiracy

He had, however, done his job well and was a different man. Now he walked with a swagger like he was somebody and he knew it. For him, there would be no more corporal punishment, for example. He grew up in Mexico and was tougher and more mature. People now looked upon him as a leader and even if they didn't step aside for him as rapidly as they would for Davis or Grover, they still stepped aside. The veterans greeted him with smiles, called him "lieutenant," shook his hand, and occasionally even offered to buy him a beer. Behind his back, gentlemen whispered to their ladies, that man was Rance Liebert, Jefferson Davis' adjutant, who was brevetted and mentioned in dispatches. He stormed over the wall at de La Teneria, fought house-to-house in the streets of Monterrey, rode beside Taylor and Davis in the great victory at Buena Vista, carried the colonel off the field when he was wounded, and both the colonel and the general thought very highly of him. That was enough to impress anybody, because Zachary Taylor was obviously on his way to the White House and Jeff Davis was looked upon as a bona fide war hero, North and South. Rance, meanwhile, swore that if anyone raised a hand to him again, it would be in peril of his life. And no one ever did.

─⌐ CHAPTER V ⌐─
LIGHTNING RODS
AND COLD BEDS

When he got back from Mexico, Rance Liebert faced the age-old question young people have faced since time immemorial: what am I going to do with my life? One evening, he joined Jonathan and Grover and sat in a rocking chair on the front porch. With a great deal of gravity, Grover offered him half a section of prime land, but Rance turned it down. Grover then raised it to a whole section. Rance declined that as well.

"Well, what the devil do you want?" Grover snapped, somewhat loudly.

Rance didn't have an answer for him.

"Well, you've got to do something!" The older Liebert said emphatically and banged his cane on the floor.

After a long pause, Rance said: "Maybe I'll become a lightning rod salesman."

"WHAT?"

"Yeah. That's it. I'll sell lightning rods."

"Lightning rods?!"

"Yeah. I'll design one people can use to cook steaks. Attach the Liebert Lightning Rod to a steer as a thunderstorm approaches. Now you won't have to kill the animal. The varmint will be both killed and cooked immediately, and the hide will be burned off, so you won't have to skin it. The carcass will be raw on one side, well done on the other, and every other shade in between. There will be a cut for every taste. It will also work on pigs and perhaps we can design a smaller one for chickens. Soon everybody will want one!" He declared enthusiastically. "I'll probably make a fortune."

Everyone smiled and Jonathan giggled. The patriarch of the family tried to remain harsh but couldn't quite do it. "Might work," he conceded.

"Sure it'll work!" Rance declared. "I'm gonna be rich!" Then he went silent.

The three men continued to rock on the veranda. The only sound was crickets and Jonathan chuckling. His giggle box had been knocked over. "Boy, you ain't right!" Was all he said.

"What are you going to do, Rance?" Grover asked again after a few minutes had elapsed.

"I don't know." Then, after another pause, he said: "I'd like to do a tour of the North. Maybe Europe. See the world."

"That costs money," Grover said and sipped his mint julep.

"Yeah. I heard that rumor."

More rocking. Jonathan giggled and resumed drinking what was left of his sweet tea. He still hadn't gotten over the lightning rods.

"You saw Mexico."

"Mexico was a war zone. That was manure. Mexico don't count."

"You saw Texas."

"Liked Texas, but didn't see any of it beyond the Rio Grande Valley. Never even went inside a private home. Texas don't count neither."

More rocking.

"Okay," Grover finally said. "Here's the deal. I'll pay for your grand tour. But if you still don't know what you want to do when you git back, I'll give you that half section, and you'll plant cotton."

"Okay. Whole section."

"Half section."

"Whole section."

"Three-quarters of a section."

"Done," Rance said. "How many slaves?"

"You askin' for a lot, boy!"

"I ain't plantin' and pickin' no 480 acres of cotton by myself."

More rocking. Grover sulked. "Or I could go back in the army," Rance said.

Grover frowned. "That's a good way to git kilt."

"General Taylor said I was real good at it. He said he'd get me a Regular Army commission if I wanted it."

Zachary Taylor said no such thing, but Rance was running a bluff. Besides, Taylor liked him and considered him efficient. He might get him a commission if Rance asked for it, although the young man wouldn't want to bet the plantation on it. Of course, Rance would rather eat a buffalo chip than accept such a commission, but Grover didn't know that.

"I've always wanted to see the Great Plains, live in a teepee and kill myself an Indian … Maybe git me a squaw and have a papoose." Rance declared. He was lying, of course, but Grover already thought he was crazy. Might as well play on that.

"All right," the grandfather snapped, abandoning the point. "I'll lease you the slaves you need when the time comes. You can pay me for them out of the profits."

"Done. But I want submarket rates."

"But you ain't gonna git 'em."

"Family rates?"

"No! Market rates!"

Rance frowned. "Okay," he said, realizing that he wasn't going to obtain any more concessions out of his grandfather that evening. But there was a way around that. He smiled. He would take up the matter with Grandmother Elizabeth at the appropriate time.

Jonathan grinned again and shook his head. "Sell lightning rods!"

———

Rance was excited about going to Europe, and everybody seemed happy for him except one person: little Sally Mae Glass. Ever since the Belle's Ball, she hugged him every time she saw him and sat by him in church every Sunday, as if that were exactly where she belonged. Unlike an adult, she did not try to hide her disappointment he was going to be gone for a year or more. She asked him to promise to send her letters from every country he visited.

Rance didn't fancy writing entire letters to a six-year-old, but he did promise to send her an occasional lithograph print.[7] She pouted.

"Tell you what," he said. "I'll send the letters to my mother and Grandma Elizabeth, but they'll be to you, too, okay? And I'll use envelopes with printed pictures on them, so you can see where I've been. I will also send Letter Cartes.[8] And I'll tell Miz Elizabeth to let you keep the envelopes and cartes."

"Well …" she muttered.

"You'll get a picture print and a letter just about every Sunday," he promised, "unless I'm on a boat somewhere."

She brightened up at this.

Dang, Rance thought. It looks as if I have a six-year-old girlfriend who feels perfectly comfortable making demands. How did I get myself into this? But he did like the little girl and, over the next 24 months, he kept his promise and sent out a great many picture envelopes and several lithograph prints. The envelopes he addressed to both grand-

---

7 Lithograph prints and envelopes with printed pictures on them were fairly common before the invention of the post card.

8 Letter Cartes were the forerunner of the postcard.

mother and Sally Mae.

Rance left Mississippi two weeks after his conversation with the Boss and spent the next two years on the road. He was thrifty, although Grover accused him of spending money with both hands. Elizabeth, naturally, defended and shielded him, so Rance never heard a word about it. He spent months at a northern university, taking courses he wanted to take, just for fun. The teenage former lieutenant spent an entire summer in Harvard's magnificent library, reading whatever interested him. Armed with a letter of recommendation from Zachary Taylor (who would soon be president of the United States), he made a special arrangement with the vice-chancellor, who allowed him to check out books and read them at his boarding house. The young Southern aristocrat went to Europe and spent three months in Oxford. He also spent months touring the Continent. He later said these were the best two years of his life. He was a different man when he got home and was exposed to views and opinions one did not get in Rainbow, Mississippi.

The day after his return, Grover asked him what he wanted to do.

"Plant cotton," he said.

"You want to be a planter?"

"Not really," Rance admitted. "But, as somebody told me, I've got to do something."

Rance went to work with his slaves, whom he acquired from Grover at submarket or "family" rates, thanks to Elizabeth. It wasn't long before Rance wished he had become a lawyer. But he stuck with planting, although he wasn't as good at it as Billy or Ambrose or Grover — or Jonathan, for that matter. He joined the local civic groups, took part in an occasional poker game at the local tavern, had an occasional beer with the boys (mostly former Mississippi Rifles), attended church with Elizabeth, and eventually courted a local belle named Mildred. He didn't want to be married, necessarily, and certainly wasn't head over heels in love; however, it was expected, and Rance tended to do what was expected of him, and he really did want to have children. He did like her, so he married her. Although he didn't see much sense in it, Grover threw them a bang-up wedding.

Their honeymoon trip began at the awesome Monmouth Plantation in Natchez. He became friends with John A. Quitman, the former governor who was his brigade commander during the war. Like many Mississippians, Quitman was a fire-eating secessionist. Rance was more a moderate, much like Jefferson Davis. Although he never said so out loud, he had serious doubts that the South could defeat the North militarily. He saw too much of their industrial plant first-hand. But that was the least of Rance Liebert's problems on his honeymoon.

Mildred was frigid.

When lovemaking happened at all, it was once every four to six weeks and with absolutely no passion on her part. She just lay there like a corpse and wanted to get it over with as quickly as possible. She was cross for two or three days afterward. One night after sex, she reproached him. "Are you through depositing your filth in me?"

"Yes," he declared, somewhat shocked by the question.

"Good," she answered, and rolled over, facing the wall opposite from him.

He got up and went to the guest bedroom.

They stayed in separate bedrooms after that. Rance would join her once every six or eight weeks because he still wanted a child or two. She submitted to the "ordeal" as part of her "marital duty," but made it plain that she would prefer not to have to endure his nocturnal advances. If that was the price of children, she didn't care ever to have any. Needless to say, their relationship became strained, and his nighttime visits became less and less frequent. Rance even considered being unfaithful to her but, despite several opportunities, couldn't bring himself to do it. It wasn't that the potential partners weren't alluring enough; it was what he perceived to be the Southern Code of Honor, combined with Christianity. He was raised in the church (thanks to Elizabeth) and he didn't want to be an adulterer. On the other hand, his life was comfortable, Mildred was reasonably pleasant when nothing was expected from her, the plantation "De La Teneria" was profitable, he had his own manor house, and Rance could and did order all of the books he wanted, so the years passed without significant complications. Liebert, however, was resigned to his lot rather than happy. In his gloomier moments, he felt he had failed to reach most of his goals in life. He wanted a life of adventure, and he had a few, but not enough, and now he was stuck on a plantation in an obscure part of Mississippi, probably forever. It was agreeable enough, to be sure, but there were no children, the Saturday night poker game usually was the most exciting occurrence of his week, and Sunday morning church services were second. That was just not enough, and sometimes he felt smothered and trapped — but trapped he was, and he saw no way out of it. He also desperately wanted children, but Mildred made it pretty clear that was never going to happen, and that made him so sad he tried not to think about it. And he wanted to be a general, even if it was only one of militia. He was not politically prominent, however, so that also seemed unlikely. He looked back on his army days with nostalgia. He wished he had stayed in and married some south Texas wench. He noticed they weren't as attractive, as well dressed, or as sophisticated as Mississippi plantation girls, but they always seemed happy, despite the fact they didn't have much in the way of possessions, and few of their men felt the urge to cheat. They must be doing something right.

In the 1850s, cotton prices remained quite high, and the South produced more than three-quarters of the world's cotton, so profits rolled in. One-half of all U.S. millionaires lived along the Natchez to New Orleans axis. The Lieberts prospered as well. Rance built a big house, and his old home (which was very nice) went to Jonathan's son, Chuckatuck.

Meanwhile, Liebert was having serious doubts about slavery. He rarely questioned the justness of the system — he had been raised in too traditional an environment for that. He did denounce its occasional excesses, like when a sorry master beat a slave too severely or even to death, but even the most pro-slavery Democrat did that. What concerned him was its inefficiency. The field hands received nothing for their labor; therefore, they worked only as hard as they absolutely had to. Some of the upper-class whites did not work at all. Northern farmers, on the other hand, prospered in direct proportion to the labor they put into it; therefore, they put in a lot of work. The same went for their industrialists and manufacturers. Rance was afraid the South would eventually be left behind economically.

Rance joined the local militia as soon as he got back from Europe. During the crisis of 1850, in which the North and South almost came to blows, the legislature authorized the formation of another regiment. John Quitman, who was governor again, nominated Rance Liebert to be its colonel. Some Mississippi politicians wanted the position as well, but thanks to the influence of General Quitman and Jefferson Davis, the legislature confirmed him by a single vote. Fear of Grover Liebert and the fact the political candidates lacked Liebert's combat experience also helped. Rance, meanwhile, felt mixed emotions. He was excited about his new position and, some days, was eager to go to war. On other days, he felt quite differently. He was relieved when the crisis passed without any shooting. Although he believed he would never reach it, he also was very proud of the fact he had come within one step of achieving his goal of becoming a general officer.

Mildred knew Rance was proud of his colonelcy and was in one of her frequent cross moods, so she decided to burst his bubble. "That doesn't mean a thing!" She snapped. "The crisis has passed. And you will never be a general! You were lucky, even to become a colonel!"

I know, Rance thought, but ignored her, as usual. By this point in their marriage, he considered anything that came out of her mouth to be irrelevant. Meanwhile, the seeds of sectional discord continued to germinate.

⟿ CHAPTER VI ⟾
RAPE

It was Sunday morning. Elizabeth Liebert was looking for her Bible, which she had misplaced the previous evening.

"Whatcha doin'?" Grover demanded.

"Gittin' ready for church," she answered. "I always go to church on Sunday. You know that."

"Hhuummpppph!" Grover snapped. "I think I'll go with ya."

If anyone ever saw Elizabeth Liebert speechless, that person was her husband and that moment was now. But she was delighted and helped him get ready.

After service, Grover approached the preacher, who literally shuddered with fear. He assumed Grover was there to cane him in front of the entire congregation, but Grover only wanted to shake his hand.

Grover never missed a service after that unless he was ill. He eventually got baptized, much to the shock of the entire community. Elizabeth wept with joy. Even though now a believer and a member of the church, he was never the devout Christian his wife was, although he did seem somewhat more mellow on occasion. He even let his Negroes go to church with them on Sunday mornings, except in planting and harvesting seasons, of course.

Like Grover, Richard Glass and his family attended the First Baptist Church in Rainbow. While Marguerite made it clear she considered herself superior to everyone her own age, Sally always ran up and hugged Rance. This ritual continued even as she grew taller. She sat by him in church every Sunday and often went to sleep during services, using him as a pillow. Mildred did not approve, and neither did Marguerite, but Sally's father didn't see any harm in it. He appreciated how Rance treated his youngest daughter the night of the ball and believed she would always have a soft spot for him, which didn't bother him in the least. The elder Glass also knew there was nothing untoward or unseemly in their relationship, and he rather liked young Liebert. When Marguerite approached her father and demanded he tell Sally to quit paying so much attention to Rance, Mr. Glass refused to do so and categorically ordered her to mind her own business. (Marguerite would eventually marry a wealthy plantation owner and move to Natchez.)

In time, Sally Mae grew into young womanhood and began entertaining beaus, of which she had several. She was an outgoing young lady with a bubbly personality. She loved to act and dance. She had long blondish-brown hair and a lovely face. But, as she looked into the full-length mirror, she knew she would never be as beautiful as her half-sister, Marguerite. Her skin was slightly olive colored, which gave one the impression of a slight suntan. This was considered an unfavorable characteristic in the Old South. Genteel ladies stayed out of the sun. A suntan suggested outside manual labor, which upper-class women did not do. If they had to go outside, they usually carried a parasol to shield themselves from the sun. Also unlike her sister, Sally was a woman of slight frame. She also didn't have much in the way of breasts; what she had was more of a gentle swelling of the chest. She frowned at the mirror. Well, if she wasn't Marguerite, God gave her some good attributes. She was attractive and had a beautiful smile. True, she couldn't stop traffic in Rainbow as Marguerite did, but then neither could anyone else. She had a more attractive personality, though, and was a lot sweeter, even if she did say so herself. And she was a whole lot more intelligent. Even at age 12, she could sometimes beat her father and twin brother at chess. She would bring much more to a marriage than mere good looks and a baby factory. She regretted for a moment she would even be required to get married. In another time, she felt she could have made it on her own without a husband. But such was not life in the United States in the 1850s. Oh, well, she thought. Accept what you cannot change. She smiled at her reflection. She intended to make the most of what she had, but she had no idea her whole Old South world was about to come crashing down about her head.

Bushrod Brown was a little drunk that afternoon. This was not particularly unusual.

He was from a somewhat disreputable family, but he was worse than anybody in his clan. Everyone was wary of him because he had a lethal combination of characteristics: he was brutal, handsome, murderous, cruel, amoral, vicious, totally self-absorbed, and a superb duelist. He had already killed one man in a duel, and it was rumored he was involved in a robbery and a couple of rapes. If he told you the truth (which was extremely unlikely), you would learn it was two robberies, four burglaries, a murder, a duel, and three rapes. He was planning his fourth.

Brown was playing a very hazardous game, but he acquired two accomplices, Josiah Hawks and Gouverneur "Goober" Norquist, who were almost as mean as he. Too lazy to work, they liked the easy money stealing and burglary brought, along with the whiskey and whores it could buy. They also enjoyed the cruelty of rape. All three men hated the planter aristocracy, Hawks and Norquist because they were considered "white trash," Brown because "quality folks" tended to look down on him. His invitations to balls and parties took a steep decline since he ruined a couple of them by starting fights. They ceased altogether when the rape accusations began. The fact the allegations were true did not make Brown any less angry.

Bushrod Brown considered himself smart. He used the aristocrats' own rules against them. In the 1850s, rape was considered an act of sex, not of violence. In many cases, all a man had to do to escape justice was accuse the victim of enticing him and leading him on, and Brown always had two witnesses (Hawks and Norquist) who would swear to anything he said. Not that most women would accuse him because any rape victim could count on having her reputation permanently besmirched. Known to be no longer a virgin, her choices for a husband would be severely limited — if she could find one at all; therefore, the victim usually remained silent, and the rapist(s) got away with it.

Because he had two witnesses who would lie under oath for him, Brown knew he would never be punished by the law if he remained careful. The only other source of potential punishment was the victim's family. This would entail a duel, but he was extremely good with pistols. One victim's brother tried it already. After taking the required ten paces, he died of a bullet through the heart before he could fire. That amused Brown greatly. Word of Brown's brutality spread throughout the area. Everyone except Grover Liebert was afraid of him — and that's the way he liked it. He intended to have more of it.

Bushrod Brown was not the only one who played dangerous games. Marguerite Glass did so as well. She had flirted with Brown (as she did with all young men). When he asked permission to call on her, she rejected him — and smiled. This made Brown furious. He and his comrades were now waiting in ambush for her carriage. Brown intended to cut a hunk out of her face when he finished using her. No man would ever look at her the same way again, and women like Marguerite needed to be worshiped. They didn't realize it, but male adulation was all they had. Bushrod Brown smirked.

That afternoon, Marguerite's carriage was driven by a young slave named Joshua. He was like many blacks in his position. He wanted to be free but didn't want to lose his family. He knew about the Underground Railroad but considered it chancy and, even if he were to escape, he would never see his family again. So he drove carriages for his owners, the Glasses. He did not like working without pay under any circumstances, but this was certainly better than picking cotton. He loved horses, liked working in the stables and — on those rare occasions when he allowed himself to dream — he dreamt about being free and owning his own livery stable.

Suddenly, three young men on horseback appeared out of nowhere. One of them grabbed the carriage horse's reins near the bridle and, at a gallop, guided it behind a clump of trees and bushes. "Now you're going to get yours, witch!" Bushrod roared. But the passenger was not Marguerite; it was her little sister, Sally.

She stood up in the carriage. "What are you doing?" She cried in alarm.

"Shut up, witch!" Bushrod cried as he rode his horse over to her and slapped her hard, right in the face. She fell back into the carriage, momentarily stunned. "Well, I guess one Glass whore is as good as another!" He laughed to his comrades.

"I'm not a whore," Sally said, looking up through her long light brown hair, tears rolling down her cheeks.

"You leave Miss Sally alone!" Joshua howled. He threw himself at Bushrod, knocked him off his horse, and hit him in the face. The two struggled, and the erstwhile carriage driver hit him again. A moment later, Josiah Hawks slugged Joshua in the head with the butt of his rifle, knocking him senseless.

"I'm gonna kill me a darkie," Hawks snarled and drew his Bowie knife. Low-class white trash hated blacks worse than anyone and felt more threatened by them than did the planter class.

"No! Wait!" Bushrod ordered, wiping the blood off his lip. "Here's what happened." He looked at Sally. "We caught this whore havin' sex with this slave. We knocked the snot out of him and, if she says anything, we'll say she's tryin' to get even with us for catchin' her and poleaxin' her lover. That's why the whore accused us of rape. At least that's our story ..."

"And we're stickin' to it!" Hawks laughed. So did Brown and Norquist.

"They'll probably lynch the darkie!" He correctly declared. "And, as everybody knows, a darkie can't testify against a white man in this state." He then turned to Sally. "Of course, we won't have to tell this story to the sheriff unless you open your stupid mouth. Now, take off your clothes and spread your legs!" Brown snapped.

"No!" She sobbed.

Without further ado, he grabbed her by the feet and dragged her out of the coach. She kicked, screamed, and fought back until one of them hit her in the face. They pulled up her dress and ripped off her underclothes.

"Please, don't …" she begged. But there was no mercy in them. They took her, and took her, and took her.

"Tell Marguerite she's next!" Brown laughed and spat on her as he rode away.

It was after dark before Joshua and Sally made it home. The entire plantation was consumed with worry by then, and Mr. Glass was organizing a search party.

Sally ran over to her mother, threw herself into her arms, and broke down completely. She could not talk. All she could do was wail mournfully. She wouldn't even let her father touch her. She didn't want to speak to any man, much less allow one to touch her — even her daddy.

One look at Joshua dispelled any suspicion the family might have had about him being responsible for this outrage. There was blood all over his face and shirt, the left side of his face was half again its normal size, and his eye was swollen shut.

"What happened?" Mr. Glass asked.

"It was Bushrod Brown and them two white trash boys what rides with him. They done it, sir."

"Rape?"

Joshua knew that the truth might get him hanged. It therefore took a considerable amount of courage for him to say: "Yes, sir!"

As soon as Dan Glass, Sally's twin brother, heard this, he jumped on his horse and applied the spurs. His father yelled at him to stop but, if Dan heard him, he ignored him. He headed straight for the town saloon. He knew Josiah, Gouverneur, and Bushrod would be there, and they were well on their way to being drunk. Without further ado, he walked up to Bushrod and slapped his face.

Brown sneered. He halfway expected this. "What's the matter, Glass? Are you mad because we caught your sister bangin' that darkie?"

Dan Glass immediately threw a punch and knocked Bushrod down. Norquist and Hawks seized him instantly and held him for Brown to work over, but before they could do any damage, there was an explosion. Rance Liebert had fired a shot into the ceiling.

Rather than go home to an unfeeling wife, Rance often liked to play low-stakes poker with some of his buddies from the Mississippi Rifles. He was doing that tonight. "Let him go!" he commanded.

"We're not in your regiment, Liebert!" Hawks snapped.

"No. You're not good enough for that. But you'll do as you're told just the same," he retorted.

Meanwhile, the four Rifles behind their former lieutenant drew their pistols and spread out, two on each side of Rance. Men who had seen combat together are often closer than brothers, especially when they were from an elite unit like the 1st Mississippi, and they did not have to be told what to do. When they cocked their weapons, the debate was over. Hawks and Norquist released Dan Glass.

"I demand satisfaction!" Brown snapped, wiping the blood off his lip.

"Rance, act as second," Glass exclaimed.

"Josiah, act for me," Brown growled.

"Weapons?" Liebert asked Hawks.

"Pistols."

"Ten paces?"

"Done. Place?"

"Graveyard," Rance replied.

"Fine. Time?"

"Two weeks from tomorrow."

"Why so long?" Brown demanded.

"I've got to teach this young hothead how to shoot!" Rance exclaimed.

"You lookin' for trouble, Liebert?" Brown snarled.

"You gonna help me find some?" Rance replied in a low, menacing voice.

For the first time, Brown sensed complications. He was not afraid of Rance Liebert. But, like everyone else, he had sense enough to be afraid of Grover. He once killed a man just for slapping one of his darkies, Brown thought. Imagine what he would do if I killed his grandson! Men like Grover lived by the law of the feud. If you hurt one of Grover's people, he didn't go to the sheriff, or an attorney, or the governor of the state. He came for you — usually in the dead of night — and

The Retribution Conspiracy

he didn't fight fair and never took prisoners. Brown respected that. He backed down slightly.

"Awright. Graveyard, two weeks from tomorrow."

"I'll escort you home," Rance told Glass. "Sergeant Leonard," he said to one of the Rifles, "make sure these boys stay here for the next two hours," gesturing toward Brown and his crew.

"Yes, sir."

"You can't give orders here, Liebert," Norquist snarled.

"The devil he can't!" The former sergeant cracked. "He just did! Didn't you hear him? Are you deaf as well as stupid?" The Rifles laughed uproariously. None of them uncocked or holstered their weapons.

Rance was walking to the door with Glass when another thought struck him. He stopped and turned around. "Oh, Hawks, I don't want you to labor under any misconceptions," he said. "I negotiated terms with you a moment ago simply to aid my friend, Mr. Glass, and at his request. It does not elevate you to the status of gentleman. That you clearly are not."

The Mississippi Rifles laughed again.

———

Rance did not get to see Sally that night. She was sick in bed. He did succeed in seeing her two days later. Convention was ignored because he was allowed to visit her in her bedroom. (Naturally, however, her maid also remained in the room, so they weren't in the bedroom alone.) When he looked into her bruised and battered face, he was filled with a cold rage.

"Oh, Rance," she said. He sat on her bed, and she buried her head in his shoulder and cried for some time. Feeling helpless, he patted her on the back. It was the first time she let a man touch her since that day.

Finally she said: "He raped me. And he's going to kill Dan." She dearly loved her twin brother.

"No, he's not."

"But the duel is set …"

"You let me handle all that. But you rest easy. Nobody's gonna kill Dan."

Finally she looked up. "What are you doing to do?" Tears were streaming down her face, and his heart went out to her.

"You just get some rest. We'll talk when you feel better."

CHAPTER VII

MURDER MOST FOUL

Grover, Ambrose, and Jonathan were sitting on the porch, rocking. They made room for Rance when he decided to join them.
"What'd ya do today, Rance?" Grover asked.

"Tried to teach Dan Glass how to shoot."

"Have any luck?"

"Nope. He's pretty hopeless."

"Too bad." Ambrose declared. "I heard Bushrod Brown raped Dan's sister."

"Yep," Rance acknowledged. "But they can't prove it."

"Too bad," Grover said. "She's a beautiful woman. Big titties."

"Naw. That's Marguerite. They raped the little girl, Sally. She ain't got no titties."

"Oh, yeah. Got a twin brother. His name is …"

"Dan. He ain't got no titties neither."

Everybody laughed except Grover. "Blackguards," he snapped. "Is that white trash Brown gonna kill Dan?"

"No, he ain't. He thinks he is, but he ain't."

"Why not? He's a lot better shot."

"'Cause I'm gonna kill him first."

Grover looked startled. He stared at his grandson.

"I know Brown needs killin', but …"

"But nuthin'," Rance snapped. Everybody shut their mouths. It was very unusual for anybody to interrupt Grover. After a long silence, he added, "Brown and people like him should be strung up, but there ain't no way we can git a conviction in a court of law," Rance declared. "Any man who rapes a woman needs to be hanged, and any man who beats a woman needs to be horse-whipped. And if the law won't do what's right, we ought to take care of him ourselves," he snapped with considerable bitterness. "I just wish I'd done it before he hurt Sally Mae."

Rance's pronouncement was greeted with nods all around. All of these men were Southerners, and some of them had been frontiersmen. The legacy of vigilantism was deeply ingrained in all of them. "You're spot-on right," Grover declared. "Kill the _____!"

"I need to borrow your Colt," Rance said.

Grover had recently purchased a newly manufactured Colt Dragoon revolver. It was expensive but had major advantages over the single-shot guns almost everyone else in Rainbow County carried; it fired six shots and never misfired. He didn't mind spending money on a superior weapon — at least not too much. After two seconds of thought, he stood up, unbuckled his belt, and handed gun and holster to his grandson without another word.

"Tell everybody you lost it or it was stolen," Rance said. "If they find the body, they'll see it's a Colt slug, and I don't want the law to think you shot him."

"Okay. But don't let 'em find the body."

"Nobody's gonna find his grave, 'less they can smell my urine," Rance exclaimed. Everybody chuckled.

Jonathan interrupted the ensuing silence. "I'll hep ya."

"Naw. I appreciate it, but if somethin' goes wrong, I don't want you to get hung." Jonathan was like a member of the family now and ranked higher with Grover and Rance than most white people — even kinfolk. Also, he was getting too old for what Rance had in mind.

Another long silence ensued. "You know Joshua?" Jonathan asked Rance.

"Yeah. Glass's slave. Smart guy. Pretty badly pistol-whipped by Brown's thugs."

"Go to him. He a good man. And he hates Brown more than he hates Satan hisself. He'll hep ya."

"Well, I know he's a brave man. That's for certain sure. Sally said he tried to defend her and attacked three armed outlaws with his bare hands." Rance thought for a moment. "Can he keep his mouth shut?"

"Oh, yeah."

It never dawned on Rance to ask him how he knew. He knew the blacks had their own secret networks to which white people were not granted access. He accepted Jonathan's word without question.

"You sure you know what you're doin'?" Ambrose asked.

"Yeah."

"You want me to do it?" Grover asked. He was anxious to participate in the killing.

"No."

"You ever kill anybody, Rance?"

"No. But I won't be able to say that in two weeks." This remark revealed the real reason there were 15 days between the challenge and the duel.

There was more silence as the four men continued rocking. It did not occur to Ambrose, Grover or Jonathan that they just made themselves accessories to murder, nor would it have bothered them if they had. Finally, Grover said: "You must like this little girl, Rance."

"Yes, I do," he said. He paused. "To tell you the truth, Granddaddy, if I had to do it over again, I'd have waited until she grew up and then married her, instead of that heifer I'm saddled with."

All three men stared at Rance. They were more startled by this announcement than they were been when Rance told them he was going to murder somebody and asked for their help. Rance, however, didn't say another word. He just kept rocking.

⸺⚬⚬⚬⸺

Rance Liebert was sitting on the overstuffed sofa in the large living room at Windrow, as the Glass mansion was called. Sally took her usual position beside him. Opposite him were Richard Glass and his son, Dan.

"I need your boy Joshua for two weeks or so," Rance declared.

"Why?" Richard wanted to know.

"Yes, Rance," Sally interrupted. "You may have him."

Richard was astonished by his daughter's pronouncement. "What? You don't even know what he wants him for."

"I don't care what he wants him for," she said, rising to her feet. Rance stood when she did. She took his arm and said: "I'll walk you to the door."

Richard Glass sat there dumbfounded. She had just loaned out his top stable man for two weeks without consulting him, and he was only a few feet away. He also noticed neither Rance nor Sally had mentioned compensation — a fact that probably indicated he wasn't planning to pay anything. (He was a Liebert, after all.) This was not only highly unusual — nothing like this had ever happened before. But it was a dead issue. "See you tomorrow, Dan," Liebert said.

"See ya, Rance!" The younger Glass grinned.

Out on the veranda, she took his hand. "He'll be home now," she said. "Third cabin on the left in the slave quarters."

"Thanks," he said, expecting her to release her grip, but she did not; instead, she took both of his hands and looked deeply into his eyes.

"I wish you weren't married," she said.

"I wish I wasn't either." He met her gaze and considered kissing her, but he did not. At this point, it would only complicate things. He released her and began walking down the stairs.

"I love you, Rance Liebert," she called out to him, softly.

Rance stopped on the stairs for about five seconds. Then he resumed his descent. He did not look back.

Rance knocked on the door of the slave cabin. Joshua's wife opened it, and her eyes got wide. What was a white Bourbon aristocrat doing here this time of night?

"I wanna talk to Joshua. Tell him to step out here, please."

"Yessur," she said, but she was clearly worried. Rance noticed she was short, attractive, and perhaps six months pregnant.

Joshua appeared a few moments later. His eyes registered surprise, or at least the one that wasn't swollen did.

"Have you finished supper?"

"Yessur."

"Then git packed. You're workin' fer me the next two weeks."

"Yessur," he declared, even more surprised. When Rance didn't say anything else, he ducked back inside. He emerged a few minutes later. He didn't have much, so it didn't take him long to pack.

"What we gon' do, Mr. Rance?"

"I'm gonna murder Bushrod Brown," he announced as if it was the most natural thing in the world, and he was talking about the weather. "You gonna help."

"Yessur," he said automatically. Then the full realization of what he had heard hit him. "YES, SIR, Mr. Rance!" He smiled widely.

"You know to keep your mouth shut, right? Don't even tell your wife."

"Yes, sur!" Joshua thought for a few minutes as they walked to the stables. "We gone kill that white trash, Josiah Hawks, too, Mr. Rance?" He knew who had butt-stroked him in the face with that rifle.

We? Rance thought. Dang. He's already taking ownership of this project. "Yeah, I'm gonna kill that son-of-a-gun. But not right away. I'm gonna kill Brown first. We're gonna let Hawks stew in his own juices for a while before we kill him. Let him think about it a while."

"Yes, sur!" Joshua — who was afraid he might be hanged for having sex with a white woman based on Brown's threat — was delighted by this turn of events and was willing — even anxious — to participate in his demise. Rance was also pleased. Jonathan was right: this man had guts.

They reached the Glass stables, and Joshua picked a horse. "Make sure you git one that ain't gun shy," Rance ordered. "You'll work in our stables during the day so that no one will get suspicious. I just bought some half-broken colts I want you to train."

The next night after supper, they went for a ride, ending up along the road which led from Brown's father's farm to the Rainbow Saloon. An abandoned farm and farmhouse were nearby. They went inside the house, where Rance retrieved a shovel. He tossed it to Joshua. "Behind the barn, there's an abandoned cotton field. Dig me a grave. Deep. At least six feet. Make sure it's out of sight from the road. Then cover it with this groundsheet. Angle it like a tent, so it won't fill up if it rains."

"Yessur," Joshua responded. Sometime later, he reappeared. "We gonna shoot Mr. Bushrod when he comes back from the saloon tonight?" He asked, expectantly.

"No. Not tonight. We'll wait for a thunderstorm. He'll have to cross the Emmet River at the Thompson Ford to get home. I want it to appear that he was drunk and, in the bad weather, got swept off his horse and drowned. We'll bury him here, and it will appear that his body was swept downriver and never recovered."

"What if there ain't no thunderstorm?"

"It's Mississippi in springtime. There'll be a thunderstorm, all right. But if there ain't, we'll kill him anyway."

"So, we wait."

"We wait."

They didn't have to wait too long. Five days later, bad weather arrived. In their slickers, Rance and Joshua sat on their horses in the downpour. Around 2:10 that morning, their target appeared. Rance rode out to meet him.

Because he was drunk, Bushrod Brown did not notice him until he was right on top of him. He was startled. "What are you doing here, Liebert?" He demanded.

Rance responded by pulling out Grover's revolver and shooting him right in the throat. The bullet severed his carotid artery. He never said a word and certainly didn't give Brown a chance — any more than he gave Sally Mae Glass.

In his last moments on earth, Brown felt his neck explode. He tried to stay on his horse, scream for help, and draw his gun, but he could do none of the above. He reeled and pitched forward into the permanent darkness. As black as that was, however, it was no darker than the night which surrounded Rainbow County, Mississippi, as the rain poured down from the pitch-black sky.

The thunder, the rain, and the dense air of the storm masked the sound of the shot and diminished in the distance the sound traveled. The rain had the added benefit of washing the blood away. Joshua ran to the body immediately. He wanted Brown to know he was involved in the murder and who was going to bury him, but he was too late: Bushrod Brown was already dead. To mask his crimes, Brown figured a way around the law and the Southern code of honor. For all of its gentility, however, antebellum Mississippi was only a decade or so removed from its frontier roots. Brown forgot about the unwritten laws of the frontier: vigilantism, which was swift and merciless; and retribution, which justified pretty much anything.

Rance dismounted and gazed down at the body with a look of pure hatred. How dare this — animal! — touch Sally — or anyone else Rance cared for! Joshua was a little frightened as he watched Liebert glare at the cadaver. Then, as the thunder rolled, he fired a "make sure" bullet into the dead man's face. He seemed to take pleasure in it. His hand didn't shake, and he even smiled a little. At that moment, Joshua realized what this man was capable of. Beneath the surface, he was not the introverted bookworm many people took him for. He was perfectly capable of harsh and violent action to protect those about whom he cared. And if it were too late to protect them, it was never too late to avenge them. He could be cold, calculating, and merciless, and could kill without remorse. Joshua was glad they were on the same side.

They threw the body over Rance's saddle, and the horse carried him to the grave. (Rance didn't want anybody to find blood on Brown's seat, so he rode the deceased rapist's horse.) They removed the groundsheet, dumped the lifeless body into the hole, and stared down at it. Suddenly the sky was lighted up by an enormous lightning bolt. Then, as the thunder rolled again, Rance fired a third shot into Brown's head. Just for fun, this time. Like Grover, he was not a "forgive and forget" sort of man. They buried Brown quickly, with Joshua manning the shovel and Rance holding the lantern.

A short time later, Rance and Joshua were on their horses, heading for the Emmet River. They released Brown's horse near the ford. They were in bed by 4:30 a.m. — half an hour before the rest of the plantation began to wake up.

The next day, Joshua asked if he could return to Windrow.

"No," Rance said. "Better work here for another few days. Then you can go home."

Joshua thought for a minute. Then he asked: "What if they find the grave?"

"Won't happen," Rance responded.

"It might, if the bank tries to sell the farm."

"It already did. I bought it a week ago. We'll be puttin' up the 'No Trespassing' signs today."

Joshua smiled. Ain't that just like Mr. Rance Liebert, he thought. Thinkin' of everythang.

Almost 70 years later, Joshua (who then went by the name Joshua Liebert) lay on his deathbed. He naturally thought back to the days of his youth, the friends he knew, the things he did, and the places he had seen. The world had changed a great deal in his 90-plus years. He recalled how he and Rance Liebert had murdered Bushrod Brown and smiled — it was a pleasant memory about which he had no regrets. It occurred to him Mr. Rance was a nineteenth century Southern gentleman and his class was dying out. They had been since General Lee surrendered. In a way, they were an odd group. Modern, early twentieth century urban males dealt with other people in one of three ways: 1) they did not verbally fight or argue, or 2) they always seemed to be in constant verbal fights, especially with their spouses, and led lives of continuous anger, frustration and stress, or 3) they resorted to violence. Number three was very rare in the 1910s and usually involved wife beating. It almost never involved fatalities. Number two was widespread — even common — in modern early twentieth century society. Joshua concluded if divorce laws ever became looser, there would be a lot of broken marriages in the future.

Nineteenth century Southern gentlemen did not approach life that way at all. Most of them treated ladies with great respect and almost never argued or bickered with their wives. There are, of course, exceptions to every rule, but in general, they would not fuss and quarrel over the little things and tended to concede minor points by default. If a wife wanted to argue about something, the gentleman either let her have her way or just ignored her, but usually only after listening to her opinion. This tended to soften the argument because the woman had "had her say" and felt her view had at least been considered, even if it was rejected — which it usually wasn't. This procedure made the men's lives much more pleasant, established harmony in their homes, and greatly reduced domestic stress. But for them, when dealing with people outside their immediate family, there was no middle ground; there was no number two. They did not argue or whine or moan or complain; they fought and frequently killed. They lived by the code *duello*, although sometimes — if the enemy needed killing — even murder was socially acceptable. ("He needed killin'" was considered a valid legal defense in the antebellum South, and in the culture of that day, such killings were not even regarded as immoral by many people.) Joshua thought of Lieutenant Liebert. He doubted if the memory of murdering Brown cost Mr. Rance five minutes of sleep over the past six decades. Murder, however, was not an option a gentleman could exercise very often. When it came to killing, the duel was much more acceptable. In the 1850s, a gentleman could fight any number of those and still be considered a gentleman. Joshua was almost sure this was already on Rance's mind when they turned their horses toward Fusilier that dark rainy night in Mississippi, so long ago.

Joshua tried to turn over in bed but couldn't. He sighed in frustration. God was switching off the various parts of his body one by one. He knew he was dying, and he was not afraid. He drifted in and out of consciousness. He heard his great-granddaughter say something but just couldn't concentrate on it. His mind drifted back to the past. His thoughts again returned to the nineteenth century gentleman, and he felt mixed emotions. No doubt about it — they were an enigma. They grew up in an era which accepted slavery, hook, line, and sinker, and they took full advantage of it, and some of them treated their slaves as subhumans. Joshua was a slave and, although he was never treated brutally, he did not like slavery one bit. Mostly he resented being treated as inferior just because of the color of his skin, the lack of opportunity to better himself, and the almost total nonexistence of a chance to improve his family's position in the world. Still, Joshua's deep hatred for slavery did not transfer itself to the individual slave owners. He found that perplexing. Mr. Glass was his master back then, but Joshua did not hate him; in fact, here at the end of his own life, Joshua admired him and felt friendly emotions toward him, and also toward Dan Glass, and especially toward Miss Sally Mae. And he felt something akin to love for Rance Liebert. That puzzled him. This man was the quintessential nineteenth century Mississippi planter, slave owner, and gentleman of the Old School and Joshua hated much of what he stood for, yet here on his deathbed he thought of him, and his eyes grew misty. Oh, he was sometimes rough and could be deadly when provoked, but he took care of the people he cared about and had set Joshua on the path to his future all those years ago. By the standards of early 20th Century America, Joshua was dying modestly wealthy, especially for a black man, his extended family was taken care of, and he had Mr. Rance to thank for much of that. Mr. Rance! Joshau still called him that after all these years. Old habits die hard, and some of them do not die at all. He wondered if Mr. Rance was still alive, where he was, and what happened to him.

He was suddenly engulfed in bright, white light as he never saw before. He knew it was other worldly, but he did not feel fear. All of a sudden he felt warm, safe, secure, incredibly comfortable, and totally at peace. So I am goin' up and not down, he thought and smiled. A tear of happiness rolled down his cheek. He felt one of his sons grab one of his hands, and a daughter grasped the other. Somehow they knew what was happening. He heard them chattering and thought he detected a sob. He loved them both dearly, and his heart went out to them, but he couldn't make out a word they said. It was as if they were blue jays or magpies. No matter, he thought. My business this side of the grave is finished. He thought of his late wife and looked forward to seeing her again. He wondered who else would greet him on the other side. He was still wondering when God threw the final switch and called him home.

But that was all far into the future.

The typical reaction to Bushrod Brown's disappearance was just what Rance hoped for: he had gotten drunk and was swept away by the river during the rainstorm. Only Josiah Hawks and Goober Norquist held different opinions. Hawks was foolish enough to say so in a drunken rant at the local saloon. Rance Liebert had his pretext. The next evening, Rance appeared at the bar and, backed by Ralph Leonard and Dan Glass, planted himself in front of Hawks.

"I understand you have accused me of murder," he declared.

"Where did you hear that?" Asked a startled Hawks.

"We can discuss that later. For now, just be glad I treat you like the gentleman which you are not." Without further ado, he slapped Hawks in the face with a pair of gloves.

Like most rapists, Josiah Hawks was much braver when he had a rifle and was working against defenseless women and slaves than he was against an armed man who knew how to shoot. On the traditional dueling ground, he hurried his shot and missed. Then, in a state of shock, he was foolish enough to turn and expose the entire front of his body, instead of just the side. For a moment, Rance Liebert thought about shooting him in the groin; instead, he aimed for "center of mass" in his chest, just as Ambrose and Grover trained him. The bullet went straight through his heart. He was dead before he hit the ground.

"Good shot, boy!" Grover shouted, beaming with delight. He had his doubts about his oldest grandson, but he had them no longer. (He knew he killed Brown, but he did not see it.) He hugged him around the shoulder. Rance was going to turn out all right after all.

A crowd of townspeople had gathered to watch the event. They broke into spontaneous applause at its conclusion. Rance waved at them and bowed slightly.

As the men stood over Hawks to examine the body, the younger Liebert addressed Norquist. "Take a good look, Goober," he said. "You're next. You are lookin' at your future."

To hades with that, Norquist thought. The next day, he disappeared. He left town without telling anybody (and without paying several debts), never to return. For a while, people wondered if he mysteriously disappeared, as had Bushrod Brown, and some wondered if one or more of the Lieberts were behind it, although none of them said a thing. Some months later, however, word arrived that he had fled to the west, where the Texans hanged him for stealing a horse.

—⊗⊗⊗—

In Sally Mae's day, North and South, and pretty much worldwide, people treated rape victims with a great deal of insensitivity. Such was the case with Sally Mae Glass. There was always a presumption among people — even women — that there was something a woman could do to prevent the rape if she really wanted to. Men — even human pond scum like Bushrod Brown — were given the benefit of every doubt. The default position was that she must have flaunted herself in front of the rapist — i.e., that she must have done something to deserve it.

Sally found she had few real friends. The young men of Rainbow County no longer considered her a fit candidate for marriage because she was no longer a virgin. All the boys who previously courted her disappeared immediately. The gossips cut her mercilessly behind her back. For several of them, it was a tactic to rid themselves of a more attractive rival, and it was very effective. Sally was no longer invited to the balls, cotillions, or parties. She was a social pariah. What hurt her more than anything was that she didn't deserve any of it.

Sally could still attend church, but she wasn't included in her former circle of friends anymore. Rance Liebert still invited her to sit by him, but Mildred Liebert (who never liked it) openly objected, on the grounds that it was unseemly. The issue obviously caused friction between the Lieberts, so Sally declined his invitations and sat by him no more. She became more and more isolated, introverted, and morose. The care, worry, and stress began to show on her face. It was only slightly relieved when she discovered she was not pregnant.

As day after weary day elapsed, Sally Mae became more and more depressed. She skipped the church picnic; then she decided not to go to church anymore. Nowadays she got up late, went to bed early, and didn't do anything in between. She sat in her room or moped around the Big House all day long. She cried a lot, and sometimes broke into sobs for no apparent reason. She no longer read or played chess. For a while, she didn't get dressed until after noon. Then, on more than one occasion, she didn't get dressed at all. She no longer talked much, which was uncharacteristic of her. She began taking her meals alone in her room. No one could cheer her up. Her family was very worried about her — even Marguerite.

Finally, she had a moment of truth. She could continue on her present path and become a recluse, and probably die an early death from depression, or she could start her life over somewhere else. She knew her life in Rainbow would never be right again. Sally Mae always loved to perform and act in front of audiences, so when she saw an advertisement for acting school, she decided to go north, where nobody knew her, to start life afresh and reinvent her persona.

Her father was concerned. This was a bold decision for a nineteenth-century woman to make. "Honey," he said to her, "you know I will back you, no matter what you do, but are you sure you want to do this?" Being a slave trader was a low-prestige, high-income profession. In the 1850s, being an actor fell into the same category, except for the high income part.[9] Being an actress was a cut below that.

Sally was sure. She wanted to go where nobody knew her. To make sure of this, she decided to change her name when she got there. The youngest Glass didn't know where she was going, but she knew where she had been, and she was excited about the change.

Rance Liebert also noticed her transformation. She was becoming more like the old Sally Mae Glass, more like herself. On her last Sunday

---

9 In the 1850s, the best actors did very well financially, but most supporting actors barely got by.

in Mississippi, she attended the First Baptist Church and sat by Rance Liebert and, when no one was looking, reached over and squeezed his hand. He visited her the day before she left. Sally smiled widely and hugged his neck, just like the old days, except her reach was much higher now. They never had any problem talking with each other. Now they sat in the sitting room and talked for three hours. There hadn't been many barriers between them since she was six years old.

When it was time for him to leave, she walked him all the way to his horse — an unprecedented gesture. She was pretty sure he had killed Bushrod Brown and knew he killed Josiah Hawks, and that elevated him even higher in her estimation. She hugged him goodbye. She wanted him to kiss her, and he thought about it, but he did not. After he mounted his horse, he looked down at her and said: "I wish I wasn't married."

"I wish you weren't married, too." Sally Mae smiled and brushed away a tear as he rode off. She watched him until he disappeared from sight.

The next day, her father helped her into the carriage and drove her to the railroad station where she took a train to New York City. By the end of the week, she was Guinevere Spring, a student at the Junius Brutus Booth, Jr., School for Acting.

—⁀ CHAPTER VIII ⁀—
SECRET SERVICE

"You went on a Grand Tour of Europe years ago. Now I want to," Mildred Liebert was speaking to her husband, Rance. It was the first time they had talked in days, which was not unusual. She looked at him with contempt.

"I have a plantation to run. I can't take you to Europe," not that I want to, Rance said and thought, respectively, as he looked up from his book.

"You don't have to. I'll go with Margo Hampshire."

Okay, he thought. He sometimes wondered if there was something beyond friendship in that relationship. But, if Rance was shocked or suspicious, he didn't show it. He really didn't care. He also wouldn't mind getting her out of his life for several months. Their relationship had deteriorated to the point that they were absolutely indifferent to each other. Mildred went back to her parents' home in Natchez at every opportunity or anytime she could think of a pretext. Rance worked his plantation during the day and snuggled up with his books or played poker with the boys at the local saloon at night. Sometimes he had an all-night poker game with the former Mississippi Rifles at De La Teneria. This annoyed Mildred, who threw occasional snide remarks her husband's way. Rance ignored her, as she by now knew he would. Very often these days, they didn't even bother to eat together. Liebert missed Sally Mae Glass, but he wouldn't miss Mildred.

"Oh. Sure. You can go to Europe, if you'd like."

"Thank you," she said, and managed a smile. It was the first time he had seen her smile in some time.

She left three weeks later and was to be gone for months. The only word he received from her was a letter, announcing she would be arriving in New Orleans aboard the *Constellation* on the 26th. She would take a steamboat to Natchez the next day, and he could send a carriage to pick her up at Margo's father's place anytime after that.

Meanwhile, the sectional conflict bubbled over.

On October 16, 1859, an abolitionist named John Brown seized the U.S. arsenal at Harper's Ferry, Virginia, in the first step of what he intended to be a slave revolt. His raiders (who the South called terrorists) killed seven people, wounded 10, and took several hostages, including Colonel Lewis Washington, a great grandnephew of George Washington, and stole the sword Frederick the Great gave the general. The slaves, however, did not flock to his banner, as Brown anticipated. The raid was soon put down by a combination of militiamen, pro-slavery citizens and U.S. Marines, all under the direction of Colonel Robert E. Lee. Ten of Brown's men (including two of his sons) were killed, seven were captured, and five escaped.

The ensuing trial polarized the nation. The South considered Brown a terrorist and a homicidal lunatic, but many abolitionists hailed him as a hero, a saint, and a martyr. After his execution, large memorials were held for him, and Ralph Waldo Emerson and Henry David Thoreau praised him lavishly. Abraham Lincoln, on the other hand, called him "insane."

Brown was hanged on December 2, 1859. The Northern reaction to his death shocked the South. Church bells were rung, funeral wreaths were attached to businesses, many women wore black, and much of the North went into mourning. Subsequent investigations proved he had received financial backing from some prominent abolitionists, convincing the South that a sizable number of Republicans were fostering servile insurrection. After Harper's Ferry, many of the South's former moderates, such as Nathan Bedford Forrest or Virginia Military Institute Professor Thomas Jonathan Jackson, were ready to embrace secession if a Republican were elected president.

—◦◦◦—

Some weeks later, Rance Liebert sent his carriage driver to Natchez, to pick up his wife. He returned without her two days later. When Rance asked where she was, the driver handed him a newspaper. There was the answer on the front page, just below the fold. The introductory headline read "*Constellation* lost at sea." There were no survivors.

Meanwhile, the Democratic Party split and, in November 1860, Abraham Lincoln was elected president of the United States with 39.6 percent of the vote. Although he promised not to disturb slavery where it existed, seven states — the entire Deep South — seceded before his scheduled inauguration date of March 4, 1861.

Meanwhile, on February 10, Jeff Davis was helping Varina prune the rose bushes at Brierfield when a messenger arrived. He learned that, the day before in Montgomery, Alabama, the Provisional Congress of the Confederate States of America elected him president. Davis paled at the news. A West Point graduate, a former U.S. secretary of war, and now a major general of Mississippi State Troops, he had expected to receive a general's appointment and possibly command an army. Unlike most other politicians, he could see beyond the initial adulation to the challenges beyond, and they were enormous.

Back in Rainbow, Rance Liebert was a little shaken up by the death of his wife, but very little. He gave her clothes to his slaves and the poor, divided her jewelry among family members (his and hers), and placed her portrait in storage. He had every visible vestige of her removed from De La Teneria. People assumed this was out of a sense of grief, and Rance let them think whatever they wanted. He felt a sense of relief, which was simultaneously mixed with a sense of guilt, although he had no idea what he felt guilty about. Possibly it was precisely because he felt no grief. In the end, he decided he really didn't known his wife — and hadn't really wanted to — which was good, since she was dead. Besides, he now had plenty of other things to do.

After Lincoln was elected, the governor of Mississippi called a secession convention and activated the militia. Colonel Rance Liebert's regiment was renamed the 12th Mississippi. His first stop was Windrow, where he visited Richard and Dan Glass. Here he bought Joshua and his entire family for a very low price. (Both men were sure Rance arranged Bushrod Brown's disappearance, although neither ever brought up the subject; they were prepared to do pretty much whatever he wanted, even if they lost money on the transaction.) Then, without telling Joshua he had been purchased, Rance went to see him.

"I've got a proposition for you. I know you want your freedom. Here's the deal. I'll buy you and your entire family from Mr. Glass. You serve with me throughout the war. If we win, I'll give you your freedom. If we lose, you'll most likely be free anyway. So you win either way. What do you say?"

Joshua's eyes got wide. "My family, too?"

"Your whole family."

"You got yo'self a deal, Mr. Rance!" He exclaimed as he extended his hand.

They shook on it.

When they were hiding in the bushes waiting for Brown, Joshua confided to Liebert that he wanted his freedom and to own his own livery stable someday. So Rance added: "And if I survive the war, I'll help you buy that livery stable."

Joshua beamed. Then a less pleasant thought crossed his mind. "You don't reckon I'll git shot, do you, Mr. Rance?"

"Couldn't say. I'm not clairvoyant."

"You ain't what?"

"Clairvoyant. I can't see into the future. I ain't got no crystal ball. You put on a uniform, you take your chances, just like everybody else."

Joshua didn't seem to be particularly reassured by this answer. "You reckon we'll win da war, Mr. Rance?" Like everyone else, he took it for granted there would be a war.

"We will if I have anything to say about it. You be at De La Teneria tomorrow at dawn. The Glasses say your family can stay in their cabin and work for them if they want to, or they can live in the slave quarters at my plantation or at Fusilier, whatever your wife chooses. In any case, you be ready to ride tomorrow morning!"

Colonel Liebert formed up his 910 men at Camp Instruction and began drilling them. Few people realized it, but he was in Heaven and definitely in his element. As he lay in his tent at night, Rance felt tired but simultaneously energized and renewed. Although it was comfortable, his life so far had not worked out as he envisioned it, and he was secretly disappointed. Now he had a cause for which to live and, for a radical change, couldn't wait to get up in the mornings, to begin drilling and preparing his soldiers for war.

Like millions of people in that time, Colonel Liebert did not believe the war was only about slavery. He was a moderate on that issue. Although it had existed since the first book in the Bible, he thought it was morally questionable, and the world had outgrown it. He believed it would eventually die of natural causes, as it was clearly doing everywhere else on the planet. He was, on the other hand, enraged at what the North was doing to the South economically. Rance felt Lincoln and his cronies intended to make the South an economic colony of the North. With roughly 30 percent of the country's population, Dixie already was paying more than 85 percent of the taxes, and the bulk of that money (at least 80 percent) was being used to finance internal improvements in the North. Liebert did not think it was right for the poor Southern farmer's money to be taken from them in the form of taxes (tariffs) and given to rich railroads and other corporations in the North, with the Federal government in Washington acting as the middle man and growing fat in the process, while Republican and Yankee

The Retribution Conspiracy

politicians (who passed the tariff laws in the first place) raked in the money in the form of bribes, kickbacks, and "campaign contributions" from the corporate elites. Say what you will about Abraham Lincoln, he made everything crystal clear. He would not lift a finger to abolish or interfere with slavery in the states where it existed, he declared, but he would go to war if the South ceased to pay its taxes and refused to return to the Union. Rance Liebert loved the poor farmers of Rainbow County he went to church with and occasionally bought a drink for them at the local saloon. He liked socializing with them and their wives, who considered him a good, Christian man, and always greeted him with smiles and handshakes. He also loved the way their children's faces lit up when the family ran into him at the General Store because they knew he would inevitably buy them hard candy or gum drops, which their fathers frequently could not often afford. Rance also knew De La Teneria and Fusilier could survive the unreasonably huge tax increases Lincoln and his partners in corruption were proposing, but most of Rance's neighbors could not. If these men went under, it would have a ripple effect on the entire Southern economy. At the local level, the general stores at Rainbow would not be able to survive if the small farmer didn't, nor would the tavern, the modest Biggun's Restaurant, the apothecary, the dry good store, the dress shop, and most of the other businesses in town. Colonel Rance Liebert was willing — and even eager — to stop such a disaster from happening. After years of floating through life, he now had a cause which he was excited about — a cause worth living for, worth fighting for, and worth dying for, if necessary. But he didn't think that would happen. At this stage of his life, Rance Liebert could not conceive of a military defeat.

When he allowed himself to daydream, which was rare enough, Rance Liebert usually dreamt of glory or being married to Sally Mae Glass. He was ambitious to be the best regimental commander in the Confederate Army. He wanted to parade his victorious legion down Main Street to the cheers of everybody in town. He hoped Sally Mae would come back home long enough to see that. There was still something there, and he hoped to be able to pursue a relationship with her after the war. He knew that, if they met again, it wouldn't take long for the old feelings to bubble to the top, and he was sure she felt as he did. They were both single now and, if circumstances allowed it, he considered a marriage with Sally Mae a distinct possibility. Violating the nineteenth century axiom that gentlemen always married virgins (unless they were widows) did not bother him one bit. I married a virgin once, he rationalized. To hell with that!

When he let his mind wander, Rance even secretly hoped to earn a brevet promotion to brigadier general. He knew Jefferson Davis would give him one if his regiment distinguished itself in combat. In his old age, he wanted to walk down the sidewalk of his home town and hear people tell their children and grandchildren: "There goes General Liebert, a man who won victories for the South in our Second War of Independence!" He was absolutely confident he could build a regiment capable of accomplishing this. He was also unequivocally certain he was a good enough tactician to make it happen. He believed he was a good lieutenant, had studied tactics under Colonel Davis, understood how armies worked, and read literally hundreds of books on military theory, tactics, and military history since then. He was ready and fully prepared.

After years of isolation and stagnation on the plantation, Rance Liebert felt renewed, as if he were a new man who just awakened from a long sleep. He swelled with pride as the 12th Mississippi improved day by day. Before long, it was clearly the best regiment in Camp Instruction, mainly because it conducted battle drills twice as often as anybody else. When this was accomplished, Rance immediately raised the bar on his mission. He intended to have the best regiment in the Southern army before he was through, and he was well on his way.

Rance paid for much of their equipment out of his own pocket, and (remembering Mexico) he was especially sure he got good tents (two men per tent). He had goals now, and he didn't care what he had to spend to make them happen. Under his determined leadership, squad drill and individual manual of arms took place between two-a-day company and regimental drills, just as Colonel Davis drilled the Mississippi Rifles in the Mexican War, in addition to routine camp duties. This drilling — which was double what the other regiments had to endure — did not improve the colonel's popularity, but it did make his men better soldiers and therefore more likely to survive than their peers. Liebert knew his men would look back on it all and appreciate it someday, just as the men of the old Mississippi Rifles appreciated Colonel Davis more after the Mexican War was over and they returned home alive, largely because of his efforts. Besides, he was easily more popular than Davis was, because he was more affable with the troops; he had an easy familiarity which did not breed contempt, largely because he was a Mexican War veteran and they knew he knew what he was talking about. He also socialized with them, broke bread with

The Retribution Conspiracy

them, and sat down with them around the campfire and explained to them why he was doing what he did. That was something Colonel Davis could never bring himself to do in Mexico, but the men of the 12th Mississippi understood Rance's reasoning, responded to his leadership, and worked with him to accomplish his goals, even if they sometimes grumbled, as soldiers often do. His reputation from the Mexican War certainly mitigated in his favor. Every day, Rance was more excited than the last with how well the regiment was shaping up. Then the telegram came.

Colonel Liebert:

Report to me in Montgomery at your earliest possible convenience.

President Davis

Rance was packed and heading for the train station within an hour.

The passenger cars were full to capacity all the way to Alabama, and the government quarters in Montgomery were a beehive of activity. Rance went at once to the capitol, where a guard directed him to Davis' office. There was standing room only. The receptionist hardly looked at him. He told Rance he could wait in the hall, but he might be there for hours. Liebert handed him the telegram. "I'll wait right here. You just tell him I'm waiting," was all he said. The man now actually looked at Liebert. His eyes opened a little wider, and he did as he was told. That's more like it, Liebert thought.

Rance correctly took the people in Davis' anteroom to be office seekers. They looked at him uncomfortably. He was wearing his Mississippi Rifles uniform with colonel's epaulets, a Navy Six pistol and a Bowie knife. The seekers frowned at him because it was obvious this colonel was not here to beg for a position or to plea for personal advancement. He was here on serious business. They were concerned he intended to go to the head of the line, putting one more person between them and Davis.

They were right. Rance didn't have to wait five minutes. "You can leave your weapons here, Colonel," the receptionist said. Rance thought about ignoring him but did not. Goodness, I hope he doesn't want me to be his adjutant again, Liebert thought. I don't want to be part of this circus every day. In his heart of hearts, Rance hoped Davis was about to give him a brigade. He might become a general faster than he'd thought possible.

"You may go in now, sir," the receptionist declared as soon as Rance deposited his knife and gun belt on the desk. The two guards in front of Davis' office door presented arms. He walked in and saluted.

Jefferson Davis beamed. "Rance!" He exclaimed. The president jumped up from his seat behind his desk and extended his hand. Liebert noticed his bad eye was now partially covered with a film. Davis had problems with it in Mexico, and now Rance wondered if the president had any vision left in it at all,[10] but the other eye was sparkling. "I haven't seen that uniform in ages!" The commander-in-chief gushed. "Sit down, colonel!" He smiled widely, for he was addressing the younger man by the title Liebert used when speaking to him for the past 15 years, and the thought seemed to please the president, as if his little boy was grown up. Davis meanwhile motioned to an overstuffed chair by the fireplace, away from his desk. "Would you like a drink or a cup of coffee?"

"No, thank you, sir" Rance responded. He liked being treated like an important person by the president of the Confederacy, but he was eaten up with curiosity about why he was here.

"I was sorry to hear about your wife," Davis said after he sat down on the couch opposite Liebert.

Rance unburdened himself to Davis like an old friend. "Thank you, sir. But our marriage was less than happy. I'm sorry she's dead, but I don't really miss her. I rather like being single."

A pained look crossed Davis' face. His second marriage hadn't always been that happy either. "Do you plan on marrying again?"

"Couldn't say, sir. Maybe, someday. Certainly I have no immediate plans."

Good, Jefferson Davis mused to himself. "Marriage can be great if you are married to the right person," he said, as he remembered Knoxie.

"And hell on earth if you're married to the wrong one," Liebert said, as Mildred's memory flashed through his mind. Jeff Davis thought of Varina.

"I know you're curious as to why you're here, so I won't keep you in suspense. I want you to head our Secret Service."

Liebert was momentarily stupefied and his mouth dropped open. He could not have been more surprised if Davis' head had suddenly

---

10 He didn't.

The Retribution Conspiracy

exploded. He searched for words. "I have little experience in military intelligence and none in undercover work," he protested.

"Neither does anybody else," Davis reassured him. "But you have all of the qualifications I need. I trust you, you are loyal and dependable, you are intelligent, you learn quickly, you are careful, and you are a wonderful organizer. I saw that in Mexico," he added, almost as an afterthought. He also thought the position needed a relatively senior officer, a relatively young man (which Rance was, for a colonel), someone at least somewhat familiar with the North and a single man, but he did not say so. Davis also liked the fact that Rance came from the world of private business and agriculture. He would likely create a functional agency, not a bureaucratic monstrosity.

Inside his head, Liebert's brain was working hard. He did not expect anything like this and was trying to devise of a way to get out of it.

Davis did not give him a chance to decline the appointment. "You will work directly for me. I have booked you a room at the Excelsior. Report back here in two days' time with your thoughts on how you intend to organize our new Secret Service. Will you need a clerk?"

"No. But I could use an aide," Rance declared. He felt as if he were in a canoe going downstream, and he noticed the current was picking up dangerously, as if there were a waterfall ahead.

"I'll assign you one. Plan everything as if the capital is Richmond."

"Richmond? Virginia?" The colonel was startled. Virginia had not seceded.

Davis smiled. He could not resist a little joke to break the tension. "No. Richmond, Louisiana. Of course Virginia." Richmond, Louisiana, was about 20 miles west of Vicksburg, and had a population of about 200.

Liebert said: "Richmond, Louisiana, might be better." He grinned at his old friend.

"Might be," Davis allowed. "I must confess it was not my first choice," he added. He had accepted the Virginia city only for political reasons. Richmond, Virginia, was only 105 miles from Washington, D.C. The Confederacy would have a frontier capital.

"Needless to say, all of this is confidential. You will not say anything about your new assignment or what you are doing. Officially, you are a special military advisor to the president of the Confederacy."

"Yes, sir."

"Any questions?"

"Not yet."

Davis picked up a small bell and rang it. But before anybody appeared, Rance declared: "I want my own people on my staff."

"Mississippi Rifles?"

"For the most part, yes. This job will require a staff in Richmond. I want people we can trust and a good number who are too old for active field service."

Davis noticed that Liebert said people we can trust, not people I can trust. This man was obviously focusing only on his new job and was not thinking about building a personal, bureaucratic empire. Davis found this a refreshing change.

The receptionist appeared at the door. "Did you summon me, sir?"

Davis momentarily ignored him. "Pick whomever you want," he told Liebert. "You have authority to appoint anyone up to the grade of captain. For major and above, come to me for approval."

"Yes, sir."

Davis addressed the receptionist. "This is Colonel Liebert," he said. "Make an appointment for him for Friday. Render him every assistance he requests. In the future, he is to have standing access to me whenever he requires it. Make sure his time is not wasted sitting in my anteroom."

"Yes, sir!"

"Assign him our most competent available man as a temporary assistant."

The receptionist looked startled. But he merely said "Yes, sir."

Davis rose and extended his hand. The interview was obviously at an end. "I'll see you Friday," he said.

"Yes, sir. And Mr. President?"

"Yes, Rance?"

"I intend to use highly selected women in my operation."

"Women?" Asked a surprised Davis. "Why?"

"Manpower issues. If there is a war, the South will need all of its men at the front. I expect the patriotic women of Richmond will volunteer in droves, and we will have our pick of very competent volunteers as office workers, and I suspect, very good staff officers. They also make excellent spies. A man will say things to a woman he would never say to a man. Besides, after a woman writes something, you can actually read it."

Davis was a little taken aback by this new development and this time didn't bother to hide it. He was a traditionalist but his own wife saw no reason a woman couldn't do anything she wished, including

The Retribution Conspiracy

vote. This was one of the reasons he and Varina had marital problems. The president was doubly surprised this idea came from Rance, who also hailed from the plantation aristocracy. *But maybe that's good*, Davis decided. The colonel was thinking outside of normal parameters, and the South might need leaders like that. The North outnumbered it three to one, after all.

Upon further reflection, the president could concede the colonel probably was right about women making better spies, but he couldn't believe Liebert wanted to use women for important office work. He decided to let his former adjutant have his way on the office worker issue but not for staff officer appointments.

"You will clear it with me before you commission any women staff officers."

"Yes, sir," Liebert said. With that, the two old friends shook hands, and the colonel walked out the door.

Outside, the receptionist said something to a runner. A few moments later, Corporal Toby Collier appeared and saluted. He was a tall, thin, dark-haired man who was wearing a brand new gray uniform. "This is Colonel Liebert," the receptionist said. "You'll be working for him for a while."

"What will we be doing?" The corporal asked.

"Collier, telegraph Lieutenant Ralph Leonard of the 12th Mississippi Infantry Regiment at Camp Instruction, Mississippi. Order him to report to me at the Excelsior Hotel in Montgomery. Tell him to bring Joshua with him." Liebert smiled internally. He just promoted his old comrade to lieutenant. "After you've done that, join me there yourself. Upgrade my room to a suite. Bring a field desk, paper, pens, and ink."

"What if they don't have a suite?" The corporal asked.

"If necessary, preempt the suite under the military necessity clause. I don't give a hoot who you have to kick out, as long as it isn't a cabinet secretary or a senator. Whoever it is can have my old room. Sign the order 'Jefferson Davis.'"

"Yes, sir," Collier exclaimed, impressed in spite of himself. He was taken aback by this officer's peremptory manner. This man obviously had authority and intended to use it; furthermore, he was clearly accustomed to being obeyed.

"I'll be at the Excelsior. Come get me when my suite is ready. Then get me a coffee pot, coffee, and enough sandwiches to last for two days. I prefer ham and mayonnaise."

"Yes, sir."

Liebert divided his suite into two parts: a bedroom and an office. He did not tell Collier what he was up to, but rather dismissed him when he had everything he needed. He didn't want anybody in Davis' office to know anything about his job, except the president himself. And he didn't intend even the president to know everything. He hung a "Do Not Disturb" sign on the door and, alone in his hotel room, stared at the empty pile of paper on the field desk. How in the world did this happen? He asked himself. The last thing he wanted was to head a department or a bureau. As for becoming a bureaucrat, that was unthinkable — even for President Davis. He wanted to be a combat commander and to lead soldiers in a desperate battle, as Jefferson Davis did at Monterrey and Buena Vista. He read history for years; now he wanted to make it. He sighed. He thought about returning to the capitol and giving the job back to Davis — but he knew he couldn't. The president was counting on him. None of this was about me, anyway, Rance thought. It was all about the Confederacy. He would have to subordinate his personal goals, wishes, desires, ambitions, and dreams for the good of the new nation. He didn't want to, but he knew he had to. Duty demanded it. Why is this so difficult? He asked himself. You were willing to sacrifice your life for the cause. Now you want to balk at creating an important agency. He closed his eyes. "To hades with what you want," he said aloud. "Get ahold of yourself, Liebert." With that remark, he pushed aside all of his more selfish aspirations, sat down and went to work on the preliminary organization of the Confederate Secret Service.

Two days later, he was back in Jefferson Davis' office.

This time, the meeting was more formal. The president remained behind his desk and was all business. "What are your conclusions?" he asked.

"The Secret Service must be predicated on the theory that, sooner or later, we will be at war with the United States. And probably sooner, rather than later."

Davis did not bat an eye, so Rance continued. "The Secret Service must have one primary purpose: obtain information for the president of the C.S.A. This can be obtained from one of two sources: public sources and U.S. government sources."

"By public sources, you mean ..."

"Newspapers and journals, but primarily newspapers. Remember what happened at Buena Vista?"

Davis looked puzzled.

The Retribution Conspiracy

"Santa Anna learned we had less than 5,000 men," Liebert elaborated, "and that southern Mexico was not in imminent danger of invasion. So he fell on us with 20,000 men."

How well I remember, Davis thought.

"And how did the Mexican dictator discover we were so weak and exposed? He learned it from reading American newspapers. It almost got both of us killed." He paused. "I intend to establish an Order of Battle section in Richmond. It will be supplied with newspapers from Washington, Baltimore, Philadelphia, Chicago, Boston, and New York — the *Herald*, the *Tribune*, and the *Times*, among others. Our agents will subscribe and immediately funnel the papers to our couriers. They will have no problem getting as far south as Washington, D.C. We will establish a courier route from Washington through southern Maryland, which is, as you know, strongly pro-Confederate. The newspapers will reach Secret Service Headquarters in Richmond within 24 to 48 hours of hitting the streets. They will immediately be screened for information on unit movements, troop and artillery strength reports, information on commanding officers, etc. We will probably have a complete Union Order of Battle within a few days and will be able to maintain it throughout the war. The most important articles, such as those dealing with Union plans, will be immediately forwarded to Your Excellency."

"How long will it take you to establish this network?"

"First we must have secret bank accounts. Then we must buy a nondescript building in Richmond. It should never be public knowledge what goes on there or even that we exist. Then we can establish our courier routes. Southeastern Maryland is strongly pro-Southern, so many willing volunteers will be available. We must impress upon them they are risking their lives if they speak of it. Lincoln would hang them as spies. Once that is clear, and we give them a minimum of training, we should have an efficient system with a month."

"Do it," Davis ordered. "What else do you have in mind?"

"The second source of information is clandestine. Washington, D.C. is a Southern town. We should be able to have an entire crop of spies from there."

"Very good," the president nodded. "I believe that is called espionage."

Rance nodded. "I want you to assign a general officer to interview a number of former U.S. officials and former members of Congress now loyal to the Confederacy, in order to obtain a list of potential informants."

"Why don't you do that yourself?"

"Because I don't want them to know who I am, what I do, or even that I exist."

"You shall have your lists, Rance," the president said. "I will send you one such list myself."

"Thank you, sir. I will need a letter of introduction from you."

"You shall have that, also. What about sabotage?"

"If it appears to be necessary, we will develop that branch as well."

Davis stared at him but didn't say anything.

"It really depends on how the war goes," Liebert said. "If we win one major battle and are able to establish our independence quickly thereafter, fine. We won't need sabotage."

"Don't you think one major battle will settle the issue?"

"It might, but I've got some doubts. Yankees can be quite tenacious, and their pride will be stung, after the first battle. In the meantime, we must continue to expand our private sources of information." He took it for granted the South would win the first major battle.

Jefferson Davis knew "private sources of information" meant spies. Like most professional soldiers, he looked upon spies with distaste. But that didn't mean he wasn't prepared to use them.

"What about misinformation? The conveyance of false information to our enemies?"

"We must develop that capacity. But, begging your excellency's pardon, I haven't gotten that far yet."

Davis smiled. It was good to have a subordinate who would so frankly admit he did not have all of the answers. "Okay. Get started on setting up your organization. I'll send you a list of names and a letter of introduction this evening."

"Thank you, sir. But don't use my name on the letter. Use Colonel Owen Dickerson."

"Okay. But you be careful about that letter. It must not fall into the wrong hands."

"It won't."

And that is how Rance Liebert began the busiest four months of his life.

—◦ CHAPTER IX ◦—
GETTING STARTED

Leonard, Julian Anderson, Collier, and Joshua entered into Liebert's suite at the Spotswood Hotel in Richmond and were immediately bombarded with a string of orders from their colonel.

"Find me a large building at least three stories tall — preferably four — that I can buy. If possible, I want the entire block. Don't worry too much about the cost. President Davis has already secured huge discretionary funds from Congress and is prepared to provide us with what we'll need. If we need more money, I'll use my personal funds." When he noticed some astonished looks, he added: "Don't worry. I'll get it back later." He did not bother to say how.

"I doubt if we can find a building like that — or at least one that's in good shape," Leonard remarked.

"Who said it had to be in good shape?" Liebert retorted. "If we have to renovate it, we will. It needs to be big, but I don't want a private residence. That would likely attract too much attention. Now, go find me a building."

The men grinned but didn't move right away.

"Are you people still here?" Liebert snapped. "Hurry up and get started. I've got to go tell a bunch of lies to the governor of Virginia."

The quartet chuckled at this remark, but the colonel did not. He saw an opportunity here to make a teaching point. "I wasn't joking," he said. "I don't want anybody to know anything about us, who we are, or what we're doing. Not even a great and powerful man like Governor Letcher. That's why I gave all of you false identities. Before this is over, we'll quite likely be keeping lots of secrets even from President Davis. Now, split up and go find me a headquarters."

The men started to leave, but Rance called them back. "Another thing. And believe this as if you heard it from God himself. If you are not prepared to act like an outlaw in the interests of your country, you have no place in the Confederate Secret Service. Remember that. It's going to be one of our guiding principles until we win this war." Once again, he took it for granted there would be war.

All four men stared solemnly at their commanding officer. The ambitious Collier, who joined up immediately after Rance offered him a promotion to second lieutenant, wondered what he had gotten himself into. The tall, black-bearded Julian Anderson, on the other hand, suppressed an urge to jump up and down and cheer. He was brought into the inner circle by Ralph Leonard and really didn't know the colonel but now decided he liked this guy Liebert, even if he was an officer. Leonard had picked Anderson because he already killed two men in gunfights and did not shown any remorse — mainly because he felt none. Anderson was a natural killer, and he was willing — even eager — to act like an outlaw in the interests of his country, precisely because he was already a bit of an outlaw. Joshua and Leonard, on the other hand, had no reaction at all to Liebert's little speech. They heard this kind of talk before.

"I hope you gentlemen have a good day," Rance concluded, "and don't trip over one another as you leave." He was ready to change and meet John Letcher.

The four men smiled nervously and departed immediately.

As soon as they got out into the hall, Anderson whispered to Joshua: "Do you think he meant what he said back there?"

The Negro looked at Julian Anderson with distaste. He already sensed this was a very dangerous man. He knew Anderson wasn't a gentleman, but Joshua wasn't yet sure if this fellow was white trash or not. Better give him the benefit of the doubt, he thought. "Mr. Rance Liebert?" He asked incredulously. "Yes, sur! Every word. Like the Lord hisself said it."

Anderson took in this remark in silence.

"He ain't no stranger to killin' them what needs killin', Mr. Julian," Joshua added. "I knows! Killin' don't bother him one little bit! He do what's right! If it come betwix doin' what the law say and what's right, he still do what's right! He don't care nuthin' 'bout no law!"

Anderson grinned widely. "Dang, boy," he exclaimed expansively as he wrapped his arm around Joshua's shoulder and hugged him as they walked down the hall. "We gonna have fun! I'm gonna enjoy workin' for this here Rance Liebert!"

Joshua's face registered a considerable degree of surprise. He never said a word, but he wondered just exactly how Julian Anderson would define the word "fun."

Now dressed in gray, Liebert wore the perfectly tailored uniform of a Confederate colonel when the receptionist escorted him into the rather luxurious office, and Rance introduced himself to Governor

The Retribution Conspiracy

John Letcher.

"I am Colonel Owen Dickerson," Liebert said as he extended his hand and told his first lie of the day.

"Yes," the governor said as they shook hands. "I received President Davis' telegram about you. What are we to discuss?"

"I am a special military advisor to the president. Here are my *bona fides*," he said and handed Letcher a letter of introduction from Jefferson Davis.

After Letcher perused the letter, he declared: "Your credentials are impeccable, colonel. What can I do to help you?"

"President Davis sent me here to organize a flow of information from Washington to Richmond and then to Montgomery. He is especially interested in the Union's plans and Orders of Battle. Can you help me?" Dickerson/Liebert did not mention the existence of a Confederate Secret Service.

John Letcher looked like a university professor. He was clean shaven, balding, with wire-rimmed glasses and a dark suit, subdued plaid vest and a bow tie. He looked like a man who never served a day in the military but might have watched a parade once. He was surprised by Liebert's request and took his story with a grain of salt but was willing to cooperate, providing everything remained under his office until Virginia joined the Confederacy. This was not a foregone conclusion in February 1861. As a former newspaper editor, Letcher knew the value of information, and his operatives already had taken steps to begin a secret courier route, along the lines Liebert suggested.

"Yes, I believe I can," the studious governor replied. After considering Dickerson for a moment, he opened one of his desk drawers, pulled out a piece of stationery, and began to write. "This is a letter of introduction to Captain Thomas Jordan," he said. "He is Virginia's unofficial chief of intelligence. His office is in the state's adjutant general's building. Do you know where that is?"

"Yes, sir. Thank you very much, Governor Letcher," Liebert said as he rose from his chair and extended his hand. He wanted to bring the interview to a conclusion as quickly as possible. This man was too sharp; he didn't want to give the governor time to ask any questions.

Letcher was somewhat surprised by this development but recovered quickly. He also arose from his chair, shook the colonel's hand, gave him the letter, and walked him to the door. The entire meeting did not take five minutes.

Rance Liebert, in fact, did not know where the adjutant general's building was, but he knew he wouldn't have any difficulty finding it. He and Captain Jordan hit it off immediately. Jordan was very professional.[11] He graduated from West Point in 1840 and was with the 3rd Infantry at Palo Alto, Resaca de la Palma, and Monterrey, among others. He knew Zachary Taylor[12] well and was acquainted with Jefferson Davis. He was a natural intelligence officer and understood that truth and openness were not virtues men like he and Dickerson (if that really was his name) could always afford. He decided to work with the colonel nevertheless.

"Let's go to Washington tomorrow," Jordan suggested. "I want to show you our courier route and introduce you to somebody."

Rance was pleased and startled by this suggestion but hoped his facial expression didn't show it. It didn't. Although he didn't realize it, all of those nights of playing poker in the saloon back in Rainbow were finally paying off. He had a good poker face.

"Can't tomorrow," Liebert replied. "How about the day after?"

"Fine," the captain responded. He did not mention he already was planning to go the next day, but he decided to delay his departure until Thursday to accommodate Rance. He was, however, indiscreet enough to ask: "What are you doing tomorrow?"

"Closing a real estate deal."

Jordan looked at him quizzically but decided not to pursue the matter any further.

"I found what may be the perfect place," Leonard beamed as soon as Rance entered their hotel room at the Spotswood.

"Where is it?"

"About 20 blocks from here. On Market Street."

"Let's go see," the colonel replied. "Collier, you and Anderson come too. Pick up Joshua and meet us there." Joshua, naturally, was billeted in the servants' quarters.

What Leonard found was an old, large, four-story building, about ten blocks from what soon would be the government quarters in Rich-

---

11 Jordan would be promoted to brigadier general for gallantry at Shiloh in April 1862. He was later chief of staff of the Army of Tennessee under Beauregard and Bragg.

12 Taylor was elected president in 1848 and was inaugurated on March 4, 1851, but died in office of acute gastroenteritis in 1852.

The Retribution Conspiracy

mond. Rance frowned but decided it might do. He decided the price was fair. "If we buy it, do we get the entire block?"

"No," the middle-age lieutenant replied. "This is a long block. There are three other lots. Two of the owners are gentlemen and were willing to sell when I identified myself as a Confederate officer and appealed to their patriotism. The third was a speculator and a donkey to boot. He refused to sell under any circumstances."

"As soon as we leave here, we're going to the Richmond State Bank and setting up a separate building account to which you, Mr. Leonard, will have access," Liebert retorted. "Buy the building and the two lots. Make sure the lot owners make a decent profit. Anderson, go to the third lot owner, put a knife to his throat and ask him politely to reconsider."

"And if he refuses to?"

"He won't, if you are convincing enough, and I'm sure you will be. But draw a little blood, if you have to."

Anderson smiled widely.

"But don't kill him," the colonel added quickly. Anderson's face fell. Then he decided to lift the man's wallet and take his watch. Maybe I'll cut off an ear, he thought. His mood immediately brightened.

"And Leonard?" Rance said.

"Yes, sir?"

"See to it that this piece of walking fertilizer loses money on the deal."

Everybody either laughed or grinned.

There was no identification on the building and there never would be. It was heavily guarded throughout the war. The edifice was not in particularly good condition, and Liebert gave Leonard the task of renovating it, with Collier acting as his assistant. He gave them the basic design and told them to hire the appropriate carpenters, plumbers, and whoever else was needed tomorrow morning. Work was to begin immediately. He also ordered that a livery stable be constructed directly behind it and told Joshua to design it.

"Colonel, do you want us to come to you at any point to approve any of this?" Leonard asked.

"No. I won't be here. I've got to go to Washington."

A surprised and somewhat unhappy look flashed across the lieutenant's face. Liebert noticed it. "Ralph," he said, "we have no time. I'd love to personally supervise the entire reconstruction of this building, but there is a laundry list of things which are more important. A war could break out between our country and the United States at any moment. I have no time. I must delegate."

"Okay, Rance …" he said skeptically. "Just don't chew my rear off if I do something you don't like."

"I won't," Rance promised. He put his hand on his old friend's shoulder. "I can think of no one more capable of performing this vital task than you."

CHAPTER X
WILD ROSES
AND RAINY PICNICS

"Have you ever been to Washington before, colonel?" Captain Jordan asked, "Several years ago, I spent two years tramping around the world," Rance replied. "I spent 24 hours of it here."

Jordan smiled. "First thing, I'll show you the sights." He did, and the colonel began to learn his way around the city. The monuments and the government buildings were impressive, and the Capitol dome was under construction, but it was still awe-inspiring. Rance was looking forward to visiting all of the libraries, museums, and famous places. The town was full of people because Abraham Lincoln was scheduled to be inaugurated in just a few days. In the confusion and excitement, the two Southerners were hardly even noticed. Although it was at first difficult for him, Liebert learned on his first trip to the North how to speak without his Southern accent. It did not occur to him until now that this talent might be classified as a survival skill.

The first person to whom Jordan introduced Liebert was Rose Greenhow, a prominent socialite who lived in a mansion just south of the White House. Her olive-tinted skin often flushed with color when she was amused, animated, or stimulated, which led to her nickname, "The Wild Rose." Her husband worked for the State Department until he was killed in an accident in San Francisco in 1854. She was a friend of presidents, generals, senators, and hundreds of less prominent people, and was currently being courted by the chairman and another member of the Senate's Military Affairs Committee.

After having four children, 45-year-old Rose's beauty was faded somewhat but certainly not completely. She was still very attractive, even if she didn't cause carriage accidents anymore. She also had a way of speaking to people which made them feel better about themselves just because she was paying attention to them, and she had a glittering circle of friends. She had a way of making people comfortable — even abolitionists — and comfortable people talk. She let them rattle on and learned everything of importance they knew. She was also passionately committed to the Southern cause. Perhaps too much.

Rance Liebert liked the charming Rose Greenhow immensely but decided not to have anything to do with her, other than to have an operative collect her information and transmit it to Richmond. (With that in mind, they established a dead drop.) She was a little too outspoken in her convictions, and Rance concluded that it was only a matter of time before the Yankees closed in on her. Before they arrested her, however, they would place her salon under observation. Liebert sensed she would not change — could not change — so he did not say anything about his decision to her. He merely had a private meeting with her and told her he would provide her with a cipher. She would then give her coded messages to a servant, who would convey them to a secret service operative, who in turn would take them to a courier. The information would be in Richmond in less than 48 hours.

Rance was walking down a sidewalk, thinking about finding a replacement for Rose, when he saw a sign advertising a Shakespearean play at the Washington Theatre. The star was John Wilkes Booth, of whom he had never heard. The name of one of the supporting actresses on the poster, however, caused him to stop and stare in amazement. It was Guinevere Spring.

Sally Mae Glass, a/k/a Guinevere Spring, took to acting immediately. Junius Booth liked her and paid special attention to her — much to the jealously of her contemporaries. At the end of the course (which was not cheap), she received several bit parts and did well. She was able to convey a certain freshness and innocence on stage — and sometimes off stage, although this was a world very much different from the old plantation. It was more exciting, more dynamic, tougher, and definitely harsher and more sexual. She made the necessary compromises to get ahead in her profession, and she made moral concessions when she deemed them appropriate, and even enjoyed some of them. She soon discovered she was good at it. Guinevere, in fact, now knew more about sex than she ever thought she would. Sometimes she looked upon that as just part of the real world, sometimes it was not without pleasure, and other times she wasn't particularly proud of herself.

During her time in New York, Guinevere developed a very pragmatic theory of life: although they were more powerful, men were generally not as smart as women; therefore, they could and should be manipulated, since it was through men that women accomplished all things. She even decided (and probably quite correctly) that the term "weaker sex" had been invented by a woman, in order to throw off-balance the man she was preparing to overwhelm. She smiled to herself.

The Retribution Conspiracy

She certainly got a great deal from men over the past few years. Sometimes more than she wanted.

After the play, she got the usual eight to a dozen notes from men, wanting to meet her for a late dinner or a drink, or just to talk. She and her understudy (who was also a friend) quickly went through the missives, laughing together and jotting down the usual polite rejection response. Guinevere was accustomed to meeting worshiping fans, who were always males. And they only wanted one thing. …

"This is a weird one," the understudy announced.

"Really? What does it say?" Guinevere loved variety.

"I am Owen Dickerson. Please meet me for dinner at the LaVere Hotel. Love: Rance Liebert."

"Let me see that!" She snapped as she snatched the note.

"Weird guy. His name is different from his signature."

"Uh … Personal joke," Guinevere muttered. "I know him from home."

"Oh! He's from New York?"

She momentarily forgot she now told everyone she was from New York. It would hardly do for her to be from Rainbow, Mississippi — especially now that it looked as if there might be a war. "Yes. I think so." She wondered if he succeeded in disguising his accent as well.

The understudy stared at her but decided not to pursue the conversation. She did notice, however, that all of sudden the usually light-hearted, fun-loving Guinevere was gone. Now she seemed to be in a big hurry — and she was a woman who never hurried, especially for a man.

She changed and got to the dining room at the LaVere as rapidly as she could. She looked at her hands: they were actually trembling. She tried to remember the last time that happened. Stop! She thought. You're supposed to be in control, like on the stage or in the bedroom. Get a hold of yourself, woman. He's just a man. Just another man. …

She found Rance at a table in the back of the restaurant. It was late, and there were few people dining. She did not know he paid the *maitre d'* to make sure the tables and booths around them were empty.

"Rance!" She smiled. She rushed up and hugged him, then took his hands and kissed him on the cheek. She stepped back, looked at him, and hugged him again. "What are you doing here?" She said, smiling from ear to ear.

"I'm here on business."

"What kind of business?"

"Oh, nothing important. We can talk about that later. Tell me about your life. Do you like being an actress?"

"Yes, I love being an actress! Well, most of the time." Guinevere sat down and went into a discussion of all her stage credits and, as she always did with Rance Liebert, just talked and talked and talked. It reminded him of when she was six years old at Windrow, and the topic was dolls.

As she rattled on, Rance scrutinized her. Physically she had changed. The teenage girl look was gone and was replaced by the glamorous young actress. Certainly she was not difficult to look at — not at all. Her smile seemed more beautiful now, and she looked more radiant. Success had clearly boosted her self-confidence. And there were other changes, perhaps even more subtle. She was always intelligent, but since many potential beaus in Rainbow County would be intimidated by an intelligent woman, she often tried to hide it. Now, the more self-assured Guinevere didn't seem to be hiding much. She was a good conversationalist, and sometimes a brilliant one, and was definitely not afraid to share her opinions. She also seemed to be trying to impress him with her professional accomplishments, which were indeed stunning. Clearly she was much more adventurous than she was back on the farm. Her world was broader, and she was not afraid of it. Rance felt flattered this beautiful and clever woman was trying to impress him. He listened in rapt attention.

On the other side of the table, Guinevere was having more fun than she had in a long time. Men listened to her all the time, but she could tell most of them wanted something or were just planning their next move. This man was different. She fell in love with him when she was six years old. True, it was just puppy love, but she fantasized about being married to him throughout her teenage years. I'll never tell him, she thought, but I cried myself to sleep the night his engagement to Mildred was announced. She had no thoughts of marrying him now, or at least not many, but she was glad he was here, she was glad he was single, and she was glad he was interested in what she had to say. She giggled. Sally Mae was happy and delighted she had come tonight.

In between the long bursts of conversation, they ordered a late dinner. He had a steak; she had a salad — most of which she didn't eat. She had too much to say ... about acting school, the plays in which she had appeared or starred, and life in New York City and Washington, D.C. She did, however, help him drink the wine — quite liberally, if fact. He learned she was part of the Washington National Theatre's "stock company," which supported "name" actors and actresses of established reputation and who got top billing and heftier paychecks. She hoped to earn such status herself one day and was clearly on her way.

Finally she reached over and squeezed his arm. "I was sorry to hear about your wife, Rance."

"Yeah … Well, it wasn't much of a marriage. I do feel guilty about it."

"Guilty? Why?"

"Because I didn't feel any particular regret over her passing."

She considered that for a moment. "If you could go back in time, would you do anything differently?"

"Would I! I wouldn't have gotten married to start with. I'd have waited for you to grow up."

Although she laughed off the compliment, she was pretty sure he wasn't joking. Many a truth was said in jest, she thought. "I meant would you have allowed her to go on that voyage. But thank you for the compliment. I'm very flattered."

They considered each other over their wine glasses for several moments. "Would I have made her stay at De La Teneria, knowing it would save her life, or let her go, knowing it would kill her? I don't know for certain, but I'm pretty sure I'd have kept her at home — even though she would have hated me for it."

Typical Rance Liebert, she thought. He'd have kept her alive, even if he had to pay for it every day for the rest of his life. She asked him to pour her another glass of wine, which he naturally did. She grinned. She normally didn't drink much and was getting a little tipsy.

They had a most enjoyable visit. They talked about old times, old friends, their current lives and her career. She couldn't remember when she enjoyed a conversation more. Finally, she brought the *tête-à-tête* back to the original topic. "But why are you in D.C., Rance? And why are you calling yourself Owen Dickerson? You'd better tell me now, or I'm going to burst!"

Rance Liebert knew this was the moment of truth. "Oh, I thought I'd mentioned it." He looked into his wine with affected nonchalance and then looked her right in the eyes. "I am a high-ranking officer in the Southern army. I am, in fact, the commander of the Confederate Secret Service, and I work directly for President Davis," he said, leaning back in his chair. "I am engaged in espionage and am committing high treason against the government of the United States. I am actively plotting to defeat the Lincoln regime and overthrow the Federal government with every means at my disposal and am establishing an under-cover network to help accomplish that purpose. The process is already well advanced. Would you care to join me?" He said that as calmly and as cavalierly as he would have said: "Would you like to dance?"

Guinevere Spring was suddenly jolted back into Sally Mae Glass again. Her hand shook so much that she spilled wine on herself and then dropped her glass on the floor. For once in her life, she couldn't speak — or close her mouth.

Rance promised the waiter an unusually large tip if he did not disturb them unless summoned. If he came unsummoned, no tip. The staff looked in their direction but ignored the broken glass. The silence was oppressive.

"It will likely be a dangerous business," he continued. "You'll be a foreign agent behind enemy lines. I can't pay you anything; in fact, you'll have to bear most if not all of your own expenses. If you get into trouble, I probably won't be able to get you out of it. You might even get hanged or shot. At the very least, if everything falls apart, you'll wind up in prison and your career will be ruined. But it promises to be one hech of a wild ride. Are you willing?"

The dumbfounded actress tried twice to speak and couldn't. But Guinevere was only rarely able to pass up an adventure, and this promised to be a big one. The biggest of her life, in fact. And it just appeared, without warning. When she partially recovered, she heard herself saying: "Yes, Rance, of course I'll join you," she said, smiling widely and using her Southern accent. "What woman could possibly resist a line like that, you silver-tongued devil, you!?"

Initially, Guinevere's career as a spy consisted of nothing except keeping her ears open and her mouth shut. Union counterespionage measures — which were never particularly good — were non-existent early in the war. Sally even invited Rance to escort her to one of Lincoln's inaugural balls, but he didn't think that was a good idea. A look of genuine hurt flashed across her face, but it was instantly masked. As a beautiful woman and a popular actress, she wasn't accustomed to being turned down, even when her ideas were not the best. After thinking about it for a moment, however, she also realized it was a bad idea. Too many people might recognize him later. Rance (a/k/a Owen Dickerson) noticed the hurt look and said: "How about a picnic the next day?" She brightened immediately. After all, she could have her choice of escorts to the inaugural ball, but of course she didn't tell him that.

Sally Mae Glass always had a soft spot in her heart for Rance Liebert. She was Guinevere Spring now, but she felt the old feelings coming back, and she did little to try to suppress them. She had the strange sensation of sinking in quicksand but not caring at all. Interestingly enough, she was actually enjoying it. The fact he was now more dangerous only heightened his allure. Since she left Rainbow, she experienced success and adulation, but not love. She missed Windrow, she missed her father and mother, she missed her twin brother, and she missed her old life. And she had been in love with Rance Liebert since they twirled across the dance floor together when she was six years old. All those feelings combined were coming to the surface now. At first she thought, how do I deal with these emotions? But he treated her with respect and tenderness. Now all she did was return the affection. She was also bothered her that she might not be in control this time. If he tried to take her to bed, she would not be able to resist. She also thought he probably would eventually, but it wouldn't be mindless, one-night sex. There would be some meaning to it. He wouldn't simply disappear the next morning, as other men did. Guinevere Spring decided then and there she would never be anybody's one-night stand again — unless she absolutely had to be. There had to be something more to it.

The hotel packed the picnic lunch for them, but the day of the event brought bitter cold and rain mixed with ice, so they spread a blanket on the floor near the fireplace and pretended they were outside. It worked for them. They always had a certain chemistry when they were together and were soon talking, joking, and laughing.

"It's too bad you didn't join me at the inaugural ball," she grinned. "Mr. Lincoln is a charming man, full of wit and humor. I think you'd have liked him."

I'm thinking about blowing his head off, Rance thought. He made a face, so she steered the conversation into safer waters. Eventually Sally asked about the 12th Mississippi. Then the conversation became more serious.

"I miss it," he said. "I miss it every day. I was very proud of that regiment. I wanted to command it in the big battle."

"So you think there'll be a war?"

"Oh, yes! Got to be." She grew reflective for a moment as Rance continued. "I've done some studying. There is only one central thing in Abraham Lincoln's political philosophy and that is Henry Clay's so-called American System. Basically, it calls for Southern money, taken from us in the form of tariffs,[13] to finance Northern internal improvements, especially railroads. The implementation of this scheme is already well advanced. The Federal budget is $80 million, of which $70 million comes from tariffs from Southern ports. The South, which makes up about 30 percent of the population, is already paying more than 85 percent of the taxes, but the Northern politicians want more. Look what the Congress just did. Last week, only a month or so after the Deep South left the Union, they passed the Morrell Tariff, which increases the duty on cotton to 47 percent. That's huge. Double what it had been, in fact. They couldn't have done it if senators like Jeff Davis remained in Congress to block it. The British don't want to pay that much, and I don't blame them. Even before that, they started their own cotton-growing regions in Egypt and India. When they are fully developed, it will be economically devastating to every man, woman, and child in the South, since everything in the South depends on cotton."

"So you don't think the war — if there is one — will be about slavery? That's what some of the Abolitionists say it's about."

"No. Certainly not at first. Lincoln has already publicly pledged he will not disturb a single Southern institution and backed a Constitutional amendment protecting slavery in the South. It's about money, power, and Southern self-determination. Lincoln is smart, but he is also calculating and cunning. And he loves money! I believe him when he says he wants to preserve the Union. That's the only way he has to finance his internal improvement schemes or even run the government. It's too late for that to happen peacefully. To do that, he'll have to get the South to rejoin the Union. There is no way we're going to return voluntarily! So he will resort to violence. He'll have to. Most likely he will try to maneuver the South into firing the first shot, if he can, but there will be violence. And war."

"Do you think we'll win?"

"I haven't got a clue. It's 50-50, I think. But I don't think about that very much. I have two jobs. The first is to establish a secret service from scratch, which isn't easy. And second, and more important, to have a fun picnic with a beautiful, intelligent, and exciting young woman whom I admire very much. And I am neglecting the second duty with all this heavy talk," he grinned.

She smiled back, but quickly got serious again.

"What about Dan?" Guinevere was a woman who often focused on

---

13 There was no income tax in those days.

things within her immediate purview. She was more interested in her home and family than the fate of the Confederate States of America. She wouldn't lose five minutes sleep if a giant outer space monster ate the entire nation of China, but she would worry all night if a single yellow fever case was reported in New Orleans. That city, after all, wasn't all that far from Rainbow.

"Well, your brother is a lieutenant in the 12th." *And not a particularly good one,* he thought, *although he does try hard.*

"Can you protect him?" Her blue-grey eyes met his. "Will you protect him?"

"I'd do anything for you," he said, seriously. "After his first battle, I'll have him transferred to my headquarters, so he won't get shot at again."

"Can't you do that before his first battle?"

Rance hoped that question would not come up. "No. I can't. He'd never forgive me or you if that happened. And he'd find a way to get back to the regiment in time for the fight anyway." He paused. "Dan is a true Southerner, and a Southerner sees participation in a war as both an obligation and a birthright. After the first battle, he'll have met that requirement. He'll see things differently then."

She did not ask, but what if he gets killed in his first battle? But she thought it. "It's the honor thing, isn't it?"

"It is."

She frowned. That "honor thing" came from their Cavalier ancestors and got a great many of them killed in England and many more exiled to the New World. It had almost got Dan killed by Bushrod Brown. Now it was putting him in danger again. But Rance was right, and she knew it. It would not go well if they interfered now; it would be counterproductive, in fact.

She turned the subject so as not to ruin the afternoon. Before long, he reached over and held her hand. It was an erotic moment for her. She felt more excited when he touched her fingers than she had when other men fondled her breasts.

The day ended with him sitting on the floor and leaning back against the couch. She crawled over, put her arms around him, lay her head on his shoulder, and hugged him. After a few moments, he put his hand under her chin and turned her face up to him, and they shared their first kiss. It conveyed more tenderness than passion, although both elements were present. He didn't pursue it any further, and she was glad — sort of. But she felt herself falling in love with him all over again, and it felt right.

Colonel Liebert (who was now using his real name with Tom Jordan) and the captain found it easy to establish their courier route in southern Maryland. It was strongly pro-Confederate, and geography was on their side. The couriers would leave Washington or Baltimore with newspapers and/or secret dispatches and travel through the turnpikes or many back roads of Charles' and St. Mary's Counties to the Potomac River, which they would cross in a small boat. They were now in Confederate territory, and it was an easy ride to Richmond. The Union cavalry would not bother them. It had other things to do — such as dealing with the Confederate cavalry. For the first two years of the war, this was a mismatch, because the Northern horsemen were not serious competition for their Southern counterparts. Even after that changed, the Union high command had few units to devote to southern Maryland. The Liebert-Jordan courier route (which included several alternate routes) continued to function throughout the war.

Back in Richmond, Lieutenant Leonard and Second Lieutenant Collier saw to the renovation of the Market Street headquarters, and the stables were rapidly nearing completion. Rance was so pleased with their progress when he returned that he promoted Leonard to captain and named him headquarters commandant and headquarters company commander. He appointed Collier headquarters company executive officer and promoted him to first lieutenant.

With the completion of the courier route, the Order of Battle Section became operative, and soon Rance (and Jeff Davis) had a pretty good idea about the Union strength and how they were organized.[14]

The Secret Service also had a signals branch. In this area, the South was extremely lucky. When secession came, almost all of the top signals experts in the nation joined the Confederate Signal Corps, which set up a station in Liebert's basement. It was soon inhabited by mentally swift Richmond women who wanted to serve their country — but did not want to be nurses. They encoded and decoded messages rapidly and knew how to keep their mouths shut.

---

14 Some readers may not believe this kind of information can be gleaned from public newspapers. Those readers would be wrong. During the Cold War, for example, an American lieutenant had nothing better to do than to try to construct the U.S.-West German Order of Battle from public newspapers. He included the locations of units down to the company level. When he showed his work to his commander, it was so accurate and so complete the astonished general had it classified "Secret."

The first floor of the building was Leonard's domain. It included the headquarters section, a mess hall, and a barracks. Liebert soon formed a company of permanent guards. They were posted just inside the building and between the floors. He believed in security. They were mostly older men armed with muskets, but some of them also carried modern Navy Sixes (six-shooters). Half the company was made up of Secret Service people who operated in the Richmond area and functioned as counterintelligence and counterespionage agents.

The second floor housed a supply section and offices. Many of the uniforms in the large supply room were blue, and there were civilian clothes there as well. The floor above that included several offices, many of which were unoccupied, although they would gradually fill up, as well as Liebert's office, his private apartment, and a couple of visitors' bedrooms.

The fourth floor was vacant, for the moment. No one was allowed up here, but everyone in Liebert's inner circle noticed that it resembled a jail. The entrance was guarded, the iron door was locked, and there were bars on the inside of the painted windows. There were jail cells in the back.

As soon as Virginia seceded, the Market Street headquarters was to be given the official cover name 125th Special Employment Battalion. [15]

The renovations on Market Street were barely complete on April 12, 1861, when Confederate guns opened up on Fort Sumter and war burst upon them. On April 15, Lincoln called for 75,000 volunteers to "suppress" the "Rebellion." This would make the Federal Army the largest military force in the history of the Western Hemisphere as of 1861.

Virginia left the Union two days later.

---

15 The term "Special Employment" was Confederate for "Secret Service."

— CHAPTER XI —
I CAN SHOOT HIM RIGHT NOW

It was a pretty spring day. Abraham Lincoln chatted happily with his aide as the carriage rolled through the countryside toward the Anderson Cottage at the Soldiers Home, in a rural area just north of Washington, D.C., and only three miles from the White House. This was Lincoln's favorite presidential retreat and would later be his residence during the summer months. He much preferred it to the White House. Dressed in his normal black suit and wearing his trademark stovepipe hat, the president and his aide rode in an open carriage, followed by a military escort of two blue-coated cavalrymen. Today, events in South Carolina dominated conversation. The week before, the Rebels fired on Fort Sumter.

Many Southerners believed that, although he would never say so in public, Lincoln was quite happy with the way things evolved.[16] The Confederates played right into his hands. Now, he could justifiably claim they fired the first shot. He wouldn't have to do it himself. With 75,000 men, Lincoln was sure he could crush the rebellion in 90 days. The chastised Southern states would be forced back into the Union, but things would be quite different when they returned. With the Southern senators gone, Congress already approved much of Lincoln's agenda, including a doubling of the cotton tariff to 47 percent, which meant he would have plenty of money to finance internal improvements in the North, Midwest, and West — all at Southern expense. His plan to ban slavery in the territories was largely approved, meaning Northern farmers and workers would not have to compete with cheap black labor.

"Sir," the aide said. He was reluctant to try to engage the president of the United States in an uninvited private conversation, but his curi-

---

16 Lincoln made this very clear in a letter to his friend, Gustavus V. Fox, whom he appointed assistant secretary of the navy shortly after Fort Sumter fell. See Egon Richard Tausch, "The American Dream: North and South (And What Became of It) in Frank B. Powell, III, *To Live and Die in Dixie* (Columbia, Tennessee: 2014), p. 401; Samuel W. Crawford, *The Genesis of the Civil War: The Story of Sumter 1860-1861* (New York: 1887), p. 420. Lincoln also sent not one but five war expeditions into Confederate waters prior to Fort Sumter (see Lieutenant Commander Richard Rush and Robert H. Woods, *Official Records of the Union and Confederate Navies in the War of the Rebellion* [Washington, D.C.: 1880-1891] Series I, Volume IV, 107ff).

osity overcame his reticence. "I share your vision about slavery in the territories, but what do you intend to do about slavery in the South?"

"Send them back to Africa!" Lincoln declared, flatly. "I have held this view for many years. I was secretary of the Illinois branch of the American Colonization Society for more than a decade. It is a major part of the 'Back to Africa' movement."

As the young captain nodded attentively, the president frowned. "I admit that I have not yet worked out all of the details, but I believe some form of compensated emancipation is perhaps in order. Slavery is morally wrong, and the blacks should never have been taken from Africa in the first place. All right: send them back! They are, as I have already made clear to Frederick Douglass, inferior to white people and always will be. So send them back. The South would be hurt economically, but it will adjust in two or three generations. After all, slavery did not work economically in the North, and now the South must follow our flourishing economic model. And they must return and be brought back into the Union. By force, if necessary."

"And the slave trade?" Asked the aide.

"I'd like to do something about that, too, but we must be careful," Lincoln warned, shifting in his seat. "One crisis at a time!" He did not tell the young, idealistic officer, but abolishing the slave trade was very low on his list of priorities. Lincoln was not sure he could get enough votes in the Senate to approve shutting down the slave traders. He calculated the numbers in his head. Since they operated their fleets out of New England, their members of Congress would likely be opposed to any restrictions on it. It certainly wasn't an issue Lincoln was prepared to waste any political capital on. "After all, what they are doing is legal," Lincoln added, almost as an afterthought, "and they don't bring their slaves to our shores."[17] He wasn't going to alienate any governors, senators, or congressmen on that issue.

Lincoln changed the subject as quickly as possible and expounded his vision for the future. "With the Southern obstructionists out of the

---

17 Between 24,000,000 and 25,000,000 slaves were transported from Africa during the slave trading era. Twenty million of them arrived alive — six percent of these in the American colonies/United States. Nothing was done to limit the Northern slave traders in the Civil War era, even when Congress was dominated by the Radical Republicans. They continued to operate until 1885, when Brazil became the last nation to outlaw the slave trade. Slavery was abolished in that country three years later. Since the slave fleet operated out of Boston, Massachusetts, and Providence, Rhode Island, which were not in rebellion against the Federal government, Lincoln knew they needed to be handled with care.

The Retribution Conspiracy

way, we can build federally subsidized railroads and canals, linking the North and the Midwest, spurring unprecedented economic growth for our two regions. Every other section of land within five miles of the rail lines will be given to the railroads, free of charge. They can to sell it to farmers and immigrants for a tidy profit and reinvest it to build more rail lines and pay dividends to their stockholders."[18] It flashed through his mind this prosperity would assure his reelection, but did not say so. A cycle of prosperity would be established. And prosperous people are happy people! The Republican Party would be returned to office election after election. "We will eliminate this so-called Southern Confederacy in 90 days or less," he declared aloud. "This unpleasantness with the South will soon be over and all but forgotten."

Are you trying to convince me or yourself? The captain wondered, although naturally he didn't vocalize this thought.

As Lincoln chatted away, he was not aware he was being watched. The sniper lined up his rifle and had Lincoln's head in the sights. He was less than 100 yards away, ready to shoot.

"No problem, colonel," Julian Anderson declared. "We can assassinate the jackass and escape at the drop of a hat. I can shoot him right now, if you want me to."

Rance Liebert looked at his tall, dark-haired corporal in the ill-fitting black suit and briefly considered the matter. "No, not yet," he said softly. "Let's put the idea on hold for now. I need to talk it over with somebody first."

"Awright," the reluctant corporal snapped. It was clear that he wanted to pull the trigger.

"And don't call me colonel when we're in civilian clothes and operating behind enemy lines. We're businessmen from Missouri, remember. Let's not arouse any suspicions we don't have to."

"Oh. Awright," the disappointed corporal said as he lowered his rifle and President Lincoln's carriage rolled out of range.

———

Two months later, Liebert, now impeccably dressed in the uniform of a colonel, entered the Confederate White House and asked to speak with President Jefferson Davis.

The receptionist glared at him with suspicion. To him, all other visitors were known qualities. But this colonel was different. The lieutenant was aware the man standing before him and Davis were old

---

18 The term "corporate welfare" was not been invented yet.

friends, and the president sometimes treated him almost like a son. But now this colonel had unprecedented access to the chief executive — access enjoyed only by Generals Samuel Cooper and Robert E. Lee, his adjutant general and chief military advisor, respectively, along with a handful of cabinet ministers. The room was full of visitors but, in accordance with Davis' orders, Liebert was admitted immediately. That was unusual at first. Now it was routine.

It irked the receptionist (a lieutenant) that he had little knowledge of who Liebert was and had no idea about what was his job. He certainly didn't look special: average height, brown hair, and eyes, and slightly overweight. One would not single him out of the crowd as an extraordinary man. But lieutenants don't get to ask many questions, Davis was tight-lipped about the matter, and Liebert was one of the most secretive men the lieutenant ever encountered.

Two senators who arrived earlier that day were mildly put out when a mere colonel cut in front of them. It did not escape their notice he was wearing a Bowie knife and an ultra-modern six-shot revolver, strapped low and in front of his hip, as if he intended to draw it quickly, and he had not bothered to take it off before he entered Davis' private office. This in itself was an unusual gesture of informality.

"Who the devil is that man?" One of the senators asked.

"Colonel Rance Liebert of Mississippi," the lieutenant responded.

"Is he a congressman?"

"No, sir."

"What is his position?" The next senator asked.

"He is a special military advisor to the president," the receptionist replied.

"What does that mean?"

"Danged if I know," the lieutenant answered, his palms open, in an "I don't know" kind of gesture. He did not forget to smile inanely, so the senator would not be offended.

They would have been astonished to learn this unremarkable looking colonel was one of the most dangerous men in the whole Rebel nation. He was here to give Jefferson Davis two new options to deal with Abraham Lincoln.

Like Liebert, Jeff Davis blamed Lincoln for the start of the war.[19]

---

19 Davis asserted at the time that the side who fired the first shot did not always start the war. He held that when the Union refused to evacuate Fort Sumter and tried to resupply and reinforce a potentially hostile foreign fort in the middle of a major Southern harbor, they provoked the hostilities. They also violated Confed-

The Retribution Conspiracy

But, despite their friendship and close personal relationship, this conversation did not go well.

"I am here to give you a couple of options *vis-à-vis* Abraham Lincoln," Rance said.

Davis leaned back in his chair and gave his former adjutant his undivided attention. "All right," he said. "What are they?"

"I can easily organize a kidnapping attempt."

"I don't think that's necessary at this time," the president replied. "He is clearly an inept commander-in-chief, and he might easily be replaced by a much abler man. Besides, such an attempt could result in Lincoln's death."

"That's the second option," the colonel responded.

"What?!" The president exclaimed.

"We can shoot the son-of-an ape," Liebert declared, evenly.

Jefferson Davis leapt up as if he had been stung by a bee. "No!" he shouted.

Colonel Liebert initially ignored the rejection. "Such an action could not help but disrupt the Union chain of command," he continued.

"No!" He bellowed. "We can't commit murder!"

"I doubt if Lincoln's agents would hesitate, if they had a clean shot at you! And I feel sure Lincoln would approve it." It was very rare for Liebert to talk back to Jefferson Davis, but this time he did.

"That makes no difference! There are some things a gentleman simply will not do! And a Christian wouldn't do it, either! Don't dare bring up another suggestion of this nature again, lieutenant!" He exclaimed, using Liebert's Mexican War rank, as he often did when they were alone. Normally, he employed it almost as a term of endearment; this time he was angry, and it just slipped out.

Now the colonel backed off. "Yes, sir," he said. "But just know these options are available, should you ever wish to use one of them."

He received another heated, emotional rejection. "No, no, no, no, no!" The Confederate commander-in-chief reiterated. The conversation ended with Jefferson Davis snapping at him: "Rance, I don't know what gets into you sometimes."

But the rejections did not particularly phase the colonel. "No," after all, doesn't mean "never," and Liebert had a thick skin. He knew how to wait.

---

erate territory when they crossed into Southern territorial waters with their ships. Lincoln, however, clearly won the battle of public opinion on this issue.

—☙ CHAPTER XII ☙—
THE DANCE BEGINS

July 9, 1861, was a hot, muggy day in Richmond. Colonel Rance Liebert only just returned from a trip to Kentucky and was seated at his desk when there was a rather loud knock on the door. He yelled, "Enter!" and Melody Herzog came in. She was obviously excited. "Dispatch from Washington! You need to read this right away!"

He raised an eyebrow and looked at her. She was short, young, about 30 pounds overweight, well dressed and normally somewhat reserved. Her long dark brown hair usually added to her attractiveness, but today it was in a bun. She also possessed a quick mind and was very efficient, and the colonel was becoming quite fond of her.

Rance picked up the dispatch. "McD. to begin advance against Manassas on July 16," it read. "Plan to feint against Beau's center and right. Main attack to turn CSA left. More info to follow soon. Blue Sparrow."

Liebert's eyes opened wide. McD. was Irwin McDowell, the commander of Lincoln's main army. Manassas was an important railroad junction 25 miles southwest of Washington and about 80 miles from Richmond. Beau referred to the commander of the Confederate Army of the Potomac, General P. G. T. Beauregard, which was deployed along Bull Run (creek), just north of Manassas. CSA stood for Confederate States Army. Blue Sparrow was the code name for Rose O'Neal Greenhow. In three sentences, she had given him McDowell's entire battle plan.

"Do you have another copy of this?"

"No, sir."

"Make another copy. In fact, make two copies. Bring them here as soon as you're finished. Send in Captain Leonard. And Melody ..."

"Yes, sir?" She had turned to leave and was a little taken aback by his informality. This was the first time he had called her by her Christian name.

"Not a word about this to anyone!"

"Yes, sir! I mean, no, sir. I mean, I'll keep my mouth shut, sir!" She blushed. He was a little amused by her discomfort but, like a true gentleman, he kept that fact to himself.

When Leonard arrived, Liebert was all business. "I am going to give you a dispatch which is of the utmost importance to the South. Go directly to General Beauregard's headquarters at Manassas. Don't stop for anything! Take two men of your choice as bodyguards. Go straight to Captain Jordan. Place this dispatch directly into his hands. Then, you and Jordan go to General Beauregard. Wake him up if you have to. Then report back here."

"Yes, sir." He paused. *Wake up General Beauregard?* He thought. This must be really important. "May I ask what the dispatch says?"

Liebert thought for a moment. "It outlines the enemy's plans for defeating Beauregard, and the timing of that advance."

"Oh, my!" Leonard muttered, turning pale as he grasped the importance of his mission. Liebert did not respond. He already decided to carry Rose's next dispatch to Beauregard himself. This way, he would be present at the battle.

Melody entered a moment later. She handed the copies of the dispatch to Liebert, who handed one copy to Leonard. "Now get goin'!" he snapped. "I'll be at the White House, conferring with President Davis."

The colonel was not trying to impress anyone, but he did.

Rose Greenhow issued her second coded dispatch on July 16. It arrived in Richmond the next day and was promptly decoded. It revealed the details of McDowell's order of battle, and order of march, and was specific about the timing. His forces should be in position to attack Beauregard at Bull Run on July 20 or 21, depending on the speed of their march. Rance Liebert met with Jefferson Davis at 10 p.m. that night. The Union plan was now crystal clear, and there would be time to reinforce Beauregard with Joseph E. Johnston's forces from the Shenandoah Valley, west of Manassas. This could be the decisive factor in the battle.

The president met with his senior military advisor, General Robert E. Lee, behind closed doors at the White House on July 18. Rance waited in the anteroom, along with several others. At last he was called into Davis' office.

Like many professional officers, Robert E. Lee looked upon spies and military intelligence people with a degree of distaste. But he was a man known for his courtesy, so he stood up when the colonel entered the room.

"Rance Liebert, this is General Lee," Davis said. "General Lee, this is Colonel Rance Liebert, the head of our Secret Service." Lee extended

The Retribution Conspiracy

his hand and Liebert shook it. The general had a firm grip.

"Pleased to meet you, General. President Davis has been highly complimentary of you."

"And of you as well," Lee declared. "Now, have you received any additional information you would like to share with us at this time?"

"No, sir. Nothing solid."

"Do you have anything that isn't solid?" Clearly this fellow Lee was alert in every cell of his body.

"Just this. Our chief informant in Washington says General McDowell has confidence in his plan but not in his army. He is worried it may fail because training time has been insufficient. He does not think it is ready for major offensive operations. A second informant, that actress we discussed," he said, nodding toward Davis, "has interviewed five Union generals. Four are of the same opinion."

"The Northern generals are probably quite correct," Davis stated coolly. "It takes longer to train a unit in the attack than in the defensive, especially if it is defending a creek, a hill, or some other useful terrain feature. This will give us an advantage. In seems our opponent's military leaders are aware of that, even if their general public is not."

"These sources. Are they reliable?" Lee asked.

"I believe the first one is. The second one definitely is."

"May I ask you a personal question, colonel?"

Rance gave General Lee a surprised look. "Certainly," he said.

"Are you romantically involved with either or perhaps both of these women?" Lee was apparently concerned that the colonel's emotions might be clouding his objectivity.

"No." Rance didn't like the question, so he left off the "sir."

He was watching General Lee when he answered. He could see in the man's face that he noticed the omission. His eyes flashed and his neck turned a little red, but he didn't say anything.[20] "Alright, then," Jefferson Davis said. "Is there anything else you think we should know, colonel?"

"No, Mr. President. Except that I will be visiting General Beauregard personally, to answer any questions."

"Do you think that's wise, Colonel?" Lee asked.

"Yes, sir," he said, restoring the amenities. "If you have a question about the information, who better to ask than the one with the access to the most information, the knowledge of how it was collected, and

---

20 Robert E. Lee's neck always reddened when he was angry or annoyed.

the most knowledge of the informants?"

Lee nodded. He knew that and realized he probably shouldn't have asked the question. He also realized at that moment he was just a little jealous. Lee knew President Davis intended to be on hand for the big battle and suspected — quite correctly — the colonel intended to be there as well. And he, after a lifetime of service, would be stuck behind a desk in Richmond.

On July 20, Rance Liebert arrived at Beauregard's headquarters. It was a busy place, but the general was not there. Liebert waited an hour and a half before Beauregard arrived. An aide introduced the two men at once.

"Thank you, Colonel Liebert, for the valuable information your organization has supplied to me in recent days," the Little Creole said, and smiled cordially. He could be quite charming when he wanted to be, which was most of the time.

"Thank you, General. I just wanted to come by to meet you and to see if you might have any questions I could answer."

"No, Colonel. I think the dispatches and your letter assessing the sources make everything very clear."

"Very good, General. I'll return to Richmond in the morning. Could you provide me with a room or a tent for the evening for myself and my aide?"

Beauregard smiled. Liebert was lying, and he knew he was lying, and he knew Beauregard knew he was lying. Liebert was here to see — and possibly to take part in — the big battle. This relieved the general slightly. He knew Liebert was Jefferson Davis' adjutant in Mexico and suspected he might have been sent here to spy on him for the president, but maybe he wasn't.

"Tell my chief of staff that I said to tend to your needs. Is the president planning to join us tomorrow, Colonel?" Beauregard asked.

"Not to my knowledge. At least he hasn't said anything to me about it. But, if I know the man, yes, he'll show up. I'd bet the mortgage on it."

Beauregard smiled. He took this to be an honest answer and Liebert to be an honest man. "Join me for breakfast at dawn, colonel?" he asked on an impulse.

"That would be an honor, sir," Liebert said, bowing slightly.

The temperature on July 21 was oppressive, even at 5:30 in the morning. Liebert was digging into his scrambled eggs and bacon when a Union cannonball hit the building in which they were eating. Fortunately, it did not explode.

"The dance begins," one of the staff officers said as he stood up. Each man rushed to his station. Rance Liebert put his bacon on a piece of bread, folded it over, and gobbled it down as he headed for his horse. As a veteran, he knew there was no telling when he might get to eat again.

The Union offensive started effectively enough, and the entire battle soon focused on the Confederate left. The Yankees charged and charged again. But more Southerners rushed into the fray, and stopped them again and again. More attacks followed until about 11:30 a.m., when the forward Rebel units finally gave way and fell back in some disorder toward Henry House Hill. At noon, Brigadier General Thomas J. Jackson's 1st Virginia Brigade made a determined stand, and the Confederates rallied. It was here that General Jackson earned the nickname "Stonewall."

Early that afternoon, Beauregard personally joined the battle. Meanwhile, the leading regiments of Joseph Johnston's forces began arriving at the Manassas railroad junction. Beauregard ordered members of his staff to bring up the unengaged brigades from his right flank, as well as the regiments from the Shenandoah, as quickly as they arrived at the railroad junction. He turned to Liebert. "You know the way from Manassas to here, colonel. Could you guide some of the reinforcements from Manassas to this place as they arrive at the railroad station?"

"Of course, sir. Where do you want them deployed?"

"South of Jackson on the far left. Just keep extending the line to the south and west until I tell you otherwise."

"Yes, sir," Liebert exclaimed and rode off at full speed. He later remarked he was a tour guide during the Battle of Bull Run. But one Confederate brigade after another came up. Rance made four trips from Manassas to the front, bringing back a brigade or a regiment each time. The tension was terrible, the sun was blistering, and the pace exhausting. His canteen was soon empty, but he kept going.

When the last brigade overlapped the Union right flank and threatened their rear, the Northerners began to waiver. Beauregard sensed his moment had come, so he ordered an advance all along the line. The Yankee front broke, and the Rebels swept them from the field.

As Rance predicted, Jefferson Davis showed up late in the battle, but Rance did not see him. He did, however, see part of the 12th Mississippi. That night, after the battle, he sought them out, especially his brother, Captain Billy Liebert, and Lieutenant Dan Glass in Company E. To his horror, Glass had a bloody bandage under his left eye.

"Dan, what happened?" He cried in alarm. "Were you wounded?"

"Not really," Dan responded. "A Union shell hit a tree near where I was. It exploded and a piece of wood hit my cheek."

"Well, thank God it wasn't a piece of shrapnel!"

"Yep … It woke me up, I can tell you that!" He paused a minute and abruptly changed the subject. "What are you doing here, Rance?"

"Well," he smiled, "I was having a nice, cordial breakfast with General Beauregard and his staff when this noisy skirmish started and interrupted my meal." It occurred to him only at that moment he hadn't finished breakfast or eaten lunch or dinner. He wondered where Beauregard was and if he was still alive.

"Well, maybe you can finish it in Washington before the week is out."

"Nope. I'm going back to Richmond tomorrow. And you'll be comin' with me," Liebert announced suddenly.

"What? Why?" Asked a startled Glass.

"Because we've got a job for you. Bring everything you own."

"What am I going to be doing?"

"You'll be working for the Confederate Secret Service," the colonel said, softly, so only Glass could hear him.

"Secret Service?" The lieutenant retorted. "I didn't know we had a Secret Service."

"You weren't supposed to know, 'til now," Liebert said sharply. "And keep the information to yourself. It could cost dozens of lives, otherwise. Don't even tell your family or your colonel. You'd been temporarily assigned to a staff job at the War Department in Richmond. That's all they need to know." Rance gave him his address on Market Street and walked farther on down the line before the lieutenant could ask any more questions. Here Rance had a late dinner (of sorts) with his brother, Captain Billy Liebert, a company commander in the 12th Mississippi. It consisted of hardtack and some form of meat that neither of them recognized but thought might be beef.

As Rance predicted to Guinevere, Dan did not object to the transfer. He fought in a big battle and did what Southerner men were supposed to do — what their birthright required them to do. He was even been slightly wounded and would be able to talk about it for the rest of his life, and he didn't feel any compunction to fight in another big fight, at least not right away.

After visiting with his brother, Rance sought out his own replacement, Colonel Griffith, the commander of the 12th Mississippi and another former Mississippi Rifle and showed him a letter from Jefferson Davis, assigning Lieutenant Glass to him. Griffith — who was afraid Liebert was there to try to take back his old job as commander of the 12th — was relieved he only wanted Glass and so did not offer the slightest objection. Dan was a good man and a likable fellow, but he was only a marginally useful field officer. He would be easy to replace; in fact, Griffith decided after briefly considering the matter, he would probably better serve the Cause in some staff job in Richmond.

Lieutenant Glass did not leave with Rance the following day because he didn't have a horse. He traveled by train, but the wounded naturally had absolute priority. It was three days before he arrived in the capital. When he did, Liebert placed him in charge of the Order of Battle Section.

President Davis later commented that Rose Greenhow won the battle for the South.

He thought she had also won the independence of the Confederate States of America, so he backed General Johnston[21] when he decided not to order a pursuit to Washington, D.C., despite the objections of Stonewall Jackson, who said he could take the capital with 10,000 men.

Jeff Davis later declared this decision was the worst mistake of his life.

Although the South was ecstatic over its victory, it was also sobered. Losses were terrible. The number of victims on both sides in a single day's action amounted to more than half of all American casualties in the entire Mexican War — and it had lasted two years.

---

21 As senior officer on the field, Johnston superseded Beauregard at Manassas after the battle.

—◦ CHAPTER XIII ◦—
LET'S START A WAR

A braham Lincoln was shocked and depressed by the South's unexpected victory, but he was also more determined than ever to win the war. Instead of suing for peace, on July 22, the day after Bull Run, he sent to Congress a request which would provide for the enlistment of 500,000 men for three years. He also began recruiting foreign mercenaries on a large scale.[22] Shocked by their humiliation at Manassas, tens of thousands of Northerners rallied to the colors. Eventually, 2,878,304 men would enroll in Lincoln's ranks (including 190,000 blacks), as opposed to about 800,000 for the Rebels.[23] The overall strength ratio against the South would be 3.6 to 1.

Although he did not know these figures, Rance Liebert sensed Davis' and Johnston's failure to advance on Washington, coupled with Lincoln's reaction, probably meant the war would be a long one. Shortly after he got back to Richmond, he called Toby Collier into his office. "I've decided to open the fourth floor," he announced as soon as the young man seated himself.

"What's it for?" The lieutenant wanted to know.

"Counterfeiting operations," Liebert snapped. "We're going to counterfeit Northern banknotes and documents — especially military documents."

Rance had more than one motive in mind. Not only would it allow his operatives to bribe Union officials and pay for information, it would free the Secret Service from Confederate oversight. He would not have to ask Jefferson Davis or Congress for monetary allocations — he would simply print his own. Colonel Liebert was very much going into business for himself. The fact it would hurt the U.S. economy by inflating the dollar was just an added bonus.

"Where are you going to find skilled counterfeiters?" The lieutenant asked.

"Not me, Collier — you! I have a blank letter of introduction from Jefferson Davis. You will operate under the name Colonel Owen Dick-

---

22 During the war, 489,920 mercenaries joined the Union Army, including 200,000 Germans, 150,000 Irish and 60,000 British and Canadians.

23 Estimates for the total number of Confederates, including State Troops, vary from 750,000 to slightly more than 1,000,000, with 800,000 being a common estimate.

erson. Here is the letter of introduction, signed by the president. Be very careful not to lose that — I will need it back! Take a dozen men. I've already arranged a special train for you and your detachment, so there won't be any prying eyes. Go to the major penitentiaries in Georgia, Alabama, and South Carolina. Get the warden to hand over the top counterfeiter and the top forger. They'll do it because they think President Davis authorized it. Then send them here. Put 'em in handcuffs. Two guards per counterfeiter. Don't even let them answer the call of nature alone. They'll work on the fourth floor and sleep in some of the cells on there. At the end of the war, if they're successful, they'll receive a full presidential pardon, an honorable discharge from the Confederate Army, and a sack full of money."

"Counterfeit bank notes?"

"Sure. Once we get the first wave of counterfeiters installed on the fourth floor, we'll get the top counterfeiters from Virginia and North Carolina. If we need more, we'll go to the other Southern states."

Collier smiled, then asked: "But what if Jeff Davis won't give them a full presidential pardon?"

"He won't have to," Rance smiled. "If they're any good, they can print their own, and forge the president's name on it."

"What if we get them here and they refuse your offer?"

"Then we'll feed one to Anderson. The rest will fall into line after that."

Collier grimaced. He did not think highly of Colonel Liebert's methods. But they were a secret service, and they were at war.

Liebert caught the grimace. "Anything wrong, Collier?"

"No, sir. Just a touch of gas from breakfast."

"Well, don't pass gas in my office."

Collier left for South Carolina the next day. Everything worked as Liebert foresaw it. The wardens were cooperative. Liebert had an all-star team of counterfeiters and forgers assembled on the fourth floor, along with several guards, and offered them the deal. Anderson was standing right behind him with a pistol in his hand. It was resting on his chest, so everyone could see it.

"And if we refuse?" One of them asked.

Anderson cocked the pistol and glared at him. The corporal was tall, dark, and menacing, and he looked sinister. Liebert didn't say a word.

The convict swallowed hard and backpedaled immediately. "Sounds like a good deal to me," he declared. All the others nodded

The Retribution Conspiracy

their approval, with varying degrees of enthusiasm.

"It won't be a luxury hotel, but I will try to make your stay here as comfortable and pleasant as possible. And it will certainly be better than a penitentiary." The prisoners looked at him hopefully. No one present even dreamed the war would last almost another four years.

August brought more bad news. As part of his redoubled war effort, Lincoln ordered the creation of his own intelligence service. Rance would have competition. The organization was headed by Allen Pinkerton of the famous Pinkerton detective agencies. Among his first acts was to order the arrest of Rose Greenhow, who had been under suspicion for weeks. She had done a huge amount of damage to the Northern war effort, and she was irreplaceable.

With Rose under house arrest (and later in the Old Capitol Prison) and exiled to England after that, Owen Dickerson made a few more trips to Washington, to reestablish the Confederate spy network. He hesitated to involve Guinevere but realized she was his best option, and she was ready and willing to go to work, although she had no idea what her first mission would be. Rance's plan was ambitious in the extreme: he intended to provoke a war between the United States and Great Britain.

His first step was to visit the hospitals of Richmond. He found a suitable candidate in Captain John Baker, a company commander in the 2nd Tennessee — or at least he had been, until Bull Run, where he lost a leg. He was just the man for whom Liebert was looking: young, ambitious, well-educated, courageous, single, and not well known in Virginia. He was just learning to walk with his wooden leg when he received an invitation to the Confederate White House. Young Baker was so anxious and nervous he arrived 45 minutes early.

Rance Liebert got there about five minutes early, wearing his colonel's uniform for a change. He smiled at the captain, who nodded, but they did not engage in conversation. Five minutes later, the colonel was admitted into the president's office. This irritated the captain slightly. Apparently the president was going to be running late for their appointment. To his surprise, Jefferson Davis emerged right on time, smiled, and extended his hand, and asked the captain to come in.

Baker was in awe. He had never met President Davis before, nor anyone else approaching his importance. The president asked him to sit in an overstuffed armchair. Davis took a seat on the sofa. A general was at the other end. The colonel was in the middle.

"Captain, I know you have courage. I trust you have discretion."

"Yes, Mr. President!"

"You understand this meeting is strictly confidential."

"Yes, sir."

"Captain Baker, I want you to meet General Samuel Cooper, our adjutant general."

The general rose, extended his hand, and smiled at the captain, who was almost overwhelmed. Cooper was the highest ranking man in the Confederate Army, and that included Johnston, Beauregard, and Robert E. Lee.

"And this is Colonel Rance Liebert, the head of our Secret Service," Davis continued.

Rance reached over and shook his hand. Baker was surprised. "I didn't even know we had a Secret Service," he declared.

"Good!" Liebert snapped as he took over the conversation. "You ain't supposed to know." He paused for affect. "Captain Baker, I have been studying you, and I have determined that, until your wound, you had the potential to advance to the highest ranks in the army. Your options are now regretfully more limited. You could, of course, request to leave the service and go back home with all honor."

"I don't want to do that," Baker replied. Liebert, of course, already knew this from his interview with Baker's physician. The loss of a limb did not take the starch out of this young warrior.

"You could go back to Tennessee and get a desk job with the State Reserves."

Baker frowned. Until now, he thought that was the direction he was heading, while people of less talent advanced ahead of him because they were able to do field service.

"Or you could advance in rank and remain on active duty. Are you interested?"

"Yes, sir!" he declared.

Rance smiled. "For the first year on your new career path, you will work in General Cooper's office as a staff officer. Then you and I will reassess each other and your situation, and determine your next assignment."

"All right," Baker declared uncertainly.

"You will be immediately promoted to major, by special order of the president."

"Yes, sir!" John Baker exclaimed. He was an ambitious man who hoped to be governor of Tennessee one day. This would be a step forward for him.

"And you will work under an assumed name for the first year and perhaps afterward. Can you do that?"

For the first time, Baker thought about objecting. "Why?"

"Your first year, you will have three tasks. First, recover from your grievous wounds. Second, provide a cover story for one of my spies. And third, perform the duties assigned to you by General Cooper. In this task, you will learn how a War Department works and will be infinitely more useful to the Confederacy than you are now. I would not be surprised if you were not promoted to lieutenant colonel at the end of that time."

"Tell me about your spy."

"You have to accept the assignment first, major," Rance declared. "You will receive no further details about Secret Service operations until you join the organization."

"All right!" Baker exclaimed. "I accept." He did not show it, but he was somewhat apprehensive because he had no idea what he was getting himself into, so he added: "Provided I get a more challenging assignment in a year."

"Oh, don't worry!" General Cooper piped up, "I'll make sure you have plenty of challenging assignments long before then!"

A look of horror flashed across Baker's face. He made a mistake! The three older men had a laugh at his expense.

"You are now Major John Spring," Liebert announced. "Your older sister's name is Guinevere Spring. She is an actress up north. You differ politically. You support the side of honor and right; she supports the Union." Davis and Cooper chuckled at that but didn't say anything. "Being from east Tennessee, people will believe that."

"And ... ?"

"And Miss Guinevere is going to become an agent for the North — or at least she's going to appear to be. Actually, she will be a double agent for us. Richmond is full of Yankee spies, just as Washington is full of Southern spies. She will tell them she has a brother in the Confederate War Department. They will check out her story. Then, if you've done your job properly, they will find you. That will confirm her story, at least in their minds."

"What is Guinevere's assignment?"

"That is something you may never know."

There was an awkward silence. Then Liebert stood up, pulled something out of his pocket, and handed it to Baker. It was a badge of rank, bearing the single star of a Confederate major. "Have that sewn on, and report to the adjutant general's office at General Cooper's convenience." He offered Baker his hand. "We'll have dinner tomorrow and go over some of the details."[24]

As John Baker, a/k/a John Spring, got up to leave, Jefferson Davis asked, "How old are you, Major Baker?"

"I'm 22 years old, sir."

"Do you know how many 22-year-old majors we have in the Confederate Army?" Davis inquired.

"No, sir."

"Not very many," he said. "Not very many at all."

With her cover story in place, Rance went to see Guinevere.

She was taking off her costume when his note arrived and, as always, it made her very happy. She didn't hurry to the LaVere anymore, as she did the first time he contacted her, but she was delighted to see him. Even if she had not had romantic feelings for him, she would have been pleased. He was a gentleman and treated her like a lady — a welcome change for an actress.

As soon as she arrived at the restaurant, he stood up. She gave him a little hug and kissed him on the cheek. He held out the chair next to his for her to sit and poured her a glass of her favorite wine. He was having both wine and coffee.

"How are you?" She asked.

"Better, now that I'm in the North."

"Why?"

"Real coffee," he announced, holding up his cup. "You can't get that back home anymore. Yamn Dankees. Our people are drinking coffee substitutes now. They call them ersatz coffee."

"For example?"

"Coffee made from sweet potatoes, peanuts, corn, acorns — even dandelions and okra."

She made a face. "Okra flavored coffee! Sounds vile!"

"The okra coffee isn't as bad as it sounds. Neither is the dandelion variety. The acorn coffee has no taste at all. The potato coffee ..." He grimaced and fell silent.

---

24 By "dinner," Liebert meant the noon meal. In the South, there were three meals: breakfast, dinner and supper. In much of the North, their three meals were breakfast, lunch and dinner. According to the Bible, the South was correct. Jesus had a Last Supper. He did not have a Last Dinner.

The Retribution Conspiracy

"What does it taste like?"

"Like something I stepped in one day while walking through a cow pasture. Certainly not like coffee. And there is no sugar. They use molasses, sorghum, or honey to sweeten the 'coffee,' as well as in pies, cakes and candies — but you can hardly find candy anymore."

She frowned.

"Well, the use of substitutes in pies and such is not so bad, unless they use watermelon syrup, which I detest, but things are going to get worse before they get better."

She leaned back in her chair with an unhappy look on her face but didn't say anything. The wine didn't taste as good as it had a minute before.

"Well, what brings you to Washington this time?" she asked.

"You."

"Aaawwwww. That's sweet. What are we going to do?" Visions of holding hands, long, romantic walks, and another indoor picnic danced in her head.

"I thought we might start a war between Great Britain and the United States."

She laughed. He didn't. He was stonefaced. Her laughter died.

"I'm serious."

She scrutinized him for a moment. "You are serious!" she declared.

"Yes, I am."

"Golly, you don't mind dropping cannon balls over dinner, do you?" She asked. "How do you plan to accomplish that?"

"We. Actually, mostly you."

"Me?"

"Yes." He thought for a moment. "Sally, can you think strategically?"

"Yes. Well, I don't know. Maybe …" she tailed off.

"The South can win the war one of three ways: diplomatically, militarily, or politically. Given the fact the North's industrial production is 10 times ours, and their manpower resources are four times ours, and they have a huge advantage over us in every category except courage and brains, defeating them militarily is problematic at best."

He continued: "Politically we could win if the North decides to let us go. This will happen only if the Lincoln regime is defeated or overthrown. Lincoln has already taken steps to prevent being deposed. He and his myrmidons have set up dungeons and arrested thousands of political opponents. They have suspended the right of *habeas corpus* and are holding them indefinitely and without charges.[25] They have already shut down about 100 opposition newspapers, sometimes using the army, and are shutting down more every day.[26] No one will be able to overthrow them. We cannot win politically unless we wait until the next presidential election. That's more than three years away."

She tried to think what life in the South would be like in three years, but it was too painful to contemplate. Even if the Northern armies did not gain another foot of territory, the effects of the blockade would be devastating. She dismissed the thought from her mind.

"For us, the easiest option is diplomatic. Provoke a war with Great Britain. The Royal Navy could easily break the blockade. And the French have ambitions in Mexico and Central America. If they join, we'll have the help of the French Army. And they are the best ground force in the world, except maybe the Prussians."

"I think they could defeat the Prussians," she commented, repeating conventional wisdom.

Rance, who educated himself on the techniques of the Prussian General Staff, had his doubts, but he ignored the interruption. "We are going to provoke an international incident," he announced.

"How?"

---

25 Lincoln suspended *Habeas Corpus* at various times in different places. The first time he did it was in Maryland on April 27, 1861.

26 See Thomas J. DiLorenzo, *The Real Lincoln* (New York: 2002; reprint ed., New York: 2003), p. 132, and DiLorenzo, *Lincoln Unmasked* (New York: 2006), pp. 146, 181; Clyde N. Wilson, "Those People — Part II," in *To Live and Die in Dixie*, Frank B. Powell, III, ed. (Columbia, Tennessee: 2014), p. 57; Edgar Lee Masters, *Lincoln the Man* (1931; reprint ed., Columbia, South Carolina: 1997), p. 411; Jeffrey Rogers Hummel, *Emancipating Slaves, Enslaving Free Men* (Chicago: 1996), p. 142; James Ronald Kennedy and Walter Donald Kennedy, *The South Was Right!* (Gretna, Louisiana: 1991; reprint ed., Gretna: 1994), p. 28. Dr. DiLorenzo is a professor at Loyola University Maryland and a senior fellow at the Ludwig von Mises Institute. Dr. Wilson is an Emeritus Distinguished Professor of History of the University of South Carolina. He is the author of more than 600 publications and edited the 28-volume *The Papers of John C. Calhoun*. Edgar Lee Masters authored 33 books and a dozen plays before he passed away in 1950. Dr. Hummel received his Ph.D. in history from the University of Texas. He is now a Research Fellow at the Independent Institute and a Professor of Economics at San Jose State University. Walter Donald Kennedy has authored or co-authored more than a dozen books, and edited, annotated and republished William Rawle's classic 1825 textbook on the Constitution. James Ronald Kennedy received his Masters in Health Administration from Tulane. He co-authored *Punished With Poverty* with his twin brother and holds the Jefferson Davis Gold Medal for Excellence in the Writing and Researching of Southern History.

                                                    The Retribution Conspiracy

"Like this. Jefferson Davis is a military man and has left the conduct of diplomacy to others. Initially, he sent a three-man delegation to Europe to achieve our recognition. They were selected for personal and political reasons — not because they had any idea what they were doing. For example, our European delegation is headed by William Yancey. He's a good man, but has no diplomatic skill or experience. He's now sick, frustrated, and wants to resign."

"That's too bad."

"You know," he said reflectively, "this has got to be the low point in North American diplomatic history. Are you aware we sent a representative to the Papal States who can't speak Italian, can't speak Latin, and isn't a Catholic?"

"You're joking!" She laughed.

"Not at all! The Yankees haven't done much better. Their ambassador to France has no diplomatic experience and doesn't speak French."

"What?" She asked. "French is the language of diplomacy!"

"I know."

"Oh my Goodness! I speak French! I learned it before I was 12."

"I know," he said. "So did I! Anyway, our new secretary of state seems to be doing better. He's picked James Mason and John Slidell as our new commissioners to Europe. As a U.S. senator, Mason chaired the Foreign Relations Committee for 13 years. Slidell, who was also a senator, negotiated the agreement with Mexico, making the Rio Grande our southern border. After the war, he negotiated the peace treaty with Mexico, and both he and Mason are fluent in French. They are good men. Neither is considered an extremist or a 'Fire-Eater,' and they will command a lot more respect than did Yancey."

"That's good."

"The problem is they're still in Charleston, South Carolina. The Yankees know this and want to capture them or at least keep them in the New World. They would even board a British ship on the high seas to get them."

"I see. But that might start a war …"

Rance smiled. "Right the first time! A reckless decision on their part! And I know the commissioners' travel agenda. Now, suppose the Yankees were tipped off by a beautiful actress where the emissaries were going to be, and the Northerners took them off a British ship at gunpoint…"

"The Yankees would have their private parts in a beartrap!" Guinevere finished his sentence, and sat back, sipping her wine. She couldn't wipe the smile off her face.

Liebert was a little surprised by her reference to male genitalia, but she had the picture.

"Rance Liebert," she said after a few minutes, "I think I love you. Or Owen Dickerson. Or whatever you're name is."

Rance wanted her to see Simon Cameron, Lincoln's secretary of war, but she objected. "He's on his way out. I should see Edwin Stanton."

The colonel knew all about Simon Cameron. He was a corrupt Pennsylvania machine politician. He'd been famously quoted as saying: "An honest politician is one who, when he is bought, will stay bought." Lincoln, however, once spoke up for him. "I do not believe he would steal a red hot stove," the president said. Under Cameron's questionable leadership, the War Department was characterized by corruption and incompetence.

"Edwin Stanton. I've heard that name," Rance said.

"He was attorney general at the end of Buchanan's term."

"Oh, yes. Tell me about him."

"He is an Ohio lawyer in his late forties. Short and ugly. If I were a man and couldn't grow a better beard than that, I'd stop trying and shave every day. He's also badly asthmatic, which may partially explain why he's always in a foul mood. Mr. Stanton is ruthless, brilliant, and a tireless worker."

"Anything else?"

"He is a fanatical abolitionist and an anti-Southern bigot. The man is eaten up with hatred, not only for the South, but for anyone who opposes him. He has absolutely zero sense of humor. He doesn't have any love for Lincoln, either, and habitually calls him 'the original gorilla.'"

"Too bad. Sounds like a real donkey's tail."

"He wasn't always," Guinevere said, looking into her wine glass. "He was once known as a joyful, cheerful man, blissfully in love with his wife and daughter."

"What happened?"

"They died. First the daughter, followed by the wife a year or two later. It changed him. He's now bitter, hateful, vindictive, and brusque. Now his main characteristic is a lust for power. He would do anything to achieve it."

Rance sat there and digested her words. He momentarily wondered how she knew so much about Stanton, but then he remembered she lived in the closed society of the Washington elites for the past few years. It occurred to him D.C. was something like Rainbow, Mississippi, or any other small town. Everyone knew everything about everyone else.

"He's also a legal genius," Guinevere continued. "Combined with his energy, hatred, and ambition, it makes for a dangerous combination."

"Military background?"

"None."

"Good. I'd hate for Lincoln to hire a secretary of war who actually knew something about fighting a war."

"He'll learn, though," the actress assured him. "Don't underestimate him. He'll be a big asset to Lincoln if the war lasts long enough. Anyway, he moved to Pittsburgh after his wife died," she continued. "His first famous case was McCormick vs. Manny."

Liebert vaguely remembered it.

"It was a patent infringement case," she said. "Cyrus H. McCormick invented the reaper. John Henry Manny's corporation copied it. McCormick sued. Both sides got the best corporate lawyers in the country. When it appeared the trial would be in Chicago, Manny's lawyers felt they needed an Illinois attorney, so they hired Abraham Lincoln, the best corporate attorney in the state. When the venue was changed to Cincinnati, they fired Lincoln and replaced him with Stanton, who they believed to be a better lawyer. Only they forgot to tell Lincoln. He didn't know until he showed up in Cincinnati."

Liebert grinned. "What happened?"

"Stanton pitched a fit. Called Lincoln a 'long-armed baboon' and threatened to quit if 'that giraffe' appeared in the case. Lincoln didn't say anything but handed Manny's lawyers the brief he wrote on the case. Stanton tossed it into the trash can without reading it and told him to go away."

"Bet that made him feel good," Rance observed sarcastically.

"He was humiliated and returned to Illinois immediately. Manny's lawyers won the case," the sophisticated Mississippi woman continued. "They got an old reaper, built the year before McCormick received his patent, and modified the divider, the key feature on the machine and the vital issue in the case. They had a blacksmith build a divider similar to McCormick's and install it on the old machine. They then coated it with a solution of salt and vinegar, to add rust. It looked so natural that the judge ruled in favor of Manny."

"So our man Stanton is not above using subterfuge?"

"No, he is not."

Neither am I, thought Liebert. "Go on," he said.

"Stanton was a big Democrat," Guinevere said, "and was a special counsel to the Buchanan administration. In 1859, he represented Democratic Congressman Daniel Sickles. Sickles was a whoremonger. He was censured by the New York legislature for taking a famous prostitute into the legislative chambers. Later, he took her to London with him — leaving his pregnant wife at home — and introduced her to Queen Victoria, calling her by the name of one of his political opponents. Meanwhile his wife, Teresa, decided two could play the infidelity game. She had married Sickles against her family's wishes when she was 15 or 16, and he was almost 40, so there was a major age difference. Anyway, she had an affair with Philip Barton Key II, the district attorney for the District of Columbia and the son of Francis Scott Key. Sickles pulled a pistol on Key and shot him to death in Lafayette Square, just across the street from the White House.

"Stanton got him out of it," she elaborated. "He had Sickles plead temporary insanity. It was the first time this defense was ever attempted in an American court, and it worked. Sickles got off. He later 'forgave' his wife and is now a brigadier general in the Yankee army."[27]

I guess if you've got the right connections, you can get away with anything, Rance decided.

"In any case," Guinevere continued, "Stanton now ranked high in Democratic political circles. When the attorney general resigned to become secretary of state, Buchanan picked Stanton to replace him. Then, when Lincoln was elected president, Stanton at once became a loyal Republican."

"That figures."

"Anything for power. But it didn't do him much good. Lincoln didn't retain him as attorney general."

"Can't say I blame him," Liebert observed.

"Stanton remained in D.C. as a special advisor to his friend, Simon Cameron, where he wrote General Dix and denounced the 'painful imbecility' of the President. Cameron, meanwhile, endorsed a speech

---

27 Sickles was later promoted to major general and commanded the III Corps at Gettysburg, where he committed a serious tactical blunder, got his command slaughtered, and almost lost the battle for the Union. Sickles himself lost a leg at the hip. He was later U.S. ambassador to Spain, where he continued his promiscuous behavior. He was reelected to Congress in 1893 and died in 1914 at the age of 94.

The Retribution Conspiracy

given by a Union colonel, calling for the arming of slaves. Lincoln — who was and is desperate to keep the slave states of Kentucky, Maryland, and Missouri from seceding, repudiated Cameron's remarks. Shortly thereafter, Cameron drafted a message to Congress, calling for the arming of the slaves. He showed it to Stanton. Stanton modified it, making it an even stronger appeal for servile insurrection. His name wasn't on it of course — Cameron's was. Lincoln demanded this portion of the message be deleted before it was sent to Congress. This was done. But someone — probably Stanton — leaked the original to the press. This made Lincoln look weak in the eyes of his Radical Republican allies, who want this to be a war about slavery, in addition to the subjugation of the South. Lincoln thinks Cameron is responsible for the leak. Now 'Honest Abe' is going to replace Cameron with Stanton as soon as a suitable post has been found for Cameron. He and Lincoln have agreed that Cameron cannot resign in disgrace."

"Why would Lincoln care about Cameron?" Rance wanted to know.

"He needs the Cameron machine in Pennsylvania."[28]

"I'm surprised Lincoln would pick Stanton. There can't be any love there."

"There isn't. Lincoln doesn't like Stanton and Stanton hates Lincoln. Very few people do like Stanton, except hardcore Abolitionists, and he wasn't Lincoln's first choice," Guinevere said. "Lincoln wanted Joseph Holt, Buchanan's last secretary of war. But two of Abe's biggest allies, Secretary of State Seward and Treasury Secretary Chase, want Stanton, so Stanton it will be."

"Then Stanton you will see," the undercover colonel retorted. She grimaced and shook her head at his lame attempt at poetry. In the other seat, Rance was more than a little impressed by how much she had learned. He already knew she was smart. Now she struck him as downright astute. He hoped that he would be able to keep up with her.

Guinevere Spring waited only about 20 minutes before being escorted into Edwin Stanton's office.

"I am Guinevere Spring, the actress ..." she began.

---

28 Simon Cameron was named U.S. ambassador to Russia in January 1862. He was succeeded as secretary of war by Edwin Stanton on January 15, 1862. Cameron returned to the Senate in 1867 and was succeeded by his son in 1877. The Cameron machine dominated Pennsylvania politics for more than 60 years.

"I know who you are," the humorless man in the wire rimmed glasses retorted, as he gave her a disapproving glare. He did not stand up and made no attempt to be friendly, nor did he offer her a seat. She noticed one of Stanton's aides had entered the room with her and made no attempt to leave or take part in the discussion. Obviously the anointed secretary of war did not want to be alone with an actress. *Like I couldn't do better than you,* she thought.

"What do you want?" He snapped. Edwin Stanton could hardly speak without snapping.

Guinevere decided to ignore his insulting behavior. "I will come right to the point, sir. I come from a divided family. I am an abolitionist and a loyal Unionist. My younger brother joined the traitors. But he is still my brother, and I still love him, no matter what he does. So, when I learned he was wounded, I went to see him. By the time I received the news and reached the Rebel capital, he had partially recovered and was working at the War Department in Richmond."

"What is his name and rank?"

"His name is Spring. Major John Spring."

"Major? He's a nobody," Stanton snapped dismissively.

"He works directly under a general named Cooper," she replied.

Stanton's eyes narrowed. This was the highest ranking military officer in the whole Confederacy.

"That's interesting. What brings you here, Miss Spring?"

She sat down without being invited. She noticed the secretary frowned, but he said nothing. "My brother told me something I think you should know," she said. "He said five U.S. warships are pursuing the CSS *Nashville,* which is heading for London, because they think the Rebel commissioners Slidell and Mason are aboard. But they are not. They are still skulking in the Mills House, a hotel in Charleston. They plan to run the blockade on a steamer called the *Theodora* and make their way to Havana. There is a mail packet ship which goes from there to England every three weeks. They intend to sail it to England."

Stanton was excited, although he didn't show it. Was this true? If it was, she knew more about what was going on than the entire U.S. military. Whether it was true or not, she certainly had access to confidential information. The general public didn't have any idea the Union navy was chasing a wild Rebel goose across the North Atlantic. The fact she came to him, and not the War Department, also suggested she knew which way the political wind was blowing.

"Where are you from, Miss Spring?"

"East Tennessee."

"And did your brother say from where he received his information?"

"A friend of his in Richmond. What was his name? ... Oh, yes, Liebert. Colonel Rance Liebert. He and General Cooper were discussing it."

Stanton heard that name before. Secret U.S. operatives had reported seeing him entering the Confederate White House or the Customs House, where the Rebel president had an office, on more than one occasion. He was some sort of military advisor to Jefferson Davis and occasionally shared a meal with the president. Nobody was sure exactly who he was or what he did, but he was obviously well connected and well informed.

"Mr. Stanton, who is Rance Liebert?" Guinevere asked, interrupting his thoughts.

"Thank you for that information, Miss Spring," Stanton replied, ignoring her question. "It may prove useful."

"Anything for my country, sir," Guinevere said. She extended her hand as she rose to leave. Guinevere Spring thus deliberately put Edwin Stanton on the spot. He didn't really like women and certainly did not wish to touch an actress, but he felt that this time he had no choice. He kept his seat but shook her hand. As she walked to the door, he asked: "Miss Spring, could we trouble you to acquire further information from Richmond for us from time to time in the future?"

She flashed him a brilliant smile. "I'd be delighted to. I want to do my part to smash the slave-owning aristocracy and save the Union." She walked out, followed by the aide.

He wondered if she meant what she said about the Southern planter aristocracy, but he knew there were a great many people in east Tennessee who hated the large slave owners and prayed fervently for their defeat. Two minutes after she left, Stanton rang a bell and summoned another aide. "Get in touch with Pinkerton," he commanded. "Order him to determine if a Major John Spring is employed by the Rebel War Department. And make me an appointment with Navy Secretary Welles for this afternoon."

Alerted by the naval department and an article in the Havana newspaper (placed there by an agent of the Confederate Secret Service, mentioning that Slidell and Mason were in town), Captain Charles Wilkes of the steam frigate USS *San Jacinto* lurked off the Bahama Channel, the only deep water route between Cuba and the Grand Bahama Bank. Around noon on November 8, RMS *Trent* appeared in the channel. Wilkes fired a shot across her bow, but she unfurled the Union Jack and did not slow down. He fired a second shot, this one much closer. Now she stopped, dead in the water. Wilkes sent two cutters, each with 20 sailors armed with pistols and cutlasses, to intercept and board her. The British captain protested, but the lieutenant commanding the boarding party demanded a passenger list, which the Englishman refused to give him. The lieutenant demanded permission to search the vessel for contraband. Again the captain said no. The Yankee officer decided not to force the issue. To search the vessel, naval law required that he seize it as a prize. That (arguably) would be an act of war, and the young officer had sense enough to know better than to do that. Finally, he asked Mason and Slidell to identify themselves. Two men in their sixties stepped forward.

"You are under arrest," the lieutenant said.

"We protest this illegal seizure of our persons," Slidell snapped.

"Noted," the lieutenant answered with a nod. "This way, gentlemen, if you please." He politely gestured toward the cutters. The two commissioners offered no further resistance. They were joined by their secretaries. All four men were taken to the Union prison at Fort Warren, Massachusetts.

When the news of the seizure of the *Trent* hit the streets, the citizens of the North were elated. Captain Wilkes was the toast of the country. The governor of Massachusetts held a banquet in his honor and Congress voted him a resolution of thanks. It was some time before reality set in.

In London, there was no elation — only fury. There was already bad blood between the British public and their former colonies, and the *Trent* incident was met with widespread indignation. How dare these upstarts seize a British ship on the high seas and cart off four passengers, who were under the protection of the British flag, to a Yankee prison!?! U.S. Secretary of State Seward "is exerting himself to provoke a quarrel with all of Europe," one London newspaper wrote, "in that spirit of senseless egotism which induces the Americans, with their dwarf fleet and shapeless mass of incoherent squads which they call an army, to fancy themselves the equal of France by land and Great Britain by sea."

The Americans very clearly had misgauged the depth of British outrage. There was serious talk of war. British public opinion was clearly in favor of it and by an overwhelming margin. Even some of the strongest anti-slavery voices in the country joined the chorus. Financial markets in New York and London cratered as if war was a certainty. The value of the U.S. dollar plummeted on the world markets. The British government sent a strongly worded dispatch, demanding an apology and the release of the Confederate commissioners. The U.S. ambassador to London signaled Washington that the British were serious about fighting. The British Army sent reinforcements to Canada, more than doubling their ground forces there, and sent 105,000 modern rifles and smoothbores to the province, as well as 20,000,000 cartridges. Two days after the news of the *Trent* arrived, the British cabinet suspended exports of rifles, percussion caps, military stores and lead to the United States. Worse still, from the American point of view, the day he learned of the seizure of the *Trent*, British Foreign Secretary Lord Russell ordered that the export of saltpeter from India to the U.S. be cut off at once. Saltpeter was a necessary ingredient in gunpowder. The Union Army was effectively paralyzed. With inadequate stockpiles of saltpeter, it was no longer capable of sustaining a major offensive.

Abraham Lincoln, who at first cheered the news of the *Trent*, was reluctant to back down. In his annual message to Congress, he stated Secretary Cameron could field a 3,000,000 man army, capable of quelling disturbances at home and protecting the United States from enemies abroad. Although he did not mention Great Britain or France by name, everyone knew who he meant. But American public opinion was also shifting. Former President James Buchanan called for the release of the Rebel emissaries, and he was soon joined by many other prominent people. Among them was Republican Senator Charles Sumner, chairman of the powerful Foreign Relations Committee.

Sumner joined Lincoln's cabinet secretaries for an emergency cabinet meeting on Christmas morning, 1861. One of the country's leading abolitionists, Sumner was beaten half to death by a South Carolina congressman over the issue of slavery. He nevertheless called for the immediate release of the Confederate commissioners. Secretary of State Seward, the treasury secretary and the attorney general all agreed, and the postmaster general already publicly declared the prisoners could not be kept.

Abraham Lincoln was the last holdout. He took the position that the entire incident should be put to arbitration, but Seward countered that time would not permit it. British patience was exhausted. London issued an ultimatum and gave Washington only seven days to accede to its demands. The United States must release the emissaries or go to war with Britain — and soon. The meeting ended without a decision. Lincoln said he wanted to prepare a written paper to counter Seward's arguments.

There was no paper. He sat down to write and, although he was one of the leading attorneys in the country, Abraham Lincoln was not able to draft a convincing counterargument to Seward's position. He could not even convince himself. When the cabinet met the next day, he capitulated completely. The Rebel commissioners were released the following day and carried to Provincetown, Massachusetts, where they boarded the Royal Navy sloop HMS *Rinaldo*. The British got their apology, and war was averted.

Some of Lincoln's supporters were disappointed by the news, as there were still a great many Anglophobes in the United States in 1862. To them, Lincoln said: "One war at a time, gentlemen. One war at a time."

So Rance Liebert's dream of an Anglo-American war disintegrated overnight. As he had predicted, the two commissioners were of more use to the South in a Yankee prison than on the loose in Europe. They were greeted as heroes in London and Paris but were unable to achieve diplomatic recognition for the Confederacy — or much of anything else.

The whole incident was a victory for the Confederacy, but only a minor one. Washington was humiliated, Lincoln had a few sleepless nights, the flow of essential raw materials and military supplies to the North were cut off for a few weeks and the recruitment of mercenaries in Britain, Ireland, and France were temporarily suspended, but nothing permanent was accomplished. In another year, hardly anyone would even remember the incident.

Rance's shoulders slumped as he sat on the couch in Guinevere's apartment in Washington, which was neat and clean, if not particularly nice. Guinevere tried to console him. "Cheer up! You almost carried the day," she declared.

"Almost doesn't count. I accomplished nothing."

"You accomplished one thing," she smiled.

"What's that?" He asked, gloomily.

"You very much impressed me, which is pretty good, since I was very much impressed by you already."

"Impressed you? How?"

"You almost changed the entire course of the war. If the British and French joined the Confederacy, the entire military situation would change. We would be well on our way to winning the war, thanks to you. Not bad for a mere colonel, without a single troop unit under his command."

He brightened. "Yes. I almost did that, didn't I?"

"Yes, you did. And I am very proud of you!" And with that, she kissed him deeply, right on the mouth.

Guinevere always managed to lighten Rance's mood, even after his most ambitious plans came apart at the seams. As usual, he took her to a nice out-of-the-way restaurant for dinner. She, as usual, took most of hers home in a paper bag. Rance ate less only after an extended period in the South. When working in the Confederacy, his stomach shrank. This was not unique to Rance Liebert; it was becoming very much the norm in Dixie in those days. There were a many fewer fat Southerners than there were before the war. Lincoln's blockade put the entire region on a diet, and it was clear the diet would become more severe as the war progressed.

Rance and Guinevere were not yet used to each other as a couple, but both were becoming more comfortable with their romance. They each were excited that they might have found the one true love of their lives, but neither wanted to pursue the notion too rapidly. The drawback was the war. Neither was particularly worried about his/her own personal safety. One was more concerned for the other than himself/herself. They both knew one or the other could disappear at any moment — perhaps forever. And neither wanted to be hopelessly involved with someone who might not be there tomorrow. They were both adults and understood that a few moments of happiness now might not be worth years of solitary misery in the future. On the other hand, that was beginning not to matter. Their romance was developing a life of its own. It was drawing them in deeper whether they wanted to go there or not. Guinevere now declined all invitations from any other man unless he was a high-ranking Union officers or somebody who was well-placed in the administration, from whom she could obtain information. She only went on work-related dates, and only then when her colonel was out of town. If he appeared unexpectedly, she would cancel with "a sick headache."

Rance grew more impressed with her by the day. He was astonished at how quickly she picked up military expertise. He only had to tell her something once. She knew the difference between a regiment and a battalion, cavalry and mounted infantry, a six-pounder and a Columbiad. She could discuss the amount of forage a horse artillery battalion needed in a week, the range of a Dahlgren rifled cannon, the coal consumption rate of every ironclad class in the Union Navy, and the difference between the military philosophies of Karl von Clausewitz and Baron Antoine-Henri Jomini. Rance enjoyed the fact he could "talk shop" with her and not feel as if he was talking to himself. And she could even beat him at chess some of the time.

Rance Liebert always liked Sally Mae Glass. Now he was falling in love with her. Slow it down, boy, he said to himself. And he did. But he had no desire to stop it completely. No desire at all.

—⌁ CHAPTER XIV ⌁—
GENERALS AND HARLOTS

J efferson Davis sat there flabbergasted, eyes wide and mouth wide open. He shook his head slightly, as if he couldn't believe what he had just heard.

"You instigated the *Trent* Affair?"

"Well, my operative did, but she was following my orders."

"What is the name of this operative?" General Joseph E. Johnston wanted to know.

They were in the president's office on the second floor of the Government Building because Jefferson Davis disliked conference rooms. The fewer people in attendance, the easier it was to control the discussion, and Davis had an ingrained need to be in control. Present in the office today were Davis, Johnston, Liebert, and Robert E. Lee. After Rance told his story, the reaction of each individual was quite different. Lee was positive, Johnston was negative, and Davis was just stunned. It was as if his six-year-old son devised a formula which would successfully turn water into gold.

"You should have cleared this operation through the White House before you acted, Colonel Liebert," Davis finally said.

"There was no time," Rance responded. "If I tried to do that, I would have had to go from Washington to Richmond and back. The opportunity would have been lost."

That seemed to satisfy Davis — or at least mollify him — but not Johnston. "You were still wrong, Colonel."

"I don't think so, sir. How do you figure?"

"I would have thought that would be self-evident," the pretentious Johnston exclaimed, looking down his nose at the colonel. He equated rank with intelligence and, as a full general, he considered himself much more intelligent than a colonel. The fact that this colonel — who did not even attend West Point — didn't seem to grasp this simple fact of life convinced Johnston that Liebert was obtuse. "You were willing to sacrifice two senior diplomats without consulting the president, any senior commanders or the secretary of state or the secretary of war. All of this is far above your level of rank. What's wrong with you?"

Liebert thought for a moment as to the best way to handle this question. Finally he said: "Tell me you wouldn't be happy to be reinforced by the entire French Army and to have the British Navy break the blockade and supply your army with everything you desire."

"That's not the issue," Johnston retorted somewhat harshly.

"That is precisely the issue," Liebert retorted. This time he omitted the "sir."

"You're right, colonel," Robert E. Lee interjected, cutting off the debate. "You have shown boldness, initiative and cunning. You almost succeeded and, had you done so, we might well be dealing with an entirely different military situation today. Had Lincoln not backed down, your actions might well have indirectly won us our independence. As it is, we weakened the credibility of the United States abroad and of the Lincoln regime at home, and all at no cost to ourselves. Thank you! Well done, colonel! And pass my personal congratulations to your operative."

Rance grinned. Their first meeting had not gone smoothly, but now he was beginning to like this Robert E. Lee!

Johnston was not placated. He stared at his old friend and classmate, General Lee, in disbelief. He looked at the president, expecting him to intervene on his side. When Davis said nothing, Johnston's glare turned into one of hatred.

Joseph Eggleston Johnston has been likened to a bantam rooster. He was short, pedantic, and sported short hair and a close-cropped Van Dyke beard. He was also fussy and bureaucratic. Rance thought his head was too large for his body as well as for his brain. A West Point graduate, he shared the nineteenth century professional soldiers' distaste for intelligence officers. And he was never prepared to let go of a disagreement or a quarrel. He was the fourth-ranking officer in the Confederate Army, after Cooper, Lee and Albert Sidney Johnston, the commander of the Western Front. Of the South's full generals, he only outranked Beauregard. And there was the source of endless friction. Johnston thought he should be Number One.

Rance Liebert did not like Joseph E. Johnston, who thought the best military record could be obtained by making the fewest mistakes. Rance heard the story of a hunting trip Johnston went on with several other officers and dignitaries. The other men shot at the pheasants. Sometimes they hit them, other times they missed, but they brought in dead birds at the end of the day. Johnston would only fire if he had a sure shot; consequently, he never fired. He alone did not miss all day long, but he killed no fowl. Rance thought Johnston approached his military commands the same way. He was more interested in not losing than in winning. And that could be very costly to the South. This was the sort of commander who would give up vital areas and even major cities without fighting for them.

"I'm waiting for my answer, colonel," Johnston declared.

"Excuse me?" Rance responded. "Answer to what?"

"Who is your operative in Washington?"

"Begging the general's pardon, but that is something you do not need to know."

Johnston turned livid. "I demand an answer!"

"I don't remember."

"That is a lie!" Johnston roared, pounding the table, his face red.

"What if it is? You have received your answer, sir! I WILL NOT SAY!" Liebert said, raising his voice almost to a shout. He was certainly not an intelligence expert yet, but he instinctively understood that loose lips were the cause of more undercover intelligence failures than any other reason. It was also the cause of many dead agents. This was not going to happen to Guinevere Spring, if he could help it. And, general or no general, he was not going to be bullied by a mediocrity like Joseph E. Johnston.

Jefferson Davis was momentarily astounded. For a moment — just for a moment — he saw a young Grover Liebert sitting there. He was glad the colonel was not armed.

"You should be court-martialed," Johnston growled.

"You may begin the proceedings immediately," Liebert responded. "I waive arraignment. These gentlemen can act as judges," he said, gesturing at Lee and Davis. "I will represent myself. Would you like to go get a lawyer?"

Johnston gasped and his face turned purple. This colonel was impertinent and insubordinate! Clearly he is unimpressed with the greatness of my rank, the status-conscious Johnston thought. But before he could frame a rebuttal, Jefferson Davis intervened. "That's enough of that! There will be no further talk of courts-martial. And you will consult with Richmond before you engage these targets of opportunity in the future, colonel!"

"Yes, sir!" Rance snapped. He was lying, of course, and Davis suspected as much. He winked at his former adjutant while Johnston was looking the other way but said nothing. He was secretly quite pleased with Rance — as much for taking on Johnston as for the *Trent* Affair. And Joseph E. Johnston hated him. That was certainly a mark in his favor.

"Shall we get back on track?" The diplomatic Lee asked smoothly, and steered the meeting into calmer waters.

"Yes," Davis responded immediately. "Colonel Liebert, we need you to infect the Union High Command with some false information."

"No problem there, as their entire existence is predicated upon false information. What exactly do you want done, sir?"

"We are numerically inferior to the Northern armies, both on the Eastern and Western Fronts. We want them to have the opposite impression," General Lee declared. "Can you accomplish this task?"

"Certainly," Liebert responded.

"I doubt it," Johnston snorted. He continued to pout.

Liebert ignored him. Addressing the president, he said: "The North has basically turned its fledgling secret service over to the Pinkerton Detective Agency. I know an actress who attends a lot of parties in Washington. She has been able to supply me with the names of two of their agents here in Richmond — not that they are all that difficult to identify in any case. We shall furnish them with false information."

"How will we accomplish that?" General Lee asked.

"We will use prostitutes," Liebert responded. "My organization knows a few high-priced ladies of the evening who can convincingly pose as Southern ladies. They will seduce Pinkerton's men and make them believe the women succumbed to their irresistible charms — mainly because that's what they want to believe. Then they will tell their new lovers they have connections in our War Department. When the Yankee agents pump them for information, they will be only too happy to supply it to the Pinkerton studs. Only it will be the information you want them to have."

General Lee was shocked. It occurred to him there were things going on in the Secret Service about which he did not want to know. He wished he hadn't asked the question.

"How do you know these prostitutes?" Johnston angrily demanded to know.

"One of my deputies was introduced to them in the Richmond Jail by the Richmond Police Department. They arrested the women in question. My deputy met with each woman in the jail house. He offered each one a deal. She gets an immediate release and immunity from prosecution for the balance of the war and two years thereafter. If she is arrested, she will be released immediately. And her record is expunged. There will be no record of any previous conviction or any prior arrests."

The Retribution Conspiracy

Johnston looked at Liebert as if he smelled rotten eggs. "What if one of the prostitutes does not remain faithful to her agreement? What if they warn the enemy?"

"It could happen, but it won't happen but once. Dead prostitutes are found in Richmond almost every morning," he growled in a low, menacing voice. It was clear he meant it.

"I don't believe I want to hear any more!" General Lee muttered.

"Yes, sir," Liebert agreed. There were some things these gentlemen did not need to know. *Such as the fact I'm also paying the women for their services out of Secret Service accounts,* Liebert thought.

"I hate the thought of having any association — even indirectly — with women of this kind," Joe Johnston declared loftily.

Rance just looked at him. *They're smarter and have better personalities than at least one general I could mention,* Liebert thought, but he said nothing.

"Are you personally receiving any favors from any of these women, Liebert?" Johnston snarled.

"Are you speaking seriously? Certainly not!" Rance retorted. *I've only had sex with one woman,* he thought, *and that was my wife, and that wasn't very good.* But that, of course, was none of Johnston's business. Still, it looked as if there might be better days ahead. He thought of Guinevere/Sally. He forced himself to concentrate.

"Are you sure the information we provide you will reach the Union War Department or White House within, say, three weeks?" Jeff Davis wanted to know.

"No doubt about it," Rance Liebert answered.

It did.

—๑ CHAPTER XV ๑—
ENGAGEMENTS
AND DECEPTIONS

In February 1862, Rance Liebert sat in the rocking chair in his rooms in Washington, watching the snow fall. He just returned from the west, where he set up courier routes and secret agents in Memphis, Nashville, and New Orleans, in a manner very similar to what he and Tom Jordan did in the Union capital. The task was much easier, however, because those cities were still in Rebel hands. He had undercover spy networks from Kentucky to the Gulf of Mexico. Most of them were just awaiting the arrival of the Union Army to be activated. Given the North's sea and river naval strength, Rance suspected this was just a matter of time.

At that moment, he heard something outside his door. He stood up and reached for his "Navy Six" revolver. He heard the sound of keys outside. Only the landlord, Guinevere, and Rance himself had those. The door opened and closed quickly. It was Guinevere, and she was about half frozen. Her smile was nevertheless wide and warm.

"Rance! You're home! It's great to see you!" She put the sacks she was carrying on the floor and bounced over to him, threw her arms around his neck, and kissed him on the cheek. She held the tight embrace for several seconds. He didn't mind and reciprocated, even though it was rather like hugging an icicle. Finally she let go and walked over to the fireplace. "Gosh, it's cold!" She declared.

"Ain't it so!" He answered.

Liebert saw the apartment just once before last night; that was the day he and Guinevere rented it. It looked very different since he left Washington several weeks before. Besides the normal kitchenwares (dishes, the coffee pot, canned goods, etc.), the female influence was now clearly present. There were rugs, curtains (instead of sheets tacked up to cover the windows), and a great many different kinds of soap, perfume, body lotions, makeup, etc., etc., and God only knew what else. Rance could correctly identify only about six of these. Even more surprisingly, she also brought in some of her clothes and a nightshirt.

When Rance rented the place, he had intended it to be a safe house for Confederate agents on the run and a place for them to meet when he was in Washington. He certainly did not intend for her to move in and convert it into a home — but she had. He realized they were going to have to have a serious talk — only he didn't have any idea what he wanted to say. He felt the plantation owner/military man inside him was trying to get out. It wanted organization and objective.

Guinevere, as had Sally Mae before her, did not appear to be organized, but she was. She also did not appear to have objectives, other than to become a great actress, but she did. Like many women of that era, however, she tended to keep them to herself. Men were scared far too easily by a woman with a brain, she had concluded long ago. Generally speaking, it was better to let them drift aimlessly and wonder where they stood.

None of this, of course, precluded small talk. Sally Mae was very good at this and Guinevere was a master. She could carry a conversation by herself or let a man join in — if he wanted to. If the man wanted a serious conversation, she could always engage or avoid, depending on her mood. Sometimes she even gave the man the impression he was leading the discussion, although this was only rarely true — unless it was Rance talking military strategy, and she felt she was picking that up rather rapidly. She had come a long way from Rainbow, Mississippi. And yet she hadn't. She was a different person now, it was true, but part of her never completely changed inside. She knew it was in her best interests to break it off with all things Southern — but she simply couldn't and didn't want to. There was something about home that remains inside you. Even though Bushrod Brown and his cronies destroyed part of that when they raped her, part of it still remained undefiled — at least in her heart. In her more reflective moments, she missed her parents, the bayou, the Magnolia trees, the cotton fields, and the sunsets of a less hurried, less exciting time. She cherished Rance because he was gallant, he treated her like a goddess, and he was simultaneously a gentleman and the most dangerous man she ever met, and that excited her. But did she love him? Sometimes she felt as if she did; other times she wanted to back away. But she never felt like backing off when he was there.

She fixed them supper. Afterward, they sat on the couch, held hands, enjoyed the fireplace, and watched it snow. Finally, he opened the subject they both knew had to be dealt with.

"Where are we going, Sally Mae?"

"Where do you want to go, Rance?" She asked, turning the conversation back on him. (She was good at this.)

"I don't know. I know I'm falling in love with you, if I wasn't there

The Retribution Conspiracy

already."

"Rance, so much has happened since Rainbow," she confessed. Something was clearly bothering her.

"You don't have to talk about it if you don't want to."

"Yes, I do." They both knew that an actress was only one step on the social scale above a prostitute — and for some of them, it was a short step indeed.

There were tears in her eyes as she spoke. "I am not as … pure … as I was in Rainbow."

"But you were raped …"

"I'm not taking about that," she interrupted. "I did certain things … after that … which I'm not proud of."

He thought for a moment and then decided to just let her talk it out.

"I made certain compromises … with other men." There! She had said it.

"Okay." He suspected as much, but the confirmation from her very own mouth made him surprisingly unhappy. But he still wasn't ready to throw her down the stairs.

"Say something, Rance," she said, after what seemed like several minutes.

"I guess I can understand it," he allowed. "Your world was torn apart, your self-confidence and self-worth had to be shattered, and you took whatever validation you could get wherever you could find it."

"Yes, I did …"

"And from whatever source."

"That's about right," she whispered.

"Only later, I suspect, you realized it was a false corroboration."

"Yes. That's all true!" Well, at least most of it, she thought. Sally Mae hung her head and looked miserable. She never felt quite so vulnerable.

"It was just a physical reaction, caused by your suffering. You would never have done it if you had been in your normal mental state. I would have been disoriented, too, had I been in your place. As far as I am concerned, this part of your past has nothing to do with the woman you are today. Let's forget about it."

"Can you forget about it, Rance?" She knew that most men of that era could not.

"Yes," he said, gently stroking her cheek with his hand. "But you can't bring it up very often."

"Fair enough," she smiled. "And you forgive me?"

"Of course. That's easy, since it's not my place to forgive."

"Well, it is and it isn't …" she conceded. "I just wanted you to know what you're getting." *And there's certainly no need to tell him I'm good at it, that I often enjoyed it, and that I even initiated some of the trysts,* she thought.

"Damaged goods?" This was a term used extensively in the nineteenth century to denote a single woman who was not a virgin. It did not apply to married women or to widows and certainly not to men. Society has never been particularly fair.

"Yes," she frowned. She'd learned to hate that term.

"But you are not damaged goods. That whole concept is stupid. You are a precious consignment whom any man worthy of the name would defend and protect with his life. Goods can be purchased. The most valuable things in life can't be. You can't be. But if you could be, I'd trade my entire plantation for you, because you are worth much more than that."

She brightened considerably. She knew he loved De La Teneria. She realized what a huge compliment this was.

"But Sally …"

"Yes," she asked, as a tear ran down her cheek.

"You need to forgive yourself."

She buried her head in his shoulder and kept it there for some time.

"Don't worry about any of this," he said, patting her on the back. "Let's just count our blessing that you didn't get the French disease or have an illegitimate child or something like that. Let's just put the past in the past and move on from here."

The young actress said nothing. She knew they had to have this talk, but she was glad it was over. Not being completely candid is not the same as being dishonest, she thought. Guinevere even thought about telling him her biggest secret but decided against it. Then she lifted herself up.

"Then you're not going to throw my past in my face every time we quarrel?" She inquired, hopefully. She felt a little like a fish who had gotten off the hook.

"First of all, we're not going to quarrel. We are not going to be one of those couples who fight all day, every day. Some people enjoy fighting with their spouse. I don't see how people live like that. If we fight at all, it will be extremely rare. Second, good marriages are built on trust. I should either trust you or run for the hills. And I ain't runnin'. So I must trust you. Third, I'm not going to throw anything in your face; in

The Retribution Conspiracy

fact, after tonight, we are never again going to mention the unsavory parts of your past. Or mine either."

She didn't know how to take this last remark. "How many women have you been with?"

"Counting my deceased wife?"

"Yes."

"Well, one, counting her."

"Really?"

"Yes. I guess I've been saving myself for you," he grinned.

She smiled back. This revelation — if that's what it was — made her happy. She decided to believe it because she wanted to.

"You must never mention that to another living soul for as long as you live," he joked. This conversation needed a light-hearted moment.

She thought for a moment. "You spoke of marriage a moment ago …"

"Yes, I guess I did."

She was silent. The initiative was now clearly his. He just wished he knew what to do with it. If he'd been completely honest, he would have admitted the word just slipped out, but it wouldn't do to tell her that. But if it slipped out, it must have been on my mind to begin with, he admitted to himself. Finally he decided to embrace that thought.

"We're kindred souls, you and I. I know that and so do you, or you wouldn't have moved in here. We've been in love for years — at least at some level. We'll be in love for many years more if I have anything to say about it. But I don't know that I will. There are no other women in my life and there probably never will be, other than kin — my mother, grandmother, and Sis. Except for you, I have no romantic interest in my life. If we get out of this war alive, I intend to marry you, Sally Mae Glass, or Guinevere Spring, or whatever your name is. I want to spend the rest of my life with you."

Rance stared at her blankly. He said more than he intended to. A lot more. He felt strange, but he really didn't feel bad about it.

Sally Mae grinned from ear to ear and hugged him again. They maintained the embrace for a long time. She heard what she wanted to hear. At this point in the relationship, with other men, the old Guinevere would have taken charge and run the show. But, somewhat to her surprise, all of her defenses against committing to a single man were completely shattered, although she kept a few secrets. At that moment, he could have swept her up, carried her to the bedroom and done anything he liked with her — including extracting a lifetime commitment and a promise of unquestioned faithfulness — and she would have happily complied. It was the first time in her life she felt so totally incapable of resisting, and it left her somewhat unsettled. But she knew she wanted him — now if possible, later if necessary, and for all time after that. She kissed him again, and Guinevere was a woman who knew how to do it. When she realized he wasn't going to try to have sex with her, she was a little happy and a little disappointed, both at once. She would have preferred that he rip off all of her clothes off and spirit her away to the bedroom, but since that wasn't going to happen, she rested her head on his shoulder and enjoyed the feeling of his arms around her for a while. Finally she sat up on the couch.

"As long as this is a night for clearing the air and exposing our deepest secrets …" she said softly, "I simply have to ask you a question."

"That sounds ominous."

"I guess it is …"

"Well, what is it?"

"Did you kill Bushrod Brown?"

This blunt question, which came out of nowhere, stunned him. His face fell and he jerked his head back and glared at her with surprise and annoyance. Hard brown eyes met beautiful, if slightly bloodshot, blue-grey eyes. Had she made a mistake? She wondered. He was clearly not ready for this. But now it had to be dealt with. Finally he took a deep breath and said: "I certainly did. I shot that son of a female dog right in the throat, put a 'make-sure' bullet into his brain, buried him in a field near an outhouse and urinated on his grave."

She was only slightly taken aback because she had suspected as much. She was more surprised by the vehemence of the answer, rather than the answer itself.

"Cold-blooded murder. With malice aforethought and no regrets. And if I had to do it over again, I'd do exactly the same thing, only a few weeks earlier. Does that bother you?" He asked.

As the memory of her rape and Brown spitting in her face and laughing at her sobs flashed across her mind, she didn't even have to think about her answer. "Not the tiniest little bit," she exclaimed. "I think you should receive Rainbow County's highest honorary award for selflessly performing a vital public service. They should give you a gold medal, have a Rance Liebert Day, close the school, and have a parade and a testimonial banquet in your honor, erect a statue of you in the town square, and name Main Street after you!" She thought for a minute more and added: "You saved my twin brother's life. Thank you

The Retribution Conspiracy

so much for that."

"I didn't do it for him," Rance responded. "I did it for you."

Thank you, she thought, but she didn't say it. A tear ran down her cheek.

"Sally ..."

"Yes?"

"There's one more question I've got to ask, as long as we're being so honest."

"Yes?"

"Can you limit yourself to just one man for the rest of your life?"

She momentarily thought *I should resent this question,* but she did not. "If that one man is you, Rance, yes I can."

He kissed her tenderly. From that moment, Rance Liebert and Sally Mae Glass, a/k/a Guinevere Spring, considered themselves engaged. From then on, every night he was in town, they slept together, but there was no sexual intercourse. Rance was very much a nineteenth century Southern gentleman. To him, sex came after marriage. And, although Guinevere was definitely unlike the average woman of her day, that was fine with her. It felt good, being with a man who actually respected her. And as her self-worth grew, so did her love for Rance Liebert.

Rance's deception plans worked perfectly. U.S. Major General George S. McClellan, General-in-Chief of the Union Army and commander of the Army of the Potomac, had more than 200,000 men, if the Washington garrison and the small armies in western Virginia and the Shenandoah Valley were counted. Joe Johnston had 43,000 men at Centreville (near Manassas), 6,000 in reserve nearby, 9,000 around the naval base at Norfolk, plus a few garrisons, reserve units, and odds and ends. To the west, in the Shenandoah, Stonewall Jackson had 17,000 men. But because McClellan believed that Johnston had 200,000 men or more at Manassas alone, he was extremely timid. Instead of attacking Johnston at Centreville (where he would have won a tremendous victory and perhaps a decisive one), he landed his army at Fort Monroe, southeast of Richmond, on the tip of the Virginia Peninsula, between the York and James Rivers. Johnston abandoned Manassas and marched south to meet him.

The South accumulated huge amounts of supplies in the depots around Manassas. Instead of properly evacuating them, as he could have done with a little foresight, Johnston burned them. It was a huge defeat for the Confederacy, even though it did not involve a battle. The main Rebel army would never be properly supplied after that.

McClellan's peninsular forces outnumbered Johnston's 121,500 to 58,000. McClellan advanced very slowly, however, because he concluded Johnston had four times as many men as he actually did. Meanwhile, Stonewall Jackson launched what many consider the most brilliant military campaign in American history. With 17,000 men, he crushed five separate Federal forces totaling 54,000 men and briefly threatened Washington, freezing the capital's garrison in place, neutralizing another 50,000 men without attacking them, and throwing the Lincoln administration into a state of absolute panic.

McClellan, meanwhile, pushed to within six miles of Richmond. He had no intention of attacking the city, however, because — based on bad intelligence reports from Pinkerton — he still believed himself to be outnumbered. Instead, he ordered siege guns be brought forward, to blast the city into submission. These, however, were so heavy, and the peninsular roads were so muddy and poor, it would take weeks to get them into position.

When Johnston realized what McClellan was doing, he launched an offensive against the dug-in Federals. The Battle of Seven Pines was not a disaster, but it was certainly a Northern victory. The Confederates lost 6,100 men, against the North's 5,000 casualties. Southern gains were negligible.

The most significant event occurred late in the first day of the battle when Joe Johnston rode forward to try to get his derailed battle plan back on track. He strayed too close to the front line. A Yankee shot him in the right shoulder. Almost simultaneously, an artillery shell exploded nearby, hurling a fragment into Johnston's chest. He fell unconscious from his horse, with his right shoulder blade and two ribs broken. It would take him months to recover.

Johnston was succeeded by Gustavus W. Smith. About nightfall, Jefferson Davis (who was on the battlefield) asked Smith what his plans were. Smith's answer amounted to incoherent babble, but he suggested that perhaps he would retreat closer to Richmond. Davis was astonished. They were only six miles from the capital now. As he rode back to Richmond, following a convoy of ambulance wagons, the president made the most propitious appointment of his life. He replaced Smith with Robert E. Lee. Lee promptly renamed his forces the Army of Northern Virginia and ordered the adoption of what became known as the Confederate battle flag. It was the genesis of what arguably became

The Retribution Conspiracy

the greatest army to ever fight on the North American continent. The situation in Richmond was stabilized, at least for the moment.

Things were much worse in the West. A fellow named Ulysses S. Grant captured Forts Henry and Donelson, forcing the evacuation of Kentucky and most of Tennessee, including Nashville. Confederate General Albert Sidney Johnston launched a counterstroke at Shiloh but was defeated and killed in heavy fighting. Memphis fell shortly thereafter, and the Yankees pushed into northern Mississippi and northern Alabama. To the south, New Orleans fell, followed by Baton Rouge, and Natchez. But there it stopped. Vicksburg held. This Mississippi town would be the focal point of the war in the west for the next year.

─◦ CHAPTER XVI ◦─
ABRAHAM "THE CORRUPT"

"What do you know about Abraham Lincoln?" Rance Liebert asked.

"I might ask you the same question," Jefferson Davis responded. He leaned back in his chair and regarded his Secret Service chief with a friendly smile. It was late Saturday afternoon, they were in Davis' small study on the ground floor of the Confederate White House, and the president decided he had enough stressful meetings for one week.

"Well, I know he's smart. And shrewd. And a little weird," Rance replied.

"Weird? What do you mean?"

"Well," Liebert answered, "I hear he lets his cats eat at the table, as if they're human."

"That is eccentric," Davis conceded.

"And he had his dead son dug up twice so he could view the body."

"That is a little odd," Jeff Davis conceded.

"A little …! Come now, colonel! That's more than 'a little odd.'"

"All right. You win, lieutenant. That's just plain weird." Jefferson Davis grinned.

The conversation lagged for a minute or so. The two men were using their old Mexican War titles, a sure sight of informality. Davis leaned back in his chair, summoned an aide, and ordered each of them a brandy. He had a tough week and decided to reward himself by enjoying a relaxed conversation with an old friend. This happened occasionally but certainly not often.

"President Lincoln is not what he pretends to be," Davis drawled. "One's got to give him a lot of credit for being what might be called a self-made man. Through hard work and education — largely self-education — he became perhaps the top corporate attorney in the United States."

"Corporate attorney?"

"Oh, yes. The Whig Party was always the party of the moneyed elite in the North, and Lincoln was a Whig until the party collapsed in 1854. Only then did he join the newly forming Republicans."

Davis paused and then continued. "Even today, he pretends to be a 'man of the people,' but he worked as a corporate attorney for the Illinois Central Railroad, the Chicago & Alton Railroad, the Ohio & Mississippi, and the Rock Island Railroad, that I know of. Erastus Corning offered him the job of chief general counsel for the New York Central at $10,000 a year a few years ago, but he turned it down."

Liebert whistled. The average farmer in 1860 made about $200 a year and the average manufacturing or industrial worker in New England was paid $323.[29] Ten thousand dollars was a huge salary in 1850 dollars. "Why did he turn it down?"

Davis smiled. "He couldn't afford the pay cut."

Liebert laughed. "He sure hid that from the general public during the election."

"One of the first things he did upon taking office as president was to propose legislation creating taxpayer subsidies for the Union Pacific." Davis paused. "He is also personally corrupt."

"What do you mean?"

"Well, I'll give you one example. In 1857, he purchased a great deal of land in Council Bluffs, Iowa, which was just another small Midwestern town at the time. The population was about 1,000. He did it because he had insider information that the transcontinential railroad's eastern terminus was going to be located there. And as president, he made it happen. The bill subsidizing the railroad — the Union Pacific — specifically gives the president of the United States the power to pick the location of the eastern terminus, as well as the power to choose all of the members of the board of directors."

"Hummpff," Liebert muttered.

"That's not all. He intends that the South pay for the railroad through the tariffs after he conquers us."

Blackguard, Rance thought.

"Oh, he's not the only prominent Republican with his hand in the till. John C. Fremont, their nominee in 1856, made sure the western terminus is in northern California, where he owns extensive acreage, and not in San Diego, where the end of the line should be. Thaddeus Stevens, the vicious chairman of the Ways and Means Committee, received a large block of Union Pacific stock in exchange for his support of the subsidy."

"An out-and-out bribe," Liebert commented.

"It certainly looks like it."

---

29 The cost of living gap was not as great as these figures suggest. The farmer grew his own food and animals and did not have to purchase food, but the factory worker did. The farmer also made his own clothes, soap and liquor.

"I understand Lincoln is unhappily married," the ex-lieutenant suggested.

"Yes, I hear that, too. His wife is, perhaps, mentally unstable. She is from a family of wealthy Kentucky slaveholders. Her mother died when she was a child, and she had, shall we say, a difficult relationship with her stepmother, who sent her to finishing school early. She is not at all attractive …"

"Neither is he," Liebert interjected.

"True," Davis smiled. "But she had money, taste, refinement, money, connections, education, and money. And Lincoln does love money! Oddly enough, Mary Todd was courted by Stephen Douglas as well as Lincoln."

"I didn't know that."

"Lincoln won, of course," Davis continued. "Or maybe Douglas pulled out. I don't know which."

"I think Douglas won," Rance interjected.

Davis smiled and continued. "In any case, Lincoln was just a poor country lawyer at that time, and she had money and connections, especially within the Whig Party. Many people believe that is why he proposed. She accepted his proposal, and her family planned a huge wedding with many out-of-town guests. For that special day, everything was ready except the groom."

"He wasn't ready?"

"Nobody could find him."

"You mean he jilted her at the atlar?" Rance asked.

"That's exactly what I mean. Or at least that's what his best friend and law partner, William Herndon, told me."

"Hummphhh!"

"Well, they tried it again a year later," Davis continued. "This time the groom actually showed up. On his way to the wedding, a young fellow asked him where he was heading. Lincoln replied, 'To hell,' and he wasn't joking. His trademark humor was totally absence." Davis paused a moment for affect. "Lincoln definitely married above his station," he continued. "You know several of her half-brothers are fighting for us, and her brother is a surgeon in our army. Anyway, some people think jilting is the source of his marital unhappiness. Mary Todd Lincoln never really forgave him for the humiliation."

"Can't say that I blame her. If she'd been my daughter or sister, he'd have had a duel on his hands."

"You fought a duel once, didn't you, Rance?"

"Yes. I killed me a thug. He raped a beautiful little girl who is now a beautiful woman. She is our top agent in Washington, D.C., since Rose Greenhow is in prison. I'd like you to meet her one day."

"That would be my honor," Jefferson Davis replied, seriously. He didn't particularly care for actors or actresses unless they worked for him. But if they did, they instantly became the most respectable of people and he took a personal interest in them. "Did she ever get over being raped?"

"Does a woman ever completely get over something like that? But I think maybe she has put it behind her. Anyway, she's now an actress in Washington and New York."

"Is she well connected?" Davis asked.

"Very. Invited me to the Inaugural Ball. Wanted me to meet Abraham Lincoln!"

Jefferson Davis got a rare belly laugh out of that revelation. He was now in a gossipy mood — something which almost never happened. "Rance, you are associating with one bold woman!"

"She was all set to do it. Unfortunately, she had to find another escort, because I was too much of a coward to go."

"Sounds like the better part of valor to me!" The president laughed. Then he got serious and added: "It sounds to me as if you like this woman, Rance."

"I really do!" He admitted. "She's clever, vivacious, and you never know what she's going to come up with next."

After a brief pause, Jeff Davis changed the subject. "Rance, did you know that Lincoln almost fought a duel himself?"

"Really? I didn't know."

"Yes, in Illinois he had a political enemy named James Shields …"

"General James Shields?" The colonel interrupted, with an incredulous look on his face.

"Yes."

Rance was impressed. Shields was the only Union general who defeated Stonewall Jackson.[30]

"Shields was the Illinois State Auditor at the time, and Lincoln was a 'low road' politician back then. Shields was a Democrat, and he and Lincoln clashed. Illinois issued its own paper money in those days,

---

30 On March 22, 1862, Shields was encamped at Kernstown, just south of Winchester, Virginia. Jackson's cavalry erroneously reported he had 3,000 men, so Jackson launched a surprise attack. The surprise was on Jackson: Shields had 9,000 men. Jackson had about 3,500 men.

The Retribution Conspiracy

but it was so useless that the state refused to accept its own worthless currency as payment on state taxes. Lincoln had already driven one man out of politics and almost to suicide by publishing scathing letters in the local newspaper. Lincoln apparently enjoyed that and couldn't wait to do it again. The second person he tried it on was Shields, who was partially responsible for the incredible decision not to accept state money for state taxes. He reacted rather differently from Lincoln's first victim."

"Did he pull Lincoln's nose or slap his face with a glove?" Rance asked. These were the two most acceptable ways to challenge someone to a duel.

"Neither the first time. Shields cornered Lincoln and told him in no uncertain terms that, if it happened again, there would be a duel, and he intended to kill him. This frightened Lincoln, who had already started a second polemic. He decided not to finish it. But his fiancée, Mary Todd, and one of her friends did finish it and sent it to the editor without his knowledge. And they signed Lincoln's name to it!"

Rance Liebert laughed. "I guess that's what you get for standing up certain women at the altar!"

"Maybe so," Davis grinned. "Anyway, Shields demanded satisfaction. He was an excellent shot, so Lincoln chose broadswords. Shields' seconds betrayed him — or maybe they were bribed. Anyway, they agreed to place a board on the ground, over which neither contestant could cross. Lincoln's arms were much longer than Shields', so he could strike at the general with little danger to himself. Before they crossed swords, however, the seconds intervened and convinced Shields not to fight, on the grounds Lincoln did not actually write the letters. Of course, I am sure the unfair advantage Lincoln secured for himself had something to do with it."

Lincoln has an irresponsible and possibly insane wife who makes stupid decisions, Rance thought. He made a mental note of this. That little piece of knowledge might come in handy later, he calculated.

"Sounds like General Shields has a problem pickin' his friends," Rance opined.

Jeff Davis smiled.

"Do you think Mrs. Lincoln really is insane? There certainly are rumors to that effect circulating in Yankeeland."

"Well," Davis remarked, "I certainly couldn't say, but it is known she has physically and verbally abused him in public on more than one occasion."

"Really?"

"Oh, yes. She likes to toss drinks in his face when she is upset," Davis revealed. "Sometimes that drink is hot coffee."

"Well, if you ever do decide you want Lincoln assassinated, we'll just have Guinevere go to one of the insiders' parties to which she's often invited, walk by the president, scream as if she has just been pinched, and turn around and slap Mr. Lincoln. Then Mrs. Lincoln will do our job for us."

Jefferson F. Davis laughed. Then he got serious again. "Does Mr. Lincoln cheat on Mrs. Lincoln?" He asked. "That might account for her instability."

"No. At least not with women."

Davis jerked his head back. "Do you mean ..."

"Yes. Exactly. He is known to sleep with one of his bodyguards, Captain David Derickson of the 150th Pennsylvania, when Mrs. Lincoln is out of town."

Davis' face looked as if he was smelling rotten eggs. "When I was in Washington, I heard rumors about Lincoln's sexual proclivities. Back in Springfield, they say he lived with a certain Joshua Speed for years. Rumor is that they slept in the same bed ..."

"Were there any children?" Rance asked. Jefferson Davis laughed. Just then there was a knock on the door.

It was the receptionist. "Dispatch from General Lee, sir."

The president held out his hand and scanned the message. "Well," he announced with regret, "it looks as if I have to get back to work. Thank you for coming by, Rance." And with that, Colonel Liebert was dismissed. As he walked slowly back to headquarters, he thought about their conversation. Future teachers would certainly have to leave out a great deal if they wanted to make Lincoln look saintly, he concluded. On the other hand, he actually felt sorry for the U.S. president. Then he recalled how many times he felt sorry for the president of the C.S.A. Finally, he thought of an earlier conversation they had and concluded Jefferson Davis was right: life can be hell if you are married to the wrong woman.

─∾ CHAPTER XVII ∾─
A SUPPER IS RUINED

When the South seceded, the foremost signals experts in the United States "went South." As a result, the North never did catch up to the Confederacy in the field of signal communications. Liebert used one of their signal systems in southern Maryland to keep his people advised of the location of Yankee cavalry patrols. It worked flawlessly, and the flow of information from Washington to Richmond remained uninterrupted during the entire war.

At first, Liebert's signals branch in Richmond was very small. It consisted of encoding and decoding sections, both headed by Melody Herzog. It grew, however, because the Secret Service needed ciphers and secret codes, and a telegraph office was added. As a businessman back in Mississippi, Grover Liebert believed in "Hire or buy the best people, and then git out of their way!" He passed this practice along to his grandson, who ingrained it in the Secret Service. But, in this case, the best man for the job was a woman. Liebert had a bit of trouble when he wanted Melody made a full-time paid employee and nominated her for the rank of second lieutenant. President Davis balked initially. Liebert assured him she would not wear a uniform.

"She's not planning to flaunt her rank, is she, Rance?"

"She's been warned not to, and she'd better not! This is a secret service, Mr. President!" Rance exclaimed.

Jeff Davis smiled and signed her commission without further ado.

One day, about the time Stonewall Jackson first threatened Washington, Major John Baker, a/k/a John Spring, showed up at Secret Service headquarters.

"What are you doing here, John?" Liebert asked. He wasn't hostile, but he certainly wasn't friendly. Baker wasn't even supposed to know where the HQ of the Secret Service was.

"I had a devil of a time trackin' you down," the one-legged Tennessean complained. "General Cooper didn't even know …"

"Let's keep in that way," Rance retorted. "He ain't supposed to know. You ain't supposed to know!"

"I had to go to the White House …"

"Why are you here, Major Baker?" Liebert said, cutting him short.

The colonel was not in a particularly good mood that day, and Baker's appearance made it worse.

"Because my sister showed up."

"Your sister? Guinevere Spring?"

"That's right."

Liebert knew she would not be here unless it was important. She went to her so-called brother only because she knew where to find him. Rance kept the location of the Secret Service building even from her, because he was afraid she might be captured one day. People will reveal anything under torture. "Where is she now?" he asked.

"At the Spotswood Hotel."

Sally Mae does travel in style, he thought. This was the best hotel in Richmond. "Go see her as her brother. Give her this note," he said, writing quickly. "You will carry her to supper at the Wright House at 7 p.m."

"Dinner with a beautiful woman, and an actress to boot!" The major smiled widely. "It's a tough job, but somebody's got to do it."

Liebert derailed his plans immediately. "Yeah. That would be me. You are going to escort her into a private dining room and exit straightaway through the back door. A closed carriage will pick you up and carry you back here, where you will spend the night. Eat before you go," he added. "The mess hall here closes at six."

Major Baker's chest fell. His visions of an exciting evening of sex with a beautiful woman vanished, although he did not give up completely. He obviously had been quite taken with his "sister."

"Perhaps we could have a supper another time, while she's here in Richmond."

"She's one of my agents, major. Besides, she has a fiancée."

"But he's not here," Baker smiled, man-to-man. He obviously thought as an actress, she must be promiscuous. It was also apparent he believed the colonel thought so, too, which is why he cut in for supper tonight. But he saw no reason he shouldn't be second.

Liebert decided to have some fun at Baker's expense. "Yes, her fiancée is here," Rance retorted. "In fact, he's sittin' right in front of you." He glared at the young officer.

Baker descended into complete confusion. He tried to stammer out an apology, but Rance cut him off. "Git yo' tail out of here, Baker," he snapped.

"Yes, sir!" The major responded.

"And, major …"

The Retribution Conspiracy

"Yes, sir?"

"Not every actress is a trollop. Some of them are actually ladies and are to be treated as such. Try to remember that."

"Yes, sir!" He got out the door as rapidly as he could.

"And make sure you're not late when you pick her up tonight!" Liebert shouted after him as he left.

Major John Spring walked Guinevere Spring through the main dining room of the Wright House and into a private dining room. Colonel Liebert stood up when she entered. She smiled and extended her hands. He grasped them and held them for a full minute. Their eyes locked and it seemed they couldn't take them off each other.

Baker broke the trance. "I'll be going now, colonel," he said.

"Thank you, major," Liebert said, softly. He was much friendlier than he was in his office.

"Goodnight, John," Guinevere called after him.

"Goodnight, ma'am," he said and tipped his hat as he departed.

Rance and Sally Mae had a laugh. It was obvious Baker was treating her with a great deal more deference than he had earlier in the day.

The room was small. It was luxurious and designed to seat no more than four people, although it usually accommodated only two. It was not business private. It was man-and-a-woman private.

"You look so beautiful," he told her. "I missed you so much."

"I missed you, too," she declared.

"I ordered your favorite wine."

"Good," she said. "I've a lot to tell you. It's been an interesting few days."

She told him how she was summoned to the War Department by the exalted Stanton himself. He was beside himself with worry. "Go to Richmond," he told me. "Leave immediately. Visit your brother on some pretext. Find out Stonewall Jackson's plans. Does he intend to attack Washington? And how many men does he have?"

"Huuummm," Liebert said, thinking deeply.

Suddenly, there was a bit of a scrap outside. Captain Leonard and three of his men entered the private dining area. In front of them was a fat, red-faced man. Corporal Anderson had the fellow's right arm bent behind his back and was holding a Derringer between the captive's shoulder blades.

"Caught this man listenin' in outside the door," Leonard said.

"I demand that you release me!" The man yelled.

"Pipe down!" Liebert commanded. "Who are you?"

"Name's Blanton. Mister Blanton to you. I am a British citizen here on business, and I demand that you release me at once!" He was almost shouting by the end of his last sentence. Obviously he wanted to attract attention.

"Shut up!" The colonel snapped and slapped him hard in the face. He glared at Liebert with a look of pure hatred.

"Search him!" Liebert demanded.

All of a sudden, a waiter appeared. "What is happening here, sir?" He asked Rance.

"Help me!" The prisoner demanded.

"He is a private detective, trying to eavesdrop on our rendezvous," said the suddenly urbane Liebert. "My dear Penelope," he said to Guinevere, "it appears your ex-husband doesn't want you but doesn't want anyone else to have you, either."

"Could be your wife," Guinevere offered, picking up the game.

"No chance," he smiled. "She doesn't care, and she's far too stupid." The waiter smiled.

"But I'm not ..." the prisoner interjected. He never finished his sentence. Julian Anderson hit him in the jaw. He fell to the floor, and Anderson kicked him in the solar plexus. He gasped for air and was unable to speak for several minutes.

"Not so violent, Detective Burns," Rance said smoothly to his agent. But that was strictly for the benefit of the waiter.

"What do you want us to do with him, sir?"

"I want to question him. Here," he said, giving the server a $100 bill. "Please go away. Come back in a half an hour to take our order. We do not wish to be disturbed until then."

"Yes, sir!"

"And make sure no one else from the staff disturbs us, either."

"Yes, sir!"

"And Mr. Waiter?"

"Yes, sir?"

"This did not happen. You never saw a thing."

"No, sir! Anything you say, sir!" One hundred dollars — even in Confederate money — bought a lot of silence in Richmond in 1862.

"Search him!" Rance ordered as soon as the waiter departed.

The snoop had a knife, a Derringer, and several hundred dollars in Confederate money and U.S. greenbacks, as well as about $200 in gold. He had no identification.

Rance handed the Confederate money to Leonard. "Divide this among yourselves," he ordered. "Blindfold this guy and take him to headquarters. If he so much as looks at you crossways, shoot him and dump his body into the river."

"Yes, sir," the men said in unison, as they carried the prisoner out the back door.

"Did you bring chloroform, Leonard?"

"You bet. You told us to always have chloroform available, sir."

"Good! You've been listening. Chloroform him good. Then come back here."

Leonard was back in four minutes. "He's asleep in the carriage, sir."

"Good. How many men do you have?"

"Myself and four others, sir."

"Does that include the carriage driver?"

"No. That's your servant Joshua, sir."

"Joshua?!" Guinevere perked up. "I want to see Joshua!" She was out the door before anyone could react.

Rance and Leonard followed the actress outside. She made a bee line to the carriage driver and couldn't wait to greet her father's former slave. "Joshua!" She cried. She would have hugged his neck had he not been perched on the driver's seat of the carriage. She took him by the hand and smiled widely.

"Miss Sally Mae!" He grinned. They held hands and smiled at each other for some time. She would never forget that this man risked his life to try to save her from Bushrod Brown and his thugs back in Rainbow County.

"How are you?" She asked him. "How is your family? How do you like Richmond?"

"I likes Richmond fine," he declared. "Mr. Rance, he done bought us a house, and lets me and my family live there for free. I likes it a whole lot better with my wife and childin here." He grinned. "And he carries me on the roles like a regular soldier, so I gets paid."

"How are Jane and the kids?" She asked.

Rance intervened. He could see that this visit would last a while if he didn't, and he was afraid the chloroform might wear off or they might be seen. Besides, these two were oblivious to the fact that they were in the middle of a kidnapping. And what could possibly be more conspicuous than a beautiful white woman holding hands with a handsome black man in the capital of the Confederacy in 1862?

She reluctantly removed her hands. "I'll be in Richmond a day or two," she declared. "We'll catch up and have a long visit before I leave, I promise!"

"Yes, ma'am!" Joshua grinned. He was delighted to see someone from back home.

Rance, meanwhile, turned to Captain Leonard. "Leave Anderson and one other man for me," he ordered.

"Yes, sir."

"Lay the prisoner on the floor of the carriage and keep your foot on the back of his neck. If he tries anything, shoot him. Have your other two men go with you. Order the other boys to shoot him if he tries to get up. If you have to shoot, shoot to kill. Take him to headquarters and lock him up. Then come back here. Knock on the back door."

"Yes, sir."

Two men entered a minute later and stood at what might have been a sloppy form of attention. They looked like soldiers, even in their badly fitting civilian clothes. "Corporal Anderson," Liebert said. "You have seen what can happen."

"Yes, Rance."

"You and Mims discretely patrol this place, front, back, and sideways. I've rented the two rooms on either side of this one, so there shouldn't be anybody in there. Make sure it stays that way! These creatures sometimes work in pairs. Above all, Miss Spring must not be spotted, and our conversation must not be overheard."

"That man ..." Anderson asked. "Is he a Yankee agent?"

"Pretty much has to be. That or a Pinkerton man, which is the same thing. He sure ain't one of ours."

Guinevere spoke for the first time. "What are you going to do with him, Rance?" She never saw Rance in action as Colonel Liebert until now, and it was just dawning on her that he might be planning to kill the Northern agent.

"First I'll interrogate him. Find out who he is and what he's up to."

"Then what?"

"Let's do Part One first," he said, forcing a smile. He wanted to recapture the original, festive mood of the evening. But he failed. The man now knew too much. She realized Rance had two choices: kill the spy or release him, in which case she and the entire organization would be compromised. And they both knew he would choose the first alternative without even thinking about it. The evening was ruined. She remained uncharacteristically quite the rest of the meal and pretty somber the rest of the trip.

The Retribution Conspiracy

Finally she said, "You are going to kill him, aren't you, Rance?"

He didn't say a word.

"I don't want you to kill him," she declared.

"He doesn't deserve to live."

"Don't kill him!" She insisted. "I don't want anyone killed because of me!"

"But ..."

"Promise me you won't kill him!"

"But ..."

"Promise!" She demanded.

"Okay!" Rance exclaimed, obviously somewhat put out. "If he co-operates with us, I'll let him live."

"And if he doesn't?"

Rance said nothing at first. He took a sip of wine. Then he declared: "He will if he knows what's good for him!"

———⚬⚬⚬———

Later, in Richmond's posh Spotswood Hotel, Guinevere Spring tossed and turned most of the night. Things had changed. Until now, everything was fun — a daring and exciting exploit, and a romantic one at that. She was reunited with her first love and they were working together for a purpose she considered noble. Life was an exciting adventure. But tonight, she saw firsthand the uglier side of the Secret Service. Rance and his men were ready to kill to keep their secrets, and Anderson was even anxious to do it. She heard of such men before but never knew one personally. Not that she was afraid of Julian Anderson — she wasn't. Colonel Liebert would keep him in check. But if the South had men like that, it was dead certain the North did also, and they were looking for people like her. And that bothered her.

She also got a glimpse of the kind of power she was acquiring. It went far beyond self-worth. Since she became Guinevere, she always had control over most men, and she enjoyed it. But that was sensual. As a secret agent, she had a different sort of power. Life or death power. All she had to do was say the word, and a man would die. Rance Liebert felt she had to be protected, even if someone else had to perish. And it really wasn't Rance ordering the killing — it was the head of the Secret Service. Any director worth his salt, she realized, would make the same decision. And, in a sense, it wasn't even about her. He would do it for any valuable asset. Asset. How she hated that word! This was a sort of power she never wanted and certainly never sought, but suddenly it was here, nevertheless. And now she had to deal with it.

She fluffed her pillow and rolled over. That didn't work. She fluffed her other pillow and rolled over on it. That didn't work either. She rolled over onto her right side. Then she rolled over onto her left side. Finally, in exasperation, she rolled over onto her back. She stared at the ceiling. It didn't move. Finally she adjusted. She thought about tomorrow. Breakfast with her brother. She missed him so much and could hardly wait to see him. But Rance said it would have to be in her room, and he was right. It would be disastrous if a Federal spy were to see the two of them together and word were to get back to Stanton. For the first time in her life, she couldn't be seen in public with her own twin brother. She hated that. The breakfast might be ruined if she couldn't get some sleep! But the sandman ignored her invitation.

She got up, pulled back the curtains, sat in the wingback chair, and stared at the moon. The full moon stared back. Just before dawn, she came to terms with her situation and made her decision. All right, I have life or death power, she thought to herself.
"I choose life," she said aloud.

The moon didn't answer.

—⁂—

The following morning, Rance walked up to the fourth floor jail cell with two of his men and confronted the spy, who was dressed in his underwear. Rance's boys had removed his cheap suit and ripped it apart, to see if there were any secret messages in the lining. There weren't any, but there were some Greenbacks, which disappeared somehow. Blanton's lip was busted and one of his eyes was swollen and turning black. He had obviously been beaten.

"What happened to him?" Liebert asked.

"He forgot where his hotel room was," Anderson grinned. "I helped him remember."

The colonel smiled. "Did you find anything there?"

"Some of the boys are searching it now," the corporal responded. A pained look came across his face. That's where he wanted to be. Instead, he was stuck here at headquarters. There was probably money in the hotel room, but Anderson knew he'd never see a penny of it. There was no money in guarding a prisoner.

"Who do you work for?" Liebert asked the Federal agent.

"Go to blazes, you stinking Rebel!" He snapped.

Without another word, Rance drew his revolver and shot off a fin-

The Retribution Conspiracy

ger from the man's left hand. Another torrent of profanity ensued.

"Oh, shut up! And quit cursing in my presence. Just be glad it wasn't your manhood! And it will be pretty soon, if I don't hear what I need to know. Now, who do you work for?"

Anderson smiled at this exchange.

"I'm a British citizen, and I demand to speak to the official at the Confederate state department who handles British affairs!" The spy asserted. "He won't be happy when he finds out what you've done to me!" His tone was definitely threatening.

Unfortunately for Blanton, Rance Liebert recognized a bluff when he saw it. "Fellar, if I couldn't lie any better than that, I'd quit lyin'!" That said, he blew off the tip of another finger.

This time the spy screamed, but he did not curse. Rance waited a minute to let him get accustomed to the pain. "Better git me another gun, Anderson," he said. "Looks like I might run out of ammunition again."

Anderson and Leonard laughed. Rance Liebert snickered.

"Who are you?" Rance asked again, "and who do you work for?"

"I am Charles Blanton."

"I didn't ask your name. I asked who are you."

"I am a private detective. I work for Pinkerton."

"I see. That means you are working for Lincoln. Who were you following last night?"

Blanton thought for a moment. "You. I was following you."

"Who am I?" The colonel asked.

Blanton couldn't answer. "Okay. I was following the whore. Eh, I mean the woman."

"You mean the lady," Rance corrected him.

"Eh … yeah. I mean the lady."

"You are learning, sir. What is her name?"

"Guinevere Spring."

Rance cocked his revolver.

"Eh, I mean Miss Guinevere Spring," Blanton hastily corrected himself.

"Get him some paper, a pen, and some ink," Rance ordered. "You're gonna write down the name and location of every spy, informant, Pinkerton man, Secret Service person, and Union sympathizer in Richmond you know. Including your boss. If I'm satisfied, I won't shoot you. And try not to get blood on the paper."

"Will you let me go if I do?"

"No. Not until Miss Spring is no longer operating behind Yankee lines. Otherwise you'd compromise her to the Federals and get her killed. You'll be right here 'til then."

This answer relieved Blanton somewhat. If Liebert said yes, Blanton would have known he was lying and intended to execute him, because there was no way the Rebel was going to release him. He knew too much. "Can I write a note to my wife?" The captured spy asked.

"No."

"My children?"

"No." Liebert looked at him sourly. He didn't believe Blanton had a wife or children. There was no wedding band on his ring finger and there was no evidence there ever was.

Blanton (who was a bachelor) looked around his cell. There were no windows. He had no money, so he couldn't bribe anyone. He couldn't see how he was going to get a message out. It wouldn't matter, even if he did. He had no idea where he was.

As if he read the Yankee's mind, Rance looked at him and said: "You are isolated, sir. Your only hope to survive is to cooperate with us."

"You might shoot me anyway."

"I might," Rance admitted. "But if you don't cooperate, I can guarantee it. And if you cooperate and I do decide to shoot you, it'll be quick and merciful, and with benefit of clergy, if you wish. If you don't cooperate, you'll suffer death by torture."

"Let me do it, colonel!" Anderson exclaimed, grinning widely.

Blanton turned pale. Rance ignored Anderson's request, turned to him and said: "I'm goin' downstairs to get him some medical help. Don't let anybody talk to him, period."

"Yes, sir," Anderson said, somewhat disappointed.

"You know, Rance," Leonard piped in, "I wish you'd built the jail cells on the first floor. Draggin' this fat piece of garbage up the stairs when he was unconscious weren't much fun!"

Liebert laughed.

The Retribution Conspiracy

_ CHAPTER XVIII _

EVEN A WOMAN
HAS HER USES

R
ance met Guinevere near an obscure country tavern several miles west of Richmond. Joshua drove her carriage via a convoluted route, while other agents made sure they were not followed. The colonel, now in uniform, entered the closed carriage and sat opposite her. He was armed with a pair of Navy sixes, but instead of a sword, he carried the Bowie knife. She had told him she was supposed to meet a Union dispatch rider at 5 p.m. the following evening. He would take her information back to Stanton. If she didn't appear as scheduled, he would be back at 5 p.m. the next evening.

Rance decided to give them some information they already knew or would soon know, as well as some information which was false but believable. She had already given him the Yankee code. He handed her two copies of a dispatch (one decoded, one not) which read:

Situation not as bleak as Washington thinks. Jackson not to attack capital. Will double back, reinforce Lee, Richmond. Has 50,000 men or more. Cooper worried. Rebel gold and archives already shipped to N.C. and S.C.

G.S.

"Copy the coded message in your own hand, give it to your messenger and burn the original. And I mean burn it. Don't just tear it up and put it in a trash receptacle," Rance said, and returned the codebook to her. One of Melody's female staff had already copied it for him. The Yankees would change the code in two to six weeks, but it would prove useful until then. "They didn't give you a code name?" He asked.

"No," she said.

Rance smiled ear to ear, shook his head and muttered: "Amateurs!" He knew the British would call him an amateur if they were to see his operation, and compared to theirs, they would be right. He felt lucky he wasn't facing the British — only Lincolnites.

"How much of this dispatch is true?" Guinevere asked.

"Most of it," Rance admitted. "Jackson doesn't have half that many men, but the Yankees probably think he does, so this will confirm it in their own minds. They will soon figure out he isn't going to attack Washington, if they haven't already, so that information won't hurt anything. And he is coming to Richmond. But they'd discover that soon enough anyway. You might be able to hide an entire Southern army in the Shenandoah, but you can't hide it that close to a big city like Richmond. We're not giving them much."

"Why give them anything?"

"Got to. We must maintain your credibility."

"Is that why you were going to kill that man who was spying on us last night? To maintain my credibility?"

He just looked at her for a long moment. She was not as miserable as she was the previous evening, but she clearly was not happy. When he remained silent, she spoke up. "I don't want you to kill him, Rance. Not because of me. And not to protect me, either."

The director of the Secret Service sighed. "Very well. You win. If he cooperates, I won't kill him."

Guinevere looked relieved. "But what if he doesn't cooperate?" She asked.

"Sally Mae, this man is in their secret service, and we are at war. He knew the chances he was taking if he were to get caught, and he got caught. Now his life is forfeit. Even so, I offered him a deal because of you — and only because of you. If he gives me the information I want, and I'm satisfied with it, I've agreed to let him live. And I will because I promised you I would. But if he lies, if he tries to deceive me, or if he doesn't cooperate, I'll have him shot."

"Thank you, Rance." She looked relieved, as if a burden was lifted.

"Sally," he said, "you need to decide if you want to be a double agent or not. If not, I'll have your 'brother' — and by that I mean Major Baker — transferred to Texas. That way, you'll be useless to Stanton. And you can continue to spy for us in Washington, if you want to. Another alternative is for you to 'go South.' But there's danger there, too. If we lose the war, Stanton will hunt you down, and he's a mean, murderous, power-hungry criminal. Or you can go to England. I've got some sizable discretionary funds, so I can give you all of the money you'll need to get started. You are a great actress, so you can pick up your career there, out of danger. But you can never come back to the United States while Stanton's alive. And please do what you think is right for you. I love you and want to marry you after the war, if you'll still have me. Nothing you decide will change that."

She moved over to his side of the carriage and sat by him. "Oh,

The Retribution Conspiracy

Rance," she said, taking his hand. "I'm sorry."

"No, you've done fine. No one could have done better and very few could have done as well. It's only that you're just now getting to see the dark side of this business, and it can get ugly. But you can still get out, if you want to."

"I don't want to," she said.

"Don't answer now," he said. "I'll be in Washington in a few weeks. Give me your answer then."

"I've already given you my answer," she retorted. "But come to Washington anyway, so I can give it to you again." She smiled. Guinevere was flirting. That was always a good sign. "And come to the Spotswood tonight," she said. "Room 318."

"It will be late. Perhaps very late."

"I don't care."

"I'll be there," he said.

When Rance returned, Charles Blanton had completed his list. It covered a page and a half. "Dang, Blanton, you done good," Rance (who was now dressed in a black suit) admitted.

"Can I shoot him now, colonel?" Anderson wanted to know. Liebert did not answer immediately. All of the blood drained from Blanton's face.

"No. But I ought to shoot him myself. He just created a lot of work for me." He grinned at Blanton, but the Pinkerton man did not appreciate his sense of humor and did not smile back. "Tell Lieutenant Glass to go get him a real doctor," Liebert ordered. "Blindfold the sawbones and bring him here. When he's finished, put Blanton into the cell at the far end of the building."

"How long do you intend to keep me here, colonel?" Blanton asked.

"Until the end of the war."

"But that could take years," Blanton protested.

"If you say so, Mr. Blanton," Liebert responded. "But if I shoot you, you'll be dead a lot longer than that. Which would you prefer?"

Blanton said nothing.

"Anderson?"

"Yes, colonel?"

"Don't ever call me colonel or use my name in front of the prisoners again. Understand?"

"Yes, colonel," Anderson said and smiled. Rance just rolled his eyes and shook his head.

As the two Rebels walked downstairs, Liebert said to Anderson: "Go see Colonel Winder, the provost marshal of Richmond. Go right now. Tell him I want to meet with him on a matter of the utmost importance at his earliest possible convenience."

Secretary of War Edwin Stanton was immensely relieved when he read Guinevere's message. He wondered if it were true, but he thought it probably was. That would be confirmed if Jackson appeared up around Richmond and did not attack D.C. The 50,000 men she said the Rebel had was close to Union Army intelligence estimate, which placed his numbers at 60,000 to 65,000 men. It seemed to him he had a pretty good agent in Guinevere Spring. Especially for a woman, Stanton thought. They're normally so stupid. And this one probably is, too, but perhaps she could be used on other assignments ... After all, even a woman has her uses.

A few days later, near Richmond, Stonewall Jackson joined forces with General Lee, just as Guinevere predicted. What she didn't predict — and what no Union leader even thought possible — happened next. Robert E. Lee attacked General McClellan's forces and, in the Seven Days campaign, defeated them. McClellan had to burn his huge supply depot and Richmond was saved, but the U.S. Army of the Potomac escaped (if barely so) and casualties on both sides were terrible. Among the dead was Brigadier General Richard Griffith, former commander of the 12th Mississippi and then commander of the Mississippi Brigade, who was shredded by a cannon ball.

The Retribution Conspiracy

—⌀ CHAPTER XIX ⌀—
YOU PILE OF REBEL DUNG!

L iebert met with the Richmond provost marshal the same day he received Blanton's list. They were only together 15 minutes before they were deeply involved in planning an operation to sweep the capital clean of Lincoln's operatives.

The next day, Guinevere sent another dispatch to Stanton. It read:

Someone named Blanton defected to the Rebels. Was paid a great deal of money. Is giving them names. All loyal agents in grave danger. Should be warned.
        G. S.

Liebert had her send this dispatch because he knew that it would arrive too late for the Yankees to warn anyone. Hiding in a clump of trees and using a pair of high-powered binoculars, Corporal Julian Anderson watched Guinevere hand the dispatch over to the courier.

"Did you get a good look at him?" Colonel Liebert wanted to know.

"Yeah," Anderson grunted.

"Good. He'll be back in two or three days and will appear again at this location at 5 p.m."

"Yeah?"

"Yeah," Liebert grunted back. "When he goes, kill him."

"Yes, sir!" Anderson grinned. It was about time he got an agreeable assignment.

"Don't fool around with him, Anderson," Liebert warned. "Just wear civilian clothes, make sure there are no witnesses around, and then just ride up to him and shoot him. Then either cut his throat or put a make-sure bullet between his eyes. Finally, check the body and his saddlebags for identification and documents, and bring everything back to headquarters."

"Yes, sir," Anderson grinned again. Of course, he won't have any money, the corporal thought, and his horse will have gotten away, along with his saddle and rifle, if they're any good, but I'll bring in everything else.

The next day, beginning at three o'clock in the morning, the provost guard from the Richmond Provost Marshal's Office, aided by some troops from the 125th Special Employment Battalion and the Richmond Police, rounded up every spy, informant, Pinkerton man, and Secret Service person on Blanton's list. Using Liebert's special interrogation techniques on the new prisoners (except on the women, of course), they acquired new names and soon crippled Lincoln's spy network in the Confederate capital. Several of the spies were never seen again. They were tried by secret military tribunals, found guilty, taken out and shot, and buried in unmarked graves. Some were spared the ordeal of a trial. No one asked questions. There were a lot of unmarked graves around Richmond in the summer of 1862.

Guinevere returned to Washington and continued to attend parties and dances, gathering information here and there, and establishing her own network of undercover operatives within the District of Columbia. She still went to an occasional party, ball, or dinner with a single Union officer. Some of them got as far as her door, but to their disappointment, none got beyond it. She even set up what might be called a "sleeper cell" under her friend and fellow actor, John Wilkes Booth, but she considered Booth too unstable to trust very far, so she used him as a source of information only. He was too outspoken to be of any real use, except in an emergency. Even so, he was a brilliant actor. On one occasion, Abraham Lincoln attended one of his performances. Lincoln joined the rest of the audience in the standing ovation at the end. The president was so carried away by the emotion engendered by the performance that he sent Booth a message. He wanted to come back stage and meet the famous actor.

Booth sent him back this reply: "I'd rather be applauded by a n**ger than by you."

John Wilkes Booth and Abraham Lincoln never met.

Most of 1862 and the first half of 1863 was a hard time for nearly everyone. With fewer men and far fewer resources, the South fought the North to a standstill in northern Mississippi and Tennessee, and even assumed the offensive on the Eastern Front, where Robert E. Lee and Stonewall Jackson won victory after smashing victory. Rance, meanwhile, made the long trip to Mississippi, Alabama, and Tennessee, and even took a few days off to visit Rainbow. He carried his dress gray uniform for this occasion. He looked good in the gold braid with the three stars of a Rebel colonel on his collar, and he had lost the ex-

The Retribution Conspiracy

cess stomach he developed before the war.

One evening, he and Grover got to sit on the porch to discuss events great and small. Ambrose and Jonathan were to the point of joining them, but Grover told them to go back inside. He wanted to speak to Rance by himself.

The plantation had changed, Grover declared. Some of the field hands ran off after the Yankees took Natchez, but there wasn't as much to do anyway, as the government asked the plantation owners to switch from cotton to food production. Fusilier was now growing corn, which was less labor intensive, so he didn't need as many field hands as before, which was a good thing, since he didn't have as many. Grover was still growing some cotton but not much. "Ain't no profit in it," Grover growled. "Next year, 'less thangs change, I ain't gonna plant none at all! Cotton prices are higher than ever, but you can't git it to New Orleans to export it. Shoot, the Yankees would steal it if you tried!"

"Why did you plant any this year, Granddaddy?"

"Money. I figure to store it. If we win the war, prices in England will be sky-high. Then I'll sell it." He paused for a minute and got very serious. "Do you think we'll win the war, boy?"

"Can't say, but I wouldn't bet on it."

"It's as bad as all that?"

"Gittin' that way," Rance admitted. He told his grandfather about how much of Lee's army was barefoot and their uniforms were barely hanging on their bodies. Rance told him of a visiting British colonel who pointed this out to Robert E. Lee, and asked: "What about the tattered uniforms on the backs of your men?"

"That doesn't matter," Lee responded, "because the enemy never sees their backs."

Grover and his grandson shared a laugh, and then the colonel grew reflective. "But it does matter, Granddaddy. Or at least it will when winter comes."

The patriarch frowned. "We ain't doin' so good here neither, Rance. There ain't no coffee, sugar, or salt. We can't preserve meat like we once could, not without no salt. New clothes is hard to get. So's cloth. Thar ain't no more shoes neither because you can't make shoes without thick cobbler's thread. It's especially tough on the childins, 'cause they outgrow everything so dang fast! And if a plow breaks, that's it. There ain't no replacement parts. That goes for a whole lot of stuff, includin' wagons. Somethin' breaks, that's it. The railroad trains don't hardly run at all no more. And the poor whites are really sufferin'. With the men folk off to war, the women and childins left behind just can't do all of the work by themselves — 'pecially plowin' and harvestin'. And nobody got no medicine! And the darkies are restless. Not so much the older ones. But the younger ones. I think they'd like to try out this freedom thing they keep hearin' 'bout."

"You don't think they'll rebel, do you, Grandpa?" said a suddenly concerned Liebert. He thought of Haiti.

"Naw. Why should they? They ain't stupid. The Yankees want 'em to, 'cause it'd make their jobs a whole lot easier, but they ain't stupid. If they rose up, the Mississippi State Troops and maybe even regular Confederate boys would come down here lickkidy split and hang every last one of them. Women and younguns too, most likely. They don't have guns, wouldn't know what to do with 'em if they did, and pitchforks ain't much use 'gainst a musket or a six-shooter. No." He paused and pointed his walking stick toward the southwest. "But 40 or so miles over yonder is the Yankee army. They ain't gonna do nothin' 'til Grant gits closer to Vicksburg. But he probably will. And when he goes, they'll sweep through here like a tornado. Most of the young darkies will go with them, and Fusilier and De La Teneria will be crippled plantations, if they ain't burned to the ground!"

Rance remained silent, so Grover continued. "They'll take all the young male darkies, rape all the purty young womens, 'nd steal all the horses, mules, beef cattle, dairy cattle, pigs, and chickens. They'll drink all the liquor and steal anythin' they figger they can sell. They'll have thairselves a big ol' time! If they burn the corn bins, I won't have nuthin' to feed them that remains. I'd git ready for that day by makin' heeps of jerky, but I ain't got no salt and can't get none. And you can't make jerky without salt. Blast them Yankees for their cowardly blockade."

Rance felt a shiver go through his body. He never heard his grandfather talk so negatively before. After a long pause, the younger Liebert said: "It's gonna git worse before it gits better."

"Yeah. I know."

After a long while, Grover spoke again and changed the subject. "What you gonna do tomorrow?"

"Ride over to Windrow. Visit with Richard Glass a little bit."

"Yeah," Grover smiled. "You was always a little sweet on that little girl of his."

"Ain't gonna mention her to him. I'm goin' to see Glass because his boy asked me to. But I'm more than sweet on Sally. I love her and am goin' to marry her after the war."

Rance surprised himself. He didn't mean to say that. But when the words tumbled out and he heard himself say it out loud, it felt good.

"She's an actress, ain't she?" Grover wanted to know. "She ain't no virgin," he pointed out. That was important to a lot of men in 1863.

"Neither am I," Rance retorted.

Grover Liebert smirked. "Well, if it don't bother you none, it don't bother me. Where is she now?"

"She's in Washington, D.C."

"Washington? Is she workin' for the Yankees?" asked the startled grandfather, as if he had just seen a coiled rattlesnake two feet from his rocking chair.

"Naw. She's workin' for me."

"In Washington, D.C.?" When Rance didn't respond, he said: "You ain't no 'special advisor' to Jeff Davis, are you, boy?"

"No, Granddaddy, I ain't."

"What do you do?" Grover asked.

Rance took a deep breath and said: "I run the Confederate Secret Service."

Grover's eyes widened. "I didn't know we had a Secret Service."

Rance smiled. "Good! You ain't supposed to know. The fewer people who know, the better. Don't tell nobody. Not even Grandma."

Grover nodded and Rance continued. "I run whole networks of spies, the whole shootin' match from Washington to New Orleans. That's why Colonel Davis made me give up command of the 12th. He asked me to do it, so I did it. I work directly for the president. I can't tell you everything, but me and my people have, as President Davis said, 'materially contributed to the success of Southern arms.' Shoot, Boss, I spend as much time behind enemy lines as I do in Richmond."

Grover Liebert stared at his grandson. Finally he asked: "So you doin' good at it?"

"I reckon so," Rance admitted. "The Yankees have got us outnumbered so bad, they ain't even careful half the time. Lincoln set up a spy network in Richmond. We got inside it and crushed it, kinda like the way you'd crush an empty tin can when you step on it. Now half the information they git, they git from me. And it ain't exactly right!"

The elder Liebert laughed. "And what about them Yankee spies you found out about in Richmond?"

"We got a few of 'em rottin' in prison. We used most of 'em for fertilizer and relieved ourselves on their graves."

Grover Liebert laughed out loud and slapped his leg. This conversation was acting like a tonic on him. "That's what I like to hear! Kill as many of them people as you can! Do it slow, if there's time! And cripple the rest!" Mercy was not exactly Grover's dominant characteristic.

After a long while, Grover concluded the conversation by declaring: "I'm proud of you, boy."

That moment was one of the high points of Rance Liebert's life. The following day, he visited Windrow, which was even more run down than Fusilier. The next day, he saddled up to head north, where he would meet with the commander of the army at Vicksburg. Then he would spend a few days in Yankee-occupied Memphis and Nashville, before visiting cavalry Generals Nathan Bedford Forrest, Earl Van Dorn, and John Hunt Morgan, if he could find them, and finally Braxton Bragg, the commander of the Army of Tennessee. Before he left, he reached into his saddlebags and gave Grover Liebert two three-pound bags of real coffee. The old man beamed at this unexpected windfall. "It ain't exactly what I'm used to!" he declared. He couldn't stop smiling until Rance was gone.

Rance embraced his parents, Elizabeth Liebert, and finally Grover, and rode off toward the war.

—————

When he finally got back to Washington, weeks had elapsed since his last visit. Guinevere threw her arms around him and hugged him like she would never let him go. But that night at their apartment, it was definitely Sally who showed up.

She was unusually quiet over supper. Afterwards, she asked: "Did you mean what you said a few weeks ago? Do you really want to marry me?"

"Yes," he replied, flatly.

"Are you sure 'bout that?" She asked, with a half-smile.

"Absolutely sure. I missed you more over the last few months than I thought it was possible to miss someone."

She smiled sweetly. (She had a disarming "little girl" smile and she knew how and when to use it.) He had talked that way before, but she wanted confirmation he meant it and still felt the same. Now she had that verification. She needed it for what she knew would have to be discussed. She thought of the letter she had received today.

"But you don't want to get married until after the war?"

"Well … I think it would be best to wait. Don't you?" he asked.

"I guess." She frowned. "And you still don't want to have marital relations until then?" She asked. Although sometimes she felt guilty about it, she enjoyed sex and missed it. Quite a lot. And she was perfectly willing to have "marital relations" before marriage.

"It's not that I don't want to. It's difficult for me to keep my hands off you, but I think I should try."

"Why?" She asked.

"It's about respect. I love you, and I don't want to treat you like a harlot."

"And honor?"

"And honor."

Guinevere thought about this for a few moments. She remembered reading history books at homeschool on the plantation, where she learned how moral codes and social mores changed over time. She felt perplexed she was living in 1863 and was in love with a man who would be perfectly comfortable in Puritan England, insofar as morality was concerned. And yet, she had her own sexual scars and mental cobwebs in her brain, and these floated to the top from time to time. Sally Mae felt guilty she had gone to bed with other men. And even after all that happened, she even felt a little guilty about being raped. Sometimes she was simply confused.

"What's bothering you, Sally?"

"I guess I'm just feeling insecure for some reason." She thought about the letter again. Is this the right time to bring it up? She wondered.

"You're a Confederate spy, operating in the heart of the enemy's capital, surrounded by tens of thousands of Lincoln's men, with very little support, and the slightest misstep could get you hanged," he declared. "Why would you possibly feel insecure?"

He smiled and squeezed her hand. He decided to remain silent and let her verbalize whatever it was that was bothering her.

She abandoned her resolve out and decided not to deal with the letter tonight, so she dodged. "Do you have other women … other than me?" She asked, even though she already knew the answer.

"No! I already told you I didn't."

"I mean I know you're in a lot of different cities … and you must have plenty of opportunities …"

"No doubt about that. We seem to be living in a world that's spiraling downhill. And my business is deception," he added. "But not to you. I couldn't …" He stopped. "I just couldn't."

She realized at that moment why he and people like Jefferson Davis, Robert E. Lee, and Bedford Forrest got along so well. Their moral compasses pointed the same direction. He could forgive her past indiscretions as long as she didn't bring them up; but, if he ever committed one, he would not forgive himself.

It's just not the right time, she decided. It will have to be dealt with soon, but not tonight. She pushed the thought of the letter out of her mind and kissed him gently, tenderly, on the lips. "I love you, Rance Liebert."

"I love you too, Sally Mae Guinevere Glass Spring."

<hr />

As Grover foresaw, the Yankees finally advanced northeast from Natchez, in what was more a raid and a diversion in favor of Grant than anything else. But he did not foreseen what happened next. A detachment of eleven bluecoat cavalrymen reigned up in front of Fusilier.

"Good morning, you pile of Rebel dung!" The major exclaimed.

"You don't talk that way in front of Miss Elizabeth," Jonathan demanded.

"Shut up, boy!" He shouted. Without further ado, the officer drew his revolver and shot him.

"Jonathan!" Elizabeth screamed. She ran over to him and began to examine his wound. Fortunately, it was in the shoulder.

"Stupid old slave!" He sneared, and added: "I'll talk to this ugly old crone any way I want to!" His men, who had obviously been drinking, laughed and snickered.

"White trash," Elizabeth said aloud.

The major ignored her. "Now you, you old Rebel turd," he yelled at Grover, "pack whatever valuables you want to keep. We're going to burn this place to the ground in 10 minutes!"

For the last time, Grover looked across the estate he named Fusilier. The large barn was already on fire, as was the wash house, the stables, the overseer's house, part of the slave quarters, and several outbuildings. Everything to which he had devoted his life was going up in flames and smoke, and he was far too old to start over.

"Yes, sir," he said dejectedly to the major.

The boys in blue roared with laughter. "That feeble, old planter ain't so powerful or high and mighty now, is he?" The major laughed.

The Yankees had a plan. Given only 10 minutes, the ridiculous old man would undoubtedly retrieve only his most valuable possessions: gold coins, money, jewelry, and the like. As soon as he came out, they

The Retribution Conspiracy

would rob him at gunpoint. This way they wouldn't have to waste time searching the house. Also, in a search, they might miss a secret hiding place. This way they would be sure to get the most valuable items. To Elizabeth, however, the most valuable item was Jonathan. She was immediately on her knees beside him, ripping off pieces of her petticoat, and using them to stop the flow of blood. "Git the family Bible!" She shouted at her husband as he went inside the Big House for the last time.

Grover realized at once what the Yankees were planning. He looked around the great hall and wiped away a tear of remorse. "Forgive me, Lord," were his last words. Then he pushed all thought of the divinity out of his mind. It was replaced with fury and hate. His face contorted with rage. The infamous Grover Liebert temper took over and then spun out of control, and he made no effort to check it.

He didn't need 10 minutes to fetch his most valuable possessions, of which he needed only three: a Colt Dragoon, a Navy Six revolver, and a shotgun. He loaded the first barrel with bear ball, the second with "buck and ball."[31]

The Yankees were dismounted when Grover reappeared. They did not expect him to return for at least 10 minutes and were chatting, joking among themselves, and passing around a bottle. Nobody paid the slightest attention to the pathetic old man who had just gone into the house. But adrenaline caused Grover to move with the speed of youth that he no longer possessed. The major was the first to see him. His eyes got wide. The old man was on the porch, aiming the shotgun at him. He was not able to speak before Grover pulled the trigger. A bear ball tore through his abdomen, severed his spine, and blew out his back. The officer fell down in agony and was soon choking on his own blood. (A merciful man would have loaded both barrels with buck and ball, or aimed at his heart, but Grover had no desire to be merciful. He wanted the major to suffer before he died.)

A split second later, Grover fired the second barrel into the first sergeant's groin. He screamed in pain as he looked at the mass of bloody pulp that, one minute before, were the testicles he was so proud of the other day, when he and his men had raped that pretty slave girl. He didn't even notice the buckshot in his legs. As he fell to the ground, he wondered where his penis was.

---

31 The projectiles were classified according to the animal they were designed to kill. The ball was designed to kill a bear and today is called a "bear ball." Buck, which is today called "buck shot," was designed to kill a deer.

"God, help me! Help me!" The formerly arrogant major cried as he vomited up masses of blood. But in the bedlam, nobody even noticed him. The permanent darkness closed in on him a half an hour later, and he died in torment.

"Grover, no!" Elizabeth screamed.

Grover ignored her. He dropped the shotgun and drew his first revolver. The other Yankees were not ready for this, so they did not go for their guns until it was too late for two of them. Liebert no longer chose the location of his shots, as he had for the major and the first sergeant. There was no time for that. He merely fired for center of mass. And he was good at it.

The first Yankee private he shot caught a bullet near the heart. He immediately went into shock and died several minutes later without regaining consciousness. The second caught a bullet in the heart, so he was dead before he hit the ground.

Then the quickest Yankee fired his revolver and a bullet struck Grover in the right lung. A bright crimson stain appeared on his white shirt. He took a step back but still had enough hate in him to fire another bullet, but now his aim was unsteady. He fired at a young private's chest, but the bullet tore into his right arm, shattering the bone. He would survive, but the arm would not. The young man — a farmer from Illinois — would never farm again.

In the next couple of seconds, four Yankees fired at Grover. One missed, but three more bright red holes appeared in Grover's chest. By main effort, he righted himself, took a final breath, fired wildly, fell backward, and expired. His last bullet hit no one.

"Grover!" His wife screamed in terror.

Except for Elizabeth's sobs, there was silence all around.

"You d_____ Yankees!" She cried, and scrambled for the Colt. As far as is known, that was the only time in her life she cursed.

"No, don't Miss Elizabeth!" Jonathan shouted.

"No, ma'am, no!" The Yankees yelled. They did not want to kill a woman. But she ignored them all. She grabbed the revolver, pulled back the hammer, and tried to aim. This time the Yankees fired in self-defense. Elizabeth Liebert survived her husband of sixty years by less than a minute. Later, it occurred to them that this might have been suicide.

Jonathan crawled over to her as tears ran down his face. "She was the kindest, gentlest, most Christian woman I ever knowed," he sobbed. "And she ain't never fired a gun or hurt a flea in her whole life."

He looked at a Union lieutenant who was coming up onto the porch. "I sho' hopes you Yankees is proud of yo'selves," he sobbed. The young officer felt a rush of shame, but it did not overwhelm his sense of self-preservation.

"Now, boy, don't go for that revolver," he warned, cocking the pistol in his hand. "Don't do anything stupid."

"I ain't, sur," Jonathan responded as he placed Miss Elizabeth's lifeless head in his lap and stroked her hair. His shoulder throbbed. "I don't even know how to shoot. But you white trash better be glad I can't call down no fire from heaven. There sho' wouldn't be much left of you if'n I could."

Rance and Guinevere had a nice supper at their shared apartment in Washington, D.C. Afterward, they sat on the couch, and she noticed that he was quieter than usual. (Guinevere was very perceptive; Sally less so.) She held his hand and asked, "What's wrong?"

The moment that he had been dreading was here. "There's no way to sugarcoat this," he muttered.

"You're scaring me, Rance."

"Get hold on yourself."

"All right …"

"Windrow's gone. The Yankees burned it."

A look of horror flashed across her face and her hands flew up to cover her mouth. "No! What happened to my mother and father?"

"I don't know. I sent Dan down there to find out and to assess the damage, along with a note asking General Van Dorn or Bedford Forrest to provide him with a cavalry escort, but I don't expect to hear from him for some time."

"What else did they burn? Did they burn the slave cabins, the stables, or …"

"We don't know very much. But Fusilier has been destroyed, and Grover and Grandmother have been murdered."

"Oh!" She cried and recoiled in horror.

"De La Teneria has been burned, too, and so has Billy's plantation. Rainbow was burned to the ground. Even the church."

She sobbed.

"Oddly enough, they didn't burn Brierfield."

"Jeff Davis' home? Why would they spare it?"

"Well, they didn't, exactly. They got to Davis Bend and saw two houses: Jeff Davis' modest home and Joseph Davis' huge, palatial mansion, Hurricane. Apparently, they looked at Hurricane and said 'This must be the home of the president of the Confederacy.' So they burned it. They didn't bother to burn Brierfield, although they did loot it — and the library as well."[32]

"Nobody told them that Brierfield was the president's home?" Sally asked.

"Nobody was there at the time."

"What about the slaves?"

"I don't know," he confessed. "I guess everybody had already headed for the hills."

"Didn't the army defend it?"

"No. His home had no military value, so the president ordered them not to defend it. He declared 'the Confederate Army does not do personal favors for its commander-in-chief.' Now isn't that just like Jefferson Davis. Always thinkin' of others. Never thinking about himself."

"My goodness. Isn't that something? They burn my home but not Jeff Davis'!"

"You know ..." he said, changing the subject. "Colonel Davis took his most trusted slaves to Richmond with him. One of them set fire to the White House and ran away."

"Really?"

"Yep. It was Henry, his butler. Fortunately for everybody, he didn't do a very good job of it, and the fire went out after he skedaddled. They only found it later."

"Did they catch him?"

"No," Rance said. "Luckily for him, he was a better fugitive than he was an arsonist. He's somewhere up North now, giving lectures for money."

She grimaced. "I thought the Davises were good to their slaves."

"They are. But I guess he wanted freedom. A gilded cage is still a cage," he observed, and then added reflectively: "I wonder how many

---

32 Brierfield survived another 68 years. It was destroyed in an accidental fire in 1931. The library is still standing, but it is so dilapidated and so unsafe that I would advise against going inside it. Davis Bend, incidentally, is now Davis Island. One has to cross a channel of the Mississippi River to get there. Crops are no longer produced there, and it has been leased by a hunting club. You can get there by boat, but watch out for snakes.

The Retribution Conspiracy

slaves Fusilier will have when we get back." He paused a moment and added: "Sometimes I wonder if we really know our darkies."

"And Windrow?" She added. "Oh, God, Rance," she gasped, "what will it be like when we get home? Will things ever be the same?"

He gently rubbed her cheek with his hand and didn't say a word. She lay her head on his shoulder. She instinctively knew that, if he were pressed to answer her question, the answer would be "No."

That night, Sally Mae Glass took off her dress but, for the first time, didn't bother to change into her pajamas. She crawled into bed in her underwear (which extended to her ankles anyway) and put her head on Liebert's shoulder, but couldn't go to sleep. She was too sad to cry.

"I hope Mother and Father are all right," she whispered.

"Me, too."

"I'm going to miss my dolls and all of the other things I left in Mississippi. I wish I had carried them with me," she said, just before he fell sleep.

She tossed and turned all night. The next morning she prepared breakfast but didn't eat any. Still obviously depressed, she didn't even get dressed at first. She just sat there at the kitchen table, drinking coffee in her underwear. She looked worse than he had ever seen her.

"I didn't hate the Yankees before last night," she said quietly. "I'm trying to now. But I just can't quite bring myself to do it."

"Don't," he cautioned. "At least, don't hate all of them. I really don't blame the individual soldiers, except those who are thugs. I know that, left alone, most of them wouldn't have anything to do with behavior of this sort. Of course, they've got their white trash element, just like we do."

Sally Mae frowned. She thought of Bushrod Brown, Josiah Hawks, and Goober Norquist.

"Even that element wouldn't be behaving like this if their generals did their duty and kept them under control," Rance thought out loud. "General Grierson's men never behaved like that, because they know their general would come down on them like white on bread if they tried. General Buell wouldn't stand for it, either. No," he reflected, "I think it's part of a deliberate policy of terror, tacitly endorsed by the Federal government in Washington."

Her eyes widened. "And they'll do anything to win the war?" She asked.

"I reckon so," he allowed.

"Do you think this policy comes from Lincoln?"

"I don't know. It may not go that high. I know Sherman would do practically anything, including personally raping chickens, if he thought it would gain him an advantage. I'm not so sure about Grant. He's bad, but not as evil as Sherman. Stanton would absolutely commit any kind of vile act — whether he had to or not. Lincoln? I'm of two minds about Lincoln. I know he often says one thing and acts the opposite way. We'll have to wait and see. If this sort of thing continues or becomes more widespread, we'll know he is at least going along with it."

"He knows," Guinevere declared. "He spends half his time in the Telegraph Office at the War Department and meets with various commanders every day. He couldn't help but know."

"Then we can expect more of this type of behavior in the future," the colonel predicted.

"Well, if he condones that kind of barbarism, he doesn't deserve to live!" She retorted sharply. "And to think I once liked that man!"

"It's war, Sally Mae," Rance responded. "He didn't burn Windrow himself. Don't take it personally."

Guinevere frowned. "The devil I won't! That was my home!" To her, Abraham Lincoln might as well have entered Windrow with a can of kerosene and a box of matches and, with malice aforethought, set the fire himself.

Rance Liebert did not know how to answer that, so he said nothing and the conversation lagged. Both of the Southerners were lost in their own thoughts.

─◦ CHAPTER XX ◦─
THE OHIO RAID

Emotionally, Rance Liebert had a tough couple of weeks. He was looking forward to a nice, quiet evening at home with Sally Mae in their rooms in Washington. What he got was by no means what he expected.

The meal was great. She prepared a steak for him. In Richmond, he usually ate in the mess at Secret Service Headquarters, where the food was neither wonderful nor plentiful. His troops got the same food as did General Lee's men, which wasn't much and wasn't good. Here in Washington, he enjoyed the mashed potatoes with real butter and asparagus. Sally was never a cook to compare with Jonathan's wife, Lora, back on the plantation, but then cooking was all Lora had to do. Guinevere had a full-time job as an actress and, if she wanted to take most of her day off and arrange a real home cooked meal for him, he appreciated it. She certainly did the best she could, and the meal was more than adequate.

She cheated on the apple pie. She bought it from a bakery and pretended to have made it. He suspected as much but kept quiet. The truth was that she recalled very little about how to make an apple pie. She was an actress, after all, so she rarely ate desserts. Her latest attempt to do so was lying on the ground in the bottom of the adjacent alley.[33] Her mother's cook had tried to teach her how to do it back at Windrow, but Sally was immune to that instruction.

Rance noticed she was quieter than usual during supper, but she drank more than her usual quota of wine. Afterward, he asked if he could help her with the dishes.

"Oh, let's just leave them for now," she said.

"All right. How 'bout a game of chess," he suggested.

"No. I don't much feel like it," she replied. "Not right now."

"Better take me up on it," he grinned. "I'm feeling fat and sluggish."

---

33 Garbage incinerators were not introduced in the United States until 1885. Until then, people tossed their garbage into alleys and into the streets. This explains why there were so many rodents and roaches in Washington who were not members of Congress. Even the White House was infested with roaches. (People in those days did not associate diseases such as typhoid with garbage or decaying animal carcasses.) New York City was an exception. It began systematically dumping garbage into the East River in 1872.

He had no idea this was what she was going for. She wanted him in a good, relaxed mood, and she succeeded splendidly.

"Let's sit on the couch for a while," Guinevere suggested.

"Fine."

After he sat down, she didn't put her head on his shoulder, as she usually did. Instead she said: "Rance, there's something I have to tell you."

"What is it?"

"You may not want me when you find out," she declared, working up her courage.

"Of course I will. What is it?"

"I love you more than anything in the world! You must believe that!"

"That's the big secret?"

"No!" She paused, working up her courage. A tear ran down her cheek. "Do you remember the night we talked … about my Bad Girl phase?"

"Yes. And I remember we agreed never to discuss it again."

"We have to … because … because … I had a baby out of wedlock three years ago!" There! I said it, she thought. Tears poured down her face and she tried to suppress a sob but didn't quite make it.

Wow! he thought and simply froze.

"She was in an orphanage here in Washington," Guinevere said. "I visit her every two weeks or so. She was up for adoption, but that business is slow during the war, and I never thought … I never thought … Anyway, I got a letter a few weeks ago. Some people wanted to adopt her. I went to sign the papers. I thought I could give her up, but I couldn't. I simply couldn't. I sat there, staring at the papers, and the head of the adoption agency and her lawyer kept badgering me to sign, and part of me wanted to, because I didn't want to risk losing you, but I just couldn't. Part of me just couldn't give her up. So they cursed at me and gave me 24 hours to collect my daughter and 'get her the ____ out of here.' So now I have a daughter. I'm in the process of hiring a permanent nanny now," she added, almost as an afterthought.

He said nothing. The silence was terrible. She would almost rather he scream at her, berate her, throw a lamp at the wall — anything but this.

"Rance, say something!" She implored after what seemed like several minutes.

He rubbed his forehead and remained silent for several more mo-

The Retribution Conspiracy

ments. He was angry. Maybe she hadn't lied to him exactly, but he definitely felt misled. They had talked about her promiscuous phase and she certainly did not mentioned this. He even commented about how fortunate she was not to have had an illegitimate child — and she hadn't said anything. He felt Grover's temper rising within him. He trusted her. How could he ever trust her again? Rance Liebert felt betrayed. And while nineteenth century Southern gentlemen raised the orphans of other men, and often made excellent parents, they never raised their bastards. It simply wasn't done. The bourbon code of honor was very specific about this. "What would you have me say?" He finally asked.

"I don't know! Tell me what you think!"

He thought for a moment. "I think I don't want to raise somebody else's bastard," he said evenly. "I've got to have time to consider this." He stood up, as if to leave.

"Where are you going?" She asked.

"I dunno," he replied. "Take a walk, I guess. I've got to clear my head. I need time to think." Despite the steak, he felt completely empty inside.

"All right," she said, dropping her eyes.

To have an illegitimate child in those days was considered a horrible thing. People who had "bastards" were ostracized, as were the children themselves. Decent people didn't even associate with them. She should have said something earlier, he thought. He felt completely deceived and let down. It hurt twice as much because this was the last place he expected to encounter such … deception.

"We've been courting for some time. You should have told me earlier," he said sharply. He vaguely wondered what else she was hiding.

She looked at the floor. *I didn't think it was necessary, she thought. I was going to give her up, and you would have never known anything about her. But when it came right down to it, I couldn't.* But the words wouldn't come. "I'm sorry!" Was all she said.

He walked to the door. She didn't move. She just sat there, feeling very vulnerable, as if she were a fragile goblet someone had dropped. She felt as if something had broken inside her.

He reached the door and turned the doorknob. Then he turned and asked: "Where is she now?"

"My place. I hired a babysitter …"

He nodded and opened the door.

Guinevere could not believe he was really leaving. "Rance, where are you going?" She called after him.

"I don't know. Out. I need some fresh air."

"Are you coming back?"

"Tonight?" He asked. "I doubt it."

"When will I see you again?

"I'll be in touch," he said.

"Rance, are we finished?" She sobbed. There was desperation in her voice.

"I don't know. Maybe. We'll see … I don't know much of anything right now," he said, and disappeared into the darkness.

———⊗⊗⊗———

That night, Guinevere returned to her apartment in a daze. She did not want to be alone, so she slept with her daughter. She was warned not to do this because children form habits very quickly, especially if it involved something they liked. But Mommie needed the physical contact, and it felt good when her child cuddled up against her.

Guinevere was too heartbroken to cry. Even as he was walking to the door, she didn't believe he would walk out. Men are so much luckier than women, she thought. If they have an illegitimate child, they can just walk away. But not women. They have to bare all the consequences. She was surprised when he walked out, but he did not shut the door completely, so to speak. It occurred to her she didn't know what she had expected. She had hoped he would be more understanding, but it also occurred to her most men would have broken up with her on the spot. At least he didn't do that.

Guinevere Spring was a strong woman. She suffered a blow, true enough, but it did not kill her. It left her weakened but, lying there in the darkness, she felt her strength gradually returning. What was it that German philosopher said? What does not destroy us makes us stronger.[34] Somewhere deep in the night, she solved the problem. I'll simply win him back, she decided. She knew she would have a chance. Many men were emotional cowards and would simply send her a farewell letter, breaking off their relationship or just never call on her again. But this did not apply to Rance Liebert. She knew she would see him again, face to face. That, too, was part of his understanding of the code of honor. And, of course, there was that Secret Service thing. Rance might not need her at this precise moment, but Colonel Liebert did, and in Rance's eyes, he outranked Rance by a wide margin. He would have to maintain some sort of relationship with her. And, if she had a toehold,

34 Friedrich Nietzsche

The Retribution Conspiracy

she told herself, she could work her way back. It might be a long, hard climb, but it would be worth it, and she felt she had reason to believe she would triumph in the end. To be fair, he was a very proper and conservative man — or at least part of him was — and she completely blindsided him. She could understand his reaction. By dawn, her confidence returned and the old Guinevere was back.

Sally Mae did not hear from him for two miserable days. Finally, she got a note, carried by a young courier. It read:

Dinner after the play? LaVere?
Owen Dickerson

She smiled. It did not escape her attention he used the Northern word "Dinner" here in the Union capital.

"I am to await a reply," the courier said.

"Tell him yes."

The courier nodded. As he turned to leave, she stopped him.

"No. Just tell him yes, that I'm looking forward to it."

"Yes, ma'am," he said, and turned to leave again.

"Wait!" She cried. It had occurred to her she might or might not be looking forward to it, depending on what he had to say. "Just tell him 'Yes, I'll be there.'"

"Yes, ma'am," the courier said, turning to go. He halfway expected her to call him back, but she did not.

For once in his life, Rance was not looking forward to an evening with Guinevere, mainly because he had no idea what he was going to say — or even what he wanted to say. But he didn't let his guard down or forget he was in an enemy capital. Making sure he was not being followed, he went into the city and paid a visit to the Surratt House, an inn/safe house for Confederate operatives. It also doubled as a post office for the Secret Service. Here, Liebert, a/k/a Owen Dickerson, received a message from "Pale Rose" (i.e., Jefferson Davis). It ordered him to return to Richmond immediately.

Rance scribbled a quick note to Guinevere, canceling their plans for the evening, and left at once. He stuck Davis' message in the envelope with hers. He thought it would be cruel just to cancel and disappear without any explanation. He didn't know what President Davis wanted, but he knew it was an emergency, or he wouldn't have contacted him this way, and now Guinevere knew it also. He wished he had time to at least say goodbye to her. Later, he wished he had taken the time, but he had no idea that he would be gone for months. He was in Richmond two evenings later and immediately went to the White House. Jefferson Davis was, as usual, still laboring well into the night, selflessly working for his people. The Secret Service chief was admitted right away.

"Rance, are you familiar with the Copperheads?" The President asked.

Liebert was aware of them, not familiar. "They are anti-war Northern Democrats who opposed Lincoln's tyranny," he responded. "And with considerable justification. Several of them have been arrested, their newspapers have been shut down, and their headquarters have been raided by U.S. cavalry units."

"How many newspapers has Lincoln shut down?" Davis wanted to know.

"About 300, as near as I can tell. Not all were Copperhead publications, however."

"And how many political opponents have the Republicans arrested?"

"I don't know exactly. Lincoln has suspended the right of *habeas corpus*. Due process no longer exists in the North, insofar as 'political crimes' are concerned. His political opponents are being arrested by the Army. We estimate that many more than 10,000 men and women are currently sitting in Lincoln's dungeons."[35]

"How does Lincoln justify that?" Davis asked.

"He doesn't. As far as I know, he has never said a word about it publicly. The Radical Republicans, on the other hand, openly boast that his actions are noble. They say he is violating the Constitution in order to save it."

Jefferson Davis responded with a short, humorless laugh. "That's totally illogical. It's like saying we should rape more nuns in order to advance the cause of virginity."

Rance chuckled. "Well, if you suppress enough newspapers, any-

---

35 About 32,000 Northern political opponents were arrested by Lincoln's supporters during the war. They were denied their Constitutional rights and were held without trial and many without charges. Most were released after a few weeks, i.e., the administration "sent them a message." Some, however, died in prison. Ironically, once of the prisoners Francis Key Howard, the grandson of Francis Scott Key, spent 14 months in Fort McHenry, Baltimore, Maryland. His grandfather watched the British bombardment of that fort and was inspired to write *The Star Spangled Banner*.

thing in the world can happen without people noticing. Did you know that, in 1861, Lincoln even signed an arrest warrant for Chief Justice Taney?" Liebert asked.

"Really? I heard that rumor."

"Apparently it is true. Lincoln was angry because the chief justice objected to his suspension of the right of *habeas corpus*. The only reason Taney was not arrested was because Lincoln could not find a single Federal marshal who would serve the warrant."

"What happened then?" The Southern president asked.

"Taney got the message. He went silent, and Lincoln did not push the matter. I suspect he cooled down and realized he would be courting yet another problem he did not need. Judge Taney was 84 years old at the time and not in good health. He would have died in one of those prisons. And arresting the chief justice of the United States Supreme Court would be viewed as extremely high-handed, even for Lincoln."

Davis shook his head. "Well, I hope you're wrong about not enough people in the North noticing. There are people in Ohio, Indiana, and Illinois who would overthrow their oppressors. There have been incidents of Union sentries being killed in those states, and several warehouses and depots have mysteriously burned to the ground." Davis paused. "General Morgan thinks they are ready to openly rebel."

He was referring to Brigadier General John Hunt Morgan, a charismatic Kentucky cavalry leader currently serving with Braxton Bragg's Army of Tennessee. Colonel Liebert said nothing so Davis pressed him. "What do you think, Rance?"

"Confidentially, I think General Morgan is letting his enthusiasm overshadow his good judgment. I have tried to avoid dealing with the Copperheads. They have been thoroughly infiltrated by Lincoln's spies, so no Copperhead Rebellion can succeed without direct Southern military intervention. Even then, it is problematic. Their leaders blow hot and cold and, in my opinion, are unreliable and cannot be counted upon."

"General Morgan is prepared to provide what you are pleased to call 'direct Southern military intervention.' I think it might work. Secretary Seddon agrees. Secretary Benjamin is convinced it will work."

He was referring to Secretary of State Judah Benjamin, who for months was trying to gain control of the Secret Service. Although Rance considered him very intelligent, he did not trust his judgment on intelligence matters and did not look upon him as a friend.

"General Lee has won a brilliant victory at Chancellorsville. He is preparing to invade the North with 70,000 men. Grant is besieging Vicksburg. What do you think we should do?" Davis asked.

Rance knew his president well enough to know that this was an impossible question. He wanted Liebert to reinforce his own opinion. He was not interested in opposing opinions, even from an old friend.

Also, Rance knew the numbers. *At Jackson, Mississippi, Joseph E. Johnston commands an army of more than 30,000 men, he thought. General Pemberton had an army of 35,000, but following several defeats probably has fewer than 30,000 left, and they are surrounded in Vicksburg. Grant has more than 70,000 men, with new regiments joining his army almost every day. With Johnston in command, there is no way his army is going to rescue that garrison. Vicksburg is doomed.*

"Well," Liebert finally said, "as I see it, you have two choices. Let Lee invade the North, or transfer Lee to the West, with orders to relieve Vicksburg. Either way, we have to put our faith in Robert E. Lee."

"We have already chosen the first alternative," Davis announced. "Secretary Benjamin believes a major military victory in Northern territory would result in England and France entering the war on the side of the South. We believe a Copperhead uprising would create a major diversion in favor of General Lee. That is what General Morgan is going to try to create. You are to go with him and assist him in every way possible."

Liebert's face registered shock and astonishment. Davis stood up. It was clearly time for Rance to go. But he remained seated and did not leave. Instead he said: "I believe the time for a diplomatic solution to our problem has passed. Economically, it is in the best interest of Great Britain to join us. But that chance was lost when Lincoln issued the Emancipation Proclamation. By proposing to abolish slavery, he seized the moral high ground, insofar as the British working class is concerned. They will not fight for the cause of preserving slavery. The British ruling class knows this, so they will not go too far. And, to them, declaring war on the United States would be going too far." The colonel paused. He noticed a look of distaste on the president's face. "No, sir," the colonel declared. "We now have only two chances to win the war: by military means or a political solution with the North."

"A political solution is impossible," Davis stated categorically. "Lincoln will not negotiate unless the South agrees to return to the Union. And that is unthinkable. Do you agree?"

This question was clearly a challenge, but for Liebert it was an easy one. "Of course I agree," he declared. "For now, a political solution is

The Retribution Conspiracy

off the table."

"I suppose you're right," Davis conceded, backing down slightly. "Political circumstances do change. But for now, we must attempt to exercise the military option." He drew himself up to his full height. "I want you to join General Morgan. He is going to launch a raid into Indiana and Ohio. Give him every assistance you can."

Grover Liebert would have cut loose with a profane tirade at this point. Although his Secret Service apparatus functioned extremely well in the East, Liebert's organization did not work as efficiently in the West. Here the distances were too great, courier routes were less certain and the couriers did not report to a central location such as the Market Street headquarters. The agents or couriers had to report instead to individual generals. And while Robert E. Lee learned to trust Secret Service reports, some of the Western generals, such as Braxton Bragg and Joseph E. Johnston, did not. Also, it was harder to find some of the key generals. Men such as Morgan, Van Dorn, Joe Wheeler, and Forrest galloped all over the map. No one knew where they might be at any one time. Often, by the time they returned to base, the information had "spoiled;" other times it was quite useful. Finally, codes were more difficult to replace. This was especially troublesome if they were compromised.

John Hunt Morgan was a highly successful raider who was much beloved in his native Kentucky. He couldn't wait to expel the Yankees from his home state. And there, to Rance, lay the rub. His plan was not well thought out. Not only did success depend on the Copperheads — survival of the command probably did as well. *And what am I doing here?* Rance Liebert wondered. He suspected Benjamin was behind that. He was sharp and devious, and he wanted control of the Secret Service, which he openly believed should be subordinate to the State Department. Rance suspected Benjamin convinced President Davis to send him on this raid in order to get rid of him.

The more Liebert learned about the proposed raid, the more uneasy he became. He suggested to General Morgan the Yankees could easily cut him off. What would he do if he couldn't get back across the Ohio, Liebert asked.

"Join General Lee in Pennsylvania," Morgan announced, grandly.

Rance Liebert was too dumbfounded to reply.

Morgan left Sparta, Tennessee, on June 11, with 2,500 men. The raid would last 46 days, and the raiders would ride more than 1,000 miles. "Thunderbolt" Morgan rode over much of Kentucky, capturing and paroling thousands of Yankees in isolated garrisons. Despite General Bragg's direct orders, however, he crossed the Ohio at Brandenburg on July 8, and pushed into the interior of Indiana.[36]

John Hunt Morgan caused a lot of panic, but his men lacked the discipline of Jeb Stuart's cavalry. They immediately began to loot, steal horses, and rob banks and other businesses. Not even the houses flying the single-star flag of the Knights of the Golden Circle — Copperheads — were spared. Morgan himself did not behave properly. He took $750 from a county treasury and accepted a $2,000 bribe (in greenbacks) from a Union businessman not to burn his flour mill. Meanwhile, he made the biggest mistake of the campaign. He could have turned west and seized Indianapolis, but he did not. Just outside the city was a prisoner-of-war camp that had 6,000 veteran Rebel infantrymen. Rather than that, Morgan turned east, into Ohio. The Indiana and Ohio militias, which were supposed to join the raiders, fought against them instead.

The Rebels bypassed Cincinnati on July 13 and headed northeast. On July 19, Morgan was trying to find a ford across the Ohio near Buffington Island when he was attacked by 3,000 Yankee cavalrymen, mounted infantrymen and militia. Morgan, who had only 1,000 men left, retreated to the northwest. Liebert, meanwhile, became good friends with Colonel Adam "Stovepipe" Johnson.

Before they left Tennessee, Liebert had visited Nathan Bedford Forrest's headquarters and told him he had grave reservations about this raid. Forrest knew Rance before the war, when the future "Wizard of the Saddle" was still a young man. In those days, Forrest was a traveling slave trader, and he sold Grover several field hands over the years. Bedford Forrest was the only slave trader Grover actually liked, so he let him spend the night at Fusilier on two or three occasions. As did everyone who met Grover, Forrest remembered him. The two men were a lot alike, so when Rance renewed their acquaintanceship Forrest greeted him like an old friend. When Liebert discussed the proposed Ohio Raid with Forrest, "the Wizard of the Saddle" recommended he attach himself to Johnson's regiment, as much as possible. "If everythin' goes wrong, you want to follow Johnson!" were his exact words.

"Stovepipe" Johnson was one of the boldest and bravest of the Reb-

---

36 As commander of the Army of Tennessee, Braxton Bragg was Morgan's commanding officer.

el officers. He fought Indians in Texas before joining Forrest's cavalry as a private in 1861. He became Forrest's chief of scouts by early 1862, but then joined Morgan and his Kentucky troops because they offered greater scope for advancement. He was a full colonel by 1863. Johnson got his nickname by forcing the evacuation of Newburgh, Indiana, the year before. It was defended by 2,000 militiamen and home guard troops. Johnson took a couple of stovepipes and mounted them to the running gear of a pair of abandoned wagons, making it appear at a distance that he had artillery. The Yankees hurriedly evacuated the town. It was the first Northern city captured by the Rebels. Johnson had only 12 men at the time.

Like Liebert, Johnson had grave doubts about the Ohio Raid. After Buffington Island, he decided to separate from Morgan and lead what was left of his command (350 men) to safety on his own. Liebert, who was looking for an opportunity to abandon the Morgan ship before it sank, fell in right beside him. They swam across the rain-swollen Ohio into the recently coined state of West Virginia and eventually made their way back to Rebel lines via back roads through the mountains several weeks later.[37]

Morgan, meanwhile, was decisively defeated at Salineville on July 26, and surrendered to the 9th [U.S.] Kentucky Cavalry near the village of East Liverpool, Ohio, that same afternoon.

Everything had changed when Rance Liebert finally arrived back in Richmond. When he left, people were optimistic and hopeful about the future. Now, after the death of Stonewall Jackson, the decisive defeat at Gettysburg, the surrender at Vicksburg, the loss of Morgan and his raiders, and the fall of Chattanooga, the entire South seemed darkened in gloom. Not even the sun seemed to shine so brightly. "I should have listened to you," Jefferson Davis told his old adjutant.

Rance stared at him. President Davis looked older. "I would have done the same thing," he lied. "You risked 2,500 cavalrymen against a chance of winning the war and achieving our independence. There are some risks you just have to take."

---

37 Stovepipe Johnson lost both eyes in a skirmish near Princeton, Kentucky, in August 1864. Totally blinded for the rest of his life, he refused to let his disability be a handicap. He founded and directed several successful businesses and founded the city of Marble Falls, Texas, in 1887. He died in 1922 at the age of 78. He was promoted to brigadier general about the time he was blinded.

"Thank you for that," Davis said, and stood up and shook Liebert's hand. *Rance has aged over the past four months*, the president thought. *He's a lot thinner. And I've never seen him with a beard before.*

"You're welcome, Mr. President. But I will tell you one thing."

"What's that?" Davis asked.

"I will never trust a Copperhead again, for the rest of my life, and I will not work with them."

Guinevere Spring waited for Rance Liebert for a few weeks and then decided maybe he wasn't going to contact her again. But she continued to wait. She still went to the occasional party, but only with a group. She tried to have fun — but she couldn't. She missed Rance, and at the very least, she needed closure. But no one seemed to know where the colonel was. He had simply vanished.

Between plays, she continued her work with the Confederate Secret Service, but her coded dispatches were now picked up by John Surratt — never by Rance. She considered making another trip to Richmond on some pretext, but decided it was best to wait on Stanton. She was even delighted one day when Julian Anderson showed up at her place.

"Julian!" She cried and took his arm. "Come in! Sit down!" The sergeant looked startled. She had never given him the time of day before. "Tell me what you've been up to. Would you like a drink?"

That's the dumbest question I ever heard, Anderson thought. "Yes ma'am" is what he said.

She poured him about a quarter of a glass of bourbon. He looked at it, disappointed.

"Would you like some water with that?"

"Oh, no ma'am," he said and downed the whiskey with one gulp. "May I have another?"

"Of course," she said. Guinevere smiled and poured him another. This time she filled the glass. Julian Anderson grinned.

Now she got down to business. "Have you seen Colonel Liebert lately?"

"No, ma'am. He seems to have disappeared off the face of the earth."

"Who's running the Secret Service in Richmond?"

"That would be John Spring. He's a lieutenant colonel now. Good man. But he ain't got the sand Rance Liebert had ... er, has."

She was startled to hear the word "had" (past tense) in connection with Rance. "You don't think anything has happened to him, do you?"

The Retribution Conspiracy

"I couldn't say. He went west. And everything's turned to _____ in the West." He immediately realized his mistake — swearing in front of a lady was against Colonel Liebert's rules of conduct, and any disrespect toward Guinevere could get your fingers blown off. "Beggin' your pardon, ma'am," he added quickly.

"That's okay, Anderson, eh, Julian," she replied. She was disappointed he didn't know anything. She just hoped he wasn't with Morgan, trapped in Vicksburg, surrounded at Port Hudson, or locked in some Yankee prison — or in a shallow, unmarked grave somewhere.

Just when she was about to give up hope, she received Rance's note, asking her to meet him in the LaVere restaurant after her last performance. Uncharacteristically, Guinevere rushed and got there as quickly as she could. The accomplished actress almost didn't recognize him at first and was astonished by his appearance. He took a couple of steps toward her and she noticed he limped. He reached out for her hands. He wasn't going to hug her, but she impulsively wrapped her arms around his neck; even though he tried to hide it, she noticed that he grimaced and involuntarily drew back in pain. "Where have you been?" She asked.

"Southern Maryland, Virginia, North Carolina, Georgia, Tennessee, Kentucky, Indiana, Ohio, West Virginia, then back to Virginia, Kentucky, Tennessee, Georgia, North Carolina, Virginia, southern Maryland, and then here." He tried to smile, but he looked tired.

She looked puzzled. "Did you have a good trip ..."

"I was with Morgan."

"Morgan!" She recoiled in horror. "The newspapers and the Yankee generals said he and his command were totally wiped out! Everyone was killed or captured."

"No," Rance said. "We lost all of the wagons and artillery, but only 85 percent of the men."

She had a million questions, but he cut her short. "Sweetheart, I'm here only for a few days, and I intend to spend a good part of my time with you. I know you've got a lot of questions, but I don't want to have to think that hard right now. Not tonight. Tonight, I'm exhausted. Tonight I just want to be with you, if you want to be with me."

Guinevere/Sally was glad he wanted to spend time with her, at least. And he was willing to talk. They would work out the rest of it later — she hoped. "Yes, I do want to be with you" was all she said. But she thought: "There's somebody I want you to meet."

She noticed he didn't eat much of his steak. "Aren't you hungry?" She asked.

"Stomach shrank," he smiled and laughed. "Weren't much to eat where I've been." They were constantly on the run from bluecoat cavalry, which gave them no time to forage for food.

He finished and ordered a paper bag and six raw eggs and some butter and bacon because "there won't be any food in our place."

When they got there, he went immediately to bed. She undressed and crawled in with him.

"Why are you sleeping in your underwear?" He asked her. "Not that I'm complaining," he added quickly.

"Intimacy," she replied. "When I'm like this, I feel more intimate with you." She paused. "After all, you're the only man who's seen me in my underwear in more than two years." *And quite possibly the only man who ever will in the future,* she thought — *at least I hope so.* But she didn't say that out loud. Not yet. Guinevere Spring was a woman who knew how to wait.

He patted her on the back and dropped off to sleep immediately.

The Retribution Conspiracy

CHAPTER XXI

HE CAN'T AFFORD TO LOSE CHICAGO

"**D**o you feel better this morning?" Guinevere asked over her cup of coffee.

"Much," he declared. "Sorry if I was so difficult last night."

"You weren't," she said, "but I'm glad to have you back. What is that bandage on your arm?"

"Grazed by a Yankee bullet. Nothing serious," he added hastily, when he saw the look of horror flash across her face. "Just cut through a couple of layers of baby fat."

"And you were limping. Did they shoot you in the leg, also?"

"Naw. We'd been riding for two straight days when my horse collapsed and landed on it. I had to go buy a new horse from a greedy farmer. And a sorry nag it was, too. Fortunately, I brought along a whole wad of counterfeit greenbacks, and ridin' her sure beat walkin' all the way back to Tennessee."

She smiled. But now she didn't know what to say. He wolfed down his steak and eggs and part of hers. He broke the ice and asked her about her latest play. He already knew where that was going to go. Because of the tension between them, she started slower than usual. But once she got going, she was hard to stop. When she got on a roll, Guinevere just talked and talked and talked — basically about nothing. Rance didn't care. She enjoyed it, and that was enough for him. Besides, for now he didn't want to deal with the other issue.

The Morgan Raid gave Rance time to think. Camping out, sleeping out in the open air, and staring up at the stars, he had time to ponder their situation but had not really drawn any conclusions. He still had a soft spot in his heart for Sally Mae, that was clear, and he missed her. The friendship which dated back to her childhood was still there and evolved into something more, but was it enough? Could he marry her with a little bastard in tow? He certainly couldn't go back to Rainbow if he did; they would all be ostracized from polite society. Of course, if the South lost the war, he'd never be able to go home anyhow — especially if he did some of the things he intended to do. And there was an increasingly good chance they would lose. What was left of Rainbow anyway? He knew one day he would have to drop Guinevere or marry her. But he didn't have to make a decision right now, so he made the conscious decision not to make a decision. He wasn't particularly comfortable with that, but he was more comfortable delaying a decision than he would have been if he dumped her. He hoped she wouldn't force him to make a choice. She certainly hadn't yet. He thought perhaps she was just giving him some space. He had no idea she already mapped out her own carefully considered romantic campaign, and he was walking into a velvet ambush.

They avoided talking about her daughter for five days, all of which they spent together. They went for picnics in the Maryland countryside, went fishing, had nice dinners together at out-of-the-way restaurants, made a day trip to Baltimore, made another to Philadelphia, read to each other, went to a couple of theatrical performances (always arriving just as the show began, sitting in the back and leaving immediately, so as few people saw them together as was possible), and they played chess. (They were rather evenly matched, but on this trip she let him win almost every game.) She kept everything as light hearted as she could. After five days with her, Rance Liebert felt like a new man, and she could tell he was warming to her again. The sixth day was more traumatic. This time, they were supposed to go on a picnic to Virginia, but Guinevere brought a little three-year-old child with her. The actress ignored the stern look of disapproval on his face. She knew his natural Southern gallantry would assert itself quickly, and he would never take out on a little girl any animosity he might feel toward Sally Mae, much less express it in her presence. Guinevere already knew he had a weakness for children.

"Rance, I want you to meet my daughter, Ginger."

"Hello, Ginger," he said, and got down on his knees to be at her level. This was a mistake because of the horse fall. He grimaced in pain but smiled through it nonetheless. He held her hands in his and said: "You sure are a pretty little thing."

"Thank you, Mr. Rance."

"You can call me Mr. Owen or Mr. Dickerson, sweetheart," Liebert said. "Most folks do."

A pained expression flashed across the actresses' face. She should have known to introduce him as Owen Dickerson.

Suddenly an unexpected event occurred. Ginger threw her little arms around his neck and hugged him. "Thank you for taking me with you and Mommy on your picnic, Mr. Dickerson," she exclaimed.

He was completely disarmed. And enchanted. The little brown-haired girl, who very much resembled her mother, was utterly charming. He stammered out a thank you while her mother climbed into the back step of the carriage, leaving Ginger and Rance to share the front seat. This wasn't how Liebert envisioned the ride, but it was exactly how Guinevere planned it. Up front, Ginger swelled with self-importance. Only adults rode in the front seats of carriages. This must mean she was almost an adult. Her face beamed.

Colonel Rance Liebert, who was a foe to be reckoned with on just about any battlefield, proved absolutely defenseless against a three-foot-tall child in a ponytail. He asked the name of her doll.

"Molly," she said, and that started something. Ginger picked up the conversation and ran with it. She talked about everything under the sun. You are your mother's daughter, he thought. It was clear she was very happy and loved not being in the orphanage. To Ginger, at this moment, life was an exciting adventure, and the world was just opening up. Rance joined in the conversation occasionally and talked about his happy childhood on the plantation. "My favorite toy was a knife, which I bought myself, with my own money," he declared. "I was very proud of that. I called it 'Mr. Bowie,' because it was designed by Colonel Jim Bowie of Louisiana. Would you like to see it?"

"Yes, sir!" She exclaimed. He handed her his knife. Ginger's mother was surprised he still carried that old knife but then remembered he was very good at throwing it. It might come in handy in his profession. "Be careful with that," he warned. "It's very sharp."

Ginger held it very carefully, like it was some kind of breakable diamond. She handed it back to him after only a few seconds.

"When you're older, I'll teach you how to throw it," he declared.

"Oh, really, Mr. Owen!" She bubbled. "Do you promise?"

"I promise."

In the back seat, Guinevere smiled widely. Although the child didn't realize it, Ginger was helping her win back Rance Liebert. Her plan was working perfectly.

After they picked a likely spot near the road, Rance lay out a blanket, and they broke out the picnic basket. They played catch and tag. Rance picked Ginger up and rolled her stomach on his head. She laughed and laughed and then said: "Do it again!" He did until his arms got too tired. The little girl even taught the Rebel colonel how to play patty-cake. The only bad moment occurred when a squadron of Union cavalry rode into view. He sat up and Guinevere got very quiet.

A tight-lipped Liebert waved at them. They waved back. He could see some of them speaking to others, who laughed. No doubt they were wishing that they could trade places with him.

"They're probably lookin' for Mosby," he said, referring to John Singleton Mosby, the "Gray Ghost of the Confederacy," who operated in this area.

"Won't do 'em any good," Guinevere retorted. "They've been looking for him for a long time."

"Without positive results, that's for sure," he observed. "They only find him when he wants to be found."

"Then they wish they hadn't, because he clobbers them," she remarked.

After a long pause, Rance said: "I guess it's gittin' time to go." Yankee cavalrymen made him nervous.

"Oh, no, Mr. Owen!" Ginger shouted at once. "Not yet. Mommy packed a book. Could you read to me, please. Ppppllllleeeeeaaaaasseeeeeeeeeeee!"

Rance smiled. He had heard that word before. So he read until it was time for supper. Fortunately, Guinevere packed quite a lot of food. The sun was setting when they headed back to town.

Both adults had a good time at the picnic, and Ginger was in heaven; however, three-year-olds can take only so much. She was dead to the world when Rance put her on the back seat. She slept the entire way home.

On the way back, Guinevere opened up a little. "After I was raped, the doctor said I was so badly injured that I'd never be able to have children," she confessed. "So I wasn't very careful. I didn't think I had to be." She paused.

"Doctors don't always get it right," he observed. This was especially true in this war. More than half the surgeons in both armies had not practiced medicine before the war began, and many who had weren't particularly competent.

They rode in silence for a long while, both of them lost in their own thoughts. "I'd be lost without you, Rance," she said shortly before they got to her building.

Liebert carried the sleeping child inside and put her to bed. As soon as he finished, Guinevere said: "I think I'll go to bed, too." She gently took his hand and almost whispered: "Join me."

"I don't have anything to sleep in," he replied.

"Yes, you do. I brought you a nightshirt. And don't worry about

The Retribution Conspiracy

Ginger. She'll sleep all night."

Later, with her head on his shoulder, Rance decided Guinevere would be a good general. She thought of everything. He wasn't yet sure he wanted her back with some other man's child to raise, but he wasn't sure he didn't, either; besides, the child was a delight, and he felt his resistance weakening. And she was smart enough not to press the matter too hard. She asked herself: Has he forgiven my sin of omission — that I didn't tell him I had a child when he first started becoming romantically involved with me? He may not want you back as a girlfriend or a fiancée, she thought, at least not yet, but he still sees you as his best friend. You can build on that. Bide your time, woman. You can win him back. Just don't move too hastily. And she didn't.

On the last day of his furlough, Rance Liebert kissed Sally Mae and Ginger goodbye. Both kisses were on the cheek. Ginger cried. "Don't go, Mr. Owen," she begged. "Please stay and play with me!"

The colonel grinned. "He has to go, honey," her mother told her.

"But why?!"

"He has to work."

Ginger paused to consider this. Rance ignored the question, mounted his horse and nudged it with the toe of his boot, but his eyes were a little misty as he headed off to visit Robert E. Lee via the usual route: southern Maryland, cross the Potomac via rowboat, and onto the Northern Neck of Virginia (the peninsula between the Potomac and Rappahannock Rivers), where a horse was waiting at a Secret Service way station.

When Rance first met that gentleman, they were not particularly friendly. In two years, however, they gained a great deal of respect for each other. Liebert decided Lee was not only a brilliant general but was also the most Christ-like person he knew, with the exception of his late grandmother, Elizabeth. He always looked forward to meeting with Robert E. Lee.

Rance was admitted to the general's tent immediately, and Lee invited him to sit down. The general always asked about Guinevere. Rance told him he took his first leave of the war and had spent more than a week with her in Washington. Lee chuckled and commented it was a strange place for a Confederate colonel to spend his leave. Rance smiled and remarked that keeping his hands off her was the hardest thing he ever did. The general assured him it was worth it and one day he would be glad he had. (Robert E. Lee frequently gave fatherly advice to his younger officers, and they almost always followed it. Rance did not tell the great commander about Ginger. He looked upon that as his own problem to work out.) With that, General Lee got down to business. "Is there anything your sweetheart would like to tell me?"

"Well, that she loves you, for starters."

Lee smiled and blushed. "That's good to know," he snickered.

"She also says that Burnside is forming a new corps in the Annapolis area."

Lee already knew that. "Does she know where Mr. Lincoln plans to deploy it?"

"Yes, sir. He plans to employ it against you. Against the Army of Northern Virginia. Most of the corps will join General Meade shortly after he begins his spring offensive."[38]

A serious look flashed across Lee's face. He had not known that. Forming at Annapolis, it would have to be used against his army or a coastal target. There was speculation that it might be employed to reinforce the Union forces at New Bern and push into the interior of North Carolina, or possibly it might be deployed against Beauregard, who was currently besieged in Charleston, South Carolina. Now that question was answered.

"They are also organizing an all-USCT division."

General Lee started at Colonel Liebert but remained silent at first. USCT stood for "United States Colored Troops." This development interested Lee, who wanted to know everything about it, including the name of its commander.

"Brigadier General Edward Ferrero."

General Lee laughed out loud.

"Do you know this man, General?"

"Yes, I do. He was an instructor at West Point when I was the superintendent."

"Oh, really?" Rance said, a little concerned. This man might know his job, he thought, but only for a moment.

"Well, I wouldn't worry too much about him. He was a dance instructor."

Rance also burst out laughing. But Jefferson Davis did not see anything funny about black troops. He sent General Lee a dispatch stating

---

[38] He was referring to General George G. Meade, the commander of the Army of the Potomac, the main Union army in the East. Meade was the victorious commander in the Battle of Gettysburg.

The Retribution Conspiracy

that Negroes in blue uniforms would be returned to slavery immediately, and their white officers would be shot if captured. Lee sent orders to his regiments that captured blacks and their officers would be treated as regular prisoners of war. Davis, who was normally pretty prickly about his authority, ignored this piece of insubordination and allowed himself to be overruled by his best general.

"The Negro regiments have some excellent human material and could be a real threat to us," Lee said, "but Lincoln's War Department is wasting them. It always assigns them the worst officers so, more often than not, they get slaughtered."

"I know that's true," Rance replied. "General Beauregard told me about that assault on Battery Wagner near Charleston last summer. They tried to storm it with a white regiment, which was decimated; then, one week later, they tried exactly the same thing, using exactly the same plan, only with a black regiment. Surely they knew it would be slaughtered also."

"You would think," General Lee responded. There was a brief silence.

"One other thing Guinevere said that might interest you," Liebert said.

"What is that?"

"She says the Spirit of Bull Run is gripping the North again."

"What did she mean by that?" The general asked.

"Well, you remember the heady days before the 1st Battle of Manassas?"

"Of course," Lee answered.

"Well, both sides thought the war would be over in ninety days. Our side averred that one Southerner could whip ten Yankees, and they were going to have your sword and Jeff Davis' hat within thirty days and were going to conquer the entire South in ninety?"

"Yes. Both sides were overconfident back then." Lee could have truthfully said he wasn't swept along with the tide, but he did not.

"Well, that same old feeling is back in the North. They are overconfident now. They believe that after their victories at Gettysburg, Vicksburg, and Chattanooga, the main Confederate armies are broken reeds. If they begin their main offensives in May 1864, they will not face serious resistance. The offensives will essentially be mopping up operations. The war will soon be over and their troops home by the time the children start school in September."

"Really?" Lee said, a little skeptically.

"Yes, sir. In addition, I have read several major Northern newspapers. The editors share this opinion."

Lee smiled and was at least partially convinced. He knew his army had been hurt at Gettysburg, but it was far from finished. He was going to have a nasty shock for some Northern editors within forty-eight hours of the commencement of the campaign.

"I can send you copies of some of these editorials if you would like to see them, sir. Just as soon as President Davis is through with them."

"Yes, I would very much like to see them, Colonel," General Lee grinned. Goodness, Liebert thought. This old man is planning to knock the overconfidence out of an entire nation. Lee, meanwhile, decided to give Rance Liebert a test. He often did this with promising junior officers.

"Colonel, what do you think of the overall war situation?"

"Well, do you remember our first conversation about strategy, two years ago?" Rance replied.

"Yes," Lee answered. "You said we had three chances to win the war: diplomatically, militarily, and politically."

"I think we're down to politically," Rance declared.

"You mean hold out until November 1864, and hope Lincoln is defeated for reelection?"

"Yes, sir. I believe it is our only chance, but it is a reasonably good chance. If you can hold Richmond, and Johnston can hold Atlanta until after the elections, I think we have a real probability of achieving our independence via a negotiated peace."[39]

"You may be right. That is why I have devised a method of trench warfare aimed at inflicting maximum casualties on those people. It features …"

Suddenly someone stuck his head into the tent. "I am sorry to interrupt, sir," Lee's adjutant announced, "but General Longstreet is outside and would like to speak with you."

A look of disappointment flashed across Lee's face. "I am sorry, Colonel," he declared, "I was, as always, enjoying our conversation, but duty calls. Give my fond regards to Miss Guinevere, and thank her for some very useful information."

The general stood up and, always the gentleman, extended his hand. Rance shook it and, in an unusually informal jest, the gener-

---

39 Joseph E. Johnston replaced Braxton Bragg as the commander of the Army of Tennessee in December 1863.

The Retribution Conspiracy

al impulsively declared: "You may tell Miss Guinevere that I love her, too!"

The two men smiled at each other. "That, sir, will make her day! And she will be insufferably pleased with herself for at least a month!" Liebert replied. With that, he left the tent and was soon on his way back to Richmond.

———✦———

Jefferson Davis greeted Rance as an old friend, but the president looked older and more careworn and his shoulders slumped. He sat on the couch and gave Liebert the overstuffed chair. He skipped the small talk and got right to the point.

"Rance, you told me once that you would never work with Copperheads again. Do you still feel that way?"

"Yes, I do."

"Secretary Benjamin, Jacob Thompson, and others believe great things can be accomplished working with them."

Not that again, he thought. "I do not believe it," Rance retorted. "I believe they are wrong."

"I want to try."

Liebert met this news with a stony silence. The South had few resources and they were dwindling daily. He had already decided not to have anything to do with this. But Davis surprised him.

"Secretary Benjamin has long wanted a second Secret Service under the State Department. In view of your attitude, I have decided to honor his request."

"Am I being relieved of my command?" Liebert demanded, clearly put out.

"Oh, no, Rance, no," Davis quickly assured him. "You have done an excellent job under very trying circumstances. You created a fine organization literally out of nothing, and don't think I don't appreciate it! I am just setting up a parallel organization under State. I am sending three commissioners to Canada, led by Colonel Jacob Thompson. They will work with the Copperheads."

Liebert knew Thompson from Mississippi. He was a friend and political ally of Jefferson Davis. He served eight years in Congress but was defeated in his last election. Then President Buchanan named him secretary of the interior. He joined the Confederate Army in 1861, and served three years in the West as a staff officer. He was a good man, intelligent, very rich, and patriotic. He was also hardheaded, opinionated, and accustomed to getting his own way.

"My plans for setting up a base in Canada are already far advanced," Rance declared. "Should I turn over my operatives and facilities to Colonel Thompson?"

"No. Continue with what you are doing."

"But our goals are different. I am setting up sabotage operations. My goals are to prevent as many newly formed Union regiments from leaving the North as possible. Secretary Benjamin wants to ferment subversion among people who are dissatisfied but are not going to rebel."

"With all due respect, Rance, what you are suggesting amounts to pinpricks."

"Pinpricks can be uncomfortable, especially if they are in the right places. If I can keep one brigade from going south, that's one brigade which won't be able to attack Lee or Johnston. And I believe I can force them to hold back the equivalent of several divisions or more."

"Do that!" Jefferson Davis ordered. "But cooperate with Commissioner Thompson also."

"Yes, sir."

"Rance," he asked, "what are your manpower requirements for these 'pinpricks'?"

"None, sir. I already have 25 Secret Service personnel, a couple of hundred trained infantrymen and several dozen trained cavalrymen at safe houses in the Montreal and Toronto areas, armed, ready, and awaiting orders. I also have a couple of hundred undergoing or awaiting training."

"That's more than 500 men!" The president exclaimed. "How did you raise a regiment of armed men — in Canada?" Jefferson Davis was genuinely shocked. He wondered what else was going on that he didn't know about.

"Escaped prisoners of war, sir. The Northerners prudently set up their prison camps far from Southern lines. But you can't do that without setting them up near the Canadian border. Some of our best fighters have escaped the Federal prisons and made their way to Canada. Here, Lieutenant Colonel John Spring takes them under his wing. They are destitute when they arrive. He provides them with food, clothing, and a place to stay. Most of them need at least some recuperation time and medical attention. We provide that. When they have recovered, some of the more daring ones are allowed to join the Secret Service and are given training in sabotage. We are receiving unofficial help from the

The Retribution Conspiracy

British and Canadians in this training. Other escaped prisoners want to return to the Confederate Army. Through Baker, eh, I mean Spring, I provide them with passage via blockade runner or let them try it on their own."

"What do you mean by that?" Davis asked.

"Give them the correct papers, a nice set of civilian clothes and money. They work their way south on their own."

"Won't some of them just go home?"

"A certain percentage will, yes, sir," Liebert confessed. "But those who don't will make a welcome addition to our army, at a time when we need every man we can get."

Ain't it so, Jefferson Davis thought. He was astonished at what Liebert accomplished without bothering to tell anyone in Richmond. This man is running his own war, Davis concluded.

"Others are willing to stay with us, to conduct sabotage operations in the North," Liebert continued. "One such man is Colonel Robert Martin of the 12th Kentucky. He rode with Morgan. A second leader is Captain Tom Hines, Morgan's chief scout. I am very impressed with both of them."

Although Davis had never met Martin, he was also impressed with him. A private in 1861, he rose to full colonel at age 23. He was captured with Morgan in Ohio but, along with Morgan, Hines, and five others, he escaped by tunneling out from under the Ohio State Penitentiary.

"Won't that bust your budget?" Davis wanted to know.

"Pretty close," Liebert admitted. But he wasn't quite telling his old friend the entire truth. Jefferson Davis was micro-managing again, and Rance didn't like it. He decided to give him only as much information as he absolutely required. He did not feel the need to tell him he was running a full-scale counterfeiting operation less than 15 blocks from the Confederate White House, or he was giving the escapees counterfeit greenbacks.

"What do Martin and Hines think about the Copperheads?" the president inquired.

"Hines thinks another attempt at a Copperhead Rebellion is worthwhile. Martin doesn't," Rance answered.

"What does Martin say?"

"Colonel Martin says 'the only difference between a Copperhead leader and a bucket of manure is the bucket,' sir."

Jefferson Davis jerked his head back and stared at his Secret Service chief. He didn't care for this kind of talk.

Liebert noticed the look. "Sorry, sir," he half apologized, "but if you didn't want to know …"

"Then I shouldn't have asked. I know, I know," Davis finished his sentence for him. He first heard that answer from Second Lieutenant Rance Liebert in Texas eighteen years ago, and several times in Mexico after that.

Jefferson Davis did not tell Liebert Thompson asked for Spring, Hines, and Martin. He just said: "Transfer Hines and Spring to Thompson. You can keep Martin."

"I need Spring." Rance exclaimed. "I have plans for him."

"What are they?" Davis wanted to know.

Liebert sighed. "First, I want him to continue doing what he is doing. I want his 'sister,' Guinevere, to visit him. Then she will tell Stanton we are planning to raid Camp Douglas in Chicago, free our prisoners, and turn them loose on the city, with orders to burn it to the ground. We are planning similar raids on Rock Island, Alton, Elmira, and Point Lookout."

"What will that accomplish?"

"I believe they will reinforce each prison with a regiment to augment the guards. Camp Douglas may get two. That's a reinforced brigade or a small division that can't be used against Lee or Johnston, or Forrest in Mississippi or General Taylor in Louisiana."

Pinpricks, Davis thought. But Liebert was right. That would be five or six regiments they could not deploy in Virginia or Georgia. "Won't that compromise Guinevere?"

"I don't think so," Rance declared. "She will just report back to Stanton that we learned he reinforced the guards and decided to delay our attacks until the new regiments depart. At that point, I believe Stanton will decide they will never depart. He can't afford to lose Chicago."

Davis did the math in his head. Rance's plan would neutralize 5,000 to 6,000 Northern infantrymen and cost the South virtually nothing. This was the easiest decision he would have to make all day. "Transfer Hines. You can keep Martin and Spring. I will have Treasury Secretary Memminger transfer $100,000 in gold to your Canadian account for continued operations."

Rance was momentarily shocked. That was a huge amount of money. After a moment, Davis asked. "Do you have any other plans?"

When Colonel Liebert answered, Jeff Davis almost fell off the sofa. He intended to rob Northern banks, derail Northern trains, burn car-

The Retribution Conspiracy

go ships and barges, blow up Yankee ammunition plants, burn Union transports with troops on board, burn New York City to the ground, and generally subject the entire North to a reign of terror.

When Rance Liebert left the White House early that morning, he carried an order to Treasury Secretary Christopher Memminger. He was to transfer $250,000 in gold to Rance's Canadian accounts.

—∘ CHAPTER XXII ∘—
SURRENDER, YOU G******
REBELS!

U.S. Brigadier General Judson Kilpatrick, the commander of the Army of the Potomac's 3rd Cavalry Division, looked at his remarkable reflection in the mirror. He could not get over how handsome he was. Even with his uncombed, unruly hair, he was still delightful to look at, especially in the nude. His untrimmed mutton-chop beard set off his manly features nicely. Twenty-eight years old and a brigadier general already! He could only marvel at himself and his remarkable achievements. He was well on his way to accomplishing all three of his life's objectives: become a great general, become president of the United States, and have sex with everyone in a skirt, except the Scottish guy playing the bagpipes. This very month, he was going to take a major step toward accomplishing all three goals.

Kilpatrick grinned at himself. He had certainly moved up in the Union's pecking order. Even though he was only a division commander, the secretary of war had ignored the chain of command and conferred with him personally, bypassing the general-in-chief, the commander of the Army of the Potomac and his corps commander. The orders Stanton gave him were dynamite. He was to capture the Confederate capital, free the Union prisoners of war in Libby and Belle Isle prisons, hang Jefferson Davis and his entire cabinet as well as a long list of other prominent traitors, and, for his grand finale, burn Richmond, the seat of the Rebellion, to the ground.

According to Stanton, these orders came from Abraham Lincoln. Kilpatrick wondered. He couldn't be certain, but he believed the orders might have come from Stanton himself, and the secretary of war was lying about Lincoln, as usual. But it really didn't matter. With Jefferson Davis' lifeless body swinging in the breeze, he, Judson Kilpatrick, would be the one true hero, the savior of the Union. He could see it now: a promotion to major general and well on his way to becoming president of the United States. And, of course, there would be thousands of women eager to give their bodies to him — just a minor fringe benefit. In gratitude, General Kilpatrick decided he would retain Edwin Stanton as secretary of war after he defeated that limp rag, Abe Lincoln, for the presidency later that year. Kilpatrick's mind continued to race. Congress would have to suppress the Constitution so I can be inaugurated, of course, but who cared? He thought. The Lincoln administration had ignored that useless piece of garbage for three years already and had gotten away with it. Perhaps it was time to revoke it altogether. What this country really needs is a military dictatorship under a handsome, dashing, young cavalry officer. ...

If Kilpatrick did not think highly of Lincoln, the feeling was mutual. The president also skipped several layers in the chain of command and personally selected Lieutenant Colonel Ulric Dahlgren to command Kilpatrick's spearhead, largely because he thought Kilpatrick was an incompetent fool. Dahlgren was a highly efficient and well-connected young officer who lost a leg in the Gettysburg campaign, but he could still ride and was eager to get back into the war. His 500 men would be the first to enter Richmond and would hang Davis and his cronies. The main body of Kilpatrick's troops would come in shortly thereafter and hunt down the cabinet secretaries, senators, and the slower congressmen, and hang them too. All would be spared the ordeal of a trial.

Kilpatrick knew better than to write down his instructions. If something went wrong, there would be hell to pay, and Judson Kilpatrick wasn't going to make the payment personally. But Ulric Dahlgren was only 21 years old. He didn't know any better. He took notes while Kilpatrick briefed him and, as soon as he got back to his tent, he used his notes to write down everything Kilpatrick said. Kilpatrick knew this but didn't object; in fact, he was pleased. Let the *naïve* Dahlgren suffer the blowback, if there were to be any.

The odds certainly favored the Yankees. Kilpatrick had 4,000 men, and the U.S. Bureau of Military Information reported the only Rebel forces available to oppose him were 1,500 motley cavalrymen under Wade Hampton, plus a few local defense and home guard forces.

Even though they were at war for three years, the Northern leaders neglected the most elementary principle of warfare: security. One Union staff officer described the preparations for the raid as "a picnic, with everybody blabbing." The worst of these was Kilpatrick himself, who bragged at a party to Guinevere Spring, in hopes that she would be impressed enough to go to bed with him.

Guinevere constituted a challenge to Judson Kilpatrick. She was short and had an alluring figure — although her breasts could be larger, he thought — but there was something about her that suggested a certain freshness and innocence. She had a peaches-and-cream complexion and flashed a naturally warm smile with well-polished, perfect

The Retribution Conspiracy

teeth. She made whoever was around her feel that she was listening intently, a characteristic that was well calculated to captivate an audience or an individual — especially a male. Despite her appearance, Kilpatrick was sure she was far from innocent. Although she had the reputation among Washington elites as being attainable by amorous men in the years immediately prior to the war, she was considered more a tease and a flirt these days. It did not occur to them to ask if a change in her nature had taken place. They merely assumed she was just being more discrete. But surely she will succumb to me, General Kilpatrick thought. He poured her some wine, told her a few *risqué* jokes, made sure to be witty and charming, and even offered to take her to dinner — on their way back to her rooms. But, to his surprise, she did not allow him to single her out from the herd, much less hop into bed with him, despite his repeated attempts. Obviously, she did not know who he was or how important he was going to be, so he reminded her. He told her just how he planned to hang Jeff Davis.

The slender, blue-grey-eyed actress with the beautiful face did laugh when he talked about how Davis would dance on air and how he intended to swing from the nearest tree every last member of the Confederate Congress on whom he could get his hands.

"But I don't think you'll be able to reach Richmond," Guinevere said coyly.

"And why not?" Asked the Federal. It was cute how she'd asserted herself, as if she had the foggiest idea about what she was speaking.

"Because of the Rebel generals and their men," she muttered softly, not forgetting to smile demurely.

This caused the bluecoat officer to give her a detailed rundown on exactly how he would succeed in completing his task, just as she calculated. He reasoned that a flood of military detail would demonstrate his genius and overwhelm his objective for the night which, of course, was Guinevere herself. He saw no harm in this; after all, she was just a little woman. She wouldn't be able to understand the nuances or the military jargon, he assumed. Judson Kilpatrick tried every way he knew to impress Guinevere, and she was impressed — with his stupidity. The actress understood every word he said, though she played dumb. By the end of the evening, she could diagram Kilpatrick's entire battle plan, including locations of assembly areas, dates of departure and arrival, order of battle, estimations of Rebel positions and strengths, Union commanding officers to the regimental level, names and personality descriptions of Union staff officers, General Kilpatrick's favorite sexual positions, check points, rally points, routes of advance, alternate routes, escape routes, rations per horse and per man per day, anticipated ammunition consumption rates, and allocations of medical provisions.

As the head of the Confederate Secret Service in Washington, Guinevere had played this game before, with officers who were much more astute than Kilpatrick. That evening, while a frustrated Kilpatrick was taking a cold bath alone, she was writing to the chief of the Secret Service. Before the sun set the next day, Rance Liebert knew all about the Yankees' plans — except for the part about Kilpatrick's favorite sex positions. She added that both Lincoln and Stanton had taken a hand in the planning, and that, for a light colonel, Ulric Dahlgren had more access to the White House than anyone of his rank.[40] So Lincoln did know, Liebert concluded.

The raid began on February 28, 1864. Initial Confederate resistance was heavier than anticipated, but Kilpatrick pushed on. He soon discovered he was facing not only Hampton but also another of Jeb Stuart's veteran cavalry divisions under Robert E. Lee's nephew, Fitzhugh Lee; Virginia Home Guard Troops; Colonel Dickerson's 125th Special Employment Battalion (whatever that was); several battalions of local defense troops; and four batteries of Virginia heavy artillery. Even the clerks from the War Department were deployed against him! Casualties were heavy. It was almost as if the Rebels were waiting for him. Ulric Dahlgren's spearhead broke off from the main body and drove to the southwest, and managed to evade the defenders and head for the James River, west of the Confederate capital. By 10 a.m. on March 1, they reached the James River Canal, 21 miles from Richmond. Along the way, they wasted time looting local homes and stores, burning plantations and barns, and destroying a grain mill, several canal boats and some canal locks.

Soon, they came upon Sabor Hall, one of the largest and most beautiful plantations in Virginia, and the home of Confederate Secretary of War James A. Seddon. They immediately began burning the outbuildings. Colonel Dahlgren dismounted with difficulty, hobbled to the front door on his crutches, and frantically beat on it.

Seddon's wife, Sarah Bruce Seddon, answered. She had once been

---

40 Ulric was the son of Admiral John Dahlgren, the inventor of the famous Dahlgren naval gun. Ulric's grandfather was Bernhard Dahlgren, a rich Pennsylvania slave trader. Ulric himself, however, was an abolitionist.

beautiful and was still attractive, and age had only increased her mental acuity. "Sallie" was quick and as smart as a whip.

"I am Colonel Dahlgren," he barked. He intended to curtly order her and her servants out of the house before he burned it.

"Are you related to Admiral Dahlgren?" She asked

"I am his son, Ulric," answered the surprised bluecoat.

She smiled genially. "I knew you when you were a child," she declared. "Your late mother and I were schoolmates in Philadelphia. Her name was Mary Bunker back then. We were close personal friends."

"You knew my mother?" Asked the astonished officer.

"Yes. I grew up in Philadelphia. She and I used to spend the night at each other's homes and gossip about boys. We had several of the same beaus."

"Really?" The colonel asked. He was clearly fascinated.

"One of them was John Adolphus Dahlgren, your father."

Dahlgren's mouth was wide open. He was completely taken off guard. Seddon had him right where she wanted him. "Yes, and I must confess that I was just a little jealous when he picked Mary. I nevertheless served as one of her bridesmaids."

Memories of his mother poured back into Dahlgren's head. "You know," Sallie declared, "I was thinking how much I would enjoy a glass of blackberry wine, but everybody's gone and I have no one to drink it with. Would you like to join me?"

"Well … I really should get back to my command. …"

"Oh, tis-tis," she retorted and, flashing him a disarming smile, said: "The war will still be there in 15 minutes or so. Let's visit for a while."

Dahlgren capitulated immediately. The gracious lady soon had him eating out of her hand. He was totally charmed. They were soon visiting like old friends, catching up and telling stories. He drank most of the bottle. The fifteen minute visit took an hour and a half. When he left, he promised to see to it that no harm would come to the Big House. She thanked him profusely as she watched her barns and stables burn, smiling on the outside yet fuming internally. She knew her neighbors had lost everything and her horses, mules, grain stockpiles, agricultural equipment, and other property were gone — her plantation crippled. She nevertheless expressed strong gratitude to young Dahlgren as he staggered to his horse. He thanked her for the visit, although his speech was slurred. She did not tell him that Brigadier General Henry Wise, the former governor of Virginia, spent the previous night at Sabor Hall and was even now rushing toward Richmond, to raise the alarm and help organize the defenses. She also sent a messenger to her husband, warning him of the impending assault from the west.

Kilpatrick, meanwhile, battered his head unsuccessfully against the Richmond defenses. He broke off the engagement and hightailed it to the east, away from the Rebel capital, toward the Union-held Fort Monroe, which he reached with what was left of his command. Dahlgren was left on his own.

Colonel Dahlgren planned to cross the James and loop behind Richmond, in order to take the city from the south and reach the prisons, but he failed. The Union's Bureau of Military Information (BMI) provided him with a guide, a free Negro named Martin Robinson, who was deemed reliable and knew the area. Robinson was supposed to be able to identify a crossing point, but the river was too high. Furious and growing desperate, Dahlgren had the black man hanged. He paid with his life because the river was too high. Dahlgren's only option now was to attack Richmond from the northwest.

But again, resistance was heavier than expected. By March 2, Dahlgren had only 100 men left. Night was falling as he neared the King and Queen County Courthouse. The road led from open country into a deep and ominous forest, and Dahlgren found his way blocked by the 42nd Virginia Home Guard Battalion, which was hidden in the brush and trees. A Rebel officer shouted and ordered him to stop, but they were only rag-tag fourth class troops, and many of them were schoolboys, aged 17 or younger. Surely I can compel them to capitulate if I demand it forcefully enough! Dahlgren thought. It was the biggest mistake of his life.

The Union colonel stood up in his stirrups, raised his sword above his head and bellowed harshly: "Surrender, you G****** Rebels!"

In doing this, Dahlgren probably unwittingly saved the lives of some of his men. The Guards were aiming at them, but now every gun turned toward the blaspheming colonel. The Rebel commander yelled "Fire!" A sheet of yellow and gray flame erupted from the forest. A bullet hit him in the arm, and another ripped into his chest. Something flew by his ear, and it sounded like an angry bee. There was a tap on his shoulder, and he felt something rip out the back of his uniform. He reeled in the saddle and dropped his sword as he was hit by another bullet, and then another, and then another. In a matter of two or three seconds, he was shot several times. The last one struck him full in the forehead, and his bullet-riddled body toppled into the darkness. He was dead before that.

The Retribution Conspiracy

Chaos ensued as the Federals watched their commander fall. Dahlgren's formation dissolved completely, and his men scattered in all directions. The surviving officers were not able to rally them. "Every man for himself!" someone cried as he rode into the night. Fitz Lee's boys rounded up most of them up the next day.

Meanwhile, 13-year-old William Littlepage groped through the darkness. Until the day before yesterday, he was just a young schoolboy, feeling the grips of puberty. Then the sergeants arrived. The Yankees were coming, they declared, and every male in the class was now drafted into the Virginia state forces, which were part of the Confederate Army for operational purposes. Barefoot and without a uniform, he was posted in the forest with the rest of the 42nd Virginia. Like his classmates, he hid in the vegetation. Despite the coolness of the late afternoon, sweat dripped from his face as he awaited the enemy, and the tension seemed unbearable. Then he saw men on horseback galloping toward him. Littlepage choked back the fear as Dahlgren and his men came nearer and nearer. Even so, he held his position and cocked the antiquated musket he was only the day before. Suddenly, the Yankees stopped. Then one Northerner, who Littlepage took to be the leader, advanced alone, in front of the formation. The teenager aimed at his chest as the Federal demanded that they surrender. When Edward Halbach — formerly his teacher and now his commanding officer — shouted "Fire!" He pulled the trigger. Littlepage never knew if his bullet found its mark, but he was proud he saw combat and was pleased with his own conduct. He even fired on an enemy officer, who toppled from his horse. He was both surprised and delighted when the Federal formation dissolved and the men in blue moved smartly to the rear.

Later that evening, after the sun fully set, Littlepage crawled forward, looking for loot and souvenirs. He found the body of the Yankee officer, lying in the mud. The decedent had a nice gold watch, so Littlepage took it and rifled his pockets. In his interior coat pocket he found a document, some greenbacks, and a few cigars.

Shortly thereafter, he offered his teacher, Captain Halbach, a cigar. The elderly reserve officer was somewhat astonished. "Where did you get such a fine cigar?" he wanted to know. Hardly anyone in the Confederacy had fine cigars anymore.

"Off a dead Yank. He also had these papers," Littlepage declared, handing them to Halbach. He never mentioned the watch or the greenbacks. He wasn't above making a modest profit from his first battle.

The Home Guard captain's eyes got really wide after perusing the blood-stained document. He immediately passed it up the chain of command until it reached General Fitzhugh Lee about an hour later. As he read the document, Lee's eyes opened so wide they almost bulged. Without further ado, the general put the spurs to his horse and headed directly for Jefferson Davis.

That night, Davis summoned Rance Liebert to the Confederate White House. Liebert just returned to his headquarters and was covered in mud, but quite happy. He spent the last two days skirmishing with Federal cavalry and was proud of his battalion's performance. Although he was careful not to show it, he was also pleased with himself. He always wanted to command a unit in battle. He now did so, and he passed the test, at least in his own mind. (No one else knew there was a test.) True, it was only a small battalion, and he wanted to lead a brigade or a regiment at least, but this would do. The 125th did not face a major attack, but the Yankees launched two moderately strong probes against his line and were beaten back twice, and left with empty saddles both times. Liebert knew that, when the history of the war was written, his little victories north of Richmond would not even warrant a footnote, but he nevertheless commanded a unit in combat, and thus fulfilled one of his life's ambitions. Rance smiled. He was also pleased that none of his men were killed, although one was severely wounded. They also captured four Yankees. Three were so seriously wounded that their colleagues left them behind, and the other was trapped under his horse when it was killed and fell on him. The veteran bluecoat cavalryman had been embarrassed he had been taken prisoner by local defense troops, but the men had been placed under the strictest orders not to tell anyone who they really were. Liebert interrogated the man, a sergeant, who told him nothing. Even so, he left with all of his fingers. The colonel rather liked the prisoner, so he also made sure the captive had a tin cup when he departed. (In a place like Andersonville, a cup was a key to survival.) Rance smiled to himself. He couldn't wait to recount his adventure to Robert E. Lee. Many years from now, he thought, I will be able to brag to my grandchildren that I served as a combat infantry officer in the legendary Army of Northern Virginia. After the last three days, no one will ever be able to take that away from me. He decided he would not mention to his unborn descendants it was for only three days and, in the excitement of battle, he forgot to fire at the enemy, as he had intended to do. That's all right, he decided. The grandchildren won't need to know everything.

Liebert's self-congratulatory interlude was interrupted by President Davis' courier. Rance was instructed to come to the White House at once. He wondered for a moment if he should change into a clean dress uniform but decided against it. Jefferson Davis had seen him dirty before.

It was very late when Liebert arrived at the corner of Clay and 12th Streets, where the White House was located. It occurred to Rance the name was a misnomer. It was a kind of dirty-gray/brownish building with white columns, but the Southerners had a president living in a White House for eight decades before secession, and the tradition continued by default, at least insofar as the name was concerned.

The receptionist stood up as the colonel entered the room, and his eyes grew wide. Rance smiled. It occurred to him the lieutenant had never seen him dirty before, and in an old fatigue uniform to boot. "Show me in, lieutenant," he said, flashing the astonished young man a big smile. Rance was enjoying his confusion. As usual, he did not remove his Navy Sixes or Mr. Bowie.

President Davis stood up when the colonel entered his private office. He did not show the fatigue he felt, but contrary to his custom, he did not smile, shake Rance's hand, or greet him verbally. He simply handed Liebert the blood-stained Dahlgren document and looked outside the window while the colonel read it.

When he finished, Liebert said: "Well, I guess that confirms Miss Spring's warning."

"It does indeed," Davis replied somberly, without turning around.

The president usually sent her his compliments at this point in the conversation, but tonight he said nothing. Tonight he was sad.

"She sent me another message, which arrived today. Shall I read it?" Liebert asked.

Davis nodded his head.

"Hereby confirm a meeting took place at the White House with Kilpatrick, Stanton, and Lincoln present. Details not known, but Lincoln personally approved the raid and named Dahlgren second-in-command. Apparently Lincoln thinks Kilpatrick is a senseless braggart."

"So Lincoln knew," President Davis muttered, more to himself than to his guest.

"She is, without a doubt, the top agent we have, since Rose Greenhow was arrested," Liebert declared. He never missed an opportunity to sing the praises of Guinevere Spring in front of Davis, as a person or as an undercover agent. The Secret Service leader had an ulterior motive here. Although he was no longer sure he was in love with her, he wanted Davis to trade a Union general for her if she was ever captured. He couldn't stand the thought of her in one of Lincoln's prisons. Just as he was about to continue, the president raised his hand, and Rance Liebert fell silent.

"Do you remember two and a half years ago, when I gave you an order, making President Lincoln off-limits to you and your men?" Davis asked, several seconds later.

"I do."

"It is revoked."

"Yes, sir."

"Make plans to abduct him," Davis ordered, still looking outside.

"Yes, sir." There was a long pause. "And if he resists? What if abduction becomes assassination?" Liebert asked.

Davis turned around, sat down at his desk, closed his eyes and, several moments later, nodded his approval.

———

For the next fortnight, Sallie Seddon was hailed as a hero and was toasted as the savior of Richmond. After a lifetime of playing second fiddle to her prominent husband, she enjoyed the limelight and being the center of attention at parties, formal suppers and the like. Newspaper reporters wrote articles praising her. Public figures declared she was a fine role model and a perfect example of what a Southern woman should be. Editors proclaimed their admiration of her, often on the front page. Veteran combat officers saluted her as she walked down the sidewalk. Even President Davis went out of his way to thank her and declare she was the woman who saved the capital. No one knew or mentioned Guinevere Spring. And that was exactly how she wanted it. She was 60 miles behind enemy lines, after all.

The Retribution Conspiracy

~⌒ CHAPTER XXIII ⌒~
DIRTY TRICKS
AND PINPRICKS

The Kilpatrick-Dahlgren Raid and the document William Littlepage found on the colonel's body sent shock waves throughout the South. The list of those earmarked for execution was a virtual "Who's Who Among Southern Political Leaders." Robert E. Lee immediately urged it be published in the newspapers so "our people and the world may know the character of the war our enemies wage against us, and the unchristian and atrocious acts they plot and perpetrate." He sent a copy of the list of men Dahlgren intended to hang without trial to Union General George G. Meade, a personal friend before the war, and forcefully demanded to know if this document reflected current Union policy. Meade quickly repudiated the document and suggested it was a forgery planted on the body by the Confederate Secret Service. Privately, however, he told his wife that Kilpatrick and Dahlgren probably did intend to burn Richmond and murder the Rebel leaders. Lee, Davis, and Secretary of War James A. Seddon did not for a moment believe Meade's explanation. Davis felt sure the document originated with Abraham Lincoln himself. Prior to the raid, Seddon opposed any and all proposals which involved killing or kidnapping Lincoln. Now he completely reversed himself. Certainly Southern opinion was on his side after the document was published.[41] Editorials from reputable newspapers called for the assassinations of Lincoln, Seward, and Stanton. Certainly none of them believed Meade's explanation. To Rance Liebert's delight, some of the editors even doubted the South had a secret service.

Canada felt a certain sympathy for the Confederate States of America. Like the C.S.A., it also was invaded by the United States, and more than once, and there were still people in their early 60s and above who remembered it. Also, Lincoln's blockade severely limited the cotton trade between Canada and the South, causing widespread unemployment in the shipping and manufacturing sectors. Additionally,

---

41 The document was first published in Richmond on March 5, 1864. By the end of the month, every major newspaper in the South had published it, along with fiery editorials, denouncing Lincoln and his associates.

the South didn't mind spending money there. The shipyards in Nova Scotia, New Brunswick, and Quebec were busy constructing Southern ships, which became blockade runners. The housing, hotel, and boarding house businesses were also profiting handsomely from the war. There were 15,000 ex-Confederate soldiers in Canada (most of them escaped POWs) and 18,000 fugitive slaves, giving Canada a nice source of cheap labor. On the other hand, the Canadian population hated slavery — but perhaps not as much as they feared their much more powerful neighbor of the southern side of the Great Lakes.

Jacob Thompson and Rance Liebert met in the Queen's Hotel in Toronto and clashed immediately. Thompson demanded all clandestine operations be handled through his "Canadian Cabinet" — a commission which consisted of himself, Clement Claiborne Clay, and James P. Holcombe. It was a strong team. Clay, a cousin of the Great Compromiser, Henry Clay, had been both a U.S. and C.S. senator, and Clement's portrait appeared on the Confederate $1 bill from May 1864 on. Holcombe was a distinguished law professor at the University of Virginia and served a term in the Confederate House of Representatives.

After Thompson made his demand, Liebert didn't say a word. He just sat there, looking at him. The commissioner was uncomfortable, but he continued. He also demanded all bank accounts be turned over to the commission and all operations be approved by them before they were initiated.

Thompson had a good argument under the military principle of unity of command, but Liebert was ordered to "cooperate," not to subordinate himself and his organization to Thompson; besides, Liebert wasn't yet sure the Canadian Cabinet knew what it was doing. He also knew there was no way he could out-debate two talented politicians and a law professor. "No" was all he said.

Jacob Thompson pressed the issue, but Rance knew he was no match for them dialectically, so he avoided getting into an argument with them. He merely repeated President Davis' orders. He also refused to divulge the names and duties of his agents, the size of his bank accounts or where they were located, or his immediate plans. Thompson got angry. He decided Liebert was just another wooden-headed soldier/bureaucrat, sticking to his orders and protecting his little kingdom, no matter what.

The Retribution Conspiracy

"What have you or your organization ever done for the South?" a frustrated Thompson finally demanded.

"I will tell you about just one incident, since it is long past, although I will omit some of the details you don't need to know."

A sour look flashed across Thompson's face. Then, without mentioning Guinevere's name, Rance told him about the *Trent* Affair, ending with the praise Robert E. Lee lavished upon him in the presence of Jefferson Davis and Joseph E. Johnston. That shut them all up.

For once, Jacob Thompson didn't know how to proceed. If this is true, this man Liebert wasn't as stupid as he initially appeared, he thought. Jeff Davis hadn't done the South any favors by setting up a system of divided jurisdictions in Canada, Thompson concluded, but it looks as if I'm just going to have to live with it, at least for now. Besides, Liebert's got some resources that could be useful. Finally he swallowed his pride and broke the silence. "How do you suggest we proceed?"

With that, an uneasy truce evolved. Liebert's War Department Secret Service and Thompson's State Department Secret Service (a/k/a the Canadian Cabinet) worked well together, with Lieutenant Colonel Spring serving as liaison officer. Colonel Liebert took the first step in making this happen by offering to let Thompson's organization send their dispatches via his courier routes. Without revealing any details, Liebert told Thompson he did not have to rely on blockade runners to get his messages to Richmond. They went overland, from Montreal or Toronto, across the United States to Washington, and then across southern Maryland to Richmond. Thompson was skeptical at first, but it worked out so well that he was impressed in spite of himself. He often got answers to his questions within two weeks of sending them off.

On the other hand, Liebert was forced to admit Thompson's Copperhead activities worked out well for the South, despite his low expectations. One day, a depressed Thompson held a meeting of the top Secret Service leaders in Canada. He didn't really want to invite Liebert, but he was in town, and he saw no way not to invite him without being overtly rude. In the conference, the commissioner expressed his frustration with the Copperheads and the resulting lack of success it entailed.

"You are lamenting your failures," Liebert asserted, "but nothing could be further from the truth. It is true your efforts have not produced a general uprising in the Northwest as you hoped, but you have achieved much more than I or anyone in my organization expected.

You have kept the entire Northwest in confusion and disarray.[42] The very threat of an uprising has kept the governors, Mr. Lincoln, and the general population nervous, in a state of turmoil, and occasionally in a state of alarm bordering on panic. You have frozen many Union regiments in place, guarding against a Copperhead revolt. Thousands and perhaps tens of thousands of Yankees are forced to remain in the North. Stationed in Indiana, in Illinois, in Ohio, or Kentucky or Michigan, they are unable to fire at my kinsmen serving in Virginia or on the Western Front, and I thank you for that. Your efforts have been noble and have been crowned with success." He paused. "I still do not believe the Copperheads will join us, but I think you should continue fomenting discord, exactly as you have been doing. What you have expended in terms of resources is nothing compared with the results you have achieved. Your success has been overwhelming in our favor. I am embarrassed to admit I initially opposed these efforts. I was wrong. The South owes you a tremendous debt of gratitude."

Thompson beamed. Clay, Holcombe, and the other men in the room applauded — even Anderson. Such fulsome praise from such an unexpected source took the former Mississippi politician aback and caused him to blush, and he stammered out a thank you. "You, sir, haven't done so badly yourself," he smiled and bowed slightly to the colonel. Liebert bowed back. Cooperation was smoother after that.

Rance had, in fact, not done badly himself. He informally renamed his organization "the Department of Pinpricks." He visited Brigadier General Gabriel Rains at the Torpedo Bureau in Richmond. In the spring of 1862, Rains commanded a brigade in the peninsula but did so poorly as a combat leader that D. H. Hill relieved him of his command. General Cooper then brought him to Richmond as a bureau chief. Not much was expected of him, but he forever revolutionized warfare worldwide. Gabriel Rains invented the anti-personnel mine and the land mine.

General Longstreet denounced the invention as improper and forbade its use. General D. H. Hill, on the other hand, saw the possibilities. "In my opinion, all means of destroying our brutal enemies are lawful and proper," he declared. Although he didn't fully agree with Hill (he refused to poison Northern municipal water supplies or derail passenger trains, for example), Liebert thought the mining idea was brilliant. He wanted to know what other ideas Rains had, and the general cer-

---

42 What was called the Northwest in 1864 is called the Midwest today.

The Retribution Conspiracy

tainly had them. From the former prisoners-of-war in Canada, Rance had dozens of volunteers willing to wreak havoc in the Northern rear, especially since they had an excellent chance of escaping without being detected. The fact they were well reward financially was lagniappe.

General Rains' bureau might have been called "the Department of Dirty Tricks." He developed a rather simple mine which could be set under a rail. When a train passed by and depressed the rail, it exploded. His people trained several Secret Service men on how to manufacture such a mine, so the Confederacy soon had its own small mine manufacturing plant in Canada. The mines were shipped south to the United States and placed under rails scheduled to carry troop trains that same day, causing a great many casualties. A pretty good pinprick.

Rains also designed a method to detonate explosives electronically. Bridges exploded just before the trains got there. Too late to stop, the locomotives and cars sailed into the river. Dozens of Federals were killed in areas thought to be "safe." As a result, nervousness increased exponentially in the North. Soon, no area was thought to be "safe," and none was. Another pinprick.

The troop train was barreling down the track at 25 miles per hour. There was an ammunition train on the siding, waiting for the troop train to pass before resuming its journey. Suddenly, someone emerged from the woods and threw the switch, diverting the train onto the siding. It was too late to stop. The engineer and the fireman jumped for their lives. The switch-thrower jumped onto his horse and fled for his life. It was too late for the troop train, which hit the ammunition train at full speed. More than a hundred Yankees were killed and dozens of others were injured, many of them maimed for life. Another pinprick.

Derailed train cars flew all over the place. One landed on top of the engineer, killing him instantly. Another bounced off the fireman, squashing him like a bug. Another pinprick.

Because there was a mountain of loaded passenger cars and freight cars on top of each other, it took the railroad days to clear the tracks. Regional train traffic was a mess for a week. Another pinprick.

Rains also designed a bomb disguised as a lump of coal. One cold winter day, explosions rocked Northern military bases throughout the country and dozens of barracks burned down. Subsequent investigations revealed the Union soldiers put coal into their stoves, which were used to heat the barracks, as they always did. Shortly thereafter, the stoves blew up, causing casualties, burns, and general consternation. Red-hot partially burned coal flew all over the place. The Rebels picked a particularly cold day. The water lines were frozen, so the fires were difficult — and in some cases impossible — to extinguish. Still another pinprick.

One Yankee officer hit upon the bright idea of having an enlisted man smash the larger lumps of coal with a hammer, in hopes of finding a mine. The soldier found one. After his funeral, this practice was discontinued. Another pinprick.

The fires and exploding coal caused the Union generals to tighten security on their bases. This required more manpower. Even the coal bins had to be guarded. None of these men could be used against General Lee in Virginia. More pinpricks.

Two Union ammunition manufacturing plants exploded on the same day, one in Pennsylvania and another in Iowa. Dozens of workers were killed, and both had to be shut down. More pinpricks.

Security had to be tightened everywhere, especially about military bases, railroad bridges, ammunition plants, and depots. This diverted men who would otherwise have been with Sherman or Grant. Another pinprick.

General Grant built an ammunition depot at his advanced supply base at City Point, Virginia, to give himself a reserve source of powder and shells for an attack against General Lee. It exploded one night, killing dozens of Yankees and wiping out the reserve. The fire could be seen for miles and the explosions were so loud they heard it in Petersburg, 28 miles away. Several nearby warehouses full of supplies caught fire and burned to the ground. The attack on Lee was postponed for a month. Another pinprick.

The Union infantry regiment marched down the company street, using the same road they always used. Suddenly there was an explosion. Five Yankees were killed outright, three were dismembered and died later, and several were injured, some of them seriously. Someone had planted a large land mine in the mud. Still another pinprick.

The freight train roared through the night through the woods of central Ohio. Suddenly, the engineer noticed the rails were gone: someone had removed them. He hit the brakes, but they work better when the train is actually on the tracks. The locomotive barreled through the forest but finally came to a stop before anyone was actually killed, although the incident created a huge pileup and one awful mess. Yet another pinprick.

Gabriel Rains and his men developed a flammable substance called Greek Fire. It could be camouflaged in a whiskey bottle or similar con-

The Retribution Conspiracy

tainer and could be detonated by throwing the bottle against a hard surface, such as the deck of a ship. The troop ship bound for South Carolina steamed under the bridge in New York City, as the crowd waved and the soldiers waved back. Someone tossed what appeared to be a whiskey bottle from the bridge into the hold. No one thought anything about it; the bottle was probably meant as a gift for someone on board the ship. Several seconds later, however, smoke rose from the hold. The caissons for the artillery carried the ammunition chests, and they were fully loaded and below deck. One of them exploded. The fire could not be extinguished, and Yankees abandoned ship left and right. The captain tried to run the ship aground, but he could not reach shore before it sank in shallow water. Very few Yankees were killed (although a few who could not swim drowned), but the regiment lost everything, including its guns, all its rifles, supplies and ammunition — even its canteens and spare uniforms. It had to be completely reequipped and never did reach South Carolina. Another pinprick.

"The Yankee nerve spot is his pocketbook. If we touch that, he'll squeal," 21-year-old Lieutenant Bennett H. Young — formerly of Morgan's Raiders — declared. On October 19, 1864, he walked onto the steps of the American House in St. Albans, Vermont, drew his Navy Colt, and announced: "This city is now in the possession of the Confederate States of America!" The New England farmers laughed, but the handsome young Kentuckian was not joking. Suddenly, there were Rebel yells, shots were fired, women screamed, and armed men forced the civilians into a circle on the main street. Young and 20 other Rebels robbed three banks of $208,000 and made the bank employees swear an oath of allegiance to the C.S.A. One civilian resisted, and Young shot him in the chest. They stole the town's best horses and were over the Canadian border before the Federals could react. Another pinprick.

The Yankee cavalry was finally organized by a 19-year-old captain, who pursued the Rebels into Canada. They captured several, but the Canadians would not let them return to Vermont with their prisoners. Instead, the British-Canadian garrison disarmed the Yankees, took their horses and weapons, and marched them back to the U.S. The pro-Confederate Canadian soldiers took particular delight in dropping the butts of their heavy rifles on Yankee toes all the way back to the border.

Stanton hired one of the best attorneys in Canada and demanded Young and the seven of his men who were captured be extradited to the United States to stand trial for arson, treason, bank robbery, horse thief, and murder. The Stanton attorney also demanded the $90,000 which had been recovered be returned. (The rest was already in Secret Service bank accounts.) Thompson and Liebert hired an equally prominent attorney to defend the Confederates. Throughout the trial, the Canadian judges sat in open admiration of the Rebels. All were set free and were allowed to keep the money. Another pinprink.

After the trial, George Sanders, the spokesman for the Canadian Cabinet, smiled and announced to the press that the St. Albans' raid was just the first of many such incursions. Given what the Federal armies were doing in the South, he declared, robbing Northern trains, banks, and other businesses was fair play, insofar as the Confederate Secret Service was concerned. He declared open season on Northern bank officers and prominent businessmen. The bankers near the border were very influential and were in full panic mode. They demanded Northern cavalry units be stationed in or near their cities to prevent a repetition of the holdups. There were no more bank heists, but none of these troops were ever used against Robert E. Lee, Joe Johnston, Forrest, or anyone else wearing gray. Another pinprick.

The ammunition train sped under the overpass at full speed when someone began tossing Greek Fire bottles on the cars. Some of the cars did not explode but others did, setting off explosions in adjacent cars, which set off explosions in cars adjacent to the adjacent cars, and so forth. The entire train was destroyed. Another pinprick. The same thing happened at four other locations throughout the North that same day. More pinpricks.

In the dead of night, large railroad trestles and bridges in multiple locations burst into flames. Greek fire again. Repairs took weeks. More pinpricks.

Now even railroads deep in Northern territory had to be guarded. The men could not be used against Lee or Johnston. More pinpricks.

Liebert's tactics were simple but brilliant. One category of targets would be attacked at a time — all in one night, if possible. Lincoln and his subordinates would shift Union army units to protect one category (such as banks, barracks, or railroads), and Liebert's operatives shifted to another category. Early one morning, the category was newspapers — specifically Abolitionist and Republican newspapers. Guards were murdered, offices exploded, bottles of Greek Fire erupted in print shops, newsrooms were set on fire, newsstands were burned, and vendors were shot, two Abolitionist editors were killed by assassins, two others were seriously wounded, and four others escaped their burning

The Retribution Conspiracy

homes dressed only in their nightshirts. Random bullets flew through the front windows of the homes of several others. All the shooters disappeared into the night. More pinpricks.

The pinpricks continued for months. Throughout the United States, people were afraid to ride the trains, even though the attackers avoided civilian targets when possible. The small attacks kept Lincoln and Stanton awake at night because they took place in the North. It seemed there was nothing to be done about them except to suppress the news, insofar as that was possible. Even on the rare occasion when a Rebel was captured, he turned out to be a Confederate infantry or cavalry private who had been fed, clothed, and given his mission by a sergeant in Canada. He was given a short training course near a safe house in Montreal, Toronto, or Quebec and sent on his way.

Stanton prepared to hang one of the captured enlisted men. Lincoln ordered him to call off the execution. He had received an anonymous letter, stating: "we will poison a Northern municipal water supply" if the captured Rebel was "martyred." The letter was signed "Josephus Longarm, Colonel, C.S.A., Commanding Secret Service Zone 20." This frightened Lincoln. He sent the Rebel back to a prisoner of war camp, from which he promptly escaped — again. Another pinprick.

Even if a prisoner gave away the location of a safe house in Canada, it was empty by the time the U.S. secret agents arrived. At least one was booby-trapped. Stanton would have pulled his hair out if he'd had any left.

———————

Meanwhile, on May 4, 1864, Ulysses S. Grant crossed the Rapidan River with 140,000 men, with almost as many in reserve or being made ready for employment, if necessary.[43] Lee met him near Chancellorsville with fewer than half as many men and practically nothing in reserve. The Battle of the Wilderness began on May 5. It was the first *mêlée* in what became known as the Overland Campaign. Grant lost as many men as Lee had, but still he kept coming, despite enormous casualty lists. Lee predicted much earlier that, if Grant could ever force the Army of Northern Virginia to undergo a siege, there was little hope for it in the long run. At Cold Harbor, Grant lost 7,000 men in one

---

43 Grant became general-in-chief of the Union Army in March 1864. Although General Meade remained titular commander of the Army of the Potomac. Grant actually directed the campaign in the East.

30-minute battle (as opposed to Lee's 600), but still he continued to try to batter his way past the seriously depleted but steadfast Army of Northern Virginia. Eventually, Grant pushed his way over the James River and Lee was confronted with a choice: undergo siege outside the railroad center of Petersburg or abandon Petersburg and Richmond, because without Petersburg's railroads Richmond could not be held.[44] Lee chose the first option. The Army of the Potomac's attempts to break his line, however, resulted only in even heavier casualties. Also, for the first time since Chancellorsville, Yankee troop morale sagged. The veteran units no longer launched wholehearted attacks, as they had in the past. Grant realized he had to stop and accept the stalemate. He reached Richmond and Petersburg, but he no longer had the strength to take them — at least for the foreseeable future. The Siege of Petersburg began on June 9. Thus started nine months of bitter trench warfare in one of the longest and bloodiest sieges in the history of North America.

---

44 Petersburg was 23 miles south of Richmond. Five railroads radiated out of Petersburg and brought in vital supplies.

The Retribution Conspiracy

─ CHAPTER XXIV ─
KIDNAP LINCOLN

"**H**ave you given any recent thought to the idea of abducting Abraham Lincoln?" Jefferson Davis asked Rance Liebert.

"I have been too busy with sabotage to give the matter more than superficial attention," the colonel admitted, "but I believe it may be possible. It certainly would have been in 1861," he said, referring to an earlier conversation they had, which ended in Liebert receiving a reprimand. "Whether or not Lincoln has become less careless about his personal security is something I do not know."

"We must determine that," President Davis declared. When Rance said nothing, he added: "General Lee and I have concluded it would be a good idea to abduct him." He did not deign to elaborate further, so Rance did not ask.

"I will initiate efforts immediately," Liebert said. "I am going back to Canada tomorrow, so I'll be passing through Washington anyway. I'll check with my operatives and send you a dispatch assessing the possibilities within three or four days. You should have it early next week."

"Good," Davis exclaimed.

"How far do you want me to go?" Liebert asked. "Should I start setting up a group of operatives to carry it out?"

"Yes."

"Do you have a codename for the operation in mind?" the colonel asked.

"Call it 'Operation Retribution,'" Jefferson Davis said.

Rance Liebert smiled.

───

Rance's operatives in Washington answered his questions quickly, and their opinions were unanimous: Lincoln was very vulnerable. Occasionally, he would even mount a horse and ride from the White House to the Anderson Cottage alone. On other occasions, he would ride in a carriage with one or two bodyguards. Only rarely were the president and Mrs. Lincoln accompanied by a cavalry escort.

Colonel Liebert would have to decide who would direct actual effort. As soon as he got to Washington, he asked Guinevere to dinner. He made the usual arrangements, so they could talk privately. She, however, noticed a man in an ill-fitting suit was nearby and seemed overly interested in them.

"That man is watching us," she whispered.

"Oh, him. He's supposed to," Rance answered back. "He's one of my agents. He's providing security for this meeting."

She nodded. *I shouldn't have been surprised,* she thought. Since the incident with that man Blanton, he was even more security conscious.

"I need a recommendation from you. If you had to pick a man for a most dangerous mission in Washington, who would it be?"

"Do you mean if I had to pick a person for a most dangerous mission in Washington, who would it be?" She asked, sipping her wine.

"Yes. Of course. That's what I meant."

She smiled. "Guinevere Spring. If not her, Sally Mae Glass."

"Nope. I can't risk either one of those. They're far too valuable."

A pleased look flashed across Guinevere's face. Her plan to become Mrs. Rance Liebert was progressing nicely. "Thank you for that," she smiled. They were not yet where they once were, but Guinevere felt she was regaining his trust. If she could do that, she reasoned, everything else would fall into place, because Ginger had already won him over completely. But back to business. She thought for a moment and said, "John Surratt or John Wilkes Booth."

Rance knew Surratt. Despite his youth, he was a courier for the Secret Service for three years. He was smart, brave, and resourceful. His mother operated a safe house for the Service. He would be a good choice except he was only 20, not a natural leader, and he probably wouldn't be able to put together an effective abduction force. Rance didn't know much about Booth, other than he was a great actor, so he inquired about him.

"He's about 26 years old. Comes from a family of actors. Depending on how you count them, he is the ninth or tenth child of the famous English actor, Junius Brutus Booth."

"What do you mean, 'Depending on how I count them'?"

"Well, Junius had nine children from his American wife. Before that, he had a Belgium wife who had one child by him. Then he abandoned them and came to America, so Wilkes has a half-brother in Europe."

"Interesting."

"I've known him for years. Remember when I left Rainbow?"

"Of course," he frowned. It was not a pleasant memory.

"I attended the Junius Booth, Jr., School of Acting in New York

City. Junius is Wilkes' brother. So is Edwin Booth, another famous actor of whom you may have heard."

"I see."

"Junius was a great teacher, but both Wilkes and Edwin are considered better actors. According to the critics, Edwin is the best actor in the United States. I owe him a debt of gratitude."

"Really?"

"Yes. At various times, both he and Junius helped me get acting jobs. Junius was especially helpful when I first started out. He opened some doors for me and helped me break into the business."

"Good man," Liebert concluded. "And he must be a good teacher, because you are a fine actress."

She beamed. She knew she was good, but compliments from men were always welcome, especially if that man was Rance.

"And a wonderful person," Liebert added.

Guinevere turned her head and looked him right in the eyes. He hadn't said anything that personal since he learned about Ginger — and he still had not kissed her passionately and certainly hadn't mentioned marriage. Clearly he was not yet there, but he was beginning to come around.

He interrupted her thoughts. "What about John Booth?"

"He prefers to be called 'Wilkes.' He is also an exceptional actor, as is his brother, Junius. But neither approaches Edwin."

When Liebert did not reply, she continued: "Junius, Senior, was also an exceptionally good actor, and he got paid well. He sent Wilkes to the best private academies, so he is cultured and well educated. Wilkes started his career in Baltimore in 1855, playing the part of Richmond in *Richard III*. He botched his lines so obviously that the audience let him know of their displeasure. Since then, he has become much better. Now he is extremely popular. He is flamboyant, personable, and handsome. Physically, he is a little above average height, slender, and muscular, with jet-black hair, dark eyes, and a black mustache."

"Tell me something about Booth, the man," the colonel interrupted. He knew he was handsome. Most actors were. But that didn't mean they had any sense.

"He is charming and urbane. He dresses elegantly, loves music, and plays the flute very well. He is also an excellent swordsman and fencer, a crack shot, a fine equestrian, and a skilled billiards player. He is also a fluent conversationalist. Men like him, and many woman fall in love with him, almost at first contact," Guinevere responded. "He takes full advantage of that fact," she added.

"Is he discrete?"

"Not entirely," she admitted. "His whole family is pro-Unionist and pro-Lincoln. He and Edwin are known to have had harsh words about it, and Edwin even told his younger brother that he was no longer welcome in his home. Wilkes, on the other hand, loves the South and is definitely pro-Confederate. It got him arrested in Missouri in 1861 or '62."

"Really? What happened?"

"The usual thing. He denounced Lincoln as a tyrant in a public place. Someone overheard him and reported him, so a Lincolnite cop arrested him and threw him in jail."

"Thus proving his point," Rance added. My goodness, the Constitution and the First Amendment really don't mean anything in Mr. Lincoln's America, he thought. "How long was he in jail?"

"Just overnight. He is charming and talked his way out of it. I suppose he told the police that he was drunk and it just slipped out, but he didn't really mean it. He is very persuasive. All he had to do was pay a fine."

"I believe that is called a bribe," Liebert inserted.

"Yes. And most people don't take actors and actresses seriously, so few really pay attention to what thespians say off the stage, unless that someone wants to take advantage of you," she remarked. There was just a touch of bitterness in her voice. "But he is one of the top actors in America and one of the few who is paid really well." She reflected a moment. "He also took part in the hanging of John Brown."

"Really?"

"Yes. As you may remember, there were rumors the abolitionists were going to swoop down and rescue Brown from the gallows, so Governor Wise ordered the Virginia Militia and the V.M.I. Cadets to provide security for the hanging. Booth wanted to be there to watch the old fanatic swing and to fight the abolitionists if they dared to show up. Unfortunately, he didn't have a uniform, so he asked two fully uniformed militiamen to share parts of their uniforms with him, so there would be three partially uniformed men instead of two fully uniformed soldiers."

"What did they say?" Rance asked.

"They declined. But Booth got his way with the application of cash. One civilian and two fully uniformed militiamen ducked into a nearby restroom, and three partially uniformed militiamen came out."

Rance smiled. "Did the boys get into any trouble?"

"No," she grinned. "Half the Virginia Militia was only partially uniformed in those days."

"Anything else about Booth?" Liebert wanted to know.

"Well, he's sexually promiscuous."

"I figured he might be," Rance allowed. "Young, handsome, rich, and constantly in the company of beautiful women, many of whom are loose. And with his father as a role model, I can see how he would be."

"He hops into and out of bed a lot. It almost got him killed."

"Really? How?"

"He was in a play in Albany, and Henrietta Irving was his leading lady, but he fooled around with another woman. Henrietta slashed his arm with a dirk. Then, like the drama queen she is, she went to her own room and cut herself in the chest. Her wound was superficial and his was painful though not serious, but he was lucky. She could have cut an artery."

She was glad he didn't ask her who the "other woman" was, because it was Guinevere herself. She knew Rance was probably wondering if she had sex with Booth during her promiscuous phase. She was hoping he wouldn't ask her. If he did, she was going to lie and say no.

Rance did wonder but decided against asking. He suspected she probably had, but he didn't want to know. Sometimes he dealt with things by simply shutting them out, and he meant it when he told her what she did before they became a couple didn't count, insofar as he was concerned, although he still had not completely gotten beyond how he felt when she sprang Ginger on him. But he wasn't entirely forthcoming with her, either. More than two years before, he had several good spies in Washington, and he asked two of them to keep an eye on her. Both reported she had dates with Federal officers (Rance already knew this), but apparently had not slept with anyone in months. As time passed, her assessment by the bachelors changed from "beddable" to "forget about it." She would go out with different men, it was true, but she would not commit to one in any way, shape, or form, and wouldn't allow anyone to take liberties. Even fondling her breasts was verboten and could result in a slap in the face. One frustrated officer remarked that she was going through her "second virginity."

She changed the subject as quickly as she could. "In the first two years of the war, Booth occasionally went south and performed in Richmond. In the process, he smuggled medicines to the military hospitals. Mostly quinine and laudanum."

"Good man," Liebert responded, somewhat against his will. Anyone who risked his freedom and career to help wounded Southern soldiers automatically went up in his estimation. That showed courage, and anyone who would attempt to kidnap the president of the United States had better have a whole sack full of that. "But why didn't he join our army?" He asked.

"His mother. When the war began, she made him promise not to join the Confederate Army, and he has kept his word."

Well, that's a small plus for him, if that's really the reason he didn't enlist, Liebert thought, although he should never have made that promise in the first place. If Mrs. Ambrose Liebert asked that of either of her sons, Rance or Billy, she would have gotten a resounding "No!" But he decided not to pursue this line of questioning any further. There was really no way to check the truthfulness of this assertion in any case.

"He also has a fiancée," Guinevere remarked.

"He does? Who?"

"Lucy Hale."

"Isn't she the daughter of ..."

"Yes, that's right," Guinevere declared, anticipating his question. "She is the daughter of Senator John Parker Hale, the abolitionist Republican from New Hampshire. But she's not the only woman in his life. He has girlfriends, actresses, co-stars, bit players, and prostitutes all over the place."

"He sounds about as faithful as an alley cat," Rance observed.

"That cuts both ways," she answered. "Lucy Hale is dark-haired, gorgeous if sometimes a little chubby, with beautiful blue eyes. I hear she sleeps with whomever she wants. She is charming and accustomed to having her way with men and can be cruel to her boyfriends if the mood strikes her. Even though she is unofficially engaged to Booth, she has kept her beaus. They include Captain Oliver Wendell Holmes,[45] who is absolutely brilliant, and John Hay, Lincoln's personal secretary."

"That could be useful information," Rance said, thinking aloud.

"It goes deeper than that," she said and paused for effect. He was hanging on her every word now, and that is how she liked it. "Captain Robert Todd Lincoln is courting her also."

"What?" Liebert exclaimed. "The president's son?"

"None other," Miss Spring pronounced, smiling widely. "He is ap-

---

45 Holmes later became a U.S. Supreme Court justice.

The Retribution Conspiracy

parently quite taken with her."

Colonel Rance Liebert shook his head. What a town Washington is, he thought. What a mess!

"Wilkes is quite jealous of her," Sally continued, "especially when it comes to Robert Lincoln. Flies into a rage when she dances with him."

"How does she react to that?" Rance asked.

"Oh, she doesn't care. I think it just causes her to dance all the more. Robert Todd is just one of the rods she uses to keep Wilkes in line. When he's in Washington, she cracks the whip and he walks the straight and narrow, at least in the public's view. Of course, I'm pretty sure she has no idea that he keeps a high-class prostitute in New York, another in Baltimore, and a girlfriend in Boston, that I know about. There are said to be others. …"

"If I choose Booth for this mission, I'm going to have to teach him discretion," Liebert declared, thinking out loud again. The colonel weighed the positives and negatives. Courage and charisma he definitely had. Discretion could be learned … he hoped. *Besides, I don't have any options,* the colonel thought. As he sat there, staring at his beautiful lady friend, Colonel Rance Liebert decided to enlist John Wilkes Booth for the task of abducting Abraham Lincoln. He leaned back. "The situation is desperate. Time is running out for the Confederacy. We've only got a few months at best. I don't have the luxury of proceeding slowly and carefully. Do you know where I might find him?"

"Oh, yes. The theater is a closed, incestuous little world," Guinevere answered. "Everyone knows everything about everyone else. He's in Boston, starring in *Hamlet*."

"Well, I've got to go to Montreal and perhaps Toronto anyway," he sighed. "If you telegraph him and asked him to meet Owen Dickerson in Boston in two days, would he do it?"

"You mean in three days," she said coyly, looking over her wine glass. It was clear she was reserving tomorrow for herself.

"Yes," he grinned. "Three days." He thought for a moment. "Since its July, it is perhaps a little too hot for a picnic, but we could take a ride in the country and maybe have supper together tomorrow evening."

"That sounds good," she smiled.

"Bring Ginger," he said on an impulse.

"Are you sure?" She was pleasantly surprised.

"Yes."

She grinned widely and felt she was gaining ground. But he quickly changed the subject.

"Back to Booth. Would he meet with Owen Dickerson in Boston if you telegraphed him and asked him to?" He asked a second time.

"I'm pretty sure he would," she answered, looking away. "By the way, am I allowed to know what this mission is?"

"I suppose I should tell you, since I aim for you to be the leader of it when I'm not in Washington," he said, matter-of-factly. He paused until she began to take another sip of wine. "We're going to kidnap Abraham Lincoln and transport him to Richmond, where we are going to deliver him to Jefferson Davis in chains. If he resists, we're going to kill him."

She choked as the wine shot out her nose. She put down the glass, blew her nose on her napkin, wiped the liquid off her dress and glared at him. He was suppressing a belly laugh.

Her shoulders slumped and she clenched her teeth in exasperation. Dadburnit, she thought. He did it to me again.

—∞∞∞—

The war ruined their ride in the country. News arrived that Jubal Early's Confederate Army of the Valley captured Frederick, Maryland, and was advancing on Washington, D.C. These were Stonewall Jackson's old men and Rance knew how fast they marched. They would likely reach the northwestern edge of the District's fortifications by late afternoon, and he did not want to take Guinevere and Ginger joy riding in a combat zone, so they went fishing instead. A farmer who lived just east of the Washington allowed the city dwellers to fish his stocked pond for a small fee. So Rance taught Ginger how to fish. He received the "honor" of baiting her hook. She caught an impressive mess of fish, but they let them go when they finished. Ginger had a marvelous time. Guinevere enjoyed herself as well. She could see the three of them becoming a family someday. True, she thought, Rance and I haven't had the talk, and he hasn't committed to marrying a woman with an illegitimate child, but he seems to be coming around. She knew she couldn't bring it up. He had to make the first move. But he was moving — very slowly — in the direction she hoped. And that would do, for now. It would have to.

She was also gratified Ginger was taking to Rance so rapidly. She needed a father, and he would be a great one. Ginger already thought he was wonderful because, in an era that believed children should not be heard, he paid attention to her and treated her as a small adult.

Dinner was also fun. Rance seated Ginger first, holding out her chair as if he were one of her beaus. Then he seated Guinevere, and finally himself. Ginger especially liked a recently popular dish called "French fries."[46] Rance decided to try them, along with fried chicken. As soon as "Owen" ordered the chicken, Ginger wanted that as well. Guinevere, as usual, ordered a large salad. It was expensive, because salad was normally consumed only by the wealthy.[47] The tall adults (as Ginger saw it) had lemon pie for dessert, while the short adult had strawberry short cake. As was standard, Guinevere didn't finish hers, so Rance ate the remnants.

On the ride back, they heard cannon fire — the distant sound of war. General Early was probing the city's defenses. Everywhere Washington residents looked worried and pensive.

"I hope he takes the city," Guinevere declared, "and hangs Lincoln, just like Dahlgren was going to hang President Davis." She still held the Union president personally responsible for burning Windrow and Rainbow.

"It'll never happen," Rance declared. "Under Lincoln, Washington has become the most heavily fortified city in the world. It also has a large garrison, which is replete with heavy artillery. And in the past week, he has reinforced it with an entire corps from the Army of the Potomac."

"Which one?"

Rance looked at her with a degree of amazement. How many ladies would have thought to ask that? It occurred to him that, if she were a man, she'd fit right in on Robert E. Lee's staff.

"The VI," he answered.

"That's Sedgwick's old corps," she said. "One of their best. Full of veterans. They captured Fredericksburg and Mayre's Heights in '63 and treated our boys pretty roughly at Gettysburg. But they suffered heavy losses in the Wilderness this spring." She paused and added: "You're right. There's no way Early's little army will capture Washington against both the garrison and the VI Corps."

"Probably never intended to," Rance observed. "Early likely just

---

46 French fries were apparently invented by Walloons in Belgium in the seventeenth century. Thomas Jefferson was eating them in the White House as early as 1802, but they did not become popular in the United States until the late 1850s.
47 Salad did not become a dish commonly eaten by the masses for a few more decades.

wanted to take some of the pressure off Lee" like I try to do every day, he said and thought, respectively.

They rode in silence for some moments, then Liebert added: "You know, it's strange. Lincoln is overly concerned with the safety of Washington and always has been, but doesn't seem to give a hoot about his own personal safety. Sometimes he rides off into the countryside all by himself. It never seems to occur to him that he might be killed." The colonel didn't know it, but that was being proven again, even as he spoke. While Early probed the Union defenses at Fort Stevens, President Lincoln decided he wanted to see what a Rebel infantry attack looked like, so he mounted a parapet and deliberately exposed himself to enemy fire. He didn't even bother to take off his stovepipe hat. A surgeon 20 yards from him was killed by a Rebel bullet. One of his aides, Captain Oliver Wendell Holmes, practically had to drag him down from the platform.

Once they got back to Guinevere's apartment, they played a children's card game for a while, and then it was Ginger's bedtime. She insisted Rance lie down and read her a bedtime story. When he finished, he stood up and said: "Time for you to go to sleep, little lady!"

She held up her arms. He bent down for a goodnight hug. It was a long one, during the middle of which she said: "I love you, Mr. Owen!"

"I love you, too, Ginger," he exclaimed with a big grin. Then he thought for a minute, and a serious look flashed across his face. Maybe I do at that, he decided. He tucked her in, wished her goodnight, and kissed her cheek.

When he exited her bedroom, Guinevere met him and handed him his nightshirt without saying a word. He took it and touched her face. He hesitated a moment; then drew her closer. The nightshirt fell to the floor. After a moment's pause, he wrapped both arms around her and kissed her passionately for the first time in months. She kissed him back and then hugged him firmly and buried her face in his chest. "Thank God," she muttered. "Oh, thank God!"

Rance didn't know exactly what to say. "Nuthin' settled yet," he muttered.

"I know," she declared. "But it's getting better."

He really didn't know what to make of this remark, so he said nothing at all. They went to bed, and she held him close all night long.

"I love you!" She whispered some time later.

But Rance Liebert was already asleep.

The Retribution Conspiracy

Two days later, Owen Dickerson and Julian Anderson knocked on the door of John Wilkes Booth's hotel room in Boston.

"Yes, gentlemen, are you the man Guinevere telegraphed me about?" Booth asked Anderson.

"No," Anderson cracked as he pushed passed the actor and into the room. He put his hand inside his coat and looked in the closet.

"See here, sir, what are you doing?" a startled Booth asked.

"Shut up," Anderson snarled. Then he checked the bathroom, behind the curtains, and under the bed. "The room's clean, sir."

Booth looked irate as Rance entered the room. "You must forgive us, Mr. Booth, but we find one can't be too careful, especially when one is operating in enemy territory."

Irritation mixed with astonishment flashed across Booth's face. "Enemy territory? Who are you?" He asked.

Liebert took a deep breath. In 1861, or even a year ago, he would have proceeded slowly and carefully with Booth. But it was not 1862. His country was dying, bleeding to death from a thousand cuts. No time for slow and careful. He was going to have to be honest and blunt with this man Booth, and he was going to have to tell him more than he would have even thought about telling him even a few months ago. He had shared this information with Anderson on the way to the room. Rance knew his approach would be reckless. If Booth reacted wrongly or even suspiciously, Anderson was prepared to kill him. With that thought, Liebert said: "I am Colonel Owen Dickerson of the Confederate Secret Service. This is my aide and chief security officer, Lieutenant Anderson."

"I didn't even know the Confederacy had a secret service," Booth declared.

"Good," Liebert smiled. "You weren't supposed to know. We have it on good authority that you are loyal to the Cause."

"Guinevere told you that?" The startled actor asked.

"Yes. She's one of our agents in Washington." Rance noted the surprised look on Booth's face. "Do not let her beauty, charm, and gentle manners deceive you," he continued. "Guinevere is as smart as any man in the Secret Service and just as cunning. President Davis and Robert E. Lee sing her praises every time I see them."

"You know the president and General Lee?" Booth asked. His eyes widened and he was almost overwhelmed. The actor was clearly impressed, which was the reaction Liebert was hoping to engender.

"Yes. Sure," Rance said, walking over to the table. "We're close personal friends. Colonel Davis and I fought together in Mexico. He is like a second father to me, and General Lee is a close friend. We talk all the time. He even gives me romantic advice," he added in an off-hand manner as he picked up a nearly full bottle of bourbon. "May I?"

"Oh, yes, certainly," Booth responded. Rance poured a small shot of bourbon into a glass and mixed it with water from a pitcher on the table.

"Anderson?" Liebert asked, tilting the bottle toward him.

"Yes, sir!" Anderson grinned, for the first time since he had left Virginia. It was rare for him to call even the colonel "sir," but this was one of those times. After all, there was free whiskey involved.

Rance poured him a healthy shot.

"More!" Anderson demanded.

Rance complied. "Water?"

"No, sir!" Anderson smiled, taking the glass. "No need to ruin good bourbon with water. I never drink the stuff. Fish breed in it, you know."

"Sound policy!" Liebert exclaimed, grinning. He turned to Booth and said, "We don't have much good bourbon available in the South anymore." Or much of anything else, he thought. Our transportation network is shot and this blockade is killing us.

Booth couldn't contain himself any longer. "What do you want me to do? And how do I know you are who you say you are?"

"Good question, Mr. Booth," Liebert said. "If you keep thinking like that, we'll make a good agent out of you yet. If we can prove we are who we say we are, will you join us? Are you willing to work for the overthrow of Abraham Lincoln?"

"Overthrow Lincoln? Darn right I will!" Booth proclaimed with enthusiasm. With that, Anderson took his hand off his pistol.

"Okay. Meet us at the Rossin House in Montreal on Sunday evening at 6 p.m. We already know you are not working Sunday and Monday, so you will have ample time to make our appointment and still be back in time for your evening performance Tuesday, if just barely." Rance reached into his pocket and pulled out an envelope. "Here are your tickets. And don't worry. Your train does not travel along one of the routes we have scheduled for demolition anytime soon."

Booth's head swam. Northern newspapers were full of stories about the rash of train derailments and mysterious explosions, but Booth did not associated them with the Confederate Secret Service until now.

The Retribution Conspiracy

"In Montreal, you will meet C.C. Clay and Professor James Holcombe, and perhaps Colonel Jacob Thompson. Do you know who they are?"

"I know Clay and Thompson," Booth answered. "They are the Confederate commissioners to Canada, according to the newspapers. I have met them both, after performances in Washington before the war."

"Good. Then you will recognize them."

"Yes, Colonel ..."

"Colonel's fine for here, but I am Mr. Dickerson or simply Owen when we are in public. Understand?"

"Yes, sir!"

"Good."

"What exactly do you want me to do?" Booth asked.

"All in good time, my dear fellow! All in good time," Rance/Owen answered. "We'll see you Sunday."

Anderson had already finished his drink. "Can I have one for the road?" He was asking Booth, not Liebert.

"Of course, Mr. Anderson. In fact, you may have the entire bottle." By nature, John Wilkes Booth was a generous man.

He didn't have to offer twice. Anderson swooped it up with lightning speed and walked for the door with his prize tucked under his arm. "You'll do," he said as he passed the entertainer on his way out the door. This was just about the highest compliment he ever paid anybody. Liebert never told Booth that Anderson was there to kill the actor if the meeting went wrong. Anderson was glad it was not necessary. This man was bighearted. Julian Anderson liked John Wilkes Booth.

—⊱⊰—

Jacob Thompson, C.C. Clay, and Professor Holcombe also liked John Wilkes Booth, who was habitually quite charming. He arrived at the Rossin House in the early afternoon and they talked for three hours. Along with Liebert, Anderson, and George N. Sanders, they had dinner at the nicest restaurant in Montreal. Then they went back to the Rossin House and talked until two o'clock in the morning. Part of the conversation was business, but mostly it was a gossip session. The principles in the Lincoln Conspiracy were getting to know each other.

Thompson was somewhat concerned about how Rance would take the presence of George Sanders. Liebert hardly knew the short, chubby, and balding Sanders and was obviously surprised to meet him in Montreal. After the first half hour of the conversation, the commissioner asked for a private word with Liebert and Clay.

"I would be pleased if you would accept George Sanders as an assistant for this project," Thompson said. Clay agreed wholeheartedly.

"If you recommend it, I shall certainly consider it," Liebert answered. "Tell me about him."

"I knew him in Washington. A native of Kentucky. He was a former political agent for the Democratic Party. He still has important contacts in the capital and is known for being well informed. He also has a well-deserved reputation for boldness and daring. He is willing to take chances, seize the initiative, and create and execute imaginative plans," Thompson declared. "I believe you will like him."

"He is also known for his strong republican views — republican as in French Revolutionary republican views," Rance added. "He looks upon Lincoln as a murderous tyrant. Sanders is a known advocate of political assassinations. President Pierce appointed him consul to London. While there, he associated closely with refugee European radicals, including Giuseppe Mazzini, who expounds the 'Theory of the Dagger,' ergo, the idea that tyranticide is justified. Sanders wanted someone to assassinate Napoleon III — with help from himself. That is why he was recalled."

Thompson's and Clay's faces fell. *And I thought this man was just another wooden-headed soldier,* Thompson thought ruefully. Liebert — or somebody working for him — has obviously done his homework. Then Rance added: "But back to your original point. Yeah, I like him, too. Tell him we'll meet for supper tomorrow. I want to interview him."

"Fine!" Thompson exclaimed, grinning broadly. This was working out splendidly — much better than he anticipated it would just a few moments earlier.

"Jacob, just be sure to impress upon him most forcefully that, in this operation, nobody is to be assassinated without my permission."

"I'll do that," he smiled, and patted his erstwhile rival on the back.

When John Wilkes Booth left Montreal that Sunday morning, he was a happy man. He was a full-fledged member of the Confederate Secret Service, and he very much liked his new colleagues. He also felt much better about himself. Because of his promise to his mother, he began to look down upon Wilkes Booth as a coward. He felt guilty because Southern soldiers were starving and being ground to bits by

The Retribution Conspiracy

overwhelming numbers while he, an able-bodied man, wasn't doing anything to help them. Now there was a good chance he would be the one to capture the tyrant Lincoln and put an end to their suffering! He would, at last, be the hero he always wanted to be. He also hated Abraham Lincoln to the depths of his soul for what he did to the South. He felt blessed that he was entrusted by God with a divine mission. He was determined not to fail.

—ᖇ CHAPTER XXV ᖇ—
PLAN B

landestine operations require more time, money, and effort than most people realize, even if specialized resources are not required — and they frequently are. As Thompson and Liebert explained to Booth, he would have to select a team of specialists to abduct Lincoln. After capturing the Union commander-in-chief, he would have to traverse southern Maryland as rapidly as possible. He would need to purchase a fairly large boat beforehand and have it ready to go with someone aboard knowledgeable about the inlets and currents of the lower Potomac, so he could transport his strike force across the river to the Northern Neck of Virginia. Simultaneously, a detachment of sailors from the Torpedo Bureau would mine the area just off the southern (Virginia) shore, to discourage pursuing Union naval vessels and landing parties. Upon their arrival in Virginia, Booth's abduction force would be met by a security detail, which would transport the captured president to the Richmond, Fredericksburg & Potomac Railroad at Milford Station. From there, a fast train — already fired up and waiting — would spirit "Honest Abe" to Richmond. What happened next would be up to Jefferson Davis and his associates. That was Plan A.

Rance already decided not to use his normal boatman or any of his previous contacts in southern Maryland on this mission because he knew the Federals would turn over every stone to find them. He suspected he could never use the men involved in this abduction again on any other mission, and he still wanted to have a route from Washington to Richmond, even after Lincoln was safely locked up. Also, he always crossed the Potomac in a canoe or rowboat, and this time he needed someone with a bigger boat who knew how to handle it. Clearly, though, this was a one-way mission. No one directly involved in the abduction of the Union president could ever return to the North. This meant an entire new team would have to be assembled.

Also in on the plan was Colonel John Singleton Mosby. Nicknamed "the Gray Ghost," he was the most famous and successful guerrilla fighter of the War. Large parts of his celebrated 43rd Virginia Partisan Ranger Battalion could be shifted to the Northern Neck when the time for action came. Liebert did not worry about the Federals detecting the movement of this Rebel unit. The Yankees never knew where Mosby was.

Meanwhile, Liebert and John Wilkes Booth began to recruit a team to help him kidnap Lincoln. After recruiting a pair of former Maryland infantrymen in Baltimore, Booth returned to Washington to report to his "boss," Guinevere Spring. He smiled to himself as he entered her living room. He was looking forward to the encounter. She was beautiful, passionate, and would do almost anything in bed. As soon as they were alone, he grabbed her, swept her up, and kissed her passionately, with his left hand on her back and his right hand on her breast. He did not notice the yielding quality he expected. She did not kiss him back and, instead of closing her eyes, they were as wide as saucers, registering surprise and shock rather than pleasure. All in all, the kiss was not particularly satisfactory.

When he finished, something totally unprecedented occurred. Guinevere Spring drew back her right hand to a point just behind her hip, clenched her fist into a ball, and swung for his face as hard as she could. Completely unprepared for this reaction, he took the full benefit of the blow just below his left eye. Being a country girl from Mississippi, she knew how to hit. He staggered backward.

"Ouch, woman!" He exclaimed. "What was that for?"

"You know what it was for. And you'd better never try anything like that again, ever!"

"Why not?" Booth said, rubbing his face. "I just wanted some lovin'." Then he added rather bitterly: "It's nothing we haven't done before."

"No we haven't. Or at least you'd better pretend we haven't."

"What do you mean by that?"

"Have you ever been shot between your legs?" She asked.

"No!"

"Well, if you try that again, you will be. And if I don't do it, Colonel Liebert will — or he'll have Anderson do it."

Booth's face turned pale except for his left cheek, which was red and swelling. He instinctively realized Liebert and Anderson were very tough and dangerous men — especially Anderson.

"I was raped back home, before the war," she said, as she tried not to cry. This was a painful subject for her, but she forced herself to continue. "Rance Liebert killed two of the men who did it, and the third ran for his life. He doesn't like men who molest me!" She paused and calmed down a little. "Wilkes, Rance reminded me who I am and that I

The Retribution Conspiracy

am worth something. If we get out of this war alive, I'm going to marry him. He doesn't know it yet, but I am. I'm going to remain faithful to him, for now and forever."

Booth dared to ask why.

"Because I love him! And because he treats me like I'm somebody!" She answered sharply. "At one time, I'd forgotten what that was like — to be treated with respect by a gentleman. But now I remember, and no man is going to treat me any other way ever again. Ever!" She brushed away a tear from her eye and added: "I am nobody's object or sex toy. Not even yours."

Booth nodded. He suddenly realized he had tread into hazardous territory. It occurred to him Guinevere was much more dangerous than she was a few years ago. He didn't believe Liebert would marry her after the war, but he certainly wasn't about to say so. He now looked upon Guinevere as Rance Liebert's woman, and he wasn't about to step out of line again. From what he heard from his new friends in Canada, the colonel could be a very unpleasant man when provoked, and he clearly headed an extremely deadly organization. If he didn't mind killing the president of the United States, he wouldn't hesitate to kill an actor.

"Now, we're going to forget this ever happened," she said, calming down, "and our casual encounters before the war — they never happened either. We're just two old friends who are now business associates, and our business is abducting Lincoln. Is that all right with you?"

Booth could only nod.

"Now," she said, "let's get down to business. Have you recruited anyone to help you?"

Booth looked at her through new eyes but, instead of answering her question, asked: "You're not from New York, are you, Guinevere?"

"No, I'm not."

"Where are you from?"

"Mississippi."

"And your real name isn't Guinevere Spring, is it?"

"No, it's not," she admitted.

"What is it?"

"You don't need to know," she said, evenly. "Now, let's get down to business," she said again. "Who have you recruited, and who do you plan to recruit?"

It was a hot day in August 1864, when Abraham Lincoln's horse barreled down the street at full speed until the tall, bare-headed president abruptly reined it up in front of the Anderson Cottage. For once, his customary stately dignity was totally absent, and he was clearly upset. The soldiers raced down the porch quickly. They didn't know what, but they knew that something unusual was happening.

"Somebody shot at me!" Lincoln shouted as he dismounted. "Somebody blew my hat right off my head!"

It only took a second or two for the soldiers to regain their composure. A cavalry lieutenant quickly organized a detail to find the would-be assassin. As they rode off, Lincoln shouted at them: "And find my hat!"

They found the president's stovepipe hat on the road about a mile south of the cottage and two miles north of the White House. There was a bullet hole through the brim. Another three inches to the left and Hannibal Hamlin would have been president of the United States.

The investigation was as thorough as 1864 criminology would allow. Abraham Lincoln was riding alone — without escort or bodyguards of any kind — when someone shot the hat off his head. But by the time the cavalry arrived, the perpetrator was long gone.

Had the would-be killer been just a little bit better shot, it would have been a perfect assassination. Behind the scenes, Rance Liebert also conducted an investigation. No one in his organization knew anything about it. Anderson allowed that the colonel knew it couldn't have been him because if it had been, "the son-of-a-gun would be dead." Jacob Thompson and his people were as shocked as anyone (well, except for Lincoln). No one ever discovered who fired that shot.

After he calmed down, Abraham Lincoln decided it was an accident. Someone discharged a gun, perhaps in target practice, and the bullet just happened to pass through the hat of the president of the United States — while he was wearing it. No one could convince Lincoln coincidences of this nature simply do not occur. For all his brilliance, Abe Lincoln was never able to comprehend anyone would attempt to harm him — not even in the middle of a civil war.

Lincoln's bodyguard was able to persuade the president to enlarge his security, at least temporarily. For a couple of months, he traveled with a strong cavalry escort. But cavalry is loud. The horses' hooves on the pavement and the clash of spur and saber made too much noise for the commander-in-chief. If he rode with Mrs. Lincoln or some important guest, the noise of the cavalry, combined with that of the carriage, made it impossible to carry on a conversation. So Abraham Lincoln dispensed with the escort and reverted back to his old ways.

August 1864 was a time of optimism for the Confederacy and deep depression for Lincoln and his associates. Guinevere was right about the Spirit of Bull Run. The vast majority of the people of the North expected the campaign of 1864 to be a cake walk — just mop up a few demoralized remnants and the war would be over. Their awakening was rude. In April 1864, U.S. General Nathaniel Banks advanced on Shreveport, Louisiana, with 32,000 men. Very overconfident, he signaled Lincoln he was afraid the Rebels would melt away into Texas without giving him a major battle. Lincoln shook his head. "I am sorry to see this tone of confidence," the Great Emancipator said. "The next news we shall hear from there will be of a defeat."

Lincoln was right: Banks walked right into an ambush. General Dick Taylor's Army of Western Louisiana attacked Banks' army with 8,800 men, completely routed it, and chased it for 200 miles, all the way across Louisiana. Admiral Porter's gunboat flotilla managed to escape as well, but only just barely. It also suffered heavy losses, including the largest ironclad gunboat in the inland fleet. But that was just the beginning.

The South still had tens of thousands of resolute men with guns, and they were especially dangerous when they were cornered. The Rebel soldiers drew upon hidden reserves of untapped strength and determination which few in the North suspected they had. They inflicted tens of thousands of casualties upon the advancing blue legions. The Northern public was horrified. Grant lost more men than Lee had, and still the thin gray line barred his way. Atlanta, Charleston, Mobile, and Richmond all held while, with 3,200 men, General Forrest crushed a Union army of 13,000, chased it out of Mississippi, and galloped through the streets of Memphis. The Northern public was shocked and appalled over the losses. Everyone knew someone who was killed, or was missing, or was in a hellhole like Andersonville, or was ruined for life. Hardly a family did not have a husband, father, son, uncle, or cousin lying in a military hospital or in a grave on some distant battlefield with a name they'd never heard before. Stunned and almost traumatized, they turned on Abraham Lincoln. His popularity hit a new low. The Democrats wanted a negotiated settlement and put a peace plank in their platform. According to all the political prognosticators, Lincoln was going to lose the election. And he believed it, too. He told his generals they must make plans to end the war by the time he left office. He projected that date to be March 4, 1865: the very next Inauguration Day.

It appeared the South would win the war politically, just as Rance Liebert hoped. Then, Jefferson Davis made perhaps the worst mistake of his professional life. Joseph E. Johnston fought his best campaign of the war and successfully prevented Sherman from taking Atlanta, but he was as surly as ever. He refused to assure the president he would not abandon Atlanta without permission and sometimes would not even communicate with Davis. Angry and frustrated, the president sacked Johnston.

John Bell Hood was a gallant soldier and an exceptionally brave one. He lost the use of an arm at Gettysburg and had a leg amputated at Chickamauga, but he continued to serve in the field. He was an excellent brigade and division commander, but that was his ceiling. Against the advice of Robert E. Lee, Hood's former commandant at West Point, Davis advanced him to corps commander, where his performance was mediocre at best. Nevertheless, the president appointed him commander of the Army of Tennessee, replacing Johnston. It was a disaster. Hood lost Atlanta and invaded Tennessee, where he lost most of his army in November and December.

After Atlanta fell on September 2, Northern public opinion completely reversed itself, because the end of the war was in sight. Lincoln's reelection was now a foregone conclusion. The political solution was no longer a realistic option. The South was out of chances.

Robert E. Lee always believed if his army settled down to trench warfare, besieged by an enemy with unlimited resources, there could be only one end for it, and that was defeat. He was nevertheless willing to endure such a siege until after Atlanta fell. Then, as autumn turned into winter, Sherman marched through Georgia virtually unopposed, burning everything in sight. With no chance of a political solution, Lee determined to manufacture victory out of nothing, as he did so many times before. He decided on a breakout strategy. He would abandon Richmond, out march Grant's forces, fall on Sherman's army, destroy it, and turn back to defeat Grant.

In a private meeting, Rance asked him: "What chance do you think we have of success?"

Lee turned the tables on him. "What do you think are our chances of success?"

"Ten percent. Perhaps less."

"Let's assume you are right. Say we have a 10 percent chance of success. Shouldn't we take it? And if not, what are our alternatives?"

Liebert thought hard for about five seconds. "The alternative is surrender and subjugation. The South would become an economic colony of the North for a hundred years — perhaps longer. Even if our chances are only 10 percent, we must take it, because we have to."

"I agree," said General Lee. "Now what can you do to help me?"

"I can continue what I am doing."

"And you are doing an outstanding job. What else can you do?"

"I believe I could disrupt the Union chain of command. As you know, I am working on a plan to abduct President Lincoln, but this is a very difficult operation. The chances of succeeding are not great," the colonel replied.

"What are your chances of success, do you think?" Lee wanted to know.

"I don't know. Better than 10 percent, I can tell you that!"

General Lee laughed. Liebert was always struck with how much younger he looked when he smiled.

"There is an operation I can conduct with a much greater chance of success, but I hesitate to mention it. …"

"Mention it," Lee ordered. "We are thinking aloud here. I want to hear every idea."

"All right. We implement Plan B."

"What is Plan B?"

"We assassinate Abraham Lincoln. We also assassinate Vice President-elect Andrew Johnson, Secretary of State Seward and Secretary of War Stanton."

Liebert expected Lee to dismiss the idea out of hand, but he did not. "Go on," he said. "Why Johnson and Seward?"

"The Presidential Succession Statute of 1792. If the president and vice president are both dead, the president *pro tempore* of the senate becomes acting president until the Electoral College can elect a new president. The secretary of state is supposed to set this process in motion. But what if he is also dead? The Republicans would have to select a new secretary of state. And who would nominate the new secretary? Would the Senate confirm him? And how long would that take? I'll bet you dollars to dog ticks they'd soon be in a political free-for-all over the selection of the secretary of state, over the control of the Electoral College, over who should be the new president, and a score of other issues. Washington would be in turmoil for weeks. It would be a perfect time for you to make your move."

Lee frowned. He was in deep thought. "I'm going to have to think about this one," he said. "Have you presented this idea to President Davis?"

"No, sir. Not yet."

"Please do so tomorrow. And make an appointment the next day for me, General Pendleton, and yourself," General Lee directed.

Liebert furrowed his brow. Pendleton was Lee's chief of artillery and a pretty nominal one at that, since Lee did not have a central artillery reserve. "I'll make the appointment," Rance said. "But, general ..."

"Yes, Colonel Liebert?"

"Why General Pendleton?"

"He is an esteemed Episcopal minister and a spiritual giant."

The colonel's mouth fell open, but he couldn't think of a word to say.

<hr />

Rance Liebert was concerned that a preacher's opinion might be decisive in getting Plan B rejected. (Pastors tend to oppose acts of murder.) But he did not know Rev. William Pendleton. No proponent of slavery, which he wanted to see gradually abolished, the gray-bearded old man was a Unionist in 1860, just as Jackson, Lee, Forrest and a great many others were, although it did not escape Pendleton's notice that all but three of the 23 pastors in Lincoln's home town of Springfield endorsed other candidates during the Presidential election of 1860. Like many others, North and South, his position hardened. He did not like Federal infringement on states' rights, Lincoln's unfair tax system, his arbitrary expansion of centralized government, his illegal arrests, or his plans to help major corporations, such as the large railroads, at the expense of the South. When Lincoln called for volunteers to suppress the rebellion, Pendleton formed the Rockbridge Artillery, which distinguished itself at 1st Bull Run as part of the Stonewall Brigade. Joe Johnston soon promoted him to colonel and chief of artillery, a post he continued to occupy under Lee.

Pendleton was outraged by the incarceration of pastors such as Rev. Kensey Johns Stewart, a highly respected minister with more than 20 years service, who was arrested at the altar. Dr. Stewart's only crime was he failed to pray for Abraham Lincoln after a sermon.[48] Pendleton also considered the Union Army's behavior in the Shenandoah Valley to be barbaric. Much of his home town of Lexington was burned. His own house escaped, but members of his vestry lost everything they had. His only son, Sandie, a 24-year-old Confederate lieutenant colonel, was killed at Fisher's Hill just a few days before, and William's civilian brother, with whom he was very close, died as the result of his treatment by bluecoats. Even though he was old and sick, he was arrested and forced to walk through the ice and snow from the Northern Neck to Fredericksburg. The ordeal killed him.

In front of Davis, Lee and Liebert, Rev. Pendleton expounded on Lincoln's sin and guilt, taking the same basic position as Stewart, Rev. Robert Gatewood, and Rev. Stephen F. Cameron, among others. No, given Lincoln's tyrannical nature, the Reverend Pendleton did not see anything morally wrong with Plan B. If Davis and Lee decided it should be implemented, Colonel Liebert should try to carry it out. As he left, General Pendleton shook Rance's hand and wished him good luck. He could not resist smiling and saying: "Ya know, colonel, I didn't even know we had a secret service."

"Good!" Rance retorted. "You weren't supposed to know!" He smiled at the preacher. Jefferson Davis and Robert E. Lee chuckled.

When he left the White House that night, Liebert had his orders: proceed with the preparations for Plans A and B.

The next day was a Saturday. Owen Dickerson appeared unexpectedly at Melody Herzog's home. This happened rarely (she was seeing a young cavalry officer now), but it was not unheard of. They had worked together for three years and became good friends, and when he came, he usually brought food. The whole South was hungry and some places were even starving. Richmond now had "Starvation Parties." The lavish entertaining of the antebellum days was gone forever. At the Starvation Parties, no food was served and only one beverage: water. Although Owen's presence filled Melody's parents with curiosity, they never said much. They knew romance was not involved and it had something to

---

48 This was also common in much of the occupied South. Sherman and other Union generals made a pastor's failure to pray for Lincoln an offense in Memphis, Vicksburg, and other towns and cities. Offenders could be and often were held indefinitely without legal recourse. In Vicksburg, five women who left church early rather than pray for Lincoln were exiled from the city for a year.

do with business. All they knew was he was a colonel in the signal services, and Melody worked for him — sometimes very late at night. Anytime they worked past about 5 p.m., he always saw to it she was escorted home by a pair of tough-looking soldiers armed with Navy Sixes. It was obvious she was very valuable to him, both personally and professionally. It was also clear to Mr. and Mrs. Herzog that neither Dickerson nor their daughter were going to talk business in their presence. Today, Owen brought an entire ham. This made him the most welcome man in Richmond insofar as the Herzogs were concerned.

Usually when Owen arrived, he also had something for her to sew. Sometimes, this meant he was joining them for supper — and he always provided the main dish for the meal. The feast was invariably several degrees above what was normal in Richmond in 1864, and it provided enough leftovers for several meals. Tonight, after the amenities were dealt with, he invited her to sit with him on the porch. She nodded but did not smile: this indicated serious business.

"Melody, I want you to hide this until after the war," he said, handing her a package.

"What's in it?"

"Money."

"Money?"

"Yes, money." He sighed and drew a deep breath. "Melody, there's a good chance we're going to lose this war."

She immediately began to protest, but he cut her short. "No!" He said, "we must face facts. If I had to bet, I'd bet we're going to lose this war."

Melody tried to breathe. She didn't want to hear this, didn't want to believe it, but here sat a man who regularly spent time with Jefferson Davis, Robert E. Lee, and Samuel Cooper and knew more about the military situation than anyone she had ever met, and he was confiding in her. A tear ran down her cheek. She felt as if she was suffocating.

"These are Yankee greenbacks, taken in fair combat from the enemies of our country," he continued. "I still hope, by some miracle, we can achieve victory. But if we can't, I at least want to provide for a few people I care about."

She nodded but still couldn't speak. Until this moment, it never occurred to her they might lose the war — mainly because she didn't want to believe it. Now, she was being forced to think about it and very much against her will.

The Retribution Conspiracy

"There are seven envelopes in that package. One is for you and your family. One is for my brother Billy and his family. The others are for Major Leonard, Captain Glass, my parents, my sister, and a couple of darkies named Jonathan and Chuckatuck. Hold on to them until the end of the war. If we are compelled to surrender, Billy or Dan will pick them up. All but yours. Do not open your envelope until you really need to."

"How much money is in here?"

"Two thousand dollars per package."

"TWO THOUSAND …"

"Ssshhhh!" He retorted. "Yes, $2,000. Needless to say, you must be very careful with it and very discrete. Don't use any of this money unless you must — but I suspect it will be necessary. And, if anyone asks you, tell them nothing about what you really did during the war. You merely enciphered and decrypted messages for the War Department, that's all."

"Yes, sir," she declared. Two thousand dollars would feed her and her family for years. "I'll be very careful where I hide this."

"You know," he smiled, trying to create a light moment, "if we win, you've just received an enormous bonus."

"But you don't think we will?"

"No," he said, serious again. "I do not."

"What about all of the other people?" She asked, gesturing toward the street and the city. "What about them?"

His eyes suddenly got very soft as he stared out toward Richmond. "I can't take care of everybody," he muttered.

—❧ CHAPTER XXVI ❧—
LET'S BURN NEW YORK CITY

S ally Mae Glass cuddled up to Rance Liebert on the sofa of their rooms, watching the fire in the fireplace. She put her head on his shoulder and closed her eyes. "Thank you for cooking supper," she purred. "It was delicious."

"Oh, it was nothing," he replied.

Rance was right: it really wasn't very much. After she'd finished work at the theater that evening, he'd prepared her ham and cheese omelets with some tomatoes and a few other vegetables thrown in. But the coffee was real and, being from Mississippi, he had fried the semi-obligatory pile of "fatty" bacon, a/k/a "greasy bacon." Prior to the war, Southerners just had bacon. Now they used terms like "fatty," "greasy" or "real bacon," to distinguish it from the Confederate Army's "blue bacon," a processed and preserved product which was better than nothing but not by a wide margin. It was inferior to regular bacon in every way, including smell. The Rebel soldiers often joked about how "Our bacon outranks General Lee." The coffee was such a welcome change from Richmond. In Virginia, the ersatz coffee resembled real coffee, except for the texture, taste, color, and smell. Before the war, acorns were for squirrels. The moonshine which now passed for whiskey tasted bad, but it made an excellent paint remover. The bread or "hardtack" which the troops lived on was simply indescribable, but it would make a good substitute for bricks. It was so hard it had to be boiled in water for an hour or two before it could be eaten at all. The troops called it "jawbreakers."

"Well, I really enjoyed my supper," she said. "Or was it breakfast?"

"I'm surprised. I figured you'd be running, screaming into the night. Or at least rushing for the privy."

"Oh …you!" She said as she sat up and playfully hit him on the shoulder.

"If we have to rush you to the hospital to get your stomach pumped out, would that be too much of a mood killer?" he asked.

"It was wonderful!" She exclaimed. "You even washed the dishes. I never knew you could cook."

"Neither did I. And I certainly didn't know I could wash dishes."

She smiled and nuzzled up to him again. "It's nice to be treated like a queen."

"No more than you deserve," he replied. *Is he going to come back to me tonight?* She wondered.

They sat on the couch and watched the fire in silence for a while. The curtains were open and he looked outside. It was beginning to rain. He loved watching rain.

"I'll be leaving tomorrow," he said.

"Where are you going?"

"New York City."

"I wish I could go," she sighed, wistfully.

"I'm meeting Colonel Martin at the Fifth Avenue Hotel," he proclaimed. "How would you like to come with me and play the part of the wife of the dashing and mysterious Owen Dickerson?"

"I'd love to, but I've got another performance tomorrow night."

"And the show must go on," he declared.

"And the show must go on," she repeated, smiling.

She put her head back on his shoulder. Finally she asked: "What are you going to do there? Have a conference?"

"No. Burn it down."

"Burn down the hotel?" She started. The Fifth Avenue was the most luxurious rental accommodation in New York.

"No. The whole city."

She looked at him. Outrageous remarks seemed to be a hallmark of the Secret Service, and she couldn't always tell when he was joking. "Are you serious?"

Hard brown eyes met beautiful blue eyes. "Yes. I am."

She thought about it for a moment. "You're improving, colonel," she said. "You usually deliver your bombshells while I'm eating or drinking wine. I remember once you caught me taking a sip."

"Oh, yeah ..."

"I'm really not at my best when I'm choking and have wine coming out my nose."

"Sorry 'bout that. But it was an accident."

"No, you're not sorry. And I think you did it on purpose," she retorted, folding her arms, sticking her lower lip out and pretending to sulk.

"Oh, no," he lied. "I'd never do that."

"Uuuuuhhhhmmm"

He quickly changed the subject. "I'll come back here afterward, but it might be a few days."

"No hurry," she commented. "Wilkes is down in southern Maryland, planning escape routes with Dr. Mudd. I probably won't have much to report until he gets back."

They talked about the details of the plot for some time; then she kissed his ear, lay her head on his lap, and fell asleep watching the rain.

———ᴂ———

Rance did not tell Sally Mae, but he was little more than a foot soldier in this operation. He was only going to be there because he wanted to be, and any competent private could have taken his place. The entire operation was planned and run by Robert Martin. It was, in fact, something of a "Plan B." Originally, Martin and the Copperhead leaders planned a full-scale uprising for election day, November 8. Then, on November 7, Union Major General Benjamin Butler entered the city at the head of 10,000 men. Martin was consternated. Liebert was pleased. That's 10,000 men Lincoln can't use against Marse Robert, he thought. Faced with Union troops, the Copperheads quickly stood down.

"They'd have backed down anyway," Rance reassured his depressed friend. "They would have found some pretext not to rebel. They always have. They always will. But think of the service you have performed for the South! You've tied down 10,000 men! That's marvelous!"

Martin grunted a thank you and an agreement, but Liebert could tell he didn't really mean it.

Checked in his primary mission, Martin lowered his goals. Availing himself of the aid of one of the more courageous Copperheads, he found a bomb maker, who produced for him 144 four-ounce bottles of Greek Fire. He then registered at the Hoffman House and the St. Denis, in addition to the Fifth Avenue. "Owen Dickerson" checked into the Astor and the Belmont. Other Confederate agents from Canada registered at 17 other hotels. Martin passed out his vials of Greek Fire and the Rebel operatives heated up the New York night.

Ironically, Martin's room was just above the floor reserved for General "Spoons" Butler and his staff.[49]

---

49 Butler was a corrupt Democrat politician before he allied with Lincoln and became a corrupt Republican politician. In one deadlocked convention, he cast his vote for Jefferson Davis for president of the United States in 56 separate ballots. He was called "Beast" for his infantile behavior toward the ladies of New Orleans when he was military governor there. He was also called "Spoons" because he would requisition a mansion as his headquarters for a short time. When the owner returned, all the silverware was gone. He later commented he was in New York to make sure Lincoln carried the state. Whether or not he intended to steal the necessary votes

Unfortunately for the Southern agents, they were amateur arsonists, including Rance. At the Astor, he didn't leave a window open, nor did he open a door or the transom. As a result, the fire spread slowly due to a shortage of oxygen and was noticed by a night watchman. Only the fourth floor was heavily damaged. Fire inspectors later declared, had the transom been opened, the entire hotel would have burned to the ground. At the Belmont, the transom was open — not that Liebert noticed it — he was simply lucky. As a result, the hotel was heavily damaged and two floors were totally destroyed. Another Southern arsonist had similar luck: the St. James Hotel was completely destroyed.

All police and fire department leaves were canceled as terror and panic gripped the city. Fire wagons were everywhere, and New York was in complete meltdown mode. A former lieutenant in Morgan's cavalry raced down the unlit North River piers, tossing Greek Fire bottles into barges and schooners. Several were seriously damaged, one merchant ship was a total loss, and the hay barge *Marie* practically exploded. Barnum's Museum caught fire and the workers released panicked animals into the streets to keep the creatures from being roasted alive. Some of the civilians also fled in terror — one would think they had never encountered a lion or a tiger while walking down the sidewalks of New York City before. Elephants stampeded into the night. The Metropolitan Hotel was in flames. Two entire floors were destroyed, and two of the remaining three were severely damaged. It was closed for months. The Lovejoy suffered only minor damage, but the Albemarle and Fifth Avenue Hotels were severely burned, and the St. Nicholas was a total loss. The United States Hotel on Broadway and the Bancroft Hotel at Broadway and 12th Street were completely gutted. The first and second floors of the New England House on Broadway and Bayard Street were write-offs. For some unknown reason, one of the boys decided that Halsted and Haines, the largest dry goods house in the city, needed to be burned. Firemen fought the blaze all night, but it was completely destroyed. Other businesses were severely damaged as well.

Several of the Rebels met in Central Park the next day. Martin ordered them to scatter; they were betrayed by one of the Copperheads. Twenty-six Copperheads were arrested by the New York Police that day, along with several blockade-runners, spies, and suspected Con-

---

for Lincoln is not clear, because it was not necessary. Lincoln carried New York easily.

The Retribution Conspiracy

federate agents, including at least two of Morgan's former officers.[50] They were all thrown into the prison at Fort Lafayette.

Most of the arsonists escaped to Canada by way of Albany. Rance, of course, hotfooted it back to Washington.

As soon as he entered their apartment, Sally Mae threw herself into his arms and kissed him passionately. "You guys did a whale of a job on New York City!" She gushed.

"How do you know about it?" He asked, as soon as he regained his breath.

"Newspapers." She paused. "You know, if we were married right now, I'd rip your clothes off you and not let you up for three days."

"Just remember that sensation if we do get married."

"Oh, I will! The Lincolnites are outraged!" She effused. "They're offering $2,000 for every one of 'Morgan's cutthroats' who is killed or captured. They got a taste of their own medicine, and they don't like it, not one little bit. I think that's funny! A little redress for their burning of Windrow, Fusilier, and Rainbow." She never forgotten the Yankees had burned her childhood home and never would, and she held Abraham Lincoln personally responsible. And, unlike General Lee, she was not an easy forgiver.

"Yeah, I kinda enjoyed it myself," he grinned. As she hugged him again, he let his true thoughts and emotions flash across his face, where she could not see them. We changed nothing, he thought. Compared to what Sherman is doing in Georgia, this hardly amounts to a pinprick.

---

50 John Hunt Morgan himself was killed by Union cavalrymen on September 4, 1864.

—୬ CHAPTER XXVII ୨—
YOU ARE A REBEL SPY!

A s Christmas, 1864 approached, the Lincoln conspirators were very busy behind the scenes. Booth was occupied by Ellen Starr (a/k/a Ella Turner and Fannie Harrison) at her sister's top-of-the-line bordello in Baltimore. She was a pretty, first-class, 19-year-old prostitute, and a beautiful one at that, with light hair, a fine figure and a sparkling personality. Booth paid a healthy sum to maintain her and receive her exclusive services — well, at least theoretically. He also had trysts with 16-year-old Isabel Sumer and a woman named Carrie Bean, and no doubt others as well.

Somehow, Booth found time to visit Montgomery's Tavern in Bryantown, southern Maryland, where he met with Dr. Samuel Mudd and Tom Wilson, the former postmaster of Bryantown and a Confederate Secret Service agent, who joined the conspiracy. Wilson was willing to help capture Lincoln and smuggle him out of Union-controlled territory and into Virginia. With that end in mind, he introduced them to George Andrew Atzerodt. Originally from a village in Thuringian, central Germany, he was brought across the ocean by his parents when he was eight. Now 29 years old, he was operating a failing carriage repair business in Port Tobacco, Maryland.

Tobacco production in the Port Tobacco area declined tremendously over the years due to soil exhaustion; so had the town and with it the demand for carriage repairs. Atzerodt, however, knew every stream and inlet in the region and was an excellent river pilot. He soon set up a small-scale blockade-running business and was willing to smuggle people and/or goods into the Confederacy — for a price. But he was willing to help in the abduction of Lincoln *frei gratis*.

Guinevere continued to be a Washington matinée idol and continued to reap a harvest of information from loose-lipped Federal officers and administration officials. She and Liebert brought John Surratt, Jr., into the plot. Surratt was 21 years old, 5' 9", with long hair and a goatee. He was young, bold, and energetic, and he knew every road in the Northern Neck and southern Maryland and, despite his youth, had already been a member of the Secret Service for three years. Other operatives continued to monitor Lincoln's movements, looking for weaknesses in his security. They found plenty of them.

The Confederate Signal Corps also joined the plot. After meeting with Liebert, their officers establish a camp and an outpost in the Potomac Hills, which were thinly populated. The camp was located near Boyd's Hole, a landing site for ferries between Virginia and Maryland during colonial times but no longer in use.

Colonel John Singleton Mosby, the "Gray Ghost of the Confederacy," was also deeply involved in the plot to kidnap or kill Abraham Lincoln. He was seriously wounded in December 1864. While recovering at his mother's house, he created a new battalion of four companies and sent them to the Northern Neck. They promptly scattered over Westmoreland, Richmond, Northumberland, and Lancaster counties, one company per county. They would deliver Lincoln, Booth, and his colleagues to the regular Confederate cavalry when the time came. Even though he concurred with it, Liebert was concerned Mosby's move would alert the Yankees, but they paid no attention to it.

Liebert also thought the conspiracy needed a very strong, fearless man, and he asked Mosby to provide one. Mosby gave him Lewis Thorton Powell, alias Lewis Payne.

One of eight children, Powell was the son of a Baptist preacher. His father owned three slaves but freed them around 1848. Lewis was quiet and introverted as a child but was hot-tempered. His siblings nicknamed him "Doc" because he was constantly doctoring injured animals. He was handsome except for the fact the side of his left jaw was more prominent than the right because a mule kicked him in the face when he was 13. He was also an immensely big and powerful man.

Powell was 17 years old when the war began. He lied about his age and enlisted in the 2nd Florida Infantry Regiment in May 1861. The 2nd Florida joined Lee's army in early 1862, in time for the Peninsula campaign. He fought at Yorktown, Williamsburg, Seven Pines, Seven Days, Second Manassas, Antietam and Chancellorsville. In the process, he became a hardened soldier and proved to be a natural killer. In combat, he placed no value on human life, including his own. His commander praised him because he always shot to kill, never to wound. He carried the skull of a Union soldier with him and used it as an ashtray. But he remained a deeply religious man, in a murderous sort of way.

Lewis Powell was shot through the wrist and captured at Gettysburg on July 2. As a prisoner-of-war, his captors employed him as a nurse and transferred him to the West Buildings Hospital in Baltimore. With the help of a volunteer female nurse with whom he had developed a relationship, he escaped on September 7, 1863. She took him

The Retribution Conspiracy

to her mother's boarding house, which was a Secret Service safe house in Baltimore. While there, Powell romanced the nurse's sister. He then made his way to Virginia, where he joined Mosby's Ranger Battalion in early October.

Lewis Powell impressed Mosby as a very effective soldier. He was such a fierce warrior his comrades nicknamed him "Lewis the Terrible." In December 1864, Mosby handpicked him to take part in the abduction of Abraham Lincoln.

On January 1, 1865, Powell "deserted." He took the Oath of Allegiance and soon met some of the other plotters at the Surratt House. They soon discovered Powell was a good natural actor. He could appear surly, stupid, suave, or cultured, depending upon the requirements of the moment. He had no problem with the idea of kidnapping or even assassinating the president of the United States. John Wilkes Booth trusted Powell from their very first meeting, and he soon became the Number Two man in the conspiracy, along with Surratt.

Everything in the District of Columbia, southern Maryland, and Virginia was ready on January 18, 1865. John Wilkes Booth planned to abduct Lincoln that day, when he went to Ford's Theater for a matinée performance. The charming Booth performed in that building many times and was always friendly with all the stage hands — even to the point of occasionally buying them drinks after performances. At other times, when he had an "engagement" with a woman after a play, he would simply give them a bottle of bourbon. Consequently, he was very popular with the crew and always had full access to all parts of the theater, whether he was performing or not, anytime he wanted it.

On the day in question, all of the conspirators were in place, and everything was ready — except for Lincoln. He failed to appear.

That night, the conspirators met at Mrs. Surratt's boarding house and shared a bottle of bourbon and then another. "Colonel Liebert was right," Wilkes Booth moaned. "That man Lincoln does have the instincts of a rat."

A week later, Guinevere Spring was arrested.

———— ∞∞∞ ————

In January 1865, Rance Liebert visited General Beauregard in Charleston, South Carolina. Beauregard did a great job defending the city in a siege which lasted almost three years. Unlike Jefferson Davis, Rance liked "the little Creole," who always greeted him with a handshake and a huge smile. But there was little left to smile about. Sherman was in Savannah, and Rance told Beau that, according to his sources, his next target would be Columbia, South Carolina. If Charleston was not evacuated by the time Columbia fell, the garrison could be cut off and loosely surrounded.

"This confirms what I feared," General Beauregard sighed. He got up and began to pace nervously. "How long do I have?"

"I'd say four weeks. Maybe a few days less," Rance replied.

The general nodded. Both officers knew Charleston already lost whatever military significance it ever had anyway. The port was bottled up by the Union blockade and had held out this long only because of the courage of its garrison and Beauregard's liberal use of torpedoes (i.e., mines) which kept the Yankee fleet at a distance. The city was under more or less continuous artillery and naval bombardment for a year and was battered beyond recognition. Charleston resembled a scene from hell. Everywhere one looked, there was desolation. But the city was still a symbol to both sides, because it was the birthplace of secession. Its loss would be a major encouragement for the North, a bitter blow to the South. Now, however, there was nothing to be done about it. Charleston was doomed.

Beauregard summoned his chief of staff, who was also his son-in-law. "Colonel Liebert has confirmed our worst fears," Beauregard announced. "Charleston must be evacuated. Prepare all that can be prepared. Projected date: February 15."

"Yes, General," the chief said.

"But first, I am going to offer Colonel Liebert a glass of wine. Would you care to join us?" Beauregard asked.

They drank mostly in silence. It was like a wake. Finally, Rance expressed concern that John C. Calhoun's grave might be desecrated after the city fell.

"We have considered that as well, colonel," Beauregard said, coolly.

"Of course you have, sir," Liebert replied immediately, realizing he had spoken awkwardly. He knew General Beauregard was touchy and did not want to offend him. "I didn't mean to infer you hadn't. How clumsy of me. It's just that I was curious as to what your plans in that area are, if you don't mind my asking."

Liebert's answer pleased Beauregard, so he said: "We have already removed the headstone, to discourage vandalism. Tomorrow night around midnight, the coffin will be dug up and reburied in a secret location." He looked at his chief of staff said, "See to that, colonel."

"Yes, sir," he replied.

As soon as he finished his wine, Liebert excused himself, on the grounds he had to leave early the following morning. He shook hands with the general, who invited him to an early breakfast. Naturally, Rance accepted. The next morning, he reminded the little Creole of the last time they ate together, north of Manassas Junction, on July 21, 1861.

"Oh, yes, I recall," he smiled. "We were rudely interrupted by a Federal cannonball, if I remember correctly."

"Yes, we were," Liebert agreed.

"I cannot guarantee it won't happen again," the general smiled over his ersatz coffee.

Rance chuckled. He could not help but recall how much better the food was that day than the fare they had now. "I wish they kept you in command in the West in '62," he declared. "We wouldn't be in this mess today if they had."

"Thank you for that, colonel," Beauregard replied with a gracious nod.

Shortly thereafter, Rance Liebert was on his way back to Richmond. He wondered if he would ever see Beauregard or Charleston again.[51]

<hr />

There was more bad news when Rance arrived back at his headquarters.

"Three of our men have deserted," Leonard reported.

Rance did not bother to respond.

"They took Blanton with them."

"What?" Colonel Liebert jumped straight up from his desk. "This is a disaster! When did this happen? I've been keeping this location secret for four years. If Blanton makes it back to Washington, they'll know where it is! In fact, we must assume they already know. And Guinevere Spring will be compromised." It dawned on him she probably already was, and there was nothing he could do about it. "When did this happen?" He shouted again.

"Three days ago, sir."

Liebert decided the most likely scenario was that Blanton offered the guards money if they would take him to Washington. There were a great many desertions these days, and many people — not without reason — believed the war was lost. These three men obviously did not

<hr />

51 Charleston was evacuated on the night of February 18/19. The Union troops arrived at 9 a.m. on February 19, 1865.

want to be there when Richmond fell and the Confederacy died. They saw helping Blanton as a way to avoid a Union prison and perhaps picking up a few Greenbacks in the process. He wondered how much Blanton offered to pay them and whether or not they would actually get it, or if they would be thrown in some Northern hellhole with the other POWs.

"Tell Lieutenant Anderson to report to me immediately," Rance ordered. Anderson stood in front of him five minutes later.

"Did you want to see me, colonel?" He asked.

"No, but that's the only way I can talk to you," he replied sarcastically. Anderson grinned.

"Did you know Blanton escaped?" Liebert asked.

"Yeah. I'd have gone after him, but he probably reached Union lines before I even heard about it."

"Probably." Union lines were only eight hours away — by foot.

"Shoulda let me kill the rat in '62, sir."

"Yeah, I know. But I promised Miss Guinevere I wouldn't. She begged, cried, and pleaded for Blanton's life, and now her tender heart has probably landed her in one of Lincoln's jails." Liebert paused. "I should've shot him and told her I didn't. It's a mistake I won't make again, I can tell you."

Both men fell silent. There was no need to fret about past mistakes. Everybody in the South was doing that these days.

"Get ready to go to Washington," Liebert ordered. "We leave in two hours. During that time, shave your beard." He noticed a hard look from Anderson. "Blanton won't recognize me because I've lost weight and grown a beard since 1862. You look exactly the same. He won't recognize you without a beard."

After waiting a moment, Anderson nodded his head, although he clearly didn't want to shave. "Blanton's gonna pay for this," he muttered.

———— ⬦ ————

"You're a Rebel spy!" Edwin Stanton shouted as soon as he entered the cell. "Don't try to deny it!"

"I wasn't going to," Guinevere Spring purred.

She was unruffled and as smooth as glass. The night before, she was severely distressed. But in the darkness of her cell, she pulled herself together, as she always did, and as strong women usually do. She thought about her situation and decided to apply the philosophy of

The Retribution Conspiracy

"Never show fear in the face of the enemy." In war, courage is never limited to the battlefield. Sally Mae was always bold and adventurous. Actresses have to have thick skins anyway and now, mentally toughened by life and four years as a spy, she was absolutely fearless when it counted. After years of living with the stress of being an undercover agent and running a spy ring in an enemy's capital, being out of the shadows was a relief — even if she was in a prison cell. And she knew Rance Liebert would bring the matter to Jefferson Davis' attention, if he hadn't already. She knew the president appreciated her service and most likely would trade for her — possibly for a captured Union colonel or general. She only wondered how she had been caught.

"And this Rance Liebert you said you didn't know is the head of the Confederate Secret Service!" Stanton barked, bringing her back to the present. He glared at her. When she didn't say anything, he sat down on the only chair in the cell, his face contorted in fury. She remained seated on the cot.

"He has been since before the war," Guinevere smiled. "He has derailed trains, robbed banks, blown up military installations, outwitted dozens of Union generals, and burned up half of New York City. And you just now found out who he is?"

"Oh, shut up, witch!" Stanton shouted.

"He's a wonderful man," Guinevere smiled, ignoring the secretary's remark. "Can't wait for you to meet him! I hope to introduce you to him real soon." She was using her old Southern drawl now.

The secretary couldn't think of anything to say, so he roared: "You are a Rebel!" in the same tone the pope might yell, "You are a devil worshipper," to a Satanist.

"Dang right I am!" She drawled. "And proud of it! And you, sir, are redundant."

Stanton's face turned red. "You saw John Wilkes Booth two days ago," he exclaimed. "The rumor around the War Department is that he is planning to kidnap Abraham Lincoln!"

"Oh, that Wilkes!" She smiled. "He's harmless. He's just one of my lovers. Has been for the longest time. Tells questionable jokes, like that thing about Lincoln. You can't take him seriously. But he's good in bed. Not as good as Colonel Liebert but still pretty good," she lied as she crossed her legs and unbuttoned the top two buttons on her blouse. Sweat broke out on Stanton's forehead. "You remember what that's like, don't you, Edwin? Having sex with a woman? Feeling hot, supple breasts in your hands. Feeling her tongue on your manhood. ..."

He jumped straight up, struggling to control himself in front of this … creature.

"Oh, come on, Eddie!" She drawled. "Y'all can tell little ol' me!" She deliberately used the wrong tense of the subject to sound more Southern. Her smile extended all the way across her face.

Secretary of War Edwin Stanton shook with rage. He refrained from striking her only with the greatest difficulty. Then he smiled, sort of. It was more of a dangerous lear. "You're deliberately trying to provoke me!" He growled. "Why?"

She couldn't say why exactly. She might have called him a male chauvinist pig, but that term had not been invented yet. She was tired of being submissive to this poisonous dwarf of a man, and she wanted him to know it. Besides, she was caught. What difference, at this point, did it make? So she ignored his question. "Why are you here, Edwin?" She asked.

"That's Secretary of War Stanton to you!"

"Why are you here, Eddie?" She smiled.

"You're a cool customer, I'll say that for you," he growled. He sat down again, looking as if someone hit him in the groin.

"What do you want, Edwin?"

"I want some information."

"Want in one hand and defecate in the other," she drawled, "and see which one fills up the quickest."

He stared at her for some time. It made her uncomfortable, but she didn't let him know that. She leaned back against the wall behind the cot. He clearly had something on his mind but did not know how to proceed. I know for a fact she's the kind of a woman who can keep a secret, he thought. Finally, he came out with it. "I want to make a deal."

She was surprised by this development, and for once, not even the actress could hide it completely. "Really? You do? What kind of deal?"

"You and your co-conspirators are planning to kidnap that ridiculous baboon, Abraham Lincoln."

"Are we?"

"Yes."

"And if we are?" She asked, leaning forward. This conversation was getting interesting.

"I want you to do it."

She was momentarily stunned. She didn't see that coming. Golly, I thought only Rance Liebert dropped bombshells like this one. At least I'm not drinking wine this time. …

The Retribution Conspiracy

"Very well …" she said awkwardly.

"If you agree to my conditions, I will let you go and help you do it. If not, prepare to spend the rest of your life rotting in some cell somewhere."

She smiled. "But I like it here. First rate accommodations, at least by Northern standards. The food is so delicious! I'm sure I've gained weight. And those daring little rats are so cute! I'm thinking about taking one home with me as a pet, when I get released. I'm going to name it Edwin."

"Do you want to make a deal or not!?" He snarled impatiently.

She thought for a moment. "Fine, Mr. Stanton, I'll play. What are your conditions?"

"Kill Andrew Johnson and William Seward at the same time."

She thought about it for about five seconds. "I can do that," she said, matter-of-factly.

"And don't even think about double-crossing me. Don't think your celebrity status will help you if you do. You'll simply disappear. You wouldn't be the first person we've made disappear," he said menacingly.

I believe that, she thought. "Good enough. I'll agree to your conditions — if you'll agree to mine."

"You are hardly in a position to negotiate," he retorted.

"Oh, but I am," she purred. "Precisely because I have nothing left to loose. You want power. And I'm your link to the Confederate Secret Service, which is the only organization in the world which can give you the power you want. Kind of ironic, don't you think?" She paused for dramatic affect and continued. "You're probably thinking Abraham Lincoln won't survive his trip to Richmond or his captivity. And he probably won't. I know some men who'd love to kill him. I know one in particular who would like to torture him first." She thought of Anderson. "Shucks, I'd kind of like to castrate him myself, if I had the chance and a dull knife. He'll try to escape, of course, and Colonel Liebert or one of his boys will shoot him. Probably several times. Then, with Seward and Johnson dead, you'd probably become president. Or dictator. That's what you're after, isn't it, Mr. Stanton? Isn't that really your goal?"

"It would certainly be the best thing for the nation!" He exclaimed. He stared at her. There is a lot more to this woman than just a pretty face, he thought. She's dangerous. He swallowed his pride. *The things I do for power!* "Okay. What are your conditions?"

"Release me, and give Rance Liebert and me one week to get out of the country after Lincoln dies. Give me $100,000 in Greenbacks within the next 48 hours. Top-notch professional killers don't come cheap. Give Wilkes Booth and his team a 24-hour head start. Then I will promise to attempt assassinations on all three men."

"No. An attempt won't get it. You must succeed."

"Nope, I can't guarantee that. Too many wild cards. My chances of killing all three men are only about 50-50," she calculated. "That gives you a 50-50 chance of being president of the United States. A little bit better than your odds are right now, wouldn't you say?"

He thought for a moment. The war was coming to an end and, with it, his dictatorial power as secretary of war. To maintain his power and even increase it, he had to take this chance. Besides, if the plot were exposed, there was no danger to him. Who would take the word of a Rebel spy over President Lincoln's secretary of war? "How many men have you had killed, Miss Spring?" He asked.

"I don't remember," she lied. But now I'm going to have to modify my list, she thought. Instead of Lincoln, Johnson, Seward, and Stanton, it will be just Lincoln, Johnson, and Seward.

He could see Guinevere was not going to be bluffed. "All right. But you must try to kill all of them."

"Agreed. That I will definitely do."

"Even Lincoln?" Stanton asked.

"Especially Lincoln!" Guinevere Spring spat these words out with some venom and without the Southern drawl. Her face was now deadly serious. She thought of Rainbow, her homeless parents, and Windrow in flames.

"Done," Edwin Stanton answered, and he almost smiled as he said it.

Guinevere did smile. She felt she handled the negotiations brilliantly. She was going to try to kill all three men anyway, and the only one she had to take off her list was Stanton. Besides, she would have settled for $50,000.

Twenty minutes later, Guinevere Spring was a free woman. She hired a carriage and began riding in circles around town. It didn't take her long to confirm she was being followed by a man on a sorrel horse, so she stopped, got out of the carriage, walked up to the man on horseback, and offered him a ride. He declined.

"Tell your buddy he is welcome to ride also, if he wishes," she said, flashing a brilliant smile. Again she used the Southern drawl.

The Retribution Conspiracy

She did not spotted the second man, but they did not know that, and she knew police and War Department operatives usually worked in pairs.

She continued to circle until she was sure the Union agents gave up. Then she told the driver, "Go to 604 H Street, Northwest."

The entire Booth team was demoralized by the news Guinevere was arrested. They were pleasantly surprised when she appeared at the Surratt House.

"How did you get out of it?"

"I talked my way out of it," she smiled. "I am an actress, you know. And they're not as smart as they think they are."

Only to Rance Liebert did she tell the truth.

"I hope you weren't followed," he said.

"No, I was very careful," she replied.

They checked into a hotel that night. "I can't go back to my room," he said. "They're no doubt watching it."

"But they won't do anything."

"No they won't — yet. But after the kidnapping, all bets are off, and I don't want them to see my face."

"I can go back," she said. "I want to pick up my envelopes and Letter Cartes."

He looked at her quizzically. "What Letter Cartes?"

"The ones you sent to me from Europe, when I was a child."

He looked at her, blinked, and did a double take. He was surprised they still existed, and she had kept them all these years. Rance Liebert was touched. But he didn't let on. Instead, he said: "Pick up Mr. Bowie while you're there." It occurred to him that knife was the only memento he had from his childhood, Fusilier, or Rainbow, or Grover and Ambrose, or anyone from back home. He thought of his parents, who were now living in one of the old barns on an isolated area of the plantation. He knew his sister Penny, who lived in Vicksburg, had survived the siege, along with her three children, but her husband — a lieutenant in the 1st Mississippi Light Artillery Regiment — had not. Because they were behind enemy lines, he hadn't heard anything from any of them in some time.

"I'll do it," she said, interrupting his thoughts and bringing him back to the moment. "Do you still intend to kidnap Lincoln?" She asked.

"Yes."

"What about the assassination?"

"Our first goal is to capture Lincoln and hand him over to Jefferson Davis. Killing him is Plan B."

She looked disappointed.

"Let's keep our objectives in mind," he said. "Kidnapping Lincoln will disrupt the Union chain of command and divert attention from General Lee, thus helping our armies in the field. Mr. Davis and the general think confusion in Washington might well translate into confusion in the field. Killing him won't do that, at least not for long. But the United States has never had a sitting president in the custody of a foreign power. They won't know how to proceed."

She nodded and said: "But that will break my agreement with Stanton."

"Yes, it will. Which is one reason why I don't want them to see my face. As an actress, you know how to make yourself look very different with makeup and such, and in short order. All I know how to do is shave my beard. In any case, we'd better be prepared to run like a greyhound in the opposite direction."

She smiled. "As long as I'm with you, dear. As long as I'm with you."

———∞———

Washington, D.C. in 1865 was a Southern town. Its Police Department was full of Southern sympathizers, spies and informants. It took Rance's operatives less than two days to acquire the information he requested.

"Charlie Blanton is staying in Room 103 of the National Hotel," Liebert told Anderson. "Go kill him. Use a knife if you can, or poison his whiskey. He'll go to breakfast, if I know anything about him. You can get him coming back, or you can get him in his room. I don't care. Just get him. Then hurry it back to Richmond."

"That'll be no problem," Anderson commented, smiling. He was always happy to get a choice assignment.

They found Charles Blanton's body the following afternoon. Someone had chloroformed a maid, taken her pass key, tied her up, gagged her, and locked her in a broom closet. Then the murderer or murderers entered Blanton's room. When Blanton returned from breakfast, he, she, or they stabbed him several times with a Bowie knife, sliced up his face, cut off his ears, slit his throat, and mutilated his body. His wallet and all of his money were missing. All of his whiskey was stolen, also. The hotel staff knew he entertained a couple of prostitutes during the

The Retribution Conspiracy

past week, so the police wrote off the crime as a robbery/murder. Edwin Stanton, whose War Department was paying the bill for Blanton's stay, knew better. *Colonel Liebert is sending me a message,* Stanton thought. But he also knew how to keep a secret.

_⌒___ CHAPTER XXVIII ___⌒_
KILL THE SON OF A GUN

Lee planned to evacuate Richmond in early or mid-April 1865. For the abduction of Abraham Lincoln to do the Confederate government any good, it would have to occur by the end of March. On March 17, John Wilkes Booth was told Lincoln was going to attend a matinée performance of _Still Waters Run Deep_ that very day at the Campbell Military Hospital, not far from the Soldiers Home, for the benefit of the wounded warriors there. Booth and his team were primed and ready, but Lincoln didn't appear. Instead, he decided to address a group of Indiana soldiers at the National Hotel in downtown Washington. "Lucky rat!" Rance Liebert snapped.

After that failure, a frustrated Booth gave up. The next day, he gave a performance in _The Apostate_ at Ford's Theater. Then he and Powell went to New York City and stayed at the fashionable Revere House. While there, he visited another of his favorite prostitutes. Booth and Powell went on to Toronto, where they met with Jacob Thompson and Clement C. Clay on March 22. Here, the eloquent statesmen rekindled Booth's waning courage and pumped him up again. The next day, Booth got aboard a train for New York. That same afternoon, Abraham Lincoln boarded the _River Queen_ and headed for City Point, Virginia. He wanted to be with Grant when the general launched his final attack on Petersburg. Booth did not know it, but this ended the last chance he had to capture the president and take him back to Richmond alive.

Rance Liebert knew what it meant. He returned to the Confederate capital straight away. He met with Jefferson Davis, who looked very careworn.

"Kidnapping Lincoln will no longer be possible," Liebert said. "Plan A is no longer an option. We must commit to Plan B, or abandon the entire enterprise."

Davis looked up sadly. Finally he said: "Execute Plan B."

"Yes, sir," Rance responded, gravely. He stood up, saluted, and prepared to leave.

"Don't go yet, colonel. I have some news for you."

Rance sat down again.

"The House of Representatives met in secret session on February 25th. They established the Bureau of Special and Secret Service. The

The Rise of the Confederate Secret Service

Senate's Committee on Military Affairs passed the same bill on March 6, and now the Senate as a whole has done the same, also in executive session. The chief of this organization will be in charge of all secret service missions, including experimental weapons. I want you to head the Bureau."

Liebert frowned. "Thank you for the vote of confidence, sir. I'm flattered, and it means a lot, coming from you, but Secret Service operations are now only conditionally possible. Tomorrow, I'm going to meet with General Ewell. I'm planning to organize the 125th Special Employment Battalion for combat and burn all of our secret papers. Except for our men in Canada and the cell in Washington, the Secret Service will cease to exist."

"Until we recapture Richmond," Davis declared. Rance said nothing. It was clear to Davis they disagreed, and Rance did not believe the Rebels would ever recapture Richmond. But the president also knew none of that mattered. Rance Liebert could be counted on to carry out his orders, whether he agreed with them or not. To break the awkward silence, the president reached into his desk drawer and handed Liebert a small box.

"What's this?" He asked.

"General's stars," Jefferson Davis said. "Rance, I know that you've always wanted to be a general. You should have been promoted earlier, but because of the secret nature of your work, the Senate was never made aware of what you have contributed to the Cause. And you never complained once that you hadn't been promoted. I appreciate that. But the Senate has now authorized that your new position may be occupied by a brigadier. Now I've decided to provisionally promote you to brigadier general, pending Senate approval. Robert E. Lee agrees.[52] Congratulations, General Liebert!" He got up from his desk, walked over to Rance and handed him his promotion papers and rank insignia.

"Thank you, sir," the newly minted general said, and tried to smile as he shook Jeff Davis' hand, although he knew this was really just an honorary promotion. He reached one of the major goals of his life, but it now felt hollow. It was far too late. He knew the Cause was lost, and the Senate would never confirm his appointment. Unless he seriously missed his guess, the Confederate Congress would never meet again.

---

52 Robert E. Lee became general-in-chief of the Confederate armies on February 9, 1865.

The Retribution Conspiracy

He doubted he would be a general for more than a week and the appointment might not even be legal, technically speaking. But not much he did over the past four years was legal, technically speaking. He also deeply regretted Grover Liebert was not alive to see this. Taking his leave, Rance thought about hugging Jefferson Davis as he left, but the president was keeping up appearances and was clinging to the myth that victory was still possible. For a moment, Rance decided not to hug his friend and benefactor, but the impulse was too strong. To Davis' surprise, he did it anyway. The president awkwardly returned the embrace. Then, with tears in his eyes, Brigadier General Rance Liebert bolted for the door and out of the mansion. He knew it was almost certain he would never see Jefferson Davis again.

It was raining when Rance Liebert left the White House for what he knew was the last time, and the weather matched his mood. He thought of his dreams at the beginning of the war: he would march down the main street of Rainbow at the head of his victorious regiment. How far away those days seemed now! The new uniforms he purchased for his men in 1861 were long gone. Their uniforms were now in tatters, faded by too many hours in the sun, rain, and snow. He had visited the regiment a few weeks ago. Only 270 men remained, and two-thirds of them had no shoes. If he were to parade them down Main Street today, it would be hard to distinguish them from a mob of tramps. Not that anybody would see them. Like Jackson, Mississippi, to which the term first applied, Rainbow was now a "Chimneyville." All of the buildings on Main Street were burned, and there was nothing left standing but chimneys. The thought he would never see Jefferson Davis again also depressed him beyond measure. He nevertheless hurried over to Melody Herzog's home and got her to sew the new insignia of rank on his coat as soon as he left the White House.

The next day, March 29, was characterized by low clouds and a hard, cold, driving rain. Rance's mood was also dark. General Liebert called in all of his senior staff and ordered all codes and ciphers destroyed and all papers burned. "Surely it's not as bad as all that?" Melody Herzog gasped.

Rance looked at her. During the war, she lost her excess weight and was a beauty, despite the old and worn dress she now wore. There were no new dresses in Richmond for some time. She was now engaged to a major in Wade Hampton's cavalry, wherever they were. The last he heard they were on the Western Front, which was now in North Carolina. Rance fervently hoped that man would survive the war.

"Yes, Melody, it is," he replied. "It may be too late to be of any use, but I am promoting you all. Here," he handed Melody her commission as a first lieutenant, signed by President Davis himself. He then stood up and hugged her — the only time he touched her in four long years. She tried to say something but choked on her tears.

He interrupted her. "Let's just say goodbye, Melody," he said, holding her hands in his. "Prolonging it makes it all the harder. Just know I love you and will pray for you and think of you often, wherever I am, and I hope your future is filled with all the love and happiness you truly deserve."

Overcome with emotion, she embraced him, and then burst into tears and fled the room. Within half an hour, she was supervising the burning of the secret documents.

Rance walked back over to his desk and pulled out more documents. One named Leonard commander of the 125th and promoted him to lieutenant colonel. Another promoted Dan Glass to major. Collier stood at attention, wondering if he too would be promoted. Although they had served together for four years, he and Rance had never developed a close relationship, and he was promoted to captain only the previous year. Liebert, however, appreciated his service and promoted him to major. Jefferson Davis himself signed the promotion document, and it would hang over Collier's fireplace for the rest of his life. (Collier never knew the signature was forged.) Joshua watched the proceedings in silence. Finally it was his turn. Rance asked the others to leave the room and gave Joshua his "papers," which meant he was no longer a slave. He and his family were thus freed five days before they would have been freed anyway. Liebert also promoted him to corporal in the Confederate Army and gave him a discharge certificate. In addition, the general had a more tangible reward for the man who served him so well throughout the war and had kept the Bushrod Brown murder a secret for all those years.

"What's this?" he asked.

"You wanted to own a livery stable. I haven't forgotten. Here is the deed to the Secret Service stables and the entire city block. It is post-dated to 1860, so it is not a Confederate deed. I suspect Confederate deeds will not be honored, once the conquest of the South is completed. Unfortunately, the white men will take all of the horses when the city is evacuated and I can't give you any; in fact, I'm taking the best one myself. So I'm including $2,500 in greenbacks. Don't let anybody

The Retribution Conspiracy

know you've got this money, and be careful who you buy horses from. You don't want to git no stolen horse."

"I don't knows what to say," he stammered as he brushed away a tear. "I ain't never seen dis much money in my whole life."

"Just say thank you."

"Thank you!" But he couldn't restrain himself. He embraced General Liebert. It was the first and only time in his life he ever hugged a white man. Rance awkwardly hugged him back.

Rance looked around his office. "I'm going to miss this place."

"Maybe you'll be back ..." Joshua muttered, trying to be supportive. A little man inside him was jumping up and down with joy, but he didn't let it show. At the same time, he felt bad about feeling so happy when Mr. Rance felt so miserable.

"No," he said. "I'm blowing it up in three or four days. Everything except the stables."

The Appomattox campaign began that same day, March 29, when, through mud and pouring rain, an entire Union cavalry corps, supported by several divisions of infantry, marched around Robert E. Lee's right flank. Unlike Lee's corps and divisions, all of these units were at or near full strength. Anticipating just such a move, Lee had positioned his reserves here under Major General George Pickett. On April 1, Pickett mishandled the Battle of Five Forks and Lee's reserves were effectively destroyed. Even most of the remnants who survived were cut off from the rest of the army.

That same day, explosives expert Lieutenant Thomas F. (Frank) Harney of the Torpedo Bureau joined John Singleton Mosby. His orders originated with Jefferson Davis and were passed along via Benjamin's State Department Secret Service: blow up the Executive Office Building across from the Washington White House while a cabinet meeting was in session. This would wipe out Lincoln and his entire cabinet. General Liebert was informed of the move but had nothing to do with it directly. Predictably, however, he did not lift a finger to try to stop it.

The next morning, April 2, the Army of Northern Virginia was attacked by overwhelming forces. After 11 months of nearly continuous fighting, the thin gray line finally broke. General Lee ordered the evacuation of Richmond before noon. After they blocked off the streets around the Market Street headquarters and made sure there was no one within two blocks of the place, the one-hundred-man 125th Special Employment Battalion marched out with about 3,500 men from Ewell's District of Richmond. General Liebert gave the engineers the signal, and the headquarters of the Confederate Secret Service disappeared in a flash of flame and smoke. As promised four years before, the counterfeiters were set free and each was given a sack full of money, which they manufactured themselves. Rance gave his coat with the general's stars on it to a homeless man before he and Julian Anderson headed north and then northeast, toward Washington, while his men headed west, toward Appomattox. The last Confederates left the city about dawn on April 3. The Union Army marched in about 8 a.m. Among the first to enter was Colonel Edward H. Ripley's 9th Vermont Infantry Regiment.

The next day, Abraham Lincoln made a tour of the city, where the former slaves treated him like a god and some even fell on their knees. He walked practically unescorted through the area that 72 hours before was the government quarter of an enemy state. One die-hard Rebel sniper could have shot him and escaped without much problem. He even visited the Confederate White House and sat behind Jeff Davis' desk. When General Liebert heard about this, he exclaimed: "How stupid I was! I should have had the desk booby trapped!"

Among those to see Lincoln was a former Confederate enlisted man from General Rains' Torpedo Bureau. The fellow was just wandering about the abandoned capital. That evening, showing considerable courage, he walked into the Vermont camp and asked to speak to the commanding officer. The sentry took him to Colonel Ripley.

Ripley was impressed by the Rebel's intelligence and sincerity. He told the colonel he believed the war was now over for all practical purposes, but not everyone thought so. Then he surprised Ripley: a team with an explosives expert was dispatched to Washington to blow up Abraham Lincoln. He wanted the Vermonter to warn the president that the lieutenant in charge really knew his business and the president was in grave danger. The following morning Ripley took him to see Lincoln, who was now aboard the USS *Malvern*, which was anchored in the James River at Richmond.

Lincoln agreed to meet with Ripley, who urged him to speak with the ex-Rebel. The president refused. He did not believe he was in any danger. "I cannot bring myself to believe any human being lives who would do me harm," were his exact words.

How someone as intelligent as Abraham Lincoln could have such a blind spot when it came to his own personal safety has baffled historians for decades.

Mosby's men ran into a Union patrol near Washington, and Frank Harney was captured, thus eliminating this particular threat to Lincoln's life. But an entire other team was waiting in the wings.

—— ∞∞∞ ——

The days of Stonewall Jackson were gone. Due to bad staff work, Lee's army reached Amelia Court House and the food which was supposed to be there was not. The soldiers had to search the surrounding countryside for provisions and found almost none. Lee had counted upon being able to out march Grant's forces and did so before Amelia. Now Grant was able to catch up, and the Army of Northern Virginia was running for its life. But the lost time could never be made good, and not even Lee's veterans could out march the enemy's horses. General Ewell's *ad hoc* corps was cut off and destroyed at Sayler's Creek on April 6, and Colonel Leonard, Major Glass, and the rest of the 125th went into captivity. Finally, Lee's last escape route was cut. He surrendered at Appomattox Court House on April 9.

Rance Liebert was in Washington when the news arrived. He was sickened by the jubilant crowds celebrating the demise of arguably the greatest army which ever fought in the Western Hemisphere.

Robert E. Lee was offered many drinks in his life and turned down all but one. In 1861, he was offered two bottles of the best, bonded Kentucky bourbon. "I am not going to have a drink now," he told his benefactor. "But the coming war is going to be more terrible than anyone realizes. I am told there are times when a man needs a drink. This may happen to me before this war ends. With your kind permission, I am going to keep these bottles against that day."

Lee placed the two bottles in his ambulance, where they remained for four long years. The day after Appomattox, two Confederate soldiers visited their General-in-Chief to shake his hand and say goodbye. Lee gave each of them a bottle of bourbon. They had never been opened.

Rance Liebert was not as strong as Robert E. Lee. On the evening of April 9 he bought a bottle of bourbon. Although he was never much of a drinker, he consumed almost half of it. Sally Mae had a small glass of wine. She didn't say much. He generally communicated only in monosyllabic grunts. Before tonight, he had always sat on the couch, so she could snuggle up against him. Tonight, he took the rocking chair and watched the fireworks. "Here's to General Rance Liebert," he said at one point.

"You can't blame yourself," she declared.

"Maybe not," he sighed. "I don't know. Sometimes I think 'My conscience is clear. I fought 'em all I could.' But I can't help but think about that day in 1861, when President Davis made me head of the Secret Service. What if I'd turned it down?"

"Best case scenario? You'd be a prisoner at Appomattox, or starving at Elmira, or some other Yankee hellhole."[53]

"Maybe. Or maybe I'd have been a corps commander by the time of the Battle of Gettysburg. You don't think I'd have made the same mistakes as Longstreet or Ewell, do you?"

Of course not, she thought, but did not engage him in that particular argument. "Who replaced you as commander of the 12th?" she asked.

"Richard Griffith."

"Where is he now?"

"In a grave in Jackson, Mississippi," Rance replied.

"That's where you'd be, in all probability. Where is the 12th Mississippi?"

"Most of them dead. According to the newspapers, it covered the army's retreat on April 2, at a place called Fort Gregg. It blocked an entire corps — 20,000 men — and held out for three hours. Only 30 men surrendered." He did not tell her that among the dead was Lieutenant Colonel Billy Liebert, the regiment's last commander. He was too sick at heart to even mention that.

"If you'd stayed with them you might have been there. Would you rather be there or here?"

He looked at her as if he just then noticed her. "Maybe you're right," he declared. After a minute's reflection, he handed her the bottle of bourbon and said: "Pour this stuff out. We'll start our new life tomorrow."

"Our new life?" She asked.

"Yes," he replied. "If you want to."

"If you want me."

"You know I do," he answered.

She immediately got up and poured the whiskey out the window.

---

53 Elmira, New York (called "Hellmira" by the Rebels) had a death rate almost as high as Andersonville.

The Retribution Conspiracy

"Aren't you coming to bed?" She asked half an hour later.

"Not right now," he answered, still watching the fireworks burst over Washington, D.C.

"They look like artillery shells," Guinevere observed.

"I wish they were artillery shells," he muttered under his breath. He was still watching when she drifted off to sleep.

As promised, Rance was more like himself the following morning, except for a headache. Guinevere also remained unusually quiet, but Rance didn't see anything wrong with that, given the horrible news from Virginia. She went to work at the theater that evening, where she received a note from "J.W.B.," asking "What does O.D. want us to do?" She also got a note from the War Department. It was unsigned and informed her Lincoln would be attending the play *Our American Cousin* at Ford's Theater on Friday, April 14.

The corporal/messenger felt very awkward in the presence of a beautiful actress. He stood at something approximating attention and said: "I'm supposed to wait for a reply."

"Very well," she said. "Just say, 'Action on the 14th.' He'll understand."

He looked puzzled. She turned away from him and resumed putting on her makeup. "Is there anything else, corporal?" She asked, when he didn't leave.

"I'm supposed to recover the original note, ma'am."

Stanton was covering his tracks. She handed it to him without turning around. "Anything else?"

"No ma'am. Except I've always enjoyed your performances, Miss Spring."

She turned in her chair, actually looked at him, and gave him a genuine smile. "Thank you, corporal," she said. Guinevere always appreciated a compliment from a man who was not trying to get into her underwear. "Have a pleasant evening."

"Goodnight, ma'am," he said, touched his hand to his cap and hurried back to the War Office.

Later, she received another note, giving her Seward's address and informing her Vice President Johnson was staying in Room 68 in the Kirkwood House in Washington for the foreseeable future. As instructed, she memorized the information and burned the note in the presence of the messenger.

On the night of Tuesday, April 11, Rance was in the huge crowd who attended a speech by Abraham Lincoln. It was a mixed message. Lincoln talked about revenge and how for every drop of blood extracted by the lash, he intended to extract a drop of blood by the sword, but he also spoke of "with malice toward none, with charity toward all."

"What did you think of the speech?" Guinevere asked when she got home from the theater.

"Don't know what to think of it," Rance responded. "Typical Lincoln! He talked out of both sides of his mouth, like he always does. He is on every side of every issue, as usual. On one hand, the South should be treated harshly. On the other hand, the South should be welcomed back into the Union as if nothing has happened. And all in the same speech! All he knows for sure is everything should be centralized and controlled by an all-powerful Federal executive."

"What do you think he'll do?" She asked, referring to Lincoln.

"Oh, he's likely to flip-flop, like he did on the slavery issue. He'll probably end up with the Radicals. He has decent enough instincts, but he suppresses them when the pressure is on. That seems to be a pattern with him."

"Shouldn't we … kill him? We can, you know."

"I've thought about it. But they'd just make a martyr of him," Liebert said bitterly. "If he lives, he'll end up being smeared and dragged through the mud by the leaders of his own party. If he dies now, it would be the best possible moment for him, insofar as his historical legacy is concerned. The newspapers and abolitionist preachers would compare him to Moses, who was allowed to see the Promised Land but not to enter it. I suspect an entire Lincoln Cult would arise, under those circumstances. In the future, all of his crimes and misdemeanors would be forgotten, and he would only be remembered only for freeing the slaves and restoring the Union. In time, it will likely be easier to question the divinity of Christ than the greatness of Abraham the Magnificent, when he is, in fact, a terrible president."

"But doesn't he then deserve to die?" She asked, referring to Lincoln. "He is responsible for a lot of innocent deaths and suffering, you know."

"Yes, he is," Rance declared. He thought of Grover and Elizabeth, of Fusilier and Windrow and Rainbow, and Billy Liebert, lying in an unmarked grave, of Rose Greenhow, killed on a secret mission in 1864, and of his father and mother and Jonathan and his family, just strug-

The Retribution Conspiracy

gling to keep from starving in a devastated land, while Lincoln's cronies got rich on plunder. "Honey, if there's ever been a man in American history who deserved to be shot, it's Abraham Lincoln. But it ain't gonna happen. At least not by us."

Don't be so sure, Guinevere thought. Visions of Windrow burning flashed through her mind, her homeless, destitute parents, now living in a dilapidated former slave cabin, Rainbow on fire, the church in which she grew up in flames, Fusilier and De La Teneria burned down, her twin brother in a Yankee prison, and all of the brave and dashing young men she knew who wore the gray and were no more. She looked at him harshly. Guinevere was not an easy forgiver; however, she decided not to argue with him about it. He was perfectly willing to assassinate Lincoln before General Lee surrendered. Appomattox changed everything. Rance was presently convinced the war was lost and would soon be over. Killing Lincoln now would serve no purpose except to enrage the North. She knew she wouldn't be able to change his mind. But he hadn't changed hers, either.

Rance, meanwhile, pushed these thoughts out of his mind. "Sit down," he said, interrupting her thoughts. "There's something we need to talk about."

She instinctively knew the moment had come. This is the talk, she said to herself.

"I really should have brought this up earlier. ..."

Sally sat very still, very quiet. She could hardly breath.

"We've all made mistakes in our lives," he declared. "You've made some mistakes during what you called your Bad Girl phase, including one very big mistake."

She nodded. She knew he was talking about Ginger. She didn't exactly see her daughter as a mistake, but she also knew this was not the time to bring that up.

"But ..." he continued, "over the past year, I've become extremely fond of your little mistake."

"She loves you, too, Rance," Guinevere interjected.

And I don't want her to grow up to be a bastard, Rance thought, but never said. Illegitimacy was a huge consideration in nineteenth century America. It was terribly unfair, but children in those days were ostracized from the day they were born, and for their entire lives, there was nothing they could do about it, even though they had done nothing wrong. The stigma already ruined many an innocent life.

"I never thought I'd say this," he stammered. "And it's still very difficult for me … I mean I never thought I'd want to help raise another man's child, but I'm willing to try — if you are."

She smiled from ear to ear. "I are," she said, and hugged his neck.

"Of course, this can only work one way."

"What's that?"

"We have to become a family. She can't be just your daughter anymore. She has to be our daughter."

Sally was never so happy in her life. She squeezed him so hard that oxygen became an issue.

"I have to treat her as my own flesh and blood — neither one of us can treat her differently from any other children we might have. And you have to agree to that."

"Oh, I do!" She exclaimed.

"And I don't want to know who the biological father is. Ever! She's mine and yours until the day we die. You understand that?"

His last sentence was more a demand than a question, but she readily agreed to it.

A few moments later, she asked, "Do you want to have more children?"

"Yes, I do. I've always wanted children. Now I've got one, but I'd like another. From the beginning, so to speak. Do you?" During the war, neither of them brought up this subject or even thought much about it.

"Yes," Sally/Guinevere answered. Since her rape, she hadn't wanted children. (Ginger was strictly an accident.) But suddenly she was at least open to the idea. She didn't know if it was because he wanted children, or if it was something inside her. Besides, if he had a child of his own blood by her, she knew he would never even think about leaving, as long as she remained faithful to him. She decided to sort out all that later.

"You know, all my life I wanted a son. But since I've gotten to know Ginger, I'd kinda like another daughter."

"I'll see what I can do," she declared, perkily.

"I always figured I'd be married before I had a child," he joked. "But I guess we can put the cart before the horse. We'll get married tomorrow or Thursday," he said. "If that's all right with you?"

"Absolutely!" She smiled and wiped a tear of joy from her face.

"Well, I guess I should do this right," Rance said. He got down on one knee, and asked: "Will you marry me, Sally Mae Guinevere?"

"Of course I will, you silly goose!" She beamed. "I've always wanted to! And I thought you'd never ask!"

The Retribution Conspiracy

It was April 12, 1865. There were some details the happy couple needed to take care of. They decided to get married on Thursday, April 13. After Guinevere's last performance on April 12, they would leave Washington under the cover of darkness, to evade Stanton's agents. Their first stop would be Canada. After wrapping up the Secret Service business, they would emigrate to England or Ireland. Both of them figured it would not be safe to live in the United States as long as Edwin Stanton was alive.

"What names should we adopt?" Guinevere asked.

He thought about it for a minute. "Yes, I don't suppose we should keep our real names, if we're trying to dodge Stanton's goons. What name have you come up with?"

"Rose-Marie Cormier. Pronounced in the French manner, Cor-me-ay. How about you?"

They tried out several names. Rose-Marie rejected Davis, Lee, Forrest and Jackson, and several others, and he rejected Ambrose, Billy, and Grover. Finally, Rance said: "Finis Randall."

"Finis?"

"Yes. Finis. I am now Finis Randall."

"Uh ..." she said, as if unsure about this.

"Good! It's settled."

"Finis!?!"

"Yes," he declared.

"Really?"

"Yes. Finis. Finis Randall." Finis was Jefferson Davis' middle name, but he didn't tell her that.

"I like Randall. But Finis?"

"Yes. Finis. Finis Randall. Or Stefanbrook Cornelius McGillicutty Katzenellenbogen. Take your pick."

"Okay. It's a tough choice, but Finis Randall it is," she said, but it was clear she wasn't completely sold on the idea.

"Any middle name?"

He thought for a moment. "William," he declared, "after my brother."

"Where are you going?" Rance asked the former Guinevere.

She walked over and kissed him. "I've got to go see John Wilkes Booth and tell him to disband the team."

"You think he'll act if you don't?" A startled Liebert asked.

"He might," she said. "General Lee only surrendered about one-fifth of the Confederate Army, John Singleton Mosby hasn't surrendered, and President Davis is still at large, and I know he hasn't given up. If I had to guess, I'd say Wilkes will grasp at straws. He will convince himself the Northern leadership will descend into chaos if Lincoln, Seward, and Johnson are all killed. He will aver that the Confederacy still has a chance."

"The only real army we have left east of the Mississippi is the Army of Tennessee," Rance said. "If Stonewall Jackson or Bedford Forrest or Dick Taylor were in charge, we might actually have a slim chance. But the army is led by Joe Johnston. There is no way anything positive will be accomplished. No, dear, it's time to quit. Tell Wilkes I said to cancel 'Retribution,' dissolve the team, and go home." He paused. "Tell him I wish him happiness and success for the rest of his life," he added as an afterthought.

"I will," she said.

"What does the colonel say?" John Wilkes Booth asked Guinevere Spring. He had an anxious expression on his face.

"He says to kill the son-of-a-gun," she replied.

"Seward and Johnson, too?"

"Seward and Johnson, too."

"How about Stanton?" He asked.

"You let me worry about Stanton," she answered.

CHAPTER XXIX

YOU AIN'T GOT HALF OF 'EM YET!

On April 13, 1865, Rance Liebert got on his knees for the second time in three days and looked into Ginger's eyes. "Can I be your daddy?" He asked. "Would you like to be my little girl, mine and your mommy's?"

Her smile extended from ear to ear. "Oh, yes, Mr. Owen. I want a daddy! I want you to be my daddy! Can I call you Daddy?"

"It would be my honor," he replied gravely.

She threw her little arms around his neck.

Finis and Rose-Marie were married that night by a preacher in rural southern Pennsylvania. Ginger stood by her mother's side, clutching Molly the doll, which was her prized possession. Afterward, they had a nice dinner and checked into the largest suite of a local hotel. Finis/Rance had enough foresight to buy a children's story book, so he went into Ginger's bedroom, lay down with her, and read until she fell asleep lying on his arm. Then he reentered his own bedroom.

"Is she asleep?" Guinevere asked.

"Yes."

"It's about time," she declared. She stood up, undid her robe, and dropped it to the floor. She was stark naked. His eyes widened as she walked over and kissed him as never before.

And that was just the start of it. Guinevere — and now Rose-Marie — enjoyed sex and knew how to please a man — and she hadn't made love in four years. She was more than ready and turned him every way but loose. The next morning, as he lay there exhausted with her nestled under his arm, he realized he was going to have difficulty getting out of bed. Wow! He thought. So that is what the hoopla about sex is all about. I've heard about it since Jefferson College. Now I understand it.

Guinevere herself felt completely satisfied as she lay there naked, with her head on his shoulder. She felt the only real romantic relationship she ever had just moved from the theoretical to the intimate. He had sworn an oath to spend the rest of his life with her — and she knew he meant it. To real men like Rance Liebert, she thought, an oath is almost a physical thing. They didn't swear them unless they meant to keep them. They would literally rather die than break one, as they proved on more than two thousand battlefields over the past four years. Yesterday and last night proven that Rance meant exactly what he had said. It was about so much more than sex — although that was definitely a part of it. She was now certain he had moved beyond her misleading him and springing Ginger on him. He would probably never bring that up again — and she certainly wouldn't. Analyzing her wedding and wedding night in the quiet of the early morning, the words of the scripture from her youth floated back to her: "and the two shall be as one." And that is how she felt.

She also decided that sex with love was vastly superior to sex without it. It occurred to her this was the first time she'd had sex with someone she loved, which — in a sense — made it like making love for the first time. Rose-Marie felt giddy. She had heard people in love could give each other so much more than two lovers who were just having sex for fun or amusement, and she had not believed it — but she believed it now. Did he know he had taken her breath away? It occurred to her that she knew why. It was because this was the first time she ever completely given herself to a man. She gave herself in a sense that was so much more than sex alone. And he did the same. That thought made her feel wonderful. "And the two shall be as one. ..."

Guinevere lay there thinking for several minutes. She knew she left him breathless also, both emotionally and physically, because she did done some things he never experienced with his frigid wife, among which was totally committing her body, spirit, heart, and mind to him. Mildred did none of that. At various points in the day, the evening, and the night, she could tell he was happy and sometimes even ecstatic. After remembering the evening for a moment, she decided he might be in something of a state of shock. She never experienced a night like that. It was certain he hadn't. Perhaps he needed some reassurance.

"Yesterday was the best day of my life. And last night was the best night of my life," she affirmed quietly, without moving her head. It was a simple, heartfelt statement of fact.

She felt his chest swell with pride. Good, she thought.

"Mine, too." He dropped his shoulder slightly. She raised her head, and he kissed her long and tenderly. Guinevere closed her eyes and lay her head back on his shoulder. I could stay here forever, she thought, as she hugged him around the waist.

Just then there was a pounding on the door between the two rooms they had rented. "Daddy!" Ginger called out. "Time to get up! Let's eat breakfast and play. Daddy?!? DADDY!?!"

"Be there in a minute, sugar!" He shouted.

He smiled down at his wife, who was grinning up at him. "I guess we have to get up," she said.

"Aaawwwww. I guess so!"

In a couple of moments, the smile vanished from her face, and she became very serious. "I'm going to make you very happy," she promised.

"You already have," he said, equally serious. It was as if the previous two years, when they were separated, had never occurred. He would never bring up their broken courtship again, and he was pretty sure neither would she. That was a past hidden behind a door which would never be reopened. Perhaps, as a married couple, they would be stronger because of it. He felt they were much stronger as a couple than they were two springs ago, and he was absolutely and completely committed to her, and would be until the day he died. Rance Liebert would never be able to put his feelings into words, the way his actress wife could, but that didn't mean the former Rebel general couldn't feel as deeply. He silently thanked God for his wife, his family, and his future.

"Daddy! Daddy!" The little girl's impatient voice intoned as she beat on the door.

"I'm coming, sweetheart," he cried, and with that, he actually got out of bed and started looking for his trousers. Rose-Marie/Guinevere grinned and retrieved her robe, and the Randalls began their first day together as a family.

It was April 14, 1865: the last day of Abraham Lincoln's life.

It is ironic Abraham Lincoln did not concern himself about his personal security until the week of his death. While at City Point, he dreamed he was in the White House, wandering about as if in a daze. There was a sinister silence except, in the distance, several people were weeping, but they were invisible. He went from room to room. Everything was familiar, but he still could not find the people. Lincoln kept searching until he arrived in the East Room. There, he found a throng of people, some of whom were gazing mournfully at a corpse.

"Who is dead in the White House?" He asked.

"The president," some answered. "He was killed by an assassin."

He awoke in a cold sweat. Lincoln placed a great deal of stock in dreams. He believed God and angels communicated to people through dreams. And this dream shook him to the core. He was glad Ulysses S. Grant was going to accompany him to Ford's Theater that night. He was always accompanied by a strong bodyguard of loyal men. But then Grant canceled.

———⊱⊰———

Robert E. Lee once said disasters often follow the pattern that everything which could go wrong did go wrong. Such was the case with Abraham Lincoln.

History often turns on small events. In late March 1865, Lincoln reviewed the troops of Edward O. C. Ord's Army of the James outside Petersburg, as they prepared to launch their final offensive against the Army of Northern Virginia. Also present on the reviewing stand was Ord's attractive wife, Mary. Arriving late in an ambulance were Mary Todd Lincoln and Julia Grant, the wife of the general. Mary Todd immediately erupted. "That woman is pretending to be me," she shouted at Julia. "The soldiers will think that vile woman is me!" She accused Mrs. Ord of flirting with the president.

Julia Grant defended Mary Ord, pointed out she was with her own husband, and certainly was not flirting with Mr. Lincoln. The president's wife immediately turned on Mrs. Grant, accusing her of wanting to get to the White House herself and taking Mrs. Lincoln's place. Julia was shocked by this unwarranted outburst, but the day was not over. When she mounted the reviewing stand, Mrs. Lincoln called Mrs. Ord a whore and unleashed a string of expletives at her. In the end, she accused Mary Ord of pretending to be her and demanded Lincoln relieve General Ord of his command. This Lincoln, of course, would not do. Edward Ord was one of the best generals in the Union Army, and the president knew it, and he had sense enough to know that, against Robert E. Lee, he needed every good general he could get.

Mrs. Lincoln continued her out-of-control behavior throughout dinner, where she ruined everyone's meal by verbally castigating the president, who bore her multiple reproaches in pained silence. It was not the first time something like this happened. Mary had a record of emotional instability dating back years. She had struck Lincoln on the head with firewood, chased him with a knife, threw hot coffee in his face, threw tomatoes at him, and pulled out part of his beard. He had spent many nights sleeping on the couch, both in his law office and in the White House. Even Lincoln himself called his wife "partially

The Retribution Conspiracy

insane." But this was the first time Julia Grant witnessed her emotional imbalance firsthand.

After storming out of the dining room, Mary Lincoln spent the next three days in her cabin before returning to Washington. Mrs. Grant never saw such abuse or disrespect in her life. She refused to socialize with Mrs. Lincoln after City Point.[54]

When General Grant told Julia they were supposed to accompany the Lincolns to Ford's Theater, she balked. She refused to socialize with that woman. Grant could not persuade her to reconsider. They were planning to meet their children in New Jersey. If they took the train departing on the afternoon of April 14, they could arrive two hours earlier than if they took the morning train on April 15. It was a thin excuse, but when a pretext is needed, any story will do.

General Grant sighed. After having to deal with Robert E. Lee for a year, now he had to deal with Julia Grant. But against Lee, he always had a possibility of winning. This was a real no-win scenario. He would offend Mrs. Grant or run the risk of offending Abraham Lincoln. Which course should he take?

Edwin Stanton, also, was concerned about Grant's accompanying the Lincolns. Having no idea she was on her way to Canada, he was at the point of sending Guinevere Spring a note, canceling the assassination, when U.S. Grant appeared in his anteroom. He presented his problem to the secretary of war. Would the president be offended if he canceled?

"No, not at all!" The secretary of war gushed. What a perfect opportunity, he thought. He encouraged Grant to leave early. Spend some time with your children, he told the general. After fighting the Army of Northern Virginia for a year, you deserve it! And Lincoln won't be offended. By the time he left Stanton's office, Grant had decided: he would not be attending the play with the Lincolns.

Not that he cared, but Stanton was wrong: Lincoln was upset. Without Grant — and his bodyguards — he did not want to go to Ford's Theater that night. After the cabinet meeting that afternoon, Lincoln walked over to the War Department, which was just west of the White House. On the way, he told his daytime bodyguard he was worried.

---

54 A few years later, after jumping out a window to escape a non-existent fire, Mrs. Lincoln was committed to an asylum. Her lawyer secured her release by threatening to embarrass the Lincoln family with a public hearing. She was released to the custody of her sister. She made at least one more suicide attempt before she died in 1882.

"Do you know, I believe there are men who want to take my life? And I have no doubt they will do it!"

When he arrived at the War Department, Stanton was hard at work. He was always hard at work. It was his job, his passion, his mistress, and his hobby. He was secretly very proud of himself. Despite his lack of military experience, he had won the war for the Union. It galled him this ridiculous baboon, Abraham Lincoln, was getting the lion's share of the credit. Stanton knew that, without him, Lincoln would be nothing. Even with me, he isn't very much, Stanton thought. He looked around his small, cramped, dingy, dirty little office. He hoped to see the last of it soon. One problem was it was too small. For another, it was square. He wanted his next office to be oval.

"President Lincoln is here to see you, sir," his secretary said.

Speak of the devil, Stanton thought. "Tell him to wait. I need to finish this important dispatch."

There was no dispatch. He just liked making the man he called "the gorilla with the stovepipe hat" wait for him. Finally, he got up and walked to the door.

"Yes, Mr. Lincoln?" He said. He did not call him Mr. President, shake his hand, offer him a seat, or offer him a beverage. On the other hand, he did not throw a lamp at him, either. This was better treatment than the president received from his wife at home. Besides, he was accustomed to Stanton's rudeness.

"Mrs. Lincoln and I are attending a play at Ford's Theater tonight," he said. "Of late, I have been concerned about possible assassination attempts. Unfortunately, General and Mrs. Grant, who were scheduled to accompany us, have been forced to cancel. I was hoping his military escort would provide security. Since they will not be at Ford's, I would like Eckert to join us as an escort and a sentinel."

The president was referring to Major Thomas T. Eckert, the head of the War Department's Telegraph Office. Lincoln, who spent a lot of time in the telegraph office during the war, got to know Eckert well. He was a perfect bodyguard: tall, muscular, immensely powerful and built like a stone edifice. Lincoln once saw Eckert break five cast-iron pokers by striking them over his arm, one after another. In addition, the major had a fierce temper and was devoted to Abraham Lincoln.

"No," Stanton said. "I cannot spare him. I have important work for him this evening."

"I will ask the major myself," Lincoln replied.

"Go ahead," Stanton barked.

The Retribution Conspiracy

Eckert was in the next room and overheard the Stanton-Lincoln exchange.

"Major Eckert," Lincoln exclaimed and gave him a disarming smile. "How would you like to escort Mrs. Lincoln and me to the theater tonight?"

"I would love to, Mr. President, but I'm afraid my duties won't allow it tonight."

"Oh, come on, Eckert! It will be fun!" The president cajoled.

"My goodness, I'd love to," he said. "But I have important work to do this evening. I couldn't possibly go." *Of course, I have no idea what this important work is,* he thought. Eckert was not going to buck the powerful, humorless, and vindictive secretary of war. Most men wouldn't. Lincoln left disappointed and dejected.

About 15 minutes later, Stanton called the major into his office. "Eckert, I've changed my mind. Go home. I won't need you until tomorrow."

Later, Stanton lied to the general public and to Congressional investigators and said Lincoln never visited the War Department on April 14.

Instead of Eckert, Lincoln picked Major Henry Rathbone to escort him to the theater. Rathbone was a dapper young man, about half Eckert's size. He was accompanied by his fiancée, Clara Harris, who was also his stepsister.[55] Although he fought at Antietam and Fredericksburg, he was by nature a staff officer. Also, he was more interested in protecting Clara than the president on April 14. For once in his life, Abraham Lincoln wanted a lot of physical security. He got almost none.

Stanton knew it was the turn of the most incompetent guard imaginable to protect the president: John F. Parker. He was a 35-year-old Virginian who, like most of the Washington Police Department, was of questionable loyalty to Lincoln. He was also a corrupt, unreliable alcoholic. He had been cited for conduct unbecoming a police officer on several occasions, as well as for insubordination and being drunk on duty. A notorious adulterer and whoremonger, he often used his position to extract sexual favors from prostitutes. Those who refused were arrested.

John Wilkes Booth, of course, knew John F. Parker, who occasion-

---

55 Ira Harris, Clara's father and Henry's stepfather, replaced Seward as U.S. senator from New York in 1861.

ally guarded important personages at various theaters. Booth knew he could be enticed to leave his post for a drink, and he could be talked into joining the conspiracy — especially if someone paid him and covered up for him.

To seduce Parker, Booth deployed Ella Starr, the pretty, 19-year-old prostitute who was in love with Booth. From there, it was easy to induct him into the conspiracy. Guinevere paid the bribe. "We got him so cheap, I thought we stole him," she laughed to Booth.

Parker received his draft notice in early April, but it was quietly quashed by someone in the War Department. After the assassination, Stanton took charge of the investigation. He arrested dozens of people who had nothing to do with the killing of Lincoln. Although it was obvious, Parker's part in the tragedy was not investigated. In May, the Washington Metropolitan Police superintendent brought charges against Parker for neglect of duty in connection with the assassination. Stanton quashed these as well. The transcripts of the proceedings and all official documents relating to it disappeared.[56]

Booth walked into Ford's Theater armed only with a single-shot, 8-ounce Derringer and a knife. This is pretty persuasive *prima facia* evidence that he didn't expect much, if any, resistance. He quietly entered the Presidential box. Booth knew the play well. He did not fire until a particular line was delivered, and the laughter of the audience would cover the sound of the shot. Then, from a distance of four feet, he put a large .44-caliber lead ball (about half an inch in diameter) into the left side of Abraham Lincoln's head. The president never regained consciousness.

Booth's timing was so perfect that no one knew a shot had been fired, not even in the box. Henry Rathbone was the first one to realize something was wrong when he saw blue smoke. He attempted to prevent Booth from fleeing the scene, but he was no match for the athletic actor. Booth pulled his dagger and slashed the major's upper left arm from the elbow to his shoulder. The assassin then jumped 12 feet from the box to the stage. In his excitement, he became entangled in a Treasury Guard regimental flag used to decorate the box. He landed off balance and fractured the fibula (shinbone) in his left leg, just above the ankle. For a moment he faced the confused audience and shouted *"Sic simper tyrannis"* (Thus ever to tyrants), a line from *Julius Caesar.*

---

56 Three years later, Parker fell asleep on duty. For this, he was finally dismissed from the force.

The Retribution Conspiracy

He scrambled out the side door, pushing aside the orchestra leader in the process. One witness thought he yelled "The South is avenged!" but this is in dispute.

Almost simultaneously, Lewis Powell rang the doorbell of Secretary of State Seward's home and pretended he was delivering medicine. The servant offered to take it, but Powell said he was told to deliver it personally to the secretary. The servant opened the door, and Powell pushed him aside and ran up the stairs. Seward's son Frederick blocked his way. Powell drew a revolver, aimed it at Frederick's head, and pulled the trigger, but it misfired. Powell (alias Lewis Paine) hit the much smaller man in the head with the gun, fracturing his skull so severely that it exposed his brain.

Powell drew his Bowie knife and found Seward's bedroom. Blocked by a male army nurse, he stabbed the sergeant in the head. A giant of a man, Powell knocked Seward's daughter across the room and slashed at Seward's throat. Fortunately for the secretary, he had a steel frame around his head and face, which the physicians placed there after the carriage accident. Powell stabbed at both sides of his throat and cut his cheek so severely his tongue could be seen through it. The steel frame saved Seward's life, though he nearly died anyway.

Major Augustus Seward, another of the secretary's sons, burst through the door and into the room. He and the nurse pulled Powell away from Seward and struggled for the knife. Powell stabbed Augustus seven times and the nurse five times. "I am mad! I am mad!" He shouted as he ran back down the stairs. A messenger entered the front door at that moment. Powell stabbed him in the chest, but like everyone else in the Seward household, he survived. The place looked like a battlefield when Powell fled; wounded people and blood were everywhere.

Ella Starr, Booth's 19-year-old prostitute/girlfriend, looked at the naked vice president. The sexual activity was finished and he rolled over, exhausted. Johnson was certainly no John Wilkes Booth when it came to sexual acrobatics, she thought. She smiled to herself. After this, Wilkes will know I would do anything for him, she decided. When he sees how much I love him, maybe he will marry me. With that happy thought in mind, she decided to make sure the vice president was asleep.

"Andy?" She called softly. No answer. "Andy?" Again, no answer. He started to snore, ever so softly. She smiled and quietly got out of bed. Johnson did not stir. She walked across the room, silently un-locked the door to Room 68, and went back to bed.

George Atzerodt was supposed to enter the unlocked room and kill Andrew Johnson. He arrived at the Kirkwood House just past 10 p.m., but his courage failed him. I signed up for a kidnapping, not a murder, he said to himself. Besides, I'm thirsty. He went to the bar instead.[57]

The dying president was carried to the Petersen House, across the street from Ford's Theater. Ironically, he was placed in a room John Wilkes Booth had once rented. Henry Rathbone followed him, but his wounds were worse than anyone realized, and he collapsed from loss of blood. Booth's knife had severed an artery, but the doctors were able to save him.[58]

Lincoln the doctors could not save. He died at 7:22 a.m. on April 15. "Now he belongs to the angels," Edwin Stanton hypocritically moaned.[59]

Always before, when a friend or close relative died, Edwin Stanton was shaken to the point of mental unbalance. Not this time. He was cool, collected, and in charge. As soon as he arrived at the Petersen House (about 10:30 p.m. on April 14), he assumed the role of unofficial acting president of the United States. His first act was to surround the Peterson House with 200 soldiers, to make sure there were no more political assassinations, especially himself. He also recalled General Grant and provided security for selected other members of the government.

A shorthand recorder lived next door to Lincoln's room. Stanton ordered him to record testimony. Within 15 minutes, the recorder said later, he documented enough evidence to hang John Wilkes Booth. Several eyewitnesses identified him, yet it was hours before Stanton sent pursuers after the assassin. Had he not broken his leg, the actor would probably have reached "Mosby's Confederacy," and it is likely he would have escaped altogether. But he had broken his leg.

---

57 Ella Starr tried to commit suicide after Booth's death. She disappeared shortly thereafter.

58 Later, Rathbone married Clara, and they had three children. Despite his growing mental instability, President Arthur gave him a minor diplomatic post in Germany in 1882. The following year, he went berserk and attacked his children. When Clara defended them, he shot and stabbed her to death. He then stabbed himself five times in the chest. He spent the rest of his life in the Asylum for the Criminally Insane in Hildesheim, Germany. He died in 1911.

59 The press changed this phrase to "Now he belongs to the ages."

The Retribution Conspiracy

Washington was in turmoil. People were sure the assassination was part of a massive conspiracy, masterminded by the Confederates and Jefferson Davis. There were riots in the streets. People who said Davis might not be involved were hanged from lampposts. One 80-year-old woman who hung out her son's recently washed gray suit to dry was thrown into jail because it looked too much like a Confederate uniform. One man was severely beaten because he smiled. The rioters said anyone who smiled on a night like this committed an act of treason.

Hundreds of people were arrested over the next two days. The entire cast of *Our American Cousin* was incarcerated, along with the theater owners and anyone else with the slightest contact to John Wilkes Booth, including his stable man.[60]

About midnight on the night of April 14/15, Stanton ordered the arrest of John Surratt, who was involved in the earlier kidnapping operation but who had nothing to do with the assassination. Stanton said Surratt attempted to kill Seward, even though Surratt and Powell looked nothing alike. Some historians suggested this was pretty good evidence Stanton knew about the kidnapping plot. Surratt was in Canada at the time. His mother Mary was arrested on April 17. Dozens of other people, most of them innocent, were arrested in the meantime.

Instead of heading directly for Port Tobacco as originally planned, John Wilkes Booth went miles out of his way to get to Dr. Samuel Mudd's house, where he received medical attention. He passed by the homes of three other physicians in the process. Then he rested for 15 hours. As a result, the Union dragnet caught up with him on April 26, at the Garrett Farm in Virginia. In the ensuing melee, Booth was shot in the neck. The bullet pierced three vertebrae and partially severed his spinal cord, paralyzing him. He died three hours later. Minutes before his death, he whispered: "Tell my mother I died for my country."

Four of the conspirators, Lewis Powell, David Herold, George Atzerodt, and Mary Surratt, were hanged at the Washington Arsenal on July 7. Three others, including Dr. Mudd, were sentenced to life imprisonment, and a stagehand received a six-year sentence, based on flimsy evidence. One conspirator died of yellow fever during his confinement. The rest, including Mudd, were released after three and a half years, once passions cooled.

---

60 To his credit, when he learned Laura Keene and Harry Hawk, the stars of the play, had been arrested, Stanton ordered they be released immediately.

Just before Powell's death, he was visited by Thomas T. Eckert. The major — who made it a point never to disagree with Stanton — recently was promoted from telegraph officer to assistant secretary of war. He visited Powell several times and befriended the former Confederate. As he was leaving Powell's jail cell the last time, Eckert stopped, turned, and asked him if they caught all the conspirators.

"You ain't got half of them yet!" Powell responded to the astonished Yankee. The ex-Mosby guerrilla, who had no reason to lie, was hanged the next day.

Meanwhile, Lafayette C. Baker, the head of Stanton's National Detective Police, handed John Wilkes Booth's diary over to Edwin Stanton. The secretary tore out and burned eighteen incriminating pages. When someone pointed out they were gone, Stanton claimed they were missing when he received the diary, but a California Republican Congressman who briefly examined the diary earlier said they were there when he surveyed the document. He also wrote: "Booth knew much which they [Stanton and the Radicals] are deathly fearful and that he, even from the grave, will tell." The diary also contained information that connected Stanton and the Radicals to the assassination. Another Radical Republican congressman read part of it and was heard to mumble several times, "Oh my God, Oh, my God! I am ruined if this ever gets out!"[61]

In April 1868, Detective Baker wrote a letter to a former congressman from New York, stating Stanton was involved with the conspirators who assassinated Abraham Lincoln. Baker was found dead on July 3, the victim of arsenic poisoning.

Stanton never sent anyone after Rance Liebert or Guinevere Spring, who disappeared from the pages of history.

---

61 The missing parts of Booth's diary were never recovered. The diary itself disappeared for a time. When it was discovered in a War Department file in 1867, only two entries survived. Stanton denied any knowledge of the missing pages.

The Retribution Conspiracy

━∽ CHAPTER XXX ∽━
FINIS

The Confederate Secret Service did not stop operating just because the Confederate States of America ceased to exist. Although no one correctly put the facts together for a hundred years, it won what may have been its greatest victory long after Appomattox.

Jefferson Davis was captured on May 10, 1865. He was taken to Fort Monroe, Virginia, and placed in chains. They tortured him by not allowing him to sleep. His cell was exposed to the elements, was painted white, and the lights were never extinguished, which aggravated his already painful eye condition. A guard entered his quarters every 15 minutes day and night, bent over and examined his face. He was only allowed one book to read and that was the Bible; at first, he was denied even that. His health deteriorated to the point the Union physician declared that his life was in danger, but still the mistreatment continued.

Finis William Randall and Rose-Marie Cormier Randall appeared in Toronto on or about April 17, 1865, with their four-year-old daughter, Ginger, and their bodyguard, Philip Warner, who looked very much like a former Confederate officer named Julian Anderson. His beard was not as long, though.

The Randalls rented a nice house, and Warner took a room in a boarding house which once was a Confederate safe house. Before long, he was practically the only one there. The rent was been paid through the end of the year, but almost all the former Rebels returned home.

In May 1865, the Randalls and Warner met with George Sanders at Warner's boarding house. Also present was Jacob Thompson, who was afraid to go home — and for good reason.

George Sanders was a charmer who ran with whores and debutantes, lawmen and criminals, and heroes and swindlers, all with equal adroitness. He had worked with Liebert before, on the St. Albans bank robberies, and with John Wilkes Booth. The Confederate War Department Secret Service still had a considerable amount of money in Canadian banks, and the accounts were controlled by Finis. Thompson controlled even larger amounts from the State Department Secret Service, and not of this included huge sums of counterfeit money.

Finis started the meeting by saying, "On April 25, Secretary of War Stanton announced he had evidence a plot was organized in Canada.

The purpose of this plot was to assassinate Abraham Lincoln, Andrew Johnson, and members of Lincoln's cabinet. Johnson has since blamed Confederate agents in Canada for the murder of Lincoln. In a few days, a conspiracy trial will begin. It has two purposes: to indict Jefferson Davis and to prosecute Booth's co-conspirators. The conviction of the eight Booth's people is a foregone conclusion. Our mission is to prevent the indictment of Davis, and to secure his eventual release." This pronouncement was greeted with nods all around.

"Our longer range goal is more ambitious," Finis continued. "We are going to deflect all blame for the Lincoln assassination away from the Confederacy. Booth's reputation must be sacrificed for the good of the South." He saw a flash of horror on Rose-Marie's face. "He would have wanted it that way," Finis concluded, looking directly at his wife. Again nods all the way around. He noticed that Rose-Marie closed her eyes and nodded also.

"Mr. Sanders, your mission is to find three witnesses who appear credible but will swear to anything we tell them to, even under oath," he continued.

"I can do this," Sanders said, "but I will need some money for expenses. Also, after my activities for the Confederate Secret Services, I will never be able to return to the United States. I will need some money upon which to retire." By expenses, of course, he meant bribes. The witnesses would have to be paid agents of the Secret Service.

"I'll go as high as $20,000 for expenses," Thompson said.

"I will pay out $10,000 for expenses and $20,000 for your retirement fund, after the mission is accomplished," Finis said.

"And I will go to $30,000 for your retirement, after you succeed in your mission," Thompson added. Like Finis, he stressed the word "after."

Sanders' eyes widened. Fifty thousand dollars was huge. (Fifty thousand 1865 dollars would equal $858,267 in 2020 dollars.)

No one could see it, but Finis nudged Anderson under the table with his foot. So Anderson said the lines he rehearsed. "And I will hunt you down and kill you if you attempt to abscond with the expense money. And I will kill you real slow!" Anderson smiled at Sanders. It was an evil grin.

Sanders looked at Anderson and quickly looked down. He then looked Anderson in the eyes and remarked, "Well, it appears that I must succeed."

"Yes, it does," Anderson growled, then smiled.

The Retribution Conspiracy

"I will do that," Sanders remarked, nervously.

"And make sure the witnesses know their life expectancy will be severely curtailed if they double-cross us," Finis declared.

"I will do that also," Sanders said.

George Sanders, master swindler, went to work immediately. He recruited three witnesses from his shadowy world: Richard Montgomery, a Union spy and Confederate courier who worked for both sides during the war; James Merritt, a medical doctor; and Charles A. Dunham, alias Sanford Conover, a freelance newspaper correspondent. Dunham was an especially skilled swindler, and Sanders took full advantage of that fact.

Sanders' trio completely fooled Stanton and his judge advocate, who played the special prosecutor's role. Dunham, Merritt, and Montgomery told huge lies about murderous Rebels and their secret meetings, bizarre intrigues and plots, spies and secret agents, secret symbols and codes and handshakes, all centering about the Confederate Secret Service leaders and the head of their Washington Bureau, John Wilkes Booth, the cold-blooded murderer, Owen Dickerson, who committed suicide at the end of the war, and homicidally insane Colonel Rance Liebert, who was fluent in Spanish and fled to South America with part of the Confederate gold — or so Sanders' witnesses said.

Although the case was presented behind closed doors to a secret military tribunal, part of Dunham's testimony was "somehow" leaked to the press, compliments of George Sanders. Newspaper pressure then forced the government to release the testimony of all three witnesses. Next, just as was planned in the beginning, Sanders released the actual facts. Not one of the men (Booth, Thompson, Robert E. Lee, or anyone else) was where the witnesses said they were on the dates cited. Meetings in Richmond between the spies and Jefferson Davis could not have taken place because Davis was in Atlanta or Montgomery or somewhere else at the time, and this was easily proven. Booth could not have been at a certain location because he was performing that afternoon on a stage hundreds of miles away. People mentioned by the witnesses — loyal, Union people with substantial credibility — swore honestly they had never met them in their entire lives. Facts did not add up. The testimony of other witnesses who were actually reliable was now not taken seriously. Public opinion shifted. It appeared Stanton and his prosecutors had presented false evidence to frame the Rebel president. Southern editors in particular hammered home the theme: "Booth was a lunatic! He and his people acted alone. He certainly wasn't one of us! We didn't want Lincoln killed! Lincoln's death was the worst thing that could have happened to the South. Booth was obviously a madman! Look at Powell. He even admitted he was mad! You can't hold the South responsible for the terrible acts of madmen! You must drop all the charges and let Jefferson Davis go!"

Events lent credibility to the editorials, and newspapers north of the Mason-Dixon Line picked up on the theme. Northern editors did not forget Lincoln and Stanton threatened them and suppressed newspapers during the war, and some of the editors were even been jailed. Lincoln was now perceived by the public as a great Union martyr and could not be attacked, but Stanton and his cronies could be — and were. Now that the war was over, the secretary of war no longer held the dictatorial power he had just a few months before. Stanton-bashing became a favorite sport of the men who bought the ink. The government lost the battle for public opinion, and the judge advocate's case collapsed. Although the judge advocate continued to push for a trial of Jeff Davis, the opportunity was lost. Even Stanton eventually gave up. A highly capable lawyer himself, he saw there was no way he was going to get a conviction. Meanwhile, Jefferson Davis — who demanded a trial in open court — became a hero throughout the South. The public often has a short memory, and all of his mistakes during the war were forgotten. Still in prison, he was seen as a Southern martyr, bearing his chains with dignity like the true hero he was — at least in Southern mythology. "Jefferson Davis Suffers For Us All!" One editorial proclaimed, and there were thousands of others written in a similar vein. More than one editorial compared him to Jesus Christ. Even the pope sent him a crown of thorns, which he constructed himself.

President Johnson also had enough. Despite his personal hatred for the man, which predated the war, he released Davis on parole on May 11, 1867.[62] When the former Rebel commander-in-chief walked out of the courtroom in Richmond, a free man for the first time in two years, thousands of people (many of them black) lined the streets, and took off their hats in respectful silence.

———

Rose-Marie Randall slept for most of three days after they arrived in Canada. Now that the pressure was off, she realized how much stress she was under during the war. She was looking forward to retirement

---

62 Davis rapidly regained his health and did not die until 1889.

The Retribution Conspiracy

with her husband. She still had more than $98,000 of the money Stanton gave her, and Finis had $50,000 from the bank robbery and more than $140,000 in gold from the Secret Service accounts. They would never even have to touch the counterfeit money because they were rich — but they kept a sizable amount just in case.

Guinevere never let on, but she got what she wanted all along. As early as 1861, she suspected the South was going to lose the war. She wanted it to win, but she wasn't planning to go down with it — and she didn't. She was happy, she was wealthy, and she lived with a child she loved and a husband she adored. Finis would have been shocked, but events transpired exactly as she planned them all along. Weaker sex indeed, she mused to herself. That was funny.

She never said anything to anyone about telling Booth to kill Lincoln and never really questioned her decision to do it. To her, "the original gorilla," as Stanton was fond of calling him, got what he deserved. Besides, it got Finis, Ginger, and herself away and out of Stanton's reach. Let the men believe they control events, she thought. That's good. It makes it easier for those of us who actually do.

But there is always a price to pay, even for success. She was, for example, sorry Wilkes been killed, although she didn't feel responsible for it. She gave him a good chance to escape, and it was not her fault he tripped over that regimental flag and broke his leg. She also regretted she could not return to Mississippi and help her family rebuild. One day, she asked Finis if they could ever go home again.

"I doubt it," he said. "We may get to visit Mississippi again, someday in the distant future, perhaps 15 or 20 years, but the place we knew doesn't exist anymore, and it will never exist again," he sighed. "We won't recognize many people. I'd like to see my mother and father again, and I sorely miss Jonathan, Colonel Davis, Joshua, and Robert E. Lee, but they'll probably all be dead before we can return, except maybe Joshua, and he'll be living in Richmond. About all we will be able to do is visit some graves, if we can find them. We won't even be able to recognize most of the buildings."

She frowned, held his hand, and wiped away a tear. There were so many ghosts! But she liked Canada and loved Toronto. She enjoyed going out to supper without looking over her shoulder, she enjoyed being able to go out in public with Finis (where did he get that name?!?), and she enjoyed going dancing and to church and to parties with her husband. He still carried a small handgun, and occasionally Mr. Bowie, but it was as much from force of habit as for any other reason.

One day, she couldn't stand it any longer. "Why do you still carry that gun?" She asked.

"I feel naked without it," he answered.

"I like you naked," she said, and was rewarded with a smile, a shake of his head, and a remark about low standards.

"I have incredibly high standards," she retorted as she left the room, her nose in the air, faking a huffy exit.

On another occasion, as she watched her husband and daughter drawing in a child's art book in the floor, it occurred to her Ginger loved Finis more than anybody. To Ginger, her father hung the moon. They were constant companions and were often laughing and playing. She made it clear her daddy was her most favorite person on the planet — and that included her mother. It seemed a little strange to her that the former Brigadier General Rance Liebert, CSA, was a very domestic man after all, and preferred a quiet family life to the wild adventures he had in two wars. Unless she did something to mess it up, she was going to have a very happy, stable life — although she did miss the stage. But life is, after all, a series of trade-offs, and she would gladly trade what she had given up for what she now had. At a minimum, she would have a country manor in England and a town house in London, and she could always act at the local theater. If there wasn't one, she could easily afford to start one. I am young, rich, retired, and married to the man I love, she thought. Not a bad future to look forward to. And she was determined never to deliberately do anything to upset it.

One thing still bothered her.

"Rance. Eh, Finis?" She said one evening after he had tucked Ginger into bed.

"Yes?" He said, looking up from his book.

"Why haven't you ever asked me who Ginger's father is?"

A harsh look flashed across his face and he glared at her. "Because I know who her father is."

"You do? Who?"

"Me!" He retorted with some venom. He gave her a razor-sharp dirty look and immediately resumed reading, not looking at her again. It was the first time he snapped at her and she was so taken aback by his harshness that she left the room, but later she marveled at his eloquence. He clearly conveyed five messages with one word: 1) Ginger was his daughter; 2) this was never to be questioned; 3) this was a sore subject with him; 4) the entire topic was off-limits; and 5) she was nev-

The Retribution Conspiracy

er to bring it up again. She never did. Rose-Marie was not one to repeat a mistake.

⸺⸙⸺

As the government's case against President Davis unraveled, Finis Randall decided he, too, was at his limit. There was nothing more he could do. Events were set in motion and, while he could no longer control them, he could see they were going to work out as he planned. Toronto was too close to the United States. Stanton's thugs might trace the three perjurers back to Sanders, and the trail might lead to him. So he paid Sanders his "retirement" money and the suave Kentuckian bowed and left town, never to return. (He did look over his shoulder for Julian Anderson for several weeks.) Jacob Thompson was already in exile in England. Against Finis' advice, C.C. Clay returned to Kentucky, where he was promptly arrested and held without trial for some time. That left only three members of the Secret Service in Canada: Guinevere, Anderson, and himself. So he called Anderson in and dismissed him. "Sanders has done his job and disappeared," he said. "There is nothing for you to do anymore and there's no reason for you to stay here." He gave him an honorable discharge certificate addressed to "Captain Julian Anderson." He also gave him $10,000 in gold dollars.

Anderson's eyes bulged. "Dang, colonel, I'm rich!" He yelped. He let out a Rebel Yell.

"I reckon so," Finis allowed. He gave him another $4,000 in greenbacks and a deed. "Go to Rainbow, Mississippi. Find a slave ... I mean a black man named Jonathan Liebert. Give him this deed and $1,000. Give $1,000 to Major Glass or his father. Tell them Sally Mae and I have gotten married and are living comfortably in England. Tell them we'll be in touch when it's safe. Give the other $2,000 to my father if he's still alive. If not, give it to my mother. I'd go myself, but I'd never get back here alive," Finis said. Always cautious, Finis was sending the people he loved funds from two different directions (via Anderson and Melody Herzog), in case one of the routes failed.

"Yes, sir," Anderson allowed. Rance hoped he meant that and wouldn't just disappear with the money. Rance didn't think he would, but there was no way to know for sure. Finis also intended to send a letter to Dan Glass, with instructions on how to receive a large payment for himself from former Secret Service funds, but he did not yet know how to do that without it being intercepted. He'd figure it out, he promised Rose-Marie and himself. If Dan were to pick up the money from Melody (and he was sure he had by now), everybody should be all right for the foreseeable future.

"Also, there's a stack of counterfeit greenbacks in Room 132 at the Rossin House in Montreal," the former general continued. "At least I guess it's still there. It's in the large safe. Here's the combination," he said, giving Anderson a slip of paper. "You can have 'em if you want 'em."

"I want 'em!" He declared.

"Be careful with that money," Finis warned. "And don't give any of it to my father, Jonathan, or Mr. Glass. They only get real money! By the way, you can have your old name back. They're not going to come after you now. Not after that military tribunal debacle with the Davis indictment."

"Are you going to take your old name back, colonel?"

"Nope. Sally ... I mean Rose-Marie and I are going to England. There's nothing left for us in Mississippi, and if we were to go back there, the Carpetbaggers would be after us like ducks on a June bug. The Yankees would steal every penny we have and probably toss us into jail to boot — although most likely we'd just disappear. I can't go back home until Stanton is dead and Reconstruction is over. No. Julian, I'm going to disappear into the British countryside."

Anderson frowned. This was it, then. All of the Secret Service business was concluded. He stood up, extended his hand, and said: "Goodbye, colonel! Eh, I mean general. It's been a pleasure serving with you!" For one of the few times in his life, Anderson's eyes were actually misty.

"It has been an adventure!" Rance replied, grinning. "I'm going to miss you, Captain Anderson." They shook hands and even embraced, although neither of them were much on hugging other men. Even Guinevere hugged the newly minted captain, something she never thought she would do. Then Julian Anderson walked out, and the Confederate Secret Service ceased to exist.

Three days later, Finis Randall, his daughter Ginger, and his pregnant wife Rose-Marie boarded a ship and began their voyage across the Atlantic Ocean to their future.

—⚬⚬⚬—

The Retribution Conspiracy

⟿ About the Author ⟿

D r. Samuel W. Mitcham, Jr., was born in Mer Rouge, Louisiana. He was educated at Northeast Louisiana University, North Carolina State University and the University of Tennessee, where he received his doctorate.

A retired professor, he taught geography and military history at Henderson State University, Georgia Southern University, and the University of Tennessee.

A university professor for twenty years, he is the author of more than forty books, including *Bust Hell Wide Open: The Life of Nathan Bedford Forrest; Vicksburg: The Bloody Siege That Turned the Tide of the Civil War; It Wasn't About Slavery: Exposing the Great Lie of the Civil War* and *Desert Fox: The Storied Military Career of Erwin Rommel.*

Dr. Mitcham is the Heritage Operations Historian for the Sons of Confederate Veterans and First Lieutenant Commander of Camp 1714. He is a former helicopter pilot and company commander and a graduate of the U.S. Army's Command and General Staff College.

He holds the Jefferson Davis Gold Medal for Excellence in the Research and Writing of Southern History.

CPSIA information can be obtained
at www.ICGtesting.com
Printed in the USA
BVHW041152290421
606133BV00007B/809